MISSING
85 Days

Based on the Diary of an Amnesiac

By

RANDY HAGLUND

To my mother

Ruth W. Haglund

(1926 -2014)

A constant source of inspiration and information
for this book.

And to her father,

John L. Olson

(1890-1939)

The grandfather I never knew. Until I started writing.

JOHN OLSON'S 85 DAYS

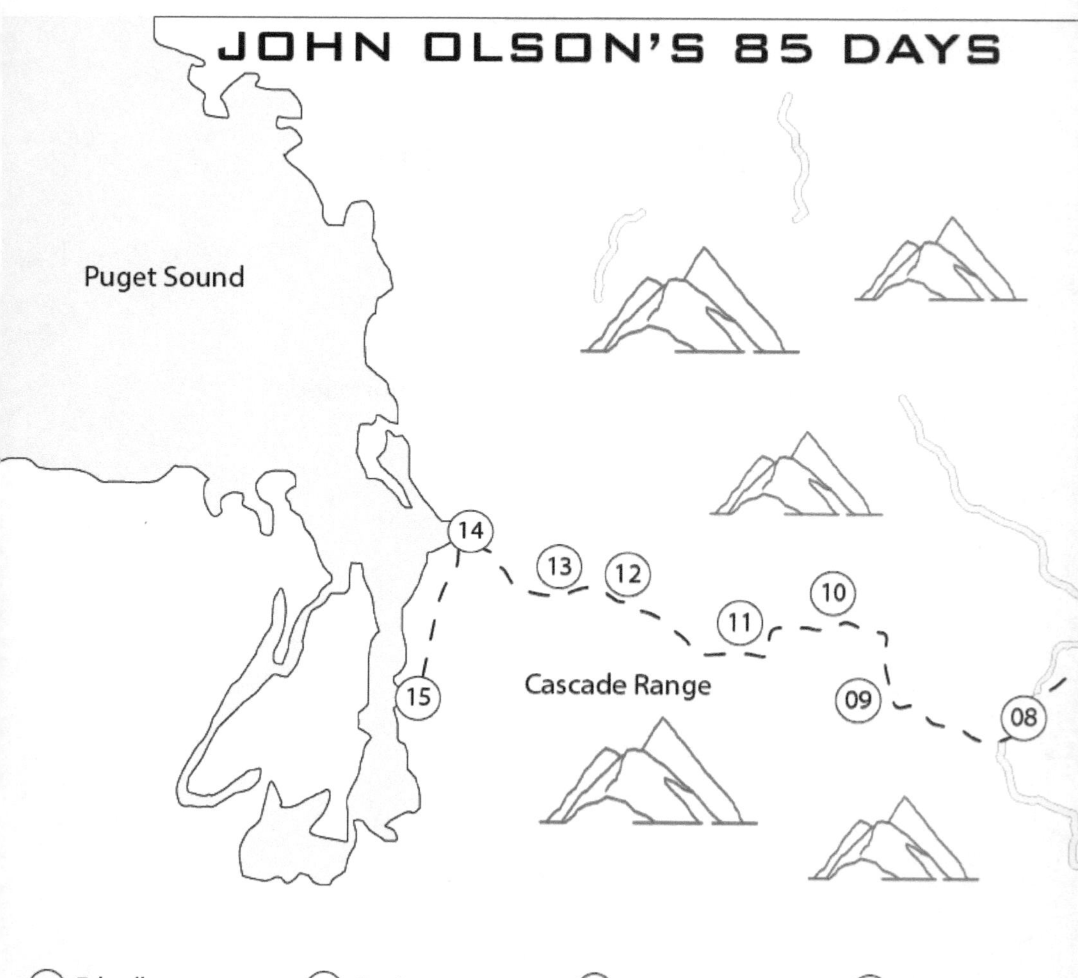

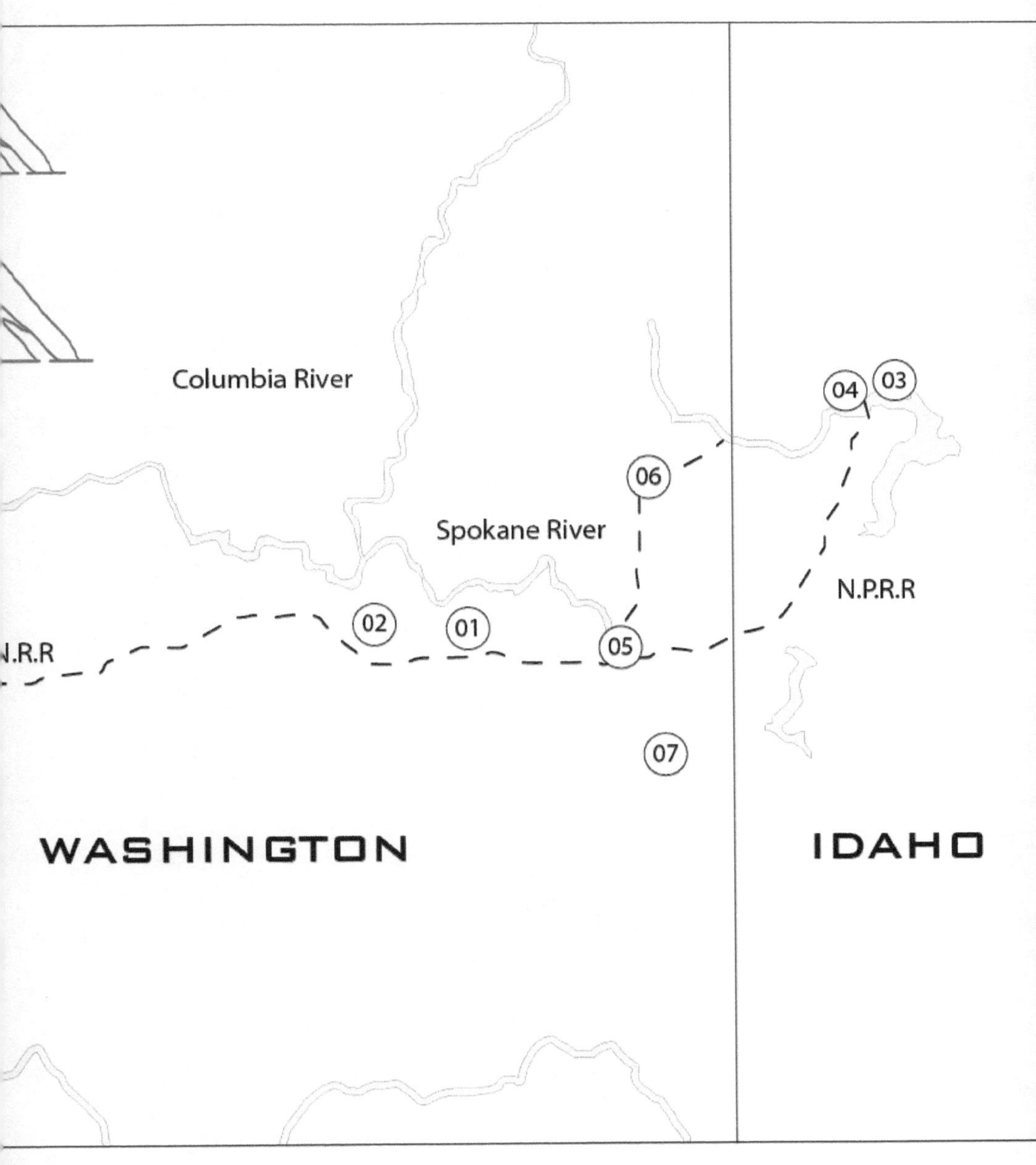

Columbia River
Spokane River
N.P.R.R
N.P.R.R
WASHINGTON
IDAHO
01
02
03
04
05
06
07

Part 1
Harrington

DAY 1

FRIDAY, APRIL 11, 1924;
LINCOLN COUNTY,
WASHINGTON

A sharp kick in his side brought him to consciousness. He groaned and wrapped his arms around his searing ribs.

"Get your miserable carcass out of here!" a gruff voice above him spoke. "If you can wear clothes like that, you can pay your fare."

Reeling with pain, he stumbled to his feet. He reached out to a wall to steady himself as the world spun around him. A fierce headache pounded in his temple as he looked up. Cold night air blew through an empty boxcar.

A railroad lantern illuminated a stern face.

Tall and muscular, his assailant stood facing him, holding the kerosene lamp. He wore a dark-blue uniform and a cap with a nickel-plated badge reading G.N. RY BRAKEMAN.

Still cradling his side, the battered man leapt out of the stationary car and into darkness. Stunned, he stood on a rocky railroad bed, his knees ready to buckle. The world seemed strange, like he had been thrust into a moving picture show without being allowed to see the script beforehand.

"Hey, stranger," the brakeman called out. "You forgot something." He threw a small black satchel out on the ground. Then, he raised the lantern above his head and down again, signaling the engineer to proceed. Hopping out of the boxcar, he latched the door and stalked past, casting a wary eye. The train lurched forward, and the brakeman jumped onto the caboose as it crept ahead. As it passed, the brakeman gave one last intimidating look and shouted at him again. "Get to hell out of here!"

Still in a fog, the stranger watched the train roll past. He stared at it for a few moments as it chugged into the distance. To his left, a lone farmhouse light interrupted the darkness. In the other direction, the train advanced through a small town.

He had no idea where he was or how he had gotten there.

Bewildered, he tried to recall his recent activity. But nothing came to him.

Alarmed, he realized he didn't even know *who* he was.

The brakeman had called him "stranger." Strange indeed. *What could be stranger than being a stranger to your own self?*

He picked up the satchel and tried to assess his situation as he trudged toward the town. The air had a chill, but his shiver came from deep inside. Pinching himself, he hoped it would wake him from this nightmare.

There has to be a simple explanation for this.

What had the brakeman shouted? "Get to *hell* out of here." Could it be?

He had heard hell was a place of darkness and separation. Was he being tortured or punished for something?

He stopped and glanced skyward, hoping to at least get his bearings, but there were no stars or moon. Only blackness. Seeing no alternative, he crossed his arms to alleviate the shaking as he pressed on toward the hamlet, slogging forward with legs like lead weights.

After about a quarter of a mile, the small community began to take shape. Grain elevators dominated the townscape, with several smaller nondescript buildings huddled together and a few dozen trees in an otherwise treeless environment. A structure that might be a fire station became evident, a few shops and some homes materialized—then a simple train depot, painted white. As he got closer, he could read the sign on the side of the terminal. EDWALL.

So that's what they're calling the Abyss now.

A flatbed truck squatted under a lonely streetlamp beside the train station. For the first time, he looked down to see his clothing—a dark-blue suit and green vest with black oxfords. The rumpled and dusty suit looked new, except there was a bad scratch on one of the vest buttons. Sitting on the bed of the truck, he opened the satchel, hoping to find a hint as to his identity. Inside he found a white shirt, two attachable collars, a pair of black socks, and a shaving kit. He examined them carefully, hoping to find a monogram or some other clue.

In his vest pocket, he found $7.20. He discovered a folding knife and a box of matches in the coat. His pants held a comb, and the shirt pocket contained two pencils and a fountain pen. No wallet. Disappointed, he then examined a pocket watch he dug out of his vest. *Cheap, with no engraving.* If it could be trusted, the hands pointed to almost ten o'clock.

******

Inside the depot, the stationmaster observed the stranger slog into town and proceed to sit on the bed of his Packard one-and-a-half-ton truck. He eyed the outsider curiously, finding it odd anyone would arrive in this remote town on foot, especially at this hour.

"Whoozat?"

The stationmaster spun.

The swing shift switchman peered over his shoulder at the same stranger.

"I don't know." The stationmaster spoke with a slow drawl.

They watched as the man explored the items in the satchel and on his person in an odd way. He kept appraising each item as if seeing them for the first time.

The switchman took off his hat and scratched his head. "What's he doin'?"

"That's a good question." The stationmaster squinted.

"Where'd he come from?"

At this, the stationmaster turned around and gave the switchman a glare. "What am I, the Great Zucchini? How am I supposed to know?" Mockingly, he repeated, "'Whoozat? What's he doin'? Where'd he come from?' I don't know any more than you do! He just came walking down these tracks like nobody's business and sat on my truck."

"He walked?" asked the switchman in a high pitch. "To Edwall?"

The two stared out the window again. The switchman dared to ask another question. "Why does he keep lookin' at his things so funny?"

"That's what bothers me." The trainmaster turned to the switchman with a knowing expression. "Maybe they aren't *his* things."

The switchman's eyes became large, and his mouth formed into the shape of an 'O' as he came to the realization that Edwall may be in the throes of a crime spree.

Turning again to the window, the stationmaster added, "And look at those nice clothes he's wearing. The suit's all dirty and wrinkled up. Doesn't really quite fit him. And his hair is all mussed up. No hat. He looks like he's been in a fight or something." He shook his head. "Something's not right."

With raised eyebrows, the switchman asked, "What are we gonna do?"

"I'll take care of it." The stationmaster spoke with an air of authority. He stood, hitched up his pants, and headed to the door. Before he left, he turned to the switchman. "But keep an eye on things. Back me up if there's trouble."

Short on stature but considerable in girth, the stationmaster stepped onto the depot platform and made his ungainly descent down the short stairway. He decided to start with a friendly disposition, in case he had misjudged the stranger.

"Pleasant evening," he began.

The strange man glanced around, apparently trying to find a sign of pleasantness.

"Where ya headed?" the stationmaster asked.

The stranger seemed almost startled by the question but answered with a bewildered, "I —I don't know."

It seemed an odd answer, but he decided to keep it light for now. "Well, where'd ya come from?"

After a pause, he repeated his reply. "I don't know."

Pursing his lips, the stationmaster shook his head. He wouldn't take chances.

He took another step toward him, abandoning the friendly approach. Snatching the satchel from his grasp, he examined the contents, ignoring the westbound passenger train arriving—cars banging and brakes hissing. Then, deciding the contents were not of much value, he thrust the bag into the stranger's chest. He didn't know what this guy was up to, but he was in no mood to deal with him.

Pointing his thumb over his right shoulder, he said, "See that train?"

As if it was possible to not notice a locomotive stopping twenty feet away, the stranger nodded.

"I want you to get on that train and get out of this town and don't come back."

******

The stranger clutched his bag and stared after the stationmaster, who turned on his heels and lumbered back up the platform steps. Before entering the depot, he whispered something to the conductor of the westbound passenger train, who stood on the platform.

Hopping to the ground, the stranger proceeded to the platform. He appeared to be the only passenger boarding. The conductor stood like a guard near the entrance to the Pullman car, not giving him notice. After a few minutes had passed, the unsmiling conductor glanced down at his pocket watch and shouted "Board!" as if he were addressing a great crowd of would-be passengers instead of a lone, rather dusty man.

Entering the coach, the stranger observed his surroundings. There were only five passengers in this car. A young couple was ensconced in the back, their attention focused on each other. Near the front sat a woman with two children—a boy approximately six years old at the window seat and an infant in her arms, asleep. The lines on her face suggested the scowl she wore was a permanent fixture. She and the boy stared at him, unblinking, making him feel like he did not quite belong there—which seemed likely.

He chose a seat two rows behind the sour woman, hoping it would prevent further gawking. It did not. The pudgy boy turned around, putting his knees on the bench, and peered over the back of the seat. After a moment, the woman elbowed the boy, who turned and sat in his seat.

The train jerked forward, reminding him of how badly his head throbbed. The motion had the added effect of waking the baby, who started crying loudly.

Closing his eyes, the stranger hoped when he opened them that the world would be alright again. But when he opened his eyes, he found the conductor hovering over him.

"Where to, mistah?" The conductor's Boston accent was clear.

Having been asked this question moments ago, he knew better than to reply the same way as he had with the stationmaster. However, not knowing the names of any stops in Hell, he couldn't be sure at first what to say.

The conductor cocked his head and tapped his thigh rhythmically with his ticket book.

The stranger blurted out, "Next stop," and handed him a dollar, hoping American currency worked here.

The conductor returned forty cents and produced a ticket. Before handing the ticket over, he studied the stranger and punched holes in strategic places. Then, the conductor turned and went through a door to a forward car. The stranger examined the ticket and saw his physical features described by the holes punched.

Gender:	Male
Build:	Stout
Age:	Middle
Eyes:	Dark
Hair:	Dark
Beard/Mustache:	None

To his relief, the movement of the train caused the baby to go back to sleep for now, and he turned to look out the window. But because of the lights in the train and the darkness outside, he could see only his own ghost-like reflection. The visage seemed unfamiliar. *Who is that person staring back at me?*

The likeness revealed his disheveled condition. Using the reflection as a makeshift mirror, he ran his fingers through his hair. *Is that dirt on my face?* He licked his fingers and tried to clean his cheek. Tightening his tie, he slapped some dust off his trousers and turned his attention back to the window. The stranger stared back.

In about a half hour, they rolled into the next town. He found it to be as unfamiliar as Edwall. "HARRINGTON," read the depot sign. Like Edwall, grain elevators dominated the skyline of Harrington, but it seemed to be a bit larger.

The station sat on higher ground, overlooking the town. Hand in hand, the young lovers got off the train. Following them, he wondered how they were able to keep their footing while staring into each other's eyes. They exited the platform to the left, then descended the short steep hill toward what appeared to be the main avenue in town. They crossed the intersection at the bottom of the hill and entered a hotel.

Pressing his aching side with his hand, he followed the route the couple had taken moments before until he came to the entrance of the hotel.

An electric neon sign read "The Hotel Harrington." Large wooden double doors with brass handles formed the entrance to a two-story brick building with a veranda on the second floor. Elegant masonry decorated the top, and lively piano music emanated from inside.

It looked expensive, but he didn't see another hotel in sight. He hoped he could sleep off this condition and get back to a normal life in the morning. That is, if morning ever came to this place.

He entered the hotel lobby.

A rather active crowd prevailed at this late hour. The couple he had seen on the train was now engaged in conversation with others in the lobby, all sitting in cozy overstuffed chairs situated on a Persian rug. A fireplace adorned with painted tiles popped and crackled in a corner. Ragtime music cheerfully emanated from an upright piano played by a man in a pinstripe suit.

"Welcome to Harrington." The voice came from behind him. Turning around, he discovered a desk clerk eyeing him with a stiff smile.

"I need a room," the stranger said.

"Well, you came to the right place." The clerk stood erect with his hands folded in front of him.

"How much?"

He cringed when the desk clerk informed him that the cheapest rooms were a dollar a night. The clerk then passed him the guest registry to sign and retrieved a key from under the counter.

Stumped, he wondered what name he would register under.

"Is there a problem?" the agent asked, bemused.

"No, no. I have it." A name popped into his head. He had no idea where it came from, but he signed the registry: "Larkin, J. A." For a hometown, he added, "Helena, Mont." He noticed some of the other guests in the registry were from Montana, and he remembered the name of its capital. Convinced his real name would be quite different, he also doubted that Helena was his hometown. But he had to write something.

When he finished signing, the clerk handed him his key. "Your room is number eight, Mister Larkin. Go to the top of the stairs and turn left down the hall. You'll see the room on the right."

Larkin retired to his room, hoping the sun would rise in the morning.

THE DAY BEFORE

THURSDAY, APRIL 10, 1924; KOOTENAI, IDAHO.

He snuck up behind his wife in the kitchen.

Helen Olson stood at their cast-iron stove, preparing oatmeal for her family of eight. A pretty thirty-four-year-old, she wore a plain, cream-colored apron over a sensible flower print dress she had made herself on her White treadle sewing machine.

Before she knew it, he pulled her apron string and bolted for the back door.

"John Olson!" She limped after him and tried to snap him with her dish towel, but he had already reached safety outside. John chuckled to himself as he filled the watering can from the hand pump. He wanted to water Helen's flower beds before leaving on his business trip to Spokane. Her white lilies were not yet in bloom, but with the dry, warm spring, he made sure they got their water.

When John returned, three of the four school-age children, Margaret, Ray, and Leonard, were at the table, eating their oatmeal. He mussed Ray's hair and asked, "Are you kids ready for school?"

They replied in unison. "Yes, Daddy."

"And we made our beds," Margaret added before he had the chance to ask.

"Where's Charlie?" John asked. The twelve-year-old was conspicuous in his absence.

"I've been meaning to talk to you about that." Helen wiped her hands on her apron.

"What, is he sick?"

"No." Helen turned from the stove. "He's suspended."

"For what?" John didn't expect this revelation. Charles may not have been a great student, but he was seldom in trouble.

"Fighting."

John's face darkened. Everyone in the family knew he did not approve of fighting, and this meant big trouble.

"John," Helen whispered. "Don't chide him. He was defending your honor."

He scrunched his face. "My honor? Since when does my *honor* need defending?"

"The Felts boy said to Charles that his dad thinks you're a coward."

"Well, that's no surprise," John said. "Consider the source. Besides, you don't solve problems by fighting."

"I told him he did the right thing." Helen pursed her lips and folded her arms in front. "Besides, he won." She turned back to the stove.

"Helen," John said with an edge in his voice, "do we really want to encourage this behavior?" In a softer voice, he added, "Especially in front of the other children?"

"Dad?" He felt a tug on his pants. Leonard, the seven-year-old, peered up at him with curious brown eyes. "What's a coward?"

A handsome and inquisitive tow-headed boy, he had a rather sensitive spirit. But he was always full of questions.

"Never mind," Helen said.

But John stooped down to within inches of Leonard's face. "Leonard, a coward is someone who runs away when things get hard." John made a fist and punched the air to emphasize his point. "But the Olsons are not afraid. We are willing to face even the most difficult things in life."

"I'm not a coward." Leonard stood at attention with his chest out.

Helen terminated the lesson. "Now, you kids get off to school. You're going to be late."

She frowned at John. He was pretty sure why, but shot back a "What?" expression, raising his hands like the victim of a holdup.

John said his goodbyes to Margaret, Ray, and Leonard as they left for school and then went in to change into his new three-piece suit. He had bought it last month at the Crescent in Spokane for thirty-five dollars. It was a lot of money but worth it if he could get some sales in Spokane. After spending that much on a suit, he couldn't afford to have it tailored professionally, but Helen shortened the cuffs of the pants on her sewing machine.

"Don't forget to talk to Charles," Helen said. "He's awfully concerned with what you're going to say."

"I won't forget. Can you help me with this tie?" When he had finished fussing with the clothes, he put on his coonskin cap.

"Oh, you're not going to wear *that*." Helen glared at the hat.

"I got to keep my wig wam."

She scrunched her nose at his feeble attempt at humor. "It just looks so silly, especially with such a nice suit." She gave a short smile. "You're so handsome—but not with *that* ghastly thing."

"But it's my lucky hat. Good things happen to me when I wear my Dan'l Boone hat."

Helen rolled her eyes.

"I'm not going to wear it to sales meetings."

"I should certainly hope not."

John studied himself in the mirror, admiring the hat. "Do you think I'm doing the right thing?"

"I already told you to forget the hat."

"No, I mean… do you think I'm cut out to be in sales? I'm so new to this. I don't really know what I'm doing." Answering an ad in *Popular Mechanics* a month earlier, John had decided to take a sixty-day leave of absence from the Northern Pacific Railroad to try his hand at selling Fyr-Fighter brand fire extinguishers.

"You're a born salesman." Helen adjusted the tie again and brushed his lapels. "Think of the success you've had here in Sandpoint."

"I've done alright," he admitted. "But that's small potatoes. Besides, everybody up here knows me. I don't know if I have what it takes to get the bigger contracts in Spokane." He straightened his cuffs. "I'm not the high-pressure type. Do you think I have what it takes to drive sales?"

"I have complete confidence in you." She held his face in her hands to fix his gaze. "Nobody likes high pressure. Just a man of his word. You'll do fine."

"I have to admit, I am nervous." He gave an uneasy smile. "But also excited about my prospects today."

"At the phone company?"

"Yes. I hear the number of phones in Spokane has more than doubled in the last ten years. Can you believe it, they say more than sixty million calls are made from Spokane every year."

"It's sure becoming popular to have a phone," Helen said. "Maybe we will even have one someday."

John furrowed his brow. "Let's not get ahead of ourselves."

He continued his point about the phone company while he fussed again with his cuffs. "They have over six hundred people working at Home Telephone and Telegraph. Can you believe that? With fire extinguishers a new safety requirement in businesses, they'll need them for their building and their truck fleet."

Helen patted his lapels again. "Should be the start of a successful sales run in Spokane if you ask me."

"I hope so. But if not, I suppose I can have my old job back with the Northern Pacific."

"Don't talk like that." She slapped him playfully on his arm. "If you think that way, you're certain to fail. And every time the rail workers go on strike, we're left without an income. With eight mouths to feed, we can't afford to have you not succeed."

Holding him close, she looked into his brown eyes. "Besides, if you do well in Spokane, maybe we can move back there soon."

John didn't answer but turned to the mirror, straightening his cap.

"Right?" Helen pondered his reflection.

"Oh, Helen." John wouldn't meet her gaze. "Are we going to go over this same thing again? I know we have some troubles here, but what good does it do to run away from troubles? They follow you wherever you go. Besides, we have friends here."

"Yes, and enemies, too. You have no idea what it's like to go to the market and have people give you that… *look*."

"You were giving *me* a look a few minutes ago." John turned and pointed at her.

"I wasn't giving you a…"

"You were giving me a look." He wagged his finger now. "I know a look."

"Really?" Helen folded her arms. "What was it like?"

"Like this." He made a face supposing it to be an accusing glare.

Helen stifled a chuckle. "When did I give you that look?"

"As you escorted Leonard out of the kitchen."

"Oh, *that*. You mean like this." She then reprised the expression she had given him in the kitchen.

"Yes. *That* one."

"Well," Helen said, "*that* look means something entirely different than the look I get around town. The one I gave you means 'See what I mean? This is the kind of trouble we have in this dirty little town. We should get out of this hole as fast as we can.'"

John frowned. "You said all that with a *look*?"

"That and several other things." She turned and headed back to the kitchen with John at her heels.

"And what, pray tell, do the looks you get around town mean?" John asked.

Turning back to him, she said, "They mean 'You're not welcome here. Why don't you go back to where you came from?'"

They argued for about five more minutes, covering the same ground they'd covered many times before. Helen making a case for moving back to Spokane, and John wanting to stay in Kootenai.

Finally, in a heated moment, Helen declared, "Fine. Just go down to Spokane for a few days and leave us here in Kootenai to fend for ourselves. Hopefully, we'll still be here when you get back."

John knew she could be huffy. But he was in no mood for empty threats. "Fine," he repeated. "I'll do that."

He grabbed his small bag, already packed with the few personal items he would need for a day or two, then two other larger bags with his sample extinguishers, accessories, and sales materials. He struggled with the front door before leaving and didn't bother to shut it.

Helen followed him to the front porch. "John, please don't go like this," she pleaded. But she knew it was too late for regrets. Her heart fell as she watched John tramp down the boardwalk toward the streetcar that would take him to the railroad depot in Sandpoint. He strode down the street without so much as a glance backward.

Sighing, she noticed her next-door neighbor, Mrs. Hoover. She stood on her front porch, broom in hand, pretending she had been sweeping. Helen knew she was really out there to hear their argument better. She gave Helen that *look*.

"Oh, shut up!" shouted Helen, and went back in the house and slammed the door. "And fly on your broom somewhere else," she muttered.

John had almost reached the station in Sandpoint when contrition set in. Why did he have to leave on such bad terms? He could have been more gracious. Besides, maybe moving wasn't such a bad idea. He decided to make it up to her somehow.

He arrived at the depot a little early. Sitting on the bench with his head in his hands, he thought about how he should have handled things.

Then he realized he had not talked to Charlie. He certainly must have heard the argument and might be upset. John wished he had told him that he loved him, and he really *was* proud of him for standing up for the Olson reputation. Still, he didn't approve of fighting, but at least Charlie wasn't one to back down, either. He admired that in his son, but it was too late to head back to the house. He'd miss his train.

"Hey, Marshal." A man in a herringbone cheviot suit and a stylish fedora appeared on the platform next to him.

Just great. The last thing he needed. A conversation with Harry Preston, one of those "enemies" Helen had referred to. John hadn't been the town marshal for over a year, of which Preston was well aware, but Harry seemed to enjoy egging Olson on. Preston's wool suit made John seem foppish by comparison. *Tailored, no doubt.* Now he felt rather silly wearing his coonskin cap.

John tried to ignore him.

Observing the bags, Preston exclaimed, "Looks like you're taking a little trip there, Marshal. Where ya headed?"

"It's really none of your business, Preston."

"Oooh, touchy."

John took a deep breath to calm himself, knowing Preston would probably not stop.

Preston seemed to be sizing him up. "I haven't seen that suit before. You must be trying to impress someone. I wouldn't blame you if you were interviewing for a job somewhere else."

Olson was silent.

Preston kept pushing. "Ever since you took Sam's side in the trial, it's made life pretty miserable for you here, hasn't it?"

John stood and eyed Preston viciously, his finger pointing an inch from Preston's chest. "I'm not on anybody's *side*. And it wasn't my testimony that's caused me problems. It's people like you who don't know how to accept the truth."

Preston backed up a couple steps and pushed John's hand downward. "Hey, don't get so excited. Just having a conversation here." Preston made a show of straightening his lapels.

Riders were beginning to assemble at the terminal as the train rolled in. Preston gave one last parting shot: "Word around town is that Helen has been lobbying for a move to Spokane. You should listen to her."

John had heard enough. He lunged toward Preston, grabbed him by the tie, and pulled his face close. "Our personal lives are none of your business. If you and your friends don't leave my wife alone, you might need to have a little talk with the sheriff."

"Relax, Olson," Preston blustered, releasing himself from Olson's grip. More people had shown up for the train and witnessed the scene developing. Preston worked it to his advantage. "I was just wishing your family well. You don't need to go off half-cocked."

As people boarded ahead of them, Preston added one more comment. A soft aside only John could hear. "Besides, the sheriff is on *my* side."

John wanted to wring his neck, but he had already overreacted. He knew he had let Preston get the upper hand and was angry with himself. Nonetheless, he began to question his own non-fighting policy. There were exceptions, he concluded.

Getting on a different car than Preston, Olson had hoped to review his sales pitch again on the ninety-minute trip to Spokane.

As the train headed south through the Idaho panhandle, John found it hard to concentrate. He stepped out onto the back platform of the car, hoping that the fresh air would clear his mind. Rathdrum was the next stop. Should he get off and head back to Kootenai, make up with Helen, and forget about the trip altogether? After all, his sales meeting would be a total fiasco if he couldn't pull it together.

But he *had* to keep his appointment. Helen was counting on him.

By the time the train arrived at the Northern Pacific Depot in Spokane, John had managed to forget about Preston. Time to focus. He still worried about Helen, but he knew the most important thing he could do was to win the contract with the Home Telephone and Telegraph Company. Nothing would make Helen happier.

John battled with his bags as he made his way across Sprague Avenue to the Arlington Hotel.

"Gotta light?"

With his mind on the upcoming meeting, he was startled by a young woman sitting on a bench near the hotel's front door. She appeared to be about twenty years old and had the flapper look that was all the rage. She wore a black straight skirt cut just below the knee, and her arms were bare. She had a boyish haircut, covered by a close-fitting hat that gave the impression she was wearing a bell on her head. A long, pink cigarette holder dangled from her lips with an unlit cigarette affixed to the end.

John faced a moral dilemma. Should he refrain from contributing to the waywardness of this rebellious young lady, or should he come to the rescue of a damsel in distress?

He chose the more chivalrous option.

Setting down his bags, he felt around in his pockets for his matchbox. Finding it, he struck a wooden match and set fire to the tip of her cigarette. Despite wearing too much makeup, she was quite attractive, with innocent hazel eyes. Her lips were full and pouty, slightly parted.

A bemused smile crept across her face. "Thanks, pal."

Distracted by the young woman, he forgot about the match until it burned his fingers. He shook the match violently and threw it to the ground.

Embarrassed and not knowing what else to say, he murmured, "Uh, sure… any time." Then, picking up his bags, he fumbled with the door. The young lady stood and helped him with it.

"Thank you," he said.

"Any time," she replied, echoing his words.

She then followed him inside.

DAY 2

SATURDAY, APRIL 12, 1924

"Coolidge Leads in Illinois Primary."

The man calling himself J. A. Larkin sat in the dining room of the Hotel Harrington sipping black coffee. Perusing the headline story in Spokane's *Spokesman-Review*, it seemed odd that he had no trouble remembering who the president was. But no, he had never forgotten that. In fact, he recalled that Vice-President Coolidge had been sworn in as president the previous year when Warren G. Harding suddenly died in California. There was no article about *that*. It was in his memory.

He took a bite of oatmeal and tried to remember other things. It came easily.

He remembered the last year when the suspension bridge in Kelso collapsed. A car had stalled on it during shift change, backing up traffic, when a cable broke. Dozens of people died or were never found. Probably more, since a lot of them were transient workers.

Drumming his fingers on the checkered tablecloth, a number of historical and current events came to mind, but not one single *personal* event. Did the brain have different compartments for different information? Maybe the part containing personal experiences had somehow been damaged. And yet, despite the continuing splitting headache, he was unable to detect any bumps or bruises. No blood in his hair or other evidence of head trauma.

Turning the page, he read an article about the ancient Temple of Apollo at Delphi. The forecourt contained the famous anonymous inscription "Know Thyself." Philosophers had debated its meaning for centuries. Socrates claimed that it was foolishness to know ordinary things if one did not, above all, know himself.

Larkin sighed.

Pushing the empty bowl away, he turned to the sports section. The baseball season had gotten underway. This reminded him that the Yankees had beaten the Giants in the World Series last season four games to two, giving the Yanks their first Series Title. It seemed ludicrous that Babe Ruth and Casey Stengel were familiar figures, but he didn't know himself.

The waitress slapped the bill onto the table. Fifteen cents.

Just for oatmeal and coffee? He pondered how much to tip. A penny seemed cheap, but two cents seemed exorbitant.

He left a penny.

Back upstairs, he went to the men's shower down the hall from his room. Examining himself in the mirror, he saw thick, dark-brown hair crowning a rugged face lined with worry. He squinted at the stranger, but the image remained a mystery. He gathered that the man in the mirror was in his mid-thirties, but no other clues to his identity emerged.

Wandering outside, he tried to come up with a plan of action. He stuffed his hands into his pockets and ruminated while exploring the town. Except for the grain elevators, no building rose higher than one or two stories. The population of the town appeared to be somewhat under a thousand, yet it seemed to be a destination for travelers. Besides the usual post office, town hall, shops, and the like, the town boasted a rather opulent opera house which, judging from its size, must have attracted out-of-towners.

The city hall doubled as the police station and jail. He stopped and considered the building, debating whether to go to the police for help. But what would he say? How would they react? They would most likely think he was some kind of lunatic and have him institutionalized. Shuddering at the thought of straitjackets, isolation rooms, and sedative drugs, he decided to move on. Remembering the glower the Edwall stationmaster had presented, he was quite sure no one would believe his story.

He would have to fake being normal and be ready with a story if anyone asked about his past.

He walked quickly past the police station. *Look normal, look normal.* Was it his imagination, or had people been regarding him suspiciously? The brakeman who kicked him off the train, the stationmaster, the conductor on the way to Harrington, and even the desk clerk at the hotel—all had given him the eye. Could his face be on a wanted poster? He was afraid to poke his head into the post office, just in case. In addition, he would avoid policemen if possible.

Since he had no idea how long his condition would last, he would need money if he was going to eat. A blacksmith shop around the corner seemed a logical place to start looking for a job.

When he walked in, the environs were familiar. Not the blacksmith shop itself, but the tools of the trade. He knew how to use the anvil and the various striking tools, as well as the turning and bending tools and even the forge. The familiar odors of molten metal and horse manure filled his lungs. *Have I been a blacksmith?*

A short, well-fed man in heavy coveralls appeared from a stable in the back where Larkin supposed he had been shoeing a horse. He had a round face, the most prominent feature being a mustache so large it obscured his mouth entirely. A mirthful walrus came to mind. Wiping his blackened hands on his dirty coveralls, he extended his right one. "Hello, there. What can I do for you on this fine day?"

Larkin shook his hand. "Well, I'm just looking for work."

"You came to Harrington to find a job?" The blacksmith chuckled. "I barely have enough work to keep me and the boys busy."

"Is there any work available in the neighborhood?"

The blacksmith scratched his chin and pondered. "The only ones doing any hiring right now are the ranchers. If you want to get on with them, you need to go to one of them pool rooms." He pointed down the street. "The farmers usually show up there to find hands. What with the spring wheat needing planting and the winter wheat harvest starting early this year, you may be able to get a job with one of them."

Larkin thanked the blacksmith and returned to exploring the town. With prohibition in full swing, there were no saloons, bars, or taverns. In their place, "pool rooms" or "soft drink establishments" had become popular across America. Harrington had three such businesses. For whatever reason, Larkin found himself attracted to The Magnet. The large glass windows in front advertised pocket billiards and soft drinks, as well as cigars and candy.

Larkin entered and sat on a dark oaken bench. Two men played pool in the smoke-filled room.

The barkeep addressed him. "Are you just going to dawdle?"

"Pardon?"

The barkeep pointed with his thumb to a sign over his shoulder. NO LOITERING.

"Oh, uh, I'll have a root beer."

The barkeep produced a frosty mug and pulled on a tap marked "Hires."

While they played pool, the two other patrons smoked and drank something from beer mugs. Larkin guessed that they were also hoping to get work today.

"Wanna play?" one of them asked as they racked up another game.

"No, thanks." He shifted in his seat as they eyed him for a moment.

"Are you here to find a job?" the other man asked.

"Yes, I am."

The man was tall and skinny and wore a cowboy hat. His bow-legged walk left the impression that he may have been born astride a horse. He turned and grinned at the other player, who wore red suspenders.

Larkin glanced down at his black leather oxfords and tucked them under the bench. The pool players wore overalls and boots. His face reddened, knowing that his dress shirt and pants were not appropriate for farm work. He wasn't even wearing a hat. He avoided eye contact by showing interest in an event calendar.

He thought about buying a change of clothes but couldn't afford the investment if employment didn't materialize. Neither did he want to miss a potential opportunity should a farmer walk in while he was away.

In addition to his odd attire, his employment rivals were younger and possibly more suited to hard labor. He felt physically fit, but based on his clothing, he had to assume that he was some sort of professional by trade, not a laborer of any kind.

Was this all a waste of his time? But he was short on options. One root beer became two root beers, and he sipped slowly so he wouldn't have to buy another.

"You sure you don't want to play?" Cowboy repeated. "Tell you what. If you win, I'll buy you your next drink. If you don't, you owe me nothing."

He had nothing to lose, so he took the man up on his bet.

"I'll let you break," Cowboy offered. "It's Eight-ball, so you have to call solids or stripes and sink the eight ball at the end."

The player with the suspenders finished racking the balls and handed Larkin the cue ball. Holding the cue awkwardly, he aimed at the white ball, pursing his lips. Cowboy elbowed his friend with a smirk.

Larkin hit the cue ball as hard as he could and got a surprisingly clean break, balls scattering in all directions. When they finally settled, the eight ball trickled reluctantly into a corner pocket. "Nuts!"

But Cowboy had already walked over to the bar. Red Suspenders pushed Larkin playfully on the shoulder. "You just won."

"What? I thought you weren't supposed to sink the eight ball until the end."

"Unless you're lucky enough to sink it on the break." Cowboy leaned an elbow on the bar. "What'll ya have?"

A big goofy grin crept across Larkin's face. "Make it a ginger ale." Then, turning to Suspenders, he said, "Talk about beginner's luck."

The day dragged on. Sometimes they played pool, but most of the time they just sat waiting and sipping soda. Although the other players' drinks smelled of alcohol. Saturday morning morphed into a long afternoon, as only a few other patrons came and went. By four o'clock, all three men sat at the oaken bench with their heads hung low.

As the sun sank lower, a tall, lean man in his mid-thirties entered and strode purposely toward the pool table, but didn't seem interested in billiards. He wore a worn-out brown Stetson and red flannel shirt with the sleeves rolled up almost to his elbows. A pair of dirty overalls had mud and dried blood stains spattered across the bib.

Cowboy crushed out his cigarette and the two players stood at attention. "Afternoon, Mr. Timm."

As a reply, the farmer nodded in their direction. At first, he didn't seem to notice Larkin sitting at the far end of the bench until he stood at attention as well. Timm gandered at him and spoke with a German accent. "Are you here for a job, too?"

"Yessir."

"On a farm?" He squinted at Larkin.

"Yessir."

"You're dressed like some sort of salesman, or a lawyer. Have you done any farming?"

"Yessir." He'd thought about that. It seemed like he had. But his answer exuded more confidence than he actually possessed.

"Like what?" The farmer squinted, suggesting doubt.

Unable to articulate anything in particular, Larkin replied, "All kinds."

Timm tilted his hat back and frowned at Larkin. "Have you ever plowed a nine-horse hitch with three bottoms?"

This time there was a pause, then a confident, "Yessir."

Timm winced at the repetitive response, removing his hat to scratch his head. "Do you like kids? And don't say 'Yessir.'"

"I love kids." He smiled.

Cowboy stepped forward. "*I* like kids."

Timm huffed. "No you don't. And neither do you." He gestured toward Red Suspenders.

Considering Larkin once again, he said, "Well, I have three kids gettin' in the way all the time. You have to like kids if you want to work for me."

Larkin nodded.

Timm put his thumbs in the straps of his overalls. "Have you got any other clothes?"

"No, sir."

"Well, I have to get some supplies at the mercantile. You can pick up some proper working clothes there." With that, he turned on his heels and left The Magnet.

Larkin followed him, then turned to the other men before he went out the door. With a grin, he said, "Beginner's luck."

Cowboy threw his pool cue to the floor.

While the farmer shopped for staples, Larkin bought a pair of overalls, two shirts, and two pairs of socks. His shoes would have to do. At the drug store next door, Larkin used his last fifty cents to buy a two-week subscription to the *Spokesman-Review* newspaper. He asked them to be delivered out to the

Timm place.

Timm was placing sacks of flour and sugar into the back of his mud-laden Model T pickup when Larkin arrived with his goods. He asked Larkin to start it.

Larkin went to the front of the vehicle, where—like second nature—he pulled the choke cable with his left forefinger and turned the crank a half a turn with his right hand. It started easily. *I wonder if I own a car.*

When Larkin climbed in, the farmer pulled the throttle toward him and headed out of town. Turning north onto Rocklyn Road, the farmer began conversation.

"The name's J. W. Timm, but you can call me Will," he said. "Everyone does." He continued to elaborate that he had a 640-acre wheat ranch but also raised mules, horses, hogs, and cattle. "I mostly hire hands to help with the plowing, mowing the hay, and the harvesting." He added that various other chores would also be expected.

Larkin nodded. He didn't mind Will doing the talking, because he was still nervous about telling anybody the truth about his situation. On the other hand, he felt guilty about lying. But is it lying if you don't know the whole truth? He decided that it probably was. Better to say nothing for now unless necessary.

"So," Will said, "are you married, and do you have any kids? Where are you from?"

"Umm…"

DAY 3

SUNDAY, APRIL 13, 1924

Larkin emerged from his bunkhouse in the predawn glow.

He rubbed his temples, hoping the raging headache would subside. After another night's fitful sleep, his spirits were lower than the sun below the horizon.

Events from the night before occupied his thoughts.

On the drive to the farm, Larkin had made up a story about how he used to be a drinking man and, without elaboration, had "lost" his family. He didn't dare say more, partly because a better story had not come to mind, but mostly for fear of being overcome by emotion. Will Timm might think he had picked up a deranged man. Fortunately, the farmer didn't probe, and Larkin left it up to him to fill in the blanks.

The sun had settled behind the western hills by the time they arrived. The farmstead provided a darkened silhouette before a sky of vibrant blue, pink, and orange. Saluting their arrival, a galvanized windmill stood in the middle of a circular gravel drive.

Mr. Timm escorted Larkin to an outbuilding about one hundred yards south of the main house. This simple shed would serve as his sleeping quarters.

After Larkin dropped off his few things there, they walked up a gentle slope to the house where the family greeted him.

Lena—Will's wife—was a smart-looking woman in her thirties, cordial but serious. Like Will, she spoke with a slight German accent. She wore a conservative light-gray dress. Not stylish, but pleasing. They had three children, ages ten to thirteen.

After a solemn prayer given by Will, the family ate a light meal of cold pork sandwiches and homemade dill pickles. Sylvia, the youngest, was a free spirit and took an interest in the new hand immediately.

"How tall are you? What is your favorite color? Do you have any kids?"

"Sylvia!" Lena's brow creased her temple. "Let Mr. Larkin be. He doesn't want to answer your silly questions."

Larkin welcomed Lena's interjection and responded to Sylvia's questions with aplomb—except for the last one, which he avoided. After all, he didn't know the answer.

When dinner was finished, Larkin helped Mr. Timm and his son, Johnny, with the evening chores, feeding the horses, pigs, and cattle. He had then retired to the bunkhouse.

That was last night. Now he had the opportunity to peruse the property in the early morning light. To the north stood the farmhouse, a well-kept two-story traditional style with clapboard siding painted white. It also had a sizable front porch with two Adirondack chairs facing the imminent sunrise.

In the opposite direction, an enormous red barn—at least 6,000 square feet, he guessed—rested on a rock foundation. A large stable conjoined on the east face. The farm road wound past the barn and extended westward, sloping down to a wooden deck bridge crossing a creek. Most of the farm acreage appeared to be on the other side of the creek.

Larkin filled his lungs with the familiar odors of manure and hay. It almost made him feel at home.

But not quite.

Lonely beyond words, he was with people, yet not with himself. *Maybe I am going crazy.* Giving the gravel drive a kick, he thought about telling somebody his true situation. If someone would just listen to his story and offer to help him sort it all out. But who?

He rubbed his temples again and tried to come up with a solution.

No, he couldn't tell the Timms. What would they think? Here they brought to their farm a man they thought they could trust around their children, but he was not who he pretended to be.

Larkin took the initiative to do the morning chores. He fed and watered the pigs, cattle, and chickens, and then the twelve horses.

The Timms mostly had Percherons and a few Shires. One splendid-looking Perch showed no interest in the fresh grass hay. Instead, he approached Larkin and gave him a playful push with his nose.

Larkin stroked his muscular neck. "Hey there, big fella. You got a name?"

"Samson." Larkin whirled around to see Will standing with one foot up on the split rail fence surrounding the stable. "My best horse. Taken a shine to you." He shook his head. "He's not like that with just anybody."

"Must be sixteen hands."

"Sixteen and a half." Will made this declaration with true pride in his voice.

Solid gray and heavily muscled, Samson was a specimen worthy of a show horse. His mane was combed and shiny. Larkin detected intelligence in Samson's large eyes.

Will glanced around. "Did you leave me any chores?"

"I hope not."

Will smiled. "Well, come on up for breakfast."

The aroma of bacon and eggs frying wafted from the direction of the house. "You don't have to twist *my* arm."

As they walked up to the house, Will explained that after breakfast, the family would be heading into Davenport to Zion Lutheran Church. "We'd be happy for you to join us."

"Uh, maybe next time. I'm not feeling up to meeting people today."

Will touched the front of his Stetson with his forefinger. "Suit yourself."

Larkin felt a bit ashamed for offering such a poor excuse, but he wasn't on speaking terms with God right now. What had he done to deserve this? In no mood to worship, he didn't even know if he was Lutheran, or Methodist, or... who knows what?

The Timms left a two-day-old issue of the *Spokesman-Review* for Larkin to read while they went into town. He retired to his quarters and studied it. Dozens of inland northwest place names seemed familiar. Spokane, Hillyard, and Coeur d' Alene. But he couldn't remember having been in a single one.

He read every article, hoping a story would give a clue or trigger some latent memory. But it was not to be.

When the Timms arrived back home, Johnny, their thirteen-year-old, came over to the bunkhouse to see him.

"Wanna go jackrabbit hunting?"

"I haven't got a gun."

"My dad'll lend ya his rifle."

Johnny led him across the wooden bridge over Cold Creek, as it was called, and they headed north along the far bank. After a few hundred yards, Johnny stopped and crouched low, signaling with his hand that Larkin should do likewise.

Pointing ahead, Johnny whispered, "Just over this rise is where I sometimes see 'em."

Larkin let Johnny lead the way. They crept up the short incline, their guns ready. With no other cover available, they used the hill itself as their hiding place, peeking over it ever so slowly.

Simultaneously, they saw one, but they were spotted right off. One shot from each hunter blasted concurrently, but the hare was gone before they could even squeeze off a second round.

Johnny pulled his cap off and hit his thigh with it. "Dagnabbit! He's gone but good."

"No rabbit stew tonight," Larkin said.

They sat together near the creek, resting their backs against a dirt bank. Larkin examined his rifle, a Mauser, admiring it.

Johnny stroked the barrel of his Winchester. "You like hunting?"

"Sure," Larkin guessed. The question made him wonder if he had a son, and if they ever went hunting together. Somehow, he thought so. He tried to conjure up a memory of it, but it seemed just out of reach.

Johnny interrupted Larkin's thoughts. "Ever play horseshoes?"

"Is that a challenge?"

A horseshoe pit occupied the north side of the house, and soon Larkin could tell Johnny had been practicing.

"Two points for a leaner," declared Johnny when he had one.

Larkin squinted. "Are you making the rules up as you go along?"

"No, it's always two points for a leaner."

"Not where I come from." Larkin thought about what he had said. Not knowing his origins and yet aware of the particulars of scoring horseshoes there. *Exasperating.*

Johnny put his hands on his hips. "It's my house, and we play by the Timm rules here. Ask my dad."

Larkin winked. "I'm only having fun with you, boy. But it's only worth two points if it stays there. I'm about to knock it off."

Despite staying busy, the afternoon dragged on. Larkin was preoccupied, his condition never far from his mind. How long had he been this way? Less than forty-eight hours, as far as he could tell. Seemed like a lifetime. It might as well *be* a lifetime, since nothing else about his existence could be substantiated.

Sipping lemonade with Johnny on the front porch, he stared out at the windmill, contemplating his situation.

Will stepped out and asked, "Do you play cribbage?"

Larkin scratched his head. "I think so."

"What do you mean? Either you play or you don't."

"Let's give it a try," Larkin said. They both laughed.

Will got out the cribbage board and a deck of cards. After Will lost two out of three, he said, "I see how you are. You like to play coy. Well, next time, you won't catch me off guard."

After supper, Larkin browsed the Timms' living room bookshelf for some reading material. A couple dozen books sat on it, mostly religious. Will gave him permission to pick whatever he wanted to take out to his bunkhouse. A heavy tome titled *John Halifax, Gentleman* caught his attention.

"It's about a man who started out with nothing," Will said. "Not even a family. But with a strong work ethic, he became successful in business, made many friends, and raised a family."

The size was intimidating, but the synopsis appealed to him, so he tucked it under his arm and browsed some more. One small red book caught his attention. Curious, he picked it up and found it to be a blank journal.

Lena came to his side. "I got it years ago as a gift from my aunt. She thought I might use it, but I never did. You can have it if you want. I'll never write in it."

"Really?"

"Please take it," she said. "I want you to have it."

His heart leapt! He immediately excused himself and nearly skipped back out to his room.

Besides a bunk and a wood stove, only a small wooden table and a sturdy oak chair served as furniture in the room. Otherwise, the Timms seemed to be using the remainder of the room to store small farm implements. Spades, shovels, and a hay fork adorned the back wall, while an assortment of handsaws and boring tools populated a corner shelf.

He lit an oil lamp, produced the fountain pen from his jacket pocket, and sat at the table with his new treasure. He made his first entry.

Harrington, Wash. – Apr. 13, 1924

Here I am on a ranch 6 miles from Harrington on a wheat ranch. I hired

out as a farm hand at $45 a month. Will try to handle 9 horses on a plow

tomorrow.

But where did I come from? Where is my home? Have I father, mother, bros.,

sisters, wife or children? Is anybody looking for me? I can think of no place

where I might have lived. Nor can I think of anyone who might be a relative or

friend.

Then he wrote all his experiences since Friday night. From getting kicked off the freight car in Edwall to the hiring on at the Timm place. Speaking from his heart, he included details of his experiences. Not just circumstances, but thoughts and feelings.

Not taking time to compose, the pen seemed to have a life of its own. He couldn't write fast enough. The words ached to get out of his head and recorded.

For the first time since his predicament, he felt a little better. He had been hiding his feelings around people, but writing it down was somehow therapeutic. Here in his little red book, he could finally express himself without fear of judgment.

Realizing how tired he had become, he lay his head on his pillow and, fully dressed, fell into a deep sleep.

******

Helen Olson pulled the floral curtains aside, gazing at the front walk for possibly the hundredth time.

The last of five daily passenger trains had already rolled through Kootenai on this Sunday night, and still no sign of John. The way he left on Thursday morning made her feel uneasy, and now she was getting worried. He never stayed angry for long, but…

Stepping outside, she sat on the porch swing. Only darkness and the chill of the spring evening air greeted her.

A cherry pie—his favorite—awaited him in the middle of the family table.

Now the kids were in bed, and she had only cold cherry pie to keep her company.

DAY 4

MONDAY, APRIL 14, 1924

His headache was gone.

Anxious to impress his new boss, Larkin wanted to confirm to himself he knew how to harness a nine-horse team and hitch them to the plow. He found the reins, chains, doubletrees, harnesses, and bits arranged neatly on hooks on one wall in the barn. The horses cooperated reasonably well as he positioned them and harnessed them. Even so, the complicated process of hitching up three teams of three took Larkin close to an hour.

The three leaders were placed in front to set the pace. The swing team was in the middle, and the biggest horses were the wheel team, closest to the plow.

The horses shook their manes and stomped their feet in excitement. Samson and his lively contingent flared their nostrils, anticipating the day's work.

Timm arrived to find his new hand sitting in the cast-iron plow seat, letting the teams step ahead to bring the leather reins tight. Larkin had tied the lines together into a knot and then slipped them over his left shoulder and under his right arm.

"My, my!" Will hooked his thumbs under his suspenders. "I was coming down to help, but I see you have it all under control." He inspected the buckles and collars and nodded. "I couldn't have done it better myself."

Larkin beamed.

Will saddled and mounted a gray shire and led the delegation toward their destination. The wooden bridge groaned as the horses crossed Cold Creek, a small bubbling stream. Once on the other side, Larkin observed the dark soil, interrupted by rocky outcroppings and scablands here and there. Rich and loamy topsoil dominated the landscape, despite the dry climate and some rocky areas.

He welcomed overcast skies. The air held a chill, but the cloud cover would keep it from getting too hot as the day wore on.

As he led the team to the edge of the field Timm designated, his earlier anxiety dissipated and he proceeded with confidence. The horses in position, he lowered the plowshares and began his first rows.

Wearing his familiar dusty Stetson, Will sat on his horse by the edge of the field to observe Larkin's work.

Driving a three-bottom riding plow with ten-inch bottoms, Larkin cultivated three furrows at a time, with an eight-inch depth. It required a combination of strength, experience, and skill.

The furrows were straight and deep. When he got to the headland, he raised the plowshares, turned the teams 180 degrees, and lined them up for the return trip. Larkin stopped momentarily to admire his work and lowered the plowshares again. Then, focusing on an outcropping he used as a guide, he made three more arrow-straight rows.

He enjoyed a rapport with the horses right off. Hardly needing any cajoling or clicking, the team cooperated with each other and with Larkin.

He crossed the headland again and turned to begin his third set of furrows.

"Very good." Will smiled and tipped his head to one side. "At the rate you're going, you'll get nine acres plowed today."

"I hope so," Larkin said.

With that, Will left to attend to other chores, entrusting Larkin to the plowing.

Everything about this labor seemed familiar. He must have been a farmer, but where? *How did I end up on an empty boxcar wearing a business suit?* However, he had little time to dwell on these thoughts, because the work required his full attention.

******

"Hello, Dad? It's Helen."

"Where are you calling from? Is everything okay?" asked Edward. Her father-in-law heard the concern in her voice.

"Fine." She tried to sound calm. "I'm calling from the store." The Bonner and Maughamer store was only a block away, and the owners were family friends. "Have you heard from John the last couple of days?"

"No. Should I have?"

"Not really." Helen gave a heavy sigh. "It's just that, well, I expected him home last night, and he didn't show. I was hoping he may have called you."

"No. Wasn't he supposed to be in Spokane selling extinguishers?"

"Yes, last Thursday he had an appointment with the phone company. Then on Friday, he was going to take a train up to Milan for a sales meeting with the school district there. After that, he was supposed to visit with Millie and Harry for the weekend and come home on the train last night." John's sister Millie lived in Milan, a community about twenty miles north of Spokane.

"And you haven't heard anything?"

"No. But, of course, we don't have a phone and neither does Millie."

"True, but Millie uses the phone at the market when she needs to."

Helen didn't answer, hoping her father-in-law would take it as a hint that he should do something. Edward lived in Freeman, only a three-hour drive from Milan. Realizing she had a death grip on the receiver, she tried to relax her hand.

"Maybe Harry asked John to help him with the porch addition."

"Yes, that's probably it. Or he could have missed the train. But still…"

"Well, I'm sure there's nothing to worry about." Edward tried to sound reassuring, Helen knew. "No doubt he will show up today. But if you still don't hear from him, call me tomorrow morning. I can run up to Millie's in the car if necessary."

"Okay, Dad." She replaced the receiver on the hook harder than she meant to.

Something was wrong.

She hobbled back home carrying baby Mary. Two-year-old Anna May toddled alongside, oblivious to the angst her mother felt.

Helen prepared wheat gruel for Mary, while Anna May ate vegetable soup for lunch. Helen had no appetite. Mechanically, she wiped down the kitchen counters in no need of cleaning.

She wrung the dishtowel and threw it on the counter. *Why didn't I push the issue harder with Edward? He thinks there's nothing to worry about. But... something's wrong. I just know it.*

Feeling helpless and abandoned, she went outside to water the lilies, hoping for any sign of John.

DAY 5

TUESDAY, APRIL 15, 1924

Helen tossed and turned in her bed.

She pushed the covers off and then pulled them back on. Sometimes she even let out a moan. She felt guilty because of her argument with John, but anger welled up in her too. *Why haven't you tried to get in touch with me? How can you be so insensitive?*

The empty side of the bed mocked her, his pillow still bearing the dent from where his head should be. She swiped it off the bed but then felt sorry and replaced it. With a tear on her cheek, she fluffed it, preparing it for his return.

After reading a few pages in a book, she realized she hadn't comprehended a single word. She slammed the book shut and laid it on the bed.

This is not like John. Something has happened to him.

By the time the sun came up, she was exhausted. With baggy cheeks, she dragged her feet out of the bedroom. She tried to hide her worry from her children, but Charles, the oldest, picked up on her mood.

"Mom? Dad's not home yet?"

"Oh, he'll be home today," she said, trying to sound convincing. But she knew Charles would see through her charade.

He split the wood and stoked the firebox for the kitchen stove without being asked. They were chores usually done by John. Then he got the oatmeal going and fed his siblings breakfast, something his mom always did. He failed to hide the worried expression on his face from Helen.

"Are you alright, Mom? Maybe I should stay home from school today."

"Don't be silly." She arose and tried to look busy in the kitchen. "Go study hard today. And try to avoid that troublesome Felts boy. Everything is fine."

But nothing was fine, and they both knew it. As soon as the kids were off to school, Helen hobbled down to the Bonner Store again with two little girls in tow.

"Hello, operator? Spokane, please. The Home Telephone and Telegraph Company. Thank you." Helen held the receiver in her left hand and spoke into the transmitter protruding from the front of the wall phone. When a receptionist answered, Helen asked for Mr. Matthews.

"He's not available right now. May I take a message?"

Helen left a message for him to call this number, explaining it was an emergency. Then, she decided to wait for a while at the store for a return call.

After several minutes that seemed much longer, the phone finally rang. Frank Bonner, the store owner, answered and said it was for her.

"John kept his appointment Thursday afternoon," Mr. Matthews said in answer to her inquiry. "But he agreed to come in again Friday morning to make his final proposal and demonstrate the use of the extinguishers to our employees. I was surprised when he never showed."

"He wouldn't do that," Helen said.

"John made a good impression with his presentation. I wanted very much to do business with him. It seemed odd when he didn't keep his Friday morning appointment. We need to hear from him. We must have fire extinguishers in place to comply with new government regulations. I hope you find out something soon."

Hanging up, Helen turned to Bonner and said, "John's missing." She tried not to sound frantic, but her voice quivered.

Frank's jaw dropped, but no words seemed forthcoming.

Helen turned the crank on the side of the phone. "Operator? Milan,

Washington. Milan Market."

But the shopkeeper there hadn't seen Millie since Friday.

Cranking again, she gave the operator the number for her father-in-law.

Helen told him what she had learned from the phone company.

"I will drive up to Milan immediately," Edward said. "I'll call the Bonner store as soon as I know something. Don't worry. I'm sure there is an explanation for this. In the meantime, go get some rest."

Sure. Nothing to worry about here.

Hanging up, she turned to Frank. Through gritted teeth, she said, "I need a phone of my own."

Frank nodded and blinked.

A sitting area located by a wood stove provided a place for the locals to exchange the latest gossip. She chose a hard oak chair instead of the comfortable stuffed chair. Some of her neighbors came in to shop and tried to make small talk, unaware of any trouble. But Helen was in no mood. Not able to sit any longer, she started to arrange the sardine cans on a nearby shelf.

"I hope you're not expecting union wages," Frank joked.

Helen emitted a sour smile.

Frank left her alone after that.

Almost three-and-a-half hours later, Edward returned the call and confirmed Helen's worst fears. Calling from Milan Market, he related that John never showed up at his sister's house. Millie hadn't worried because she assumed there had been a change in plans.

"I'm driving back to Spokane now," Edward said. "I'm going to start looking for him. I'll leave a message with Frank if I find out anything."

Helen made one more phone call—to the Spokane Police Department.

******

Larkin retired to the bunkhouse right after supper. After another long hard day of plowing, he plopped onto his bed. The workday wasn't any more arduous than the first day of plowing, but more mentally fatiguing because he could not get his mind off his troubles. He had started to hum some familiar tunes while working, but they only brought tears to his eyes.

Why did they elicit an emotional response? Did they bring up some memories? If so, they didn't surface to his *conscious* memory. Is there such a thing as an *un*conscious memory? He wondered how he could access it. Could he do something that would retrieve memories stored somewhere in his cranium?

Thinking about it only made him more dismal. Yet he could think of nothing else.

He pondered these things while he watched the fire in his stove slowly burn out. Then, opening the little red book, he penned these few words.

There is something wrong somewhere. I've lost something dear to me.

DAY 6

WEDNESDAY, APRIL 16, 1924

Detective Paul Bucholz of the Spokane Police Department reviewed the reports from the prior evening.

His simple wood desk sat in a private office where he conducted interviews or interrogations. His uncluttered workspace comprised three items: last night's reports, Tuesday evening's *Spokane Daily Chronicle,* and a Royal #10 typewriter.

Despite his rank as a detective, he insisted on wearing a meticulous standard issue uniform, navy blue with a double-breasted military-type jacket. Two rows of gold buttons ran vertically in front. His badge read "#13."

As he perused the reports, two items caught his interest.

The first involved an anonymous call the department received about a woman attempting to commit suicide at the mill pond. The caller claimed to be at the Happy Jack soft drink establishment located at the north end of the Monroe Street Bridge. Attempts to trace the call were unsuccessful. Officers hurried to the scene but found no woman or evidence of an attempted suicide.

But they did discover that the Happy Jack didn't have a telephone.

The other item of interest was a phone call from a woman in Kootenai, Idaho, late Tuesday afternoon. She claimed her husband, John L. Olson, had been missing since last Friday. He was last seen in Spokane.

The second story caught his interest for two reasons. First, he already had Olson's wallet, with his railroad union membership card inside. Second, it seemed an odd coincidence that the wallet had been found along with a fire extinguisher sample case at the south shore of the very same mill pond where the anonymous caller had claimed a woman was attempting suicide. However, Olson had disappeared Friday night, while the anonymous call came on the following Tuesday night.

By the time Helen Olson called late Tuesday afternoon, Bucholz had already gone home for the day. Police Chief Wesley Turner had conveyed to Mrs. Olson and later to the press that his items had been found. It was the top story in Tuesday night's evening paper, *The Spokane Daily Chronicle*.

MAN GONE; FEAR FOUL PLAY

The detective grumbled to himself as he eyed the headline. He needed to know more. The chief had arranged for Mrs. Olson to be in this afternoon to identify the personal effects. He could question her then.

Bucholz had been on the force for almost twenty-five years. He had been the chief detective in missing person cases for half his career. Detective work was his true calling. He liked solving puzzles. You gather up all the clues and see where they lead you. Each case introduced a new mystery. Sometimes it could be frustrating, but those were the most rewarding ones to solve.

The detective shoved his chair back and carried the paper to Chief Turner's office. He knocked on the opaque glass window in the wood panel door. Without waiting for an answer, he walked in, as was his custom.

"What can I do for you, Paul?" Wes Turner barely glanced up, concentrating on a pile of papers on his desk. But he never seemed to mind interruptions. The two had a casual relationship. Although Turner was in charge, Bucholz had by far more experience as a policeman. They sometimes butted heads, but the chief seemed to appreciate having an old hand around.

Bucholz cleared his throat. "Did you tell the *Chronicle* that Olson's disappearance was due to 'Foul Play'?"

"I may have inferred it," Turner said. "I told them what we had found Friday night, and that Mrs. Olson thinks he may have been robbed. You said his wallet had no money in it."

Bucholz didn't answer. Instead, he shut the door quietly and sat down in a padded chair across from Chief Turner's desk.

"Why?" asked Turner. "You don't think it was foul play? The wallet was torn in half."

"Could be foul play, Wes." Shrugging, the detective produced his burl pipe and made a show of lighting it. "A ripped wallet might suggest anger or frustration. But by who? Muggers, maybe. Or Olson. Anyway, since when does the family of the victim tell the newspapers what the police think?"

"I didn't tell them what the police think—"

"But you implied it."

"I told them what we know right now. Which is not much." Chief Turner tapped his right forefinger against his desk.

Bucholz puffed on his pipe while an awkward silence ensued.

"So you have a different take on the Olson case?" Turner finally asked.

"I don't have a take yet, Wes. Like you said, we don't know much. I'll be talking to Mrs. Olson today, and perhaps I'll know more then. I'm just saying you have to be careful what you say to that daily rag."

"I know your opinion about the *Chronicle.* 'It's a gossip tabloid.'"

"Worse. It doesn't *repeat* gossip. It starts it." Bucholz slapped the paper down on Turner's desk. "Anyway, my experience has been that the families of missing persons always suspect foul play. They want to think somebody else is the bad guy, not their loved one."

"But you have to admit, the way his things appeared along the bank of the river gave us reason to believe he ran afoul of someone," the chief said. "Unless, of course, he set it up to look that way so he could make a getaway."

Bucholz pointed at Turner. "Now you're talking like a cop. If you want to tell the paper something, tell them we are investigating all possibilities. They're going to make up stories anyway; let them run with it."

Turner shook his head slowly. "I don't know, Paul. It seems best to first follow the obvious, and if it becomes a dead end, then explore other alternatives. I don't see the need to hurt people if we don't need to."

"It's not about who gets hurt. It's about finding the truth." He exhaled a cloud of smoke and peered at Turner through it. "Sometimes the truth hurts."

Turner sighed. "When you see Mrs. Olson today, do me a favor and take it easy on her. Naturally, she is very distraught. There is no need to exacerbate her trauma."

Detective Bucholz rose from his chair. "That's always been my problem, Wes. Missing persons I can handle. It's the live *in-person* persons I'm not so fond of."

******

An enormous dust storm made its way across Lincoln County. The morning had been alright, but by lunchtime, there was no point in even trying to plow. Larkin couldn't see his furrows, and the horses got skittish. So he gave up and helped Will with some projects in the house.

Soon the three kids arrived home from their one-room schoolhouse about two miles east of the farm. Johnny had driven his two sisters there and back in an old buckboard wagon. As soon as they arrived home, the whole family pitched in hanging wallpaper and painting trim.

Like plowing, Larkin became convinced he had done this work before. Probably in his own house, wherever that was.

Will supervised the painting in the hall with Johnny and Dorothea. Sylvia, the youngest, washed walls—where she could reach—in the girls' second-floor bedroom, preparing them for new wallpaper. Lena glued the paper with a brush and Larkin hung the paper, aligning the patterned edges expertly and smoothing them out. The acrid odor of paste filled the room.

Sylvia scrubbed dingy spots with great enthusiasm. Turning to Larkin, she said, "I got to help pick out the wallpaper. Isn't it beautiful?"

Larkin nodded. "Very colorful and flowery."

Wind gusts rattled the windows, and the howling outside made Sylvia shudder. "Where does wind come from?" she asked, wringing out her sponge.

"From windmills of course," shot back Larkin without skipping a beat. Lena peered over her glasses at Larkin with an expression of reproof.

Sylvia's lower lip protruded as she regarded Larkin with doubt. "That's just silly."

"No, it's true. Come here, let me show you." Larkin escorted Sylvia to her window. "See the windmill out there? It's spinning like crazy. Now look down over there." Larkin pointed to an area downwind. "The windmill is blowing so hard that those weeds by the drive are whacking the ground."

Sylvia twirled the collar on her dress with her fingers as she considered this.

Larkin leaned down close to Sylvia. "What do peppermills make?"

Sylvia stared up at Larkin with doleful eyes. "Pepper."

"What about lumber mills, what do they make?"

"Lumber," she said with some hesitation.

"And what comes out of papermills, Sylvia?"

"Paper, I s'pose."

Larkin stood erect. "You see, it just makes sense that windmills make wind."

At this point Lena cleared her throat to get Larkin's attention. She glanced down at the paper she had ready for him to hang and raised her eyebrows in mock disapproval.

"Oh, got to get back to work," he announced, ending his meteorological lesson.

When Sylvia went down the hall to help Will with something, Lena quietly admonished, "Mr. Larkin, really!"

"Well, how are kids supposed to learn anything if they don't ask questions?" They both shared a laugh.

******

Across the desk from Paul Bucholz sat a glowering Helen Olson. "Mrs. Olson, I *have* to ask these questions."

Her father-in-law, Edward Olson, sat with her, hunched forward and holding his hat in his hand. "Helen and my son live in the happiest of circumstances, Detective. They love each other and their six children. John has shown no sign of depression, and he is financially stable. He would not leave his family nor take his own life. It is just unthinkable."

That's what they all say. "Okay, then. Did he have any enemies?"

Helen continued to frown but seemed distracted, staring at nothing.

Edward spoke again. "I thought the circumstances pointed to a robbery.

His things were found strewn along the bank of the mill pond, along with his empty wallet."

"As I said, Mr. Olson, we have to ask these questions in *all* missing person cases. As a police detective, I am trained to examine every possible explanation. We don't even know if he's dead or alive."

"We don't believe he's dead." Edward turned his hat in his hands. "Something has just happened to him is all."

"I understand, Mr. Olson. But please try to see my position. The more cooperation we get, the faster we can come to a conclusion in this case. That's what we all want, right? Mrs. Olson?"

As if coming out of a trance, Helen distractedly replied, "Uh, yes. Of course." Helen stood, suggesting she thought this brought the interview to a conclusion.

She's hiding something. She's been able to conceal it from Edward, but not all is well in the Olson home.

Helen had already identified his effects and given a full description of John Olson and what he had with him when he disappeared. Bucholz had asked the hard questions, some of them more than once.

"Alright then." Bucholz stood. "I want you to know we will do everything in our power to find out what has happened to your husband, Mrs. Olson. Thank you for providing a photograph. I understand you have a phone now?"

"Yes," she replied. "Just today. The number is…" Pulling a slip of paper from her purse, she read the number to him. "Sandpoint 295-J-1." Then she turned and walked out without saying goodbye.

With Helen out of earshot, Edward turned to Bucholz and asked him, "You're going to drag the pond, right?"

"But you said you believed he's not dead."

"And *you* said you had to explore every possibility." Edward drilled a finger into the detective's desk.

Touché. "That is an option being considered."

******

When Edward caught up to Helen outside, she turned and said, "Can you believe the nerve of that man? And did you see his badge?"

"I guess I didn't notice."

She shuddered. "His badge number is thirteen."

"So? You aren't superstitious."

"I didn't use to be, but I'm beginning to reconsider." Helen continued striding down the hall to the exit door. "Just my luck the man investigating my husband's disappearance is number thirteen on the force."

Three men waited outside the police station for Helen and Edward as they left the building. John's younger brother, Eddie Jr.; Charles Gifford, Helen's father; and Harry White, John's brother-in-law.

Helen started barking orders like a drill sergeant.

To Edward, she said, "Dad, I want you to search the downtown area again. Eddie, you cover north of the river, including Hillyard. Harry, check the south hill and the east end." Turning to her own father, she said, "I need you to take me to the depot. I have some business to take care of in Kootenai. I'll be back in Spokane tomorrow morning."

Everyone followed orders without question.

Helen Olson was on a mission.

******

As soon as the Olsons left his office, Detective Bucholz placed two calls, making appointments. The first one went to the Home Telephone and Telegraph Company, and the other to Washington Water Power Company. Then he left his office and walked to the Arlington Hotel to question individuals who had seen John Olson last week. On the way back, the detective kept his appointment with Philip Matthews at the phone company to get more details about his encounter with Olson.

After returning to department headquarters and eating a sack lunch in his office, he left the building again and walked north on Howard. Crossing Front Avenue and passing under the railroad viaduct, he came to the location at the mill pond where Olson's belongings had been found on Friday night. He had only walked a little more than a block from the police station to arrive here.

For the first time, Bucholz investigated the scene. Before now, he had just been in possession of someone's missing items. Now he had a missing *person* to find.

Stooping down, he inspected the hard ground packed with dense gravel. It seemed undisturbed. He took note of the short, steep drop-off to the water.

If Olson had been mugged and thrown into the pond, there would be drag marks. He checked around the vicinity for other possible clues but saw none.

Bucholz stared into the pond's dark water. The south channel of the Spokane River formed the mill pond. The north channel tumbled over the upper falls in a spectacular display that sprayed bystanders with its mist. But from where Bucholz stood, this portion of the river remained calm and serene. Washington Water Power had built a dam there four years earlier, holding the water back. Across the pond from where he stood, he could see the Phoenix Lumber Company. They used the pond created by the dam to float their logs to the mill.

Seeing nothing that would indicate what had happened to Olson on Friday night, Bucholz walked one more block west to keep his appointment with a dam engineer.

The dam served to accommodate the astronomical rise in electrical demand. During his tenure as a policeman, Bucholz had seen Spokane go from a dusty frontier town to the hub of the inland northwest. Electric lights shone from the windows of every building, and streetlights stood at attention on each corner.

"On the surface, it seems like the water is hardly moving!" The dam's chief engineer had to shout to be heard above the noise of the mill and the dam's turbines. "But five hundred cubic feet of water per second continually flows through the dam's gate." Dressed in blue-and-white striped overalls and a cap, he pointed. "So you see those gratings that cover the entrance to the intake channel?"

Bucholz nodded.

"Well, if there was a dead body in this pond, the considerable undertow would have washed it up against these grates by now." He wiped his brow with a sleeve. "What has it been? Three or four days?"

"Almost a week."

"We would have found him by now. We have to clean out debris from these grates every couple of days," the engineer said.

"What do you do with it?" asked Bucholz.

"With what?"

"The debris."

"It gets hauled away. Well, first it goes into that pile over there." He gestured with his head to the north side of the dam. "We dispose of it every couple of weeks."

Bucholz didn't expect to see anything of interest, but he walked over to the conglomeration of wood chunks, weeds, garbage, and other less identifiable items. He stepped back when he got a whiff of the fly-covered mound.

"What's that?" Bucholz pointed toward something in the pile.

"What's what?" asked the engineer.

Bucholz grabbed a nearby stick. Grimacing as he handled the grimy implement, he started poking at something furry.

"It's some dead critter." The engineer scowled.

Bucholz continued poking at the specimen. After a couple of attempts, he retrieved it with the stick. He pulled out the mess of fur and held it close to his face. He wrinkled his nose, but then raised it into the air in triumph, like a trophy.

"This, sir, is what you call a coonskin cap."

******

When Bucholz arrived back at the office that afternoon, he saw the headline on the front page of the early edition of the *Spokane Daily Chronicle*:

"MYSTERY WOMAN" IN DISAPPEARANCE CASE

JOHN L. OLSON OF KOOTENAI, IDAHO, MISSING ON TRIP TO SPOKANE – BELONGINGS FOUND ON RIVERBANK – POLICE GET MYSTERIOUS TELEPHONE CALL.

The article included a picture of John Olson as well as his description. It also featured some rather imaginative conjectures.

Was Olson slugged by thugs, robbed, and his body dumped in the mill pond of the Phoenix Lumber Company near Howard Street?

Did he leave his grip and papers on the bank of the stream as a ruse to go to parts unknown?

Did he end his life in the black waters of the mill pond of his own volition, or did he accidentally fall in?

The lengthy article also quoted various family members, each of whom denied that John would kill himself or run off with a strange woman.

Bucholz took note that the story failed to explain a connection between Olson's disappearance and the anonymous phone call, other than the location—the mill pond. He shook his head and threw the paper in a wastebasket. *Only a two-bit reporter would link the disappearance of Olson on Friday night with a phony call that came in four days later.*

******

While the detective worked on the case in Spokane, Helen pursued her investigation in Kootenai. She got off the train and went straight to Sam Clark's house and knocked sharply. Sam and John were coworkers, and he owed John a favor. A big favor.

She could hear his muffled yell from inside. "Who's at the door?"

His wife's voice called back. "Go back to sleep. I've got it."

Sam often worked a graveyard shift, and Helen had known he might be sleeping.

"Hello, Helen," Meta said when she opened the door. She held a wooden spoon with flour on it. "Nice of you to stop by."

"This isn't a social call," Helen said. "I need to see Sam."

"Well, he's sleeping— "

"I need to see him right now." Her voice quivered. She regretted sounding so forceful. Unclenching her fists, she struggled to calm herself. "It's important," she added in a quieter voice.

Meta dropped the towel and hurried to wake her husband.

Helen could hear grumbling and low talk from the bedroom as Sam's wife summoned him to the front door. Soon Meta reappeared. "I'm sorry. Where are my manners? Come inside, Helen,"

Helen entered, but she wouldn't sit down. Soon a rumpled and hastily dressed Sam Clark eased into the living room.

"What's all the fuss?" Sam rubbed the sleep from his eyes.

"John's missing."

Meta gasped.

"What do you mean?" Sam shoved his hair back.

After she explained the situation briefly, she said, "Sam, I need you to tell the police the names of the men who threatened you—and John."

"You know about that?"

"I heard you and John discussing it on the front porch a couple of months ago. I just never talked to John about it." Helen frowned. "I could tell he was trying to keep it from me."

"Well, that's true. He didn't want you to worry. But the sheriff and I aren't exactly on speaking terms, you know." Sam shuffled his feet. "He thinks I should be dangling from a rope."

"None of that matters. I need you to tell the police those names." She paused and then added in a softer voice, "John needs you."

He took a deep breath. "Okay. First thing in the morning—"

"Please, Sam. Time is wasting. I need you to come with me on the next train to Spokane so we can tell the police there. The sheriff in this county may not be so cooperative."

On the train with Sam back to Spokane, Helen remembered what John had told her about that fateful night two years ago at the Bonner Store.

Two years earlier, Monday, March 13, 1922

The late winter snowstorm was all the talk at the Bonner Store.

John Olson and four other locals lounged in the gathering area, discussing the latest news, gossip, and weather. The combination mercantile and meat market also served as the Kootenai Post Office. The men stood, warming themselves at the potbelly stove in the center of the room.

Everyone turned to face the door when Bert Partridge stormed in, his face red and frowning.

"Have any of you seen Clark?"

Partridge stood over six feet tall and was in the prime of his life. Everyone in the room knew about the long-standing feud he had with Sam Clark, and now it seemed it had come to a boil.

Olson exchanged glances with the other men. "I haven't seen him since this morning."

"Well, if you see him, tell him I'm looking for him. He's crossed the line this time."

"What now?" Frank Bonner stood behind the counter.

"I'll tell you what." Partridge took off his trilby and brushed the snow onto the area rug by the door. "As usual, that no-account liar can't be trusted with anything. Least-wise money."

Olson picked an apple from a barrel and took a bite. "Are you talking about the pledge drive?"

The men all knew Partridge and several other townsfolk had been gathering pledges to help support a local family. Tuberculosis had claimed the life of a husband and father, their only wage-earner.

"Yes." Partridge screwed his hat back on. "I have reason to believe he has gathered more funds than he is admitting to, and is keeping some of the money."

"That's a serious accusation, Bert." Frank glanced out the window. "But you can ask him yourself. Here he comes now."

Sam walked in the front door stomping snow off of his boots. Seeing everyone staring at him, he looked at first like he might bolt back out.

Instead, he bowed his head and approached the bread counter, avoiding eye contact. No one spoke at first, until he asked Frank for a slice of cake. The proprietor wrapped a piece of chocolate cake and handed it to Sam.

Frank broke the awkward silence. "Sam, could we talk?"

"I've got nothing to say."

"Come on, we can go into the storeroom, just the two of us. You can tell me your side."

In silence, Sam drummed his fingers on the counter.

Bert Partridge announced, "I am going to leave the room. I want Sam Clark to give an account to you gentleman as to the money collected. If you find his answer satisfactory, so will I. Otherwise, he will have to settle up with me." Partridge walked out the front door, brushing past Olson on his way out.

Everyone waited for Sam to say something, but instead, he inspected the apple barrel.

Like Sam, Olson worked for the railroad, but they both had unpaid positions with the town of Kootenai as well. Sam was the mayor; Olson held the position as the town marshal. He didn't want this to develop into a situation. "Sam, we're all friends here."

Sam's face reddened, but he continued in his resolve, choosing to look anywhere but at any of the men in the room. They all glanced at each other and shrugged.

After a moment, Partridge re-entered. "Well?" he asked.

Olson shook his head.

Bert removed his coat and hat and set them on a crate next to the front door. He pulled the rubbers off his shoes.

"I have nothing to say to you or anybody else." Sam Clark's hands shook. "There has been too much said already. If I say anything else, I am apt to regret it."

If a fight ensued, the mismatch would be significant. Partridge's lean, muscular body made Sam seem pudgy and small. In his mid-fifties, Sam had two decades on Partridge.

"Bert," Frank said. "Forget it, and shake hands."

"I can't," Bert snarled through clenched teeth. "I have to do it."

Sam Clark stuffed the cake into his coat pocket and forged his way toward the door, but Partridge blocked him. Three times Sam attempted to get around him, and the third time, he almost got there. But Partridge grabbed him by the lapel of his coat with his left hand, spun him around, and laid a vicious blow to the face with his right.

Blood immediately began to flow from Sam's nose. Stunned, he kept both hands in his pockets and stooped forward, pressing his face against Partridge's torso in an apparent attempt to avoid further injury to it. But Partridge was ferocious, shoving him backward and laying blow after blow. Sam absorbed the punches, staying tucked, but the barrage sent him reeling back, and he let out a loud grunt at each jab.

Olson, ready to step in to stop the salvo, was surprised to see the tide turn. Bert Partridge retreated, and Sam Clark's hands were out of his pockets in a clench with Partridge. Somehow, Sam had gotten the upper hand.

They were both stooped over, and Clark had Partridge in a headlock. Frank cringed when Partridge fell back against a glass cigar case. Boxes of cigars fell out the back, and Frank reached out with his right hand to keep the case from tipping over altogether.

As they separated, Bonner saw blood coming from Partridge's chest. "What's wrong, Bert?"

"He stuck me!" Bert Partridge slumped against a wall, his face contorted. His voice was strained and high-pitched and his lips were turning blue.

Confused, Olson grabbed Clark by the arm and pulled him away from Partridge. He turned in revulsion when he saw Clark's blood-covered face.

"Come on." Olson pulled Clark out to the wooden porch in front. He stooped down and picked up some snow. "Here, use this to clean up." Clark smeared the snow over his face and scooped up more. When Olson decided it was good enough, he told Sam to follow him back into the store.

Olson saw Frank stooped over Partridge, applying rags to his bloody chest. With an urgent tone, Frank turned to Olson. "Go get Hazel."

Olson immediately charged back outside. Getting in Frank's Ford truck, he drove the three blocks to Partridge's house and brought Bert's wife back to the store. When they returned only a few minutes later, Bert's unconscious body lay limp on the floor. Frank said the doctor was on his way.

Olson glanced around. "Where's Sam?"

DAY 7

THURSDAY, APRIL 17, 1924

The windmill stood at rest.

Johnny used an old rag to dust off the seats of the buckboard before he and his sisters climbed aboard, heading for Cold Springs School. As was his custom, Larkin came to help the girls on.

Larkin lent a hand to Sylvia, but she didn't take it. Folding her arms across her chest, she frowned at Larkin. "Dorothea says you were joshing about the windmill."

"Did she now?" Larkin smiled at Dorothea, who already sat beside Johnny. He winked at her and then lifted Sylvia by her waist and set her on the other side.

"Be sure and tell your teacher about everything you're learning on the farm." Larkin waved and turned to start another day of plowing.

******

Detective Paul Bucholz sat at his desk in the Spokane Police Station, straining to hear Sheriff Hanson through a bad connection. The detective had called the Bonner County Sheriff in order to get more information on

Clark's murder trial in Kootenai from two years ago. The night before, Clark had come in with Helen to report the names of two men who had uttered threats to himself and Olson in connection with the trial.

"Partridge was dead before he arrived at the hospital due to blood loss," Sheriff Fred Hanson said. "After the fight in the store, one of the witnesses noticed a broken knife blade lyin' on a glass case in a pool'a blood. Later, Olson found the handle to the same knife with the broken stub behind the store. Clark musta heaved it as far as he could over the roof when no one was lookin'," Hanson said.

"Where did they find Clark?" Bucholz asked.

"Olson found him at home and turned him over to the sheriff's department, where they questioned him."

"Did they arrest him?"

"Not then," the sheriff said. "The coroner's inquest found him to have acted in self-defense. It wasn't until the hearin' about two weeks later they filed formal charges and he was bound over for trial. Some six months later, a jury acquitted him."

"So what's your take on the whole thing?" Bucholz banged the receiver against his desk to see if he could clear up the problem.

"Partridge was a hothead, but he didn't deserve to get stabbed in the heart. And frankly, I think it was a setup."

"What do you mean?"

"Well, take the murder weapon, for example," Hanson said.

Bucholz found it interesting Hanson used the term "murder weapon" even though there had been an acquittal. "What about it?"

"A pocket knife. Clark contended throughout the trial it wasn't his. He claimed he found it in the store just sittin' on the counter. None of the witnesses corroborated his claim. So it's likely the knife was in his pocket all along. Several other witnesses testified that Clark routinely carried a pocketknife."

"So? Many people do."

"Well, none of the witnesses actually saw him draw it out of his pocket, either. You know, in the scuffle and all. None too surprising. But when did he have time to open it?" The sheriff paused, and when Bucholz didn't respond, he continued. "I think it hid in his pocket, opened up and ready for service."

"You think Clark planned on killing Partridge?" the detective asked.

"They had been feudin' for years. Pretty public too. Everyone knew about it."

"But I thought Clark tried to avoid the fight." Bucholz thumped the receiver with his finger.

"It was all an act, if ya' ask me. You know he's a politician, don't ya?"

"I thought he was an engineer for the Northern Pacific."

"Yeah, but they also elected him mayor of Kootenai shortly before the murder," Hanson said.

There he went again, calling it a murder.

Hanson continued. "I don't trust politicians, do you?"

Bucholz remembered Hanson had obtained his office by appointment, not election. It happened after the previous sheriff found himself in jail for using his position to distribute alcohol.

The detective answered Hanson's question. "As a cop, I arrest petty thieves every day. But for some reason, the biggest thieves manage to get elected to office. I'd like to lock them all up."

"I have to agree. Thieves and liars. So the way I see this is, Clark put on an act, you see. Pretendin' he didn't want to get into a fight, figurin' that Partridge would initiate one. Besides, if Clark *really* didn't want to get into a fight, all he would have had to do was explain what he was intendin' to do with the charity money."

"Do you think Olson and the others were in on it?" Bucholz asked.

"Nah. Clark duped them, too. But I do think they were all a little bit too anxious to help out their friend at the trial. That's what has some people up here all steamed up. Some are saying a lot of things didn't come up at the trial that should have."

"Like what?" The detective shoved the receiver hard to his ear and leaned forward as if that would help him hear Hanson better.

"Like the open knife. For some reason, the prosecutor never pursued that line of questionin'. To be honest with you, the former sheriff kind of botched the whole investigation. No coincidence he's pretty good friends with Olson and the others, too."

"So tell me about the two men Clark named as people posing threats toward himself and Olson." Bucholz shifted in his chair.

"Jack Sperry I don't know much about, except he works at the Humbird Lumber Mill up here. Harry Preston I know quite well. He's a traveling salesman. Sells magazines. He was a friend of the Partridges, and I know he is none too happy about the way the trial went. But he's not the malicious type. I know. I've gone huntin' with him a couple times."

So the new sheriff of Bonner County and Harry Preston are chums. "Do you think you could run down these two men and ask them about their whereabouts for last Friday? That's when Olson disappeared. I don't know yet if they *need* an alibi, but we might want to start laying the groundwork."

"You really think somebody did Olson in?"

"I'm running down all the possibilities." Bucholz knew Helen Olson would be back in today and would want to know what he found out about the suspects. "Could you also find out something else for me? See what you can find out about the Olsons. She got all prickly when I asked questions about their marriage. Maybe you could nose around up there and see if you can learn anything about their relationship. I wonder if it's as idyllic as they want us to think."

"Sure thing. I have a few sources that can help me. I'll get back to you as soon as I know somethin'."

******

Lena Timm liked keeping her home neat and tidy. Especially the kitchen. She didn't hear Mr. Timm come in behind her as she worked.

"You're going to rub a hole clean through that bowl if you're not careful," the farmer said.

Startled, Lena nearly dropped the bowl. "Oh, Will. See what you almost made me do." She set the bowl on the counter harder than she meant to.

"What's wrong, Teacup?"

"Nothing, I'm just trying to get the stain out of that blessed bowl."

Will put his hand on Lena's shoulder. "Now, after fourteen years of marriage, I can tell when you're fretting about a bowl stain or something else. What's on your mind?"

Lena set down the washrag. "Well, I am rather concerned about Mr. Larkin."

"Seems to me he's working out fine," Will said.

"Oh, it's not that. It's just, well, I'm worried about him. I took a sandwich out to him a bit ago. Before he saw me, I heard him singing."

Will tipped his head. "I've heard him out there too. Doesn't seem like such a bad thing to me. Most times he sings hymns."

"No, I don't mean it's bad; he has a wonderful voice." She picked up the washrag and wrung it out. "It's just that he sings them so sorrowfully."

"He does seem to be a rather melancholy person sometimes. Although he cheers up when he's around the children."

"Well," she sighed, "he looked to me like he may have been crying. What do you think he's not telling us?"

"It's none of our business, Lena. More work gets done in less time than any hired hand I've ever had. He could run this farm if I was out." Will took off his Stetson and beat it against his leg once. "I say it's best not to be too nosey. If he wants to tell us something, he will."

Lena sighed. "I invited him to come to church with us again this Sunday. I told him he should join the choir. We could use another tenor. I figured with it being Easter and all it would lift his spirits."

"What was his reply?"

"He said 'maybe.' He seems nice, but a little odd, don't you think?"

"I'd say he's odd enough to make life on the Timm farm a little more interesting."

******

"What have you been telling the papers, anyway?" Helen Olson spread a copy of last evening's paper on Bucholz's desk.

Bucholz didn't look at it. He scooted a chair over for her to sit in. She didn't.

"The newspapers are in the business to sell papers," he said. "Headlines like that sell. I, on the other hand, am in the business of solving crimes. Reporters come in here and read police reports and write their own headlines. The *Spokesman-Review* got it right in this morning's paper. The 'Mysterious Woman' was a hoax."

"Hmm. The *Chronicle* put their story about my husband running off with someone as the main headline. The *Review* mentioned it as a hoax at the end of a short article on page seven."

"Like I said, whatever sells papers. I've asked the *Chronicle* to print a retraction in tonight's paper."

"That's kinda like putting the wax back on the candle, isn't it?"

"Which is why I don't work for the *Chronicle*."

"No, you work for me." She sat down across from the detective's desk. "So what can you tell me about the men that threatened John?"

The detective sat straight in his chair. "First of all, I don't work for you. I work for the City of Spokane. You don't even pay taxes here.

"Secondly, I know you've already seen this morning's paper, so you know we are working on the 'new angle,' as they are calling it in the *Review*." He pointed to the headline. I have people exploring the theory that somebody may have wanted revenge on your husband because of his testimony in the Clark trial. We should know something later today."

******

In fact, Paul Bucholz was very busy exploring a number of angles. Not only did he have Sheriff Hanson working on the investigation up in Bonner County, but two people were dragging the river.

The coonskin cap sat hidden in a drawer in the basement evidence room at the station. Only he and Chief Turner had a key to this room. Bucholz had decided to keep the discovery of the cap to himself unless they found Olson's body in the pond. Why present evidence that would detract from his theory that Olson left town on his own recognizance?

He stood on the south shore of the mill pond directing the two men who were dragging bars connected to chains behind their boat. "Have you done over there yet? No, over there. Do that area." Bucholz squeezed his temples. The slow process and all the shouting and pointing and miscommunication tested his patience. He had better things to do.

******

A trim, matronly woman in a conservative black dress and a wide-brimmed feathered hat positioned herself at the police desk. She stood stock-straight and gave the desk officer the name of Dinah Richardson.

"I wish to report information relevant to the disappearance of Mr. Olson."

"Uh, well, Detective Bucholz is out right now. He's the one handling that case. Can I take the information?" the police sergeant said.

Chief Turner overheard the conversation and introduced himself. "I'd be happy to take any information you can give us in the Olson case."

Once seated in the chief's office, she gave her story through pursed lips. "Last week, I was walking home from the meeting of the Maccabee Lodge with another one of the ladies, and we noticed a man acting quite strangely at the Howard Street Bridge."

"What night was that?" The chief wrote in a notebook.

She lowered her eyebrows and frowned at Turner as if she believed he had not been paying attention. "Why, it was the same night as the disappearance of Mr. Olson."

He glanced up. "Go on."

"Well, he ran up and down the riverbank at the mill pond right there at the bridge. We thought he looked like he was about to jump in. So we decided to get closer to investigate, and when he saw us he became alarmed."

"What did he do then?"

"He ran. He ran across the bridge to the other side." She stretched her right arm and flitted her fingers as if shooing a dog away.

"The north side?" Turner paused in his notetaking.

"Yes. And then he ran down to the bank over there, and it appeared to us he was trying to get through the iron railings to get to the river."

"What did you do then?"

"Well, as Ladies of the Maccabees, we felt it our duty to help someone in need."

Chief Turner nodded.

"So we tried to approach again. We hoped we could stop him from making a terrible mistake. But when he saw us, he panicked again and ran away farther." She made the same gesture with her arm and, wide-eyed, gazed in the distance. "We couldn't keep up with him."

When the chief asked for a description of the man, she said, "It was John Olson. Just like the picture in the paper."

✶✶✶✶✶

Paul Bucholz returned to his office desk and plopped down in his chair. Somehow, standing around watching other people work—dragging the pond—was more tiring than actually working. Before he had the chance to write a report, the chief came in with some papers in his hand.

"Find anything at the bottom of the mill pond?" Turner asked.

"Yeah," Bucholz said. "Chunks of wood, garbage, an old rubber boot—size ten. Oh, yeah, there was one body part."

"Oh?" Turner raised his eyebrows.

"The fender of a Stutz Bearcat."

"Well, something came up here." The chief handed Bucholz a report. "Seems that a certain Mrs. Richardson saw Olson acting erratically on Friday night."

Bucholz browsed the report and frowned. "Hmm."

"What's wrong?" Turner asked.

"I don't know. I'll have to think about it." The detective rubbed his eyes. "I'm calling it a day."

******

"Plowed all day. No change," read the curt entry in J.A. Larkin's journal. He had already begun to lose track of time with each long and monotonous day. His hope of getting his memory back began to fade.

He turned down the wick in the oil lamp until the flame went out. Heaving a sigh, he felt like the fire in his soul was quenched as well. He felt terribly alone.

******

Detective Bucholz sat on the front porch of his home on West Gardner, smoking his pipe. He enjoyed the warm mid-April evening air. Though he was trying not to think about work, something about the report from Mrs. Richardson bothered him.

His neighbor, Mrs. Daily, strolled past his gate and gave a friendly "Hello." Nodding back, he remembered something. "Mrs. Daily?"

"Yes."

"You belong to the Ladies of the Maccabees, don't you?"

"Why, yes. I'm returning home from our weekly meeting." Mrs. Daily wore a floppy hat adorned with daisies. She smiled cheerily, her disposition matching her festive hat.

"You must know a Mrs. Richardson?" he asked.

"Of course, she's our treasurer. Why?"

"Was she there tonight?"

"She's there every Thursday night. Do you know her?"

Bucholz nodded. "I'm about to."

DAY 8

FRIDAY, APRIL 18, 1924

The office doorknob came off in his hand Friday morning.

Just typical of the way Detective Bucholz's morning was going. Several people ducked when he raised his arm in a motion suggesting he would throw the offending handle at someone. His face glowed red but not from taking the streetcar in the brisk morning air.

Instead of throwing the knob, he forced himself to be calm. Grinding his teeth, Bucholz serenely set the knob down on his desk. He would call maintenance later with some choice words. Storming back out of his office, he approached the desk sergeant, growling. "Who read the police report to the *Review* last night?"

The wide-eyed and trembling twenty-something recoiled but managed to stammer, "Ch-Chief Turner, sir."

Bucholz's eyes narrowed, and his lips squeezed together. He went back into his office for a few minutes in an attempt to calm his nerves further. Tapping his fingers on his desk, he tried to concentrate on the police reports. It was no use.

Leaving his office once again, he took a deep breath and crossed the hall to

Chief Turner's office. "Wes, we have a problem."

Wearing a dark-blue tie against a pressed white shirt, the Spokane Police Chief glanced up and then returned to his paperwork. "What is it now, Paul?"

"Sir, I read this morning's paper."

"Yes," Turner said without looking up. "They ran the story about Mrs. Richardson's sighting of John Olson."

"About that," Bucholz said. "It's not true."

That got Turner's attention. "What do you mean, it's not true?"

Bucholz remained standing. "Well, she may have seen somebody down by the river that night, but it wasn't John Olson."

"How could you know that?"

"Because she saw the deranged man on Thursday night. Olson didn't disappear until Friday night."

"She told me she saw him on Friday night." The chief tapped his pencil on the desk with each syllable.

"I confirmed it with her." Bucholz sat on the corner of Chief Turner's desk. "I went to her house to ask her specifically. Her meetings are always on Thursdays. She thought Thursday was the night he disappeared."

The chief threw his head back and stared at the ceiling.

"I see the paper reported that the police are going on a theory that Olson got hit on the head by thugs and is wandering around somewhere with amnesia."

The chief didn't respond.

"Is that what *you* told them?" Bucholz knew the answer to the question.

Chief Turner let out a long breath. "I told them it was one *possibility*." He stood and walked over to a wall and leaned against it. "I thought we finally had a lead. Are you sure about this?"

Bucholz nodded.

Chief Turner sighed. "I'm beginning to wonder if *you* shouldn't be our liaison to the newspapers."

"Might not be a bad idea," Bucholz said.

"But *you* never tell them anything," the chief said.

"Precisely."

******

The wind had picked up again on the farm in Harrington.

Will Timm made a decision. "We can't afford to waste another day working in the house. But it's too windy to plow. So we are going to bring the harvester down to the south forty and bring in the winter wheat. It's ready, and it could rain soon."

"It's not too windy for harvesting?" Larkin asked.

"It won't be easy." Will tipped back his Stetson. "But at least it won't be as dusty. You up to it?"

"Sure." Larkin slapped his hands together. Work kept his mind off of his troubles.

"I'll drive the horses while you gather the shocks," Will said. "When you get tired, we'll trade places."

The two of them worked hard all morning, and Lena brought out lunch. They sat with their backs leaned up against the wheels and ate pork sandwiches with cheddar cheese.

"So," Will said between bites, "you never have told me where you got your farming experience. Somewhere around here?"

Larkin's food stuck in his throat. He shook his head. "No. Grew up on a farm in Montana."

"Wheat farm?"

"Yeah." Larkin nodded and swallowed hard. "Wheat farm."

The pause in the conversation told Larkin he needed to elaborate, but since he had made it up on the fly, he didn't want to say anything that could be doubted. So he let the terse response stew there for a moment, making a show of his mouth being full.

"How 'bout you?" Larkin asked. "Where'd you learn to farm?"

"Goes back generations." Will brushed a dirt clod off of his pants. "I never even finished elementary school. Just worked on the farm. My father, August, came over here from Germany when I was very young. My whole family has been farming in Lincoln County ever since. You can't spit in these parts without hitting a Timm."

Larkin managed to keep the conversation away from his past for the rest of lunch, but he wondered how long he could keep it up.

*****

Helen Olson sat in Detective Bucholz's office in the Spokane police station for her daily update. Once again, Edward, her father-in-law, attended for moral support. They sat as the detective paced behind his desk.

"As you know, the story of your husband's disappearance is still a favorite with the local papers." Bucholz lit his pipe and puffed out a cloud of gray smoke.

"Can't anything be done about them?" Helen sat up straighter.

"They will always speculate, but they will tire of it soon." Bucholz continued to pace. "They'll make up lies about some other poor soul and then move on to the next."

"What is this about amnesia?" Helen asked. "Is there something we should know?"

"We know nothing about amnesia. Pure speculation. But I can assure you no more information about this case will go to the papers without first going through me and getting my approval."

Helen and Edward nodded. Before they could ask more questions, the detective forged ahead.

"I have a report from the sheriff of Bonner County on the two men who allegedly made threats toward your husband." Bucholz sat down at his desk.

"Not 'allegedly,'" Helen blurted. "They did."

"You have proof?" When he exhaled, the thick gray cloud failed to conceal Mrs. Olson's displeasure.

The detective continued. "One of the two men worked all day at the mill in Kootenai on the day your husband disappeared. The other one, however, rode the same train as John Olson on Thursday morning when they arrived here in Spokane."

Wide-eyed, Edward said, "So you've questioned him."

"Not yet. I still have to check sources here in Spokane," he replied, "but it's not likely he could have been near the river Friday night."

"But you're still investigating the possibility." Edward looked hopeful.

"Of course."

Bucholz set his pipe in its stand. "Now, there are a couple of other items we need to cover, Mrs. Olson."

Helen fidgeted in her chair.

"I have a report," Bucholz spoke slowly, "that you and your husband had an altercation on the Thursday morning when he left the house."

Helen took a deep breath and opened her mouth, but Bucholz did not pause.

"According to the report, your husband left the house with several pieces of luggage, and you were begging him not to leave."

"That's a lie!" She stood up so fast she almost lost her balance. Edward steadied her, holding his arm around her, but now she raged. "That busybody, Mrs. Hoover, has nothing better to do than to make up lies and spread them around like manure in the garden."

Bucholz rather enjoyed these kinds of confrontations. It gave him the chance to see what people were made of. Sometimes getting people all riled up would be the avenue to bring out the truth. People would come in with their prepared answers, all neat and tidy. But when you put them on the spot, they didn't have time to make up carefully worded replies.

"You already know what I told you, Detective. When he left the house, he did not carry *luggage*. Only a small satchel with a few personal items. The other bags were full of Fyr-Fyter samples and promotional literature and the like. You found those things yourself down by the river. Which proves she's a liar."

"So you didn't have a fight?"

Helen turned red. "We had… an argument."

The detective waited for her to elaborate.

"People have arguments."

Paul Bucholz could easily imagine having an argument with Helen Olson. It seemed like he might be having one right now. "Yes, people do. But they don't usually end with one begging the other not to leave."

"He wasn't *leaving*. I mean, he *was* leaving, he just… wasn't leaving *me*. John was just coming to Spokane. And now everybody is twisting everything and making things out to be different." Helen fidgeted with the front of her dress and stared at the floor.

Bucholz waited.

"I didn't want him to leave angry." She sat down again, calmer now. Her eyes were wet and her body shaking. There were a few moments of silence, and Edward reached over and held her.

"Can you tell me what the argument was about?"

She took a couple of deep breaths. "We were talking about moving. I mean, *I* talked about moving. To Spokane. John wanted to stay in Kootenai."

Bucholz let her words marinate a little and then continued. "We have one more report to discuss."

"Haven't you done enough?" Edward glowered.

"No, I'm okay." Helen straightened her dress and seemed to have collected herself.

Bucholz surged forward. "According to a report, a witness saw John Olson go into the Arlington Hotel Thursday morning with a young woman."

Bucholz did not get the expected response from Helen Olson. He thought she would go through the roof, but she controlled her emotions.

"Now that's simply ridiculous," she stated in a calm voice. Bucholz sensed conviction in her reply. "I know it's not true. And if you knew John, you would also know it's not true. All you have to do is a little investigating to find out somebody made it up." She glanced at Edward and then back to the detective. "Isn't that what you are supposed to do? Investigate?" She scowled at Bucholz.

Bucholz had, in fact, asked around at the Arlington. He already knew it wasn't true. But it didn't change the fact someone said it. And word got around. The sheriff in Bonner County had heard it too. But Detective Bucholz found Helen Olson's response very telling. She had confidence in her husband. John Olson apparently did not have the capacity to dally with other women.

"Yes." Bucholz jotted down some notes. "I will continue my investigating. But remember, Mrs. Olson. I'm merely filling you in on what I hear. Isn't this what you want?"

"Fine." Helen stood. "But let's not blab all this horse excrement to the papers. Enough damage has been done, don't you think?"

******

As much as Larkin yearned for human companionship and someone to talk to, he usually retired early to his quarters, sequestering himself after supper. Partly, he didn't want to interfere with the lives of the Timm family. But avoiding the subject of his past was paramount.

So he lived in lonely solitude. Self-banishment was preferable to utter exile. This evening he commiserated with his only true friend, the little red book.

How long have I lost my memory? I can't recall a place I've lived in or the name of a single acquaintance. If I have a mother, she must be worried to death. It nearly breaks my heart to think that some loved ones may be looking for me. I don't even know how old I am. Must be between 32 and 36 years old. Have I a wife and babies anywhere? And if I have, what will they do without me?

******

About the same time, Edward Olson got a call on the phone at his home in Freeman.

"Is Helen there?" Bucholz was on the other end.

Helen had stayed with her in-laws temporarily so she could be closer to the investigation.

"She's asleep. It's been a long day. Can I help?" Edward glimpsed the kitchen clock. Seven P.M. He, too, had fallen asleep reading in his chair.

"I need you to bring her in by eight tomorrow morning. She needs to identify something," Bucholz said.

"What is it?" Edward asked.

The detective paused. "I found your son's watch."

DAY 9

SATURDAY, APRIL 19, 1924

"Yes." Helen choked out the words. "It's John's watch."

A tear crept from her eye as she held the gold pocket watch in her trembling hands. She had given the watch to John as a special gift five years earlier when they first moved to Kootenai.

"The Northern Pacific required all their employees to have a watch with a minimum of seventeen jewels," Helen said. "The more jewels, the more accurate the watch. It had to be within a thirty-second variation over a one-week period."

Helen sniffled. "I ordered this watch from the Bonner store in Kootenai. Twenty-three jewels." Her eyes widened as she emphasized the number of jewels.

"So, it's an expensive watch." Bucholz did not state it as a question.

Helen nodded. "It's a forty-dollar watch. It's an Illinois Bunn. John is seldom seen without it." She sniffled again. "He regarded it as a prized possession."

A shudder ran through her as she pressed the timepiece close to her heart, wishing John were the one she held.

"Where did you find it?" Edward asked.

"At a pawn shop down on Main." Bucholz pulled his pipe from his lips and pointed the stem in the general direction of Main Avenue. "The suspect got ten dollars for it."

"Did the man give a name to the pawnbroker?" Edward asked.

"Yes," Bucholz said. "Does the name A.J. Larkin mean anything to you?"

Helen and Edward exchanged glances. With perplexed frowns, they responded by shaking their heads.

"Did the pawnbroker say what he looked like?" Helen asked.

"Oh, we can do much better than that, Mrs. Olson," Bucholz replied. "We have his picture."

Helen's astonishment turned to horror when the detective slid a copy of the suspect's photograph across his desk.

******

After plowing all day, Larkin went into nearby Davenport with Will after supper. He needed a distraction, so he picked up a copy of the *Spokane Daily Chronicle* while at the mercantile store.

Spokane's evening paper printed five editions daily. Headlines varied in each edition, and sometimes newer items appeared in later releases. Outlying towns like Davenport only got the "Fireside Edition"—the earliest printing.

Larkin found little of interest in this edition. The main headline was about the threat of foot and mouth disease coming to Spokane County. The usual political bantering of a presidential election year comprised much of the front page. The inside comprised a great deal of religious news, normal fare for a Saturday paper. Being the day before Easter, there was even more church publicity than usual.

He did not see later editions containing an article about a missing North Idaho man that pawned his watch the day he disappeared a little more than a week ago. His name was John Olson, but he had used an alias: A.J. Larkin.

DAY 10

SUNDAY, APRIL 20, 1924

Bright sunshine accosted worshippers on Resurrection Sunday. The J.W. Timm family attended Easter services at the Zion Lutheran Church in Davenport. Participating in the Sunday School pageant, the three Timm children dramatized the events at the garden tomb. Will and Lena sang in the choir as they presented a special Easter cantata.

Once again, they invited Mr. Larkin to come with them, but he declined. Lena believed the celebration would help lift his spirits, but Will insisted she avoid pushing the point.

******

In Spokane, the downtown streets were jammed with automobiles when the churches let out between noon and one o'clock. The latest fashions were on display. Women wore their fur chokers, stoles, and their tailored suits. Young ladies sported wide-brimmed hats and swagger sticks that were all the rage. Streetcars overflowed with passengers headed to Natatorium Park for baseball or Manito Park for the Spring Flower Show.

But Helen Olson wasn't interested in the festivities. For five straight mind-numbing days, she had been in Spokane and away from her family. Exhausted, she had returned to Kootenai to celebrate Easter with her truncated family. Her cousin, Cora Mae, helped watch the children in her absence. Cora had offered to stay and help with Easter dinner, but Helen had declined. She had already done enough for now but would be needed again in the coming week.

The Olsons worshipped at The First Congregational Church, where Pastor Munton offered a prayer for the family. He noted what a respected citizen John was. "A member and staunch supporter of the church, on the school board, and a trusted employee of the Northern Pacific."

When the congregation stood to sing "Up from the Grave He Arose," Helen choked on the words. One of her all-time favorite hymns sounded hollow. Grasping the pew in front of her to steady herself, she could only hope for the return of her husband. Jesus resurrected on the third day, but her husband had now been gone ten whole days. Was she still expecting a miracle?

After church, they walked home for an elaborate Easter dinner. The oldest children were especially helpful. Margaret assisted her mother with the cooking of the ham and asparagus. Raymond helped prepare deviled eggs. Charles and the other kids set the table and carried the food out to the table.

Helen had prepared peach cobbler for dessert, but she stumbled coming to the table, her knees weak. *Why is he gone?* Once again, she glanced at the top of the bookcase where his pocket watch rested. *Why would he pawn it?* She had never doubted John before, but now a battle raged in her soul. The evidence pointed down a road that she could not traverse.

Tomorrow she would be back on the train heading to Spokane. But this time, instead of going to the police station, she would ride with Edward to his home in Freeman.

Time for a new game plan.

******

It was even quieter and more lonesome than usual on the Timm farm. Being alone on a 640-acre wheat ranch on a Sunday with little to do made him feel downright forsaken. He had already read last night's paper, so he busied himself with some chores.

First, he straightened up his room. His personal effects were so slight the chore was complete in two minutes.

Then, an idea occurred to him. He changed into his suit pants and dress shirt and gathered up the rest of his clothes. Borrowing the wash tub, washboard, and a bar of Naphtha soap from the Timms' back porch, he carried them to the hand pump. He pulled his folding knife from his pocket and peeled a few shavings of soap. Dropping them into the bottom of the tub, he filled it with water.

He soaked his overalls, two shirts, one pair of underwear, and two pairs of socks in soapy water. Then he scrubbed and rinsed them right there at the pump. Wringing them out as much as possible, he took them back to his quarters. He hung them on a string near the wood stove to dry.

He was out of things to do again.

Percolating some coffee on his wood stove, he sipped his drink, careful not to burn his lip on the tin cup. *Maybe if I don't try so hard to think of my past, something will come to me by accident.* So he counted the number of floorboards in his room. It was necessary to move some furniture to accomplish this task. One hundred and seventy-six.

"Hmm." Still nothing.

He was almost sorry he hadn't taken them up on their offer to go to church. It could have been a well-needed distraction. But something about going to church still made him feel uncomfortable.

When the Timms arrived back home, he breathed a sigh of relief. They wore their Sunday best. Will looked dashing in a black suit, and the girls showed off their flowery homemade dresses to Larkin. He still wore his rumpled suit.

Lena started a lamb chop dinner complete with corn on the cob and baked potatoes with gravy. After dinner, the family invited him to browse a Montgomery Ward's catalog with them to order some goods. He sent for some underwear and work gloves.

That evening, the Timms urged him to take part in family activities.

"Come," Will said. "The cribbage board awaits. And I intend on evening up the score."

Larkin enjoyed the time spent with the family. He forgot about his troubles for a while, laughing, joking, and listening to stories.

But when he retired for the night, he collapsed into his oak chair, feeling a wave of emotion. The deep sorrow he often felt was absent, apparently spent, though the usual ones weighed on his shoulders. Fear, anger, disillusionment.

And now, a new emotion haunted him.

Guilt.

He thought about what his family must be going through. Here he was, laughing, eating good food, playing games. What about his family—if he had one—on this Easter Sunday? He could only imagine what they might be feeling. Heartbreak? Anger? Or maybe relief that he was out of their life. He could not imagine what circumstances brought him to this horrible condition, but something told him he must have a family.

The bed creaked when he sat on it. Sleep would not be coming soon. He stared into the nothingness of his room without the illumination of his lamp. His face hardened, his jaw clenched. He sat there and felt everything.

And nothing.

What a dilemma. He couldn't decide if it made him feel worse to have fun and feel guilty about it, or to just be miserable. In either case, it seemed his lot in life was to suffer.

******

With the Timm children in bed, Lena could talk to Will. "Mr. Larkin certainly was in high spirits tonight, wasn't he?"

"Yes." Will glanced up from his current issue of *Farm Journal Magazine*. "I haven't seen him so lively since he's been with us."

"Yet, I still worry about him." Lena dropped her knitting into her lap. "Will, what are we going to do about him?"

He set down his article on wheat co-ops. "Does something need to be done? Including him in the family seemed to help him a great deal. I think we should continue to do that and mind our own business about his personal concerns."

Lena tried not to sound preachy, but failed. "I suppose so long as we don't care anything about this poor soul. He's troubled and needs our help."

"Just what do you propose?" Will asked. "He has not sought our help in whatever is bothering him."

Lena picked up her knitting again but thought out loud. "I'm not so sure. I think without saying it, he is asking for help."

"But if he doesn't want to open up and tell us the problem, we can hardly offer advice." Will turned to his article again.

Lena stared off. "Have you noticed the way he reads his newspapers? Rustling through them like he's looking for something specific."

Will squinted at Lena. "You're not saying you suspect the law is after him, are you?"

"No," replied Lena. Her quiet voice exuded confidence. "He's no criminal. Criminals are shady. Mr. Larkin is as transparent as a Coke bottle."

"What then?"

"He's not running," Lena said, pointing at Will. "He's searching."

DAY 11

Monday, April 21, 1924

One way to get your mind off your troubles is to stay busy.

That was true in the case of Mr. Larkin today. He had his hands full, literally. He was back to plowing after a restful Sunday. He was glad to have fresh horses, but they were not as easy to work with. He struggled to plow a steep side hill all day, which was much more difficult than flat ground.

"Gee!" Larkin pulled the reins to coax the team left. Keeping the furrows straight on this side hill was a challenge because the plow had a tendency to slide. Controlling the horses was tricky and physically tiring. He was also careful to have the furrows turned downhill to prevent having any dead rows, which meant he couldn't just turn around at the end of the run like he could on flat ground. When he reached the headland, he had to run clear around the perimeter of the field with the team so he could come at it again from the same direction.

As a result, far less work got done in a day, and it made Larkin and the horses more exhausted. Yet, to his advantage, he hardly ever had time to think about the pickle he was in. He marveled at what he *could* remember. Personal memories were still not forthcoming, but as he worked, he recited aloud a Bible verse he had once memorized.

"Whatsoever thy hand findeth to do, do it with thy might; for there is no work, nor device, nor knowledge, nor wisdom, in the grave, whither thou goest."

Ecclesiastes 9:10

This verse brought some comfort because it gave him several clues about his past. First of all, he must have come from a Christian family to have memorized Biblical verses. It also told him that he must have come from a family convinced of the moral value of hard labor. In addition, the verse energized him because it made him remember that work is a blessing, not a curse. The ground had been cursed, to be sure. But to work the hard soil was far better than the alternative.

There had been times since his episode began when he felt so afflicted he had wished to die. But not today. Ironically, a day full of trials brought him an inner peace he could not explain even to himself.

******

On Monday morning, Detective Paul Bucholz had his notes with him along with a written report the chief required. Chief Turner met with his senior staff individually to get updates on the latest cases. Sitting in Turner's paneled office, Bucholz waited for the chief to start with the questions.

"Hmm…" The chief kept his eyes trained on the report. "In your estimation, how does the pawned watch affect the case?"

"It tells me Olson wasn't mugged or murdered. He didn't commit suicide. He disappeared on his own." The detective tried not to appear smug, but he conveyed confidence in solving the case.

The chief drummed his fingers on the desk. "Could you go over the timeline for me? Start from the beginning."

"Sure." Bucholz flipped through his notes. "On April tenth, let's see, that was a Thursday, at about ten A.M., Olson left his home in Kootenai, Idaho, to sell fire extinguishers in Spokane. After a loud argument with his wife, he went straight to the train station in Sandpoint, arriving in Spokane at about eleven-thirty that morning."

Turner nodded, rubbing his chin as he concentrated on the information.

"Olson crossed the street to the Arlington Hotel. His room wasn't ready that early, so, leaving a few personal items at the desk, he left. His whereabouts are not known until three P.M., when he arrived at Home Telephone and

Telegraph for his first sales appointment with Phillip Matthews."

The chief took notes. "Keep going."

Bucholz shuffled through his papers. "Matthews cut the meeting short. He asked Olson if they could continue again at nine o'clock in the morning, and Olson agreed. Olson left the building at about three-thirty. He returned to the Arlington and checked into his room, leaving again a couple hours later."

The detective paused and glanced up at the chief, who twirled his finger to indicate he didn't want Bucholz to stop.

"He returned to the Arlington at approximately eleven o'clock P.M. and apparently stayed the night. A desk clerk saw him leave the hotel before nine the next morning."

"Did anyone see anything unusual about Olson's behavior at the hotel?"

"No, sir."

"Continue." The chief examined the ceiling while Bucholz searched his notes.

"Olson did not show up for his appointment at H.T. &T but was seen about an hour later at Bister and Tillman's Pawnshop on Main. There he pawned his railroad watch given to him by his wife as a gift. He used the alias A.J. Larkin."

"The pawnbroker identified him?"

"He gave me a perfect description, and later I showed him the picture." Bucholz produced the photograph of John Olson from the folder and placed it on the chief's desk.

Chief Turner picked up the photo, mulled on this a moment, and pursed his lips. "Did the pawnbroker say anything about Olson's behavior?"

"He said Olson appeared nervous." The detective let out a big puff from his pipe.

Turner shuffled in his seat. "How did you discover the watch?"

"Deductive reasoning." Bucholz pointed to his temple and could not contain a wry smile.

"Okay, Sherlock." Turner smiled back. "Tell me about it."

"The pawn ticket appeared Friday night on the floor of the Hippodrome Theatre. Somebody turned it in to the office, and someone there turned it in to us. I heard about it, and went over to the pawn shop on a hunch."

"A hunch?" Turner narrowed his eyes, expressing doubt.

"Well, Helen Olson told me he had an expensive pocket watch. When I saw the pawn ticket was a pocket watch, I decided to investigate." He blew a smoke ring to accentuate the triumph.

"Nice work, but it doesn't prove that Olson made a run for it."

Bucholz sighed. "He's using an *alias*, Wes. Who uses an alias unless they're hiding?" The detective stood and started counting points on his fingers. "Olson was short on funds. He needed cash to get out of town. Mrs. Olson told me he had only enough for one night's stay at the Arlington, a couple meals, and train fare back home. Why would he pawn his watch and use an alias unless he was planning on disappearing?"

Turner rested his elbows on his desk and pressed his mouth into his folded hands, thinking. "You don't think he had a liaison, do you?"

"I doubt it." Bucholz shook his head. "The *Chronicle's* 'Mystery Woman' headline turned out to be a hoax. I never saw a connection between the phone call and Olson. And the girl at the hotel was just someone he talked to. I know the girl. She's not the type, and neither is he, from what I gather."

The chief leaned forward, hunching his shoulders. "Who told you about the girl in the first place?"

"Now *that's* interesting." Bucholz thumbed through his notes. "His name is… Preston. He is one of the people I investigated as a suspect that had supposedly threatened Olson and his friends. By coincidence, Olson and Preston arrived in Spokane on the same train Thursday morning. He witnessed Olson go into the Arlington at the same time she did."

"The suspect was on the same train as Olson? You call that a *coincidence*?" Turner's eyes widened. "And then he insinuates Olson had an affair?"

Bucholz cleared his throat. "Preston commutes to Spokane frequently from Kootenai. He's a magazine salesman. He and Olson are not on friendly terms, but he traveled back to Kootenai before Olson disappeared. He told the truth about the girl being there, but she didn't know Olson."

Turner leaned back in his chair, steepling his fingers. "You forgot something."

The detective let out a puff of smoke. "What would that be?"

"Mrs. Richardson."

Bucholz grunted. "That's not part of the timeline, remember? She saw somebody on Thursday night. Olson disappeared on Friday night."

Turner spread his hands. "So? Olson was in town that night. You said you didn't know his whereabouts during that time, and she seemed certain of his identity."

The detective pointed the stem of his pipe at the chief. "She backed down when I talked to her. And still, the timing isn't right. A passerby discovered his belongings along the bank on Friday night, next to the Howard Street Bridge. Everyone else that saw him—before and after Mrs. Richardson's description of a crazy man—described him as being of sound mind."

An awkward silence filled the room for a few moments. But then the chief seemed to concede, raising his hands in surrender. "What's next?"

"Well," Bucholz began. "I've got the Smithson forgery case I've been neglecting. I can spend more time on that."

"You're done with the Olson case?"

"If something else comes up, I'll investigate, but I can't waste more department money on someone who doesn't want to be found."

******

"What do we do now?"

The question was uttered by Edward Olson, Helen's father-in-law. She sat with him at his kitchen table along with his wife, Annie. The setting sun painted reds and yellows against the white paneled walls as they sipped coffee. Helen's in-laws looked to Helen, hoping she had a plan.

She didn't.

For the past week, she had called all the plays, but now she sat with her in-laws at the table, out of energy and ideas.

"Why don't we make wanted posters and distribute them all over town?" Edward asked.

Annie frowned. "And make him look like some kind of criminal?"

Edward shrugged. "But we have to get the word out somehow. Somebody *had* to have seen him."

Helen's face grew dark. "Detective Bucholz told me the case was all but closed."

Annie gasped. "Why?"

"He said they had exhausted their resources for an entire week and came up with nothing except the pawned watch. According to him, the watch indicates that John disappeared on his own accord."

"That's ridiculous," Annie said with a huff. "Anyone who knows John knows that isn't true."

"Well, the police *don't* know John." Helen took a deep breath and shuddered. "To them, he's not a victim—he's a suspect."

"So are they giving up?" Annie held her china cup in both hands but didn't drink.

"Unless new information comes in…" Red-eyed, Helen shook her head, unable to finish the sentence.

Over the past week, they had searched throughout the city several times. The newspapers had published John's picture and had given the case plenty of publicity. Not all of it good.

They sat in silence for a few moments.

"No, not 'Wanted,'" Annie said. It should say 'Missing.' That way, it doesn't look like the federal authorities are after him."

Edward pulled at his chin. "I have an even better idea."

REWARD
DEAD OR ALIVE

JOHN L. OLSON
Age 34, Height 5ft
11 inches, Wht. 195,
stout build. Thick
dark brown hair co-
bed pomp. Blue-gray
eyes. Full face, medium
complexion. Wen on left
wrist, long, slender white
mole at base of neck.

Left home at Kootenai,
Idaho, Thursday, April 10,
for Spokane, Wash. Was
last seen April 11th in the
afternoon at Spokane, Wn.
A Reward of $200.00
will be paid for information
leading to Olson's disco-
very if alive, and $100.00
for parties giving information that will lead to the
recovery of body if dead.

**Call Police Dept., Spokane or
Sheriff's Office, Spokane, Wn.**

DAY 12

TUESDAY, APRIL 22, 1924

REWARD

DEAD OR ALIVE

Edward suggested this headline for the flyer they would distribute all over the region. In Spokane, Sandpoint, Freeman, Kootenai, Milan, and any other areas John Olson might turn up.

"Reward," he had said. "*That* will get people's attention."

Helen was grateful that her father-in-law paid for the printing and put up the money for the reward: $200 for information leading to his discovery if alive and $100 for the recovery of the body if dead.

The poster included two portraits of John Olson. One matched the picture Helen had given the police and newspapers. She'd cropped it from a family portrait taken about ten years earlier. The other came from his days as a motorman on the streetcars in Spokane, wearing his uniform. Helen added the second one because she thought he looked quite different wearing a cap. Helen wished she had a more recent photo of John, but his appearance had changed little since the pictures were taken.

A full physical description followed, including details such as a birthmark on his left wrist and a slender white mole at the base of his neck.

While Helen designed the notice and its contents, Edward contacted the newspapers to let them know about the cash reward. Anyone with information could call the police or Orchard 25J2, Edward's phone number in Freeman.

Helen and Edward spent the morning getting two hundred copies made at McKee's Printing at the north end of the Monroe Street Bridge. Then they distributed them to other family members. Many friends also volunteered to post them at local businesses and on telephone poles in places where they would be seen.

Helen tried to be hopeful about the new poster, but she found they did little to lift her spirits. Despondent, she returned to Kootenai to be with her family after an absence of four days. While there, she and other relatives hung notices around Sandpoint, Kootenai, and nearby Ponderay.

After arriving at the train station in Sandpoint, she caught herself staring into the brown water of Sand Creek. A tear ran from her eye as she prepared to post a notice on a pole at the terminal. With a small hammer in her right hand and a tack in her left, she attached the poster. A shudder ran through her as she noted the wedding band that adorned her left ring finger.

The possibility she might not ever see John again was too much to bear. How would she be able to cope? What could she do for income? How could she be the rock for her family when she was an emotional wreck?

Her dark hair fell on her face as she leaned against the post for support and tried to tell herself they would find her husband. Something had just happened to him, that's all. The mystery would be solved and everything would be normal again, wouldn't it?

Oh, who am I kidding?

DAY 13

WEDNESDAY, APRIL 23, 1924

Edward had decided it was time for him to conduct his own investigation. It wasn't that he didn't trust Paul Bucholz.

Or was it?

Not completely, he decided. He didn't doubt the detective's competence, but felt he jumped to conclusions. Bucholz might know the criminal mind, but he didn't know John. The idea that his son would fake his own demise and disappear was not a possible explanation. He had to know more.

"Hello, my name is Edward Olson."

Mrs. Richardson had cracked her door only slightly to the stranger. She peered through the opening with a suspicious sneer. "What are you selling?"

"I'm not selling anything." He removed his bowler and held it with one hand against his chest. "I'm John Olson's father."

At first she frowned, but then her eyes widened and she opened the door fully. "Oh, I'm terribly sorry. I didn't mean to cause your family any grief. I thought the man I saw that night—"

Edward held out the reward poster displaying the two images of John.

She gasped. "Oh, my. Oh, my, my."

"Is this who you saw that evening?"

Mrs. Richardson caught her breath. She pressed her hands against her cheeks and closed her eyes as if envisioning that night. "I thought so. I mean, the police are convinced it *can't* be. You see, they told me it couldn't have been—"

"But you think the person you saw that night was John Olson?"

Mrs. Richardson held an open hand over her mouth and stared at the poster for a long moment. "Well, I am almost certain. You see, I felt so sorry for him. He looked so panicked. I was afraid he was going to jump into the river."

"I see. Were there other witnesses in the area?"

"Just Mrs. Miller, who was with me." She paused thoughtfully. "Oh, and there was another man. On the bridge."

"Another man? What did he look like?"

"Well, I wasn't paying much attention to *him*. He was walking behind us, and I was concentrating on Mr. Ols… your son."

"You have no description?"

"Let's see." She looked off, squinting. "He was about average height, I suppose. He was wearing a nice suit. Like he was a lawyer or salesman or some such thing. Anyway, after your son fled, I turned around and the man was gone. He must've changed his mind and gone back down Howard Street."

Edward talked to Mrs. Richardson for about twenty minutes. Each time she glanced at the picture, she gasped and buried her face in her hands. Edward could tell she recognized him.

But it didn't add up. If something traumatic had happened to John on Thursday night, why would witnesses that saw him on Friday say he acted normal?

Next, he went to the pawn shop on Main. This time, Edward did not identify himself, just that he wanted to ask a few more questions about John Olson. He said he came from the police station. If the proprietor took that to mean he was an officer, so be it.

Barney Tillman, the store owner, identified the picture and showed him the ledger signed "A.J. Larkin." Edward recognized the handwriting.

"Did he act unusual in any way?" asked Edward.

"Oh, I don't know. He acted pretty normal, I guess. Just nervous. He kept looking around, and barely glanced at me," replied the pawnbroker, a tall skinny man Edward thought acted a bit nervous himself. He kept wiping his nose with his finger and then onto the seat of his pants.

"In your opinion, did he act in his right mind?"

"I guess so. I mean, I don't know what he was like before that day." The shop owner chuckled at himself.

"But you didn't think he acted odd?"

The pawnbroker seemed to give it some thought. "Not really," he concluded. "I mean, I get all types in here, ya' know. I try not to be a judge of character, but with thieves and criminals everywhere, well, you have to keep an eye out." He pointed to his temple, which indicated to Edward that Mr. Tillman considered himself to be of very sharp mind.

"I knew something wasn't quite right when he came in, all twitchy and all, but I didn't take him to be suspicious or anything." Tillman hitched up his pants, which seemed ready to cascade to the floor at any moment. "Except for one thing. Between you and me, I knew he wasn't who he said he was."

"How so?"

"He had to think about it. I've seen it often enough. Only people that are making up a name have to think about it. It was a slight hesitation, but enough to know."

Edward browsed the merchandise near the counter as he listened to the pawnbroker. "You said that he wouldn't look at you, right? Did he pay attention to anything in particular?"

"No. Most of the time, he just kept looking here and there." The store owner mimicked the behavior, swiveling his head about the room. "My experience is that when people won't look you in the eye, they're liars."

"I see." Edward nodded and scratched his chin. "When he spoke to you, where did he stand?"

"Oh, most of the time, right about where you are. I stood here at the counter, and he more or less stood across from me." Tillman smiled nervously.

"Did he ever look at these?" Edward held up a green box of matches from a display near the counter. They had the word "Martyr" on them and were imported from Ireland.

"Yeah, I think he bought some of those, too."

"I'll take three boxes."

The seller hesitated, apparently surprised at the turn in the conversation. "Okay." He banged down some keys at his cash register. "That will be six cents."

Edward handed over the pennies and thanked him for his time. On the way out, he noticed the glass case displaying timepieces. Turning back to Tillman, he said, "Ten dollars?"

"Huh?" The pawnbroker acted bewildered. "Those are railroad watches. They start at about *forty* dollars."

"You gave him ten dollars for a twenty-two-jewel railroad watch. That's highway robbery."

"That's business!" The pawnbroker took a step backward, his contorted face showing indignation.

"I know how you pawnbrokers work. You took advantage of him because you sensed he was desperate, right?"

Tillman didn't speak, leering back at Edward with a curled lip.

"I'm not sure if I could sleep at night if I was you." Edward turned to leave once again.

As Edward opened the door, the pawnbroker shot back, "Yeah? Well, I wouldn't be able to sleep at night if I accepted ten dollars for a watch that my wife had given me just so I could run off with some... some floozy!"

Edward felt the blood rush to his face but managed to shut the door calmly behind him.

The five-story Arlington Hotel sat five blocks away from the pawnshop. It was Edward's next stop. By the time he got there, he had regained his composure, but was disappointed when he couldn't talk to the clerk who saw John leave the hotel on Friday morning. Nor the one who saw him come in Thursday night. He would have to come back tomorrow when they were on shift.

Leaving the building, he noticed a young lady sitting on the bench outside. She was a flapper girl. Holding the poster in his hand, he asked, "Excuse me, miss, but have you seen this man before?"

She barely glanced up from filing her fingernails. "Who wants to know?

Are you another cop?"

"No, I'm his father."

Her countenance, which had been hard upon his approach, changed dramatically. She gave him a warm smile.

"Let me see that." She seemed like a different person than she had been seconds ago. "Yeah, I seen 'im." She held the poster with both hands and read it like she was studying for a test.

Sitting down on the bench next to her, Edward asked, "Can you tell me about it?"

She handed the paper back to Edward, pulled a long cigarette holder out of her little bejeweled purse, and secured a cigarette to the end. "Gotta light?"

Edward pulled a green matchbox from his vest pocket. Using his thumbnail to strike the match, he deftly lit her cigarette.

After a couple of puffs, she produced a smoke ring and smiled again, triumphantly. Then she turned her head away and replied while staring off as if recalling a distant, glorious memory. "He was so cute. He came across the street there with a bunch of baggage." She nodded toward the train station. "I think he was going on some big trip somewhere, you know? But he wore this silly hat. It had a tail!" She giggled.

"Then what?" asked Edward, leaning forward.

"Well, I asked him to light me up, just like you. Heh. Like father like son, huh?" She laughed at her own little joke.

Edward waited for her to continue her story, but she seemed to be finished. "And…?"

"No, that's it," she said. "That's the only time I seen 'im."

"Did you talk to him?"

"Not really." She let out another smoke ring. "He just went inside. Well, I got up and opened the door for him 'cause his hands were so full."

"And is that the last time you saw him?"

"Yeah, but the police seem to think that I'm some sort of a gold digger or something. Some jerk told the cops that he saw me go in with 'im."

"But you didn't?"

"You kiddin? I'm not that kinda girl, ya know." She swung one leg over the other, exposing her leg almost to the knee. "I mean, he wasn't as old as *you,* but *way* too old for me."

She seemed to be completely unaware of any offense given, but he ignored it anyway.

"Besides," she continued, "I already told the cops all that. Didn't they tell you?"

"No, I'm afraid they omitted some details." He laid the flyer on his lap. "So, you stayed out here? I mean, after you opened the door for him?"

"Yeah. I sat back down here, and after a couple minutes, I went in to flirt with him." She pointed to the front door of the hotel.

Edward felt confused. "You… flirted with him?" he asked.

"Not *him*, silly," she snickered, pointing at the poster. "Him!" She extended her index finger to the front door of the hotel.

Craning his neck, Edward could see her pointing to a young red-headed bellhop. He nervously waved, conscious they were talking about him.

"Isn't he the bee's knees?" She waved her fingers back at the bellhop. "It worked, too."

"What worked?"

"The flirting. Now he's my boyfriend. His name is Wally, *and* he has a car. Well, it's his dad's car, but he takes me for rides in it."

"He sounds pretty special," Edward said. "So, I hate to get off the subject, but can I ask you one more question?"

"Sure," she replied, oblivious they had ever gotten off track.

"When you went back in—to flirt with Wally—did you see my son then?"

"Nope. By the time I came in, he must have already gone to his room or somethin'."

Edward stood. "Well, it's been a real pleasure, uh…"

"Betty," she filled in.

"Betty," he repeated. "I enjoyed our chat."

"Wanna kiss?" She flashed that winning smile again.

"Pardon?" Edward started at her forwardness.

"Hold out your hand and close your eyes," she said in a sing-songy voice. Grabbing his left hand before he could comply, she put something in it. Then she forced his fingers to close. "There."

He opened his hand and found a foil-wrapped candy in it.

"It's called a kiss," she said. "Funny, huh? They call them that because of the sound they make when they come out of the candy-making machine." She followed this revelation with an exaggerated kissing sound. "I give 'em only to people I like, and I like you."

"I like you, too." Edward unwrapped the chocolate and popped it into his mouth. As he left, he added, "Oh, and Betty—thanks for the kiss."

******

"Ooh, ooh! Hot! Hot!"

Larkin gingerly eased into the galvanized washtub. "Aaaahhh, yes." He had heated up six buckets of water—two at a time—on the potbelly wood stove in the corner of his sleeping quarters. The tub he'd used to wash his clothes he borrowed again and had hauled it approximately one hundred yards downhill to his room, where he had a hot fire going. Then he had filled the buckets with water from the hand pump—also up near the house—and carried them with minimum spillage to his room. The entire process of preparing the bath took nearly an hour. But now he got in it.

"Oh, that feels good."

He finally settled into the vessel and closed his eyes, the back of his neck resting on its edge. Because of his length, or rather, the tub's lack of it, he had to splash the warm water repeatedly on his exposed knees. Two weeks of rigorous farm labor, and now he enjoyed his first bath.

After a few minutes of extravagant relaxation, he began with the business of his overdo ablutions. Wielding a bar of Proctor and Gamble White Naphtha Soap, he took his time getting every part of his body clean. Then, satisfied with his cleanliness, he relaxed, simmering like turkey giblets after Thanksgiving dinner. For a while, he felt privileged and genteel, relishing this luxury.

He would have spent more time savoring the pleasure, but before long, the water cooled, and then it became just plain cold. Shivering, he conceded it was time to return to his less opulent lifestyle. After drying off, he got dressed in the same drab and dusty clothes and emptied the tub bucket by the bucketful, pouring the used bathwater down the creek bank behind the house. He cleaned the tub and buckets and returned them to the back porch, thanking the Timms for their use.

It was late, but Larkin didn't feel like sleeping. A stack of *Spokesman-Review* newspapers had arrived that day and waited on a simple pine table next to his bed. He was eager to read them to see if something might help him remember anything about anything. When he first came to Harrington, he had paid for a two-week subscription but had not received anything until today, when his first three copies of the twice-a-week "farmers" edition arrived.

After stoking the fire, he pored over the three editions by the light of his oil lamp. Nothing gained his attention. He got out his fountain pen and underlined the names of several towns that seemed familiar, but he could not capture a specific memory related to any of them. Tapping his pen against the paper, he pondered the geographic locations ringing a bell. Four states stood out to him; Idaho, Montana, North Dakota, and Washington. He also thought Oregon could possibly be somewhere he had been.

After midnight, he finally went to bed, frustrated at not getting closer to discovering his identity. The bath had made him feel new on the outside, but it had not renewed the spirit within.

Staring up from the pillow into the darkness, he declared, "Lost as ever."

DAY 16

SATURDAY, APRIL 26, 1924

"Let me help you with that, Mom."

The voice came from a twelve-year-old, but the maturity was not lost on Helen. Charles offered to take the watering can from her as she tended to the white lilies. The chore didn't seem like a burden to her. It was relaxing and took her mind off her troubles. But she knew that he needed to feel helpful.

She handed him the watering can. "Thank you, Charles."

At first she watched from the back porch as her oldest child performed the simple task. Then she came up next to him, just so that she could be closer to him. He was already an inch taller than she, and it seemed that he had become more handsome every day. Girls were already showing an interest. How could they resist his dark-brown eyes and that unruly black hair? As she studied his features, she was surprised to see some dark fuzz developing on his chin.

"You're going to have to start shaving soon."

"I already have."

Helen raised her brows. "You have?"

He shrugged. "Coupl'a times. Borrowed Daddy's razor."

"Well, you need to borrow it again."

He turned from his work to face her. "It's not here."

She shuddered. *I can't even have a normal conversation with my son without it always turning to the same overwhelming burden. I need John to be here. His children need him.* Charles interrupted her thoughts.

"I heard you and Daddy that morning." He stared down at the lilies as he spoke. "Fighting."

"We weren't fighting." There was an edge to her voice. She regretted it immediately and spoke in a more even tone. "We… had a disagreement." Charles continued watering, not responding.

Helen closed her eyes and sighed. "You're right. It was a fight." She slapped her legs and turned away. "I don't know why I had to push it. Maybe… "

He turned to see her trembling lip. "Mom…" He set the can down on the wood railing and stepped timidly toward her. But he had never been very good at offering consolation.

Helen composed herself and said, "You're hearing it at school, aren't you?"

"I'll tell you what." Charles worked up a scowl. "If Becky Simmons wasn't a girl I'd knock her but good!"

"Don't blame Becky," Helen said calmly. "It's not her fault. It's her parents that help spread the rumors."

He stared out at the garden. "Why do they do that?"

"People gossip about others to feel better about their own miserable lives." Helen picked up the watering can and used the hose to refill it. "They figure that if they can expose the failings of others, then their own shortcomings won't seem so bad."

"But don't they know how they hurt people?" He pounded his fist into his thigh. "Especially when they spread lies?"

Helen heaved another deep sigh. "I would rather they just stab me with a knife. Their gossip is more destructive than being attacked with bare fists. Because you can't fight back." She stroked his hair back. "I know it hurts, son. We are all hurting right now. It's bad enough Daddy is missing. But dealing with all the slander…"

She put one arm around his shoulder. "So what are they saying at school?"

Charles's face turned red. "They say that you—that Daddy left us. For good."

She turned and held his face with both hands, looking into his wet eyes. "You know better than that, don't you?"

He nodded slowly, his shoulders heaving.

"Daddy and I have disagreements sometimes." Helen brushed his cheek with her thumb. "Yes, even arguments. But he will never stop loving us. He would never leave us. You have to believe that, Charles."

"I do," he said. There was conviction in his voice. "I guess… I guess I'm just glad to hear you say it." He let out a deep breath. "Do you think—" He couldn't finish the thought, and his eyes fell.

"No," said Helen. "I can still feel him with us." Helen visibly trembled. "I'm not saying I don't sometimes have my doubts, but… I just somehow know that we will see him again. Soon."

He stared out again at the lilies. "What do you think happened?"

"I haven't the foggiest."

DAY 17

SUNDAY, APRIL 27, 1924

Another week gone, and if I don't get away from here or locate myself, I will go mad. Have felt sick and blue for 3 or 4 days now. Will try to stay out the month and then go to Spokane. If I don't know anyone, maybe someone will recognize me. I am satisfied that Larkin is not my name.

The cathartic, cleansing experience of writing in the little red book had waned. Still, he was averse to relating his despair to his hosts, and the diary was the only place he could go. *I hope that the words I write now will somehow come in handy later.*

He set down the diary and picked up the other book he borrowed from the Timms—*John Halifax, Gentleman.* He had been reading the tedious novel off and on for several days. He opened it in the way that had become his habit. Instead of turning to the bookmarked page where he had left off, he first opened the front cover to gaze at the frontispiece engraving. It was an image of Ursula March, the only love of John Halifax. He touched the image with soft hands, as if it could bring comfort.

It was this engraving that had caught Larkin's attention in the first place, and was the primary reason he kept reading it. The illustration was of a beautiful young girl bestowing a loaf of bread to a young Halifax, who at this tender age was nothing more than a street urchin.

Perhaps it was the beauty of the girl that drew him, or it may have been her gracious act that caught his attention. It could have been the hope that resided in the person of John Halifax, who, in early nineteenth century England, had little chance of rising from his meager beginnings to attain any success in life. But because of his persistence and faith, he became a "gentleman"—a person of wealth and influence in his society. It was most likely a combination of all these things.

But what captivated Larkin the most was simply her name. "Ursula," he said out loud as he ran his fingers down the image. Something about it haunted him. He knew the name, and not as a casual acquaintance. Someone who had a prominent place in his life, someone who cared for him—someone he loved. But while it struck a responsive chord in his memory, it remained an evasive clue to his identity. Oh, how he wished this image could tell him who he was.

He read a few pages but soon grew tired. The fire in the stove had gone cold, and he needed to get up early. Extinguishing the lamp, he crawled under the wool blanket, holding the closed book to his chest. Before he went to sleep, he uttered one more time the name that was haunting him.

"Ursula…"

DAY 20

WEDNESDAY, APRIL 30, 1924

"T'was a summer's night in winter
And the rain was snowing fast.
And a barefoot boy with shoes on
Stood a-sittin' in the grass!

It was evenin' and the rising sun
Was settin' in the west.
The little fishies in the trees
Were huddled in their nest.

Well the rain was pourin' down
And the moon was shinin' bright.
And everything that could be seen

Was hidden out of sight!"

The three Timm children were giddy as Mr. Larkin recited from memory the silly poem entitled "The Barefoot Boy with Shoes On." Larkin repeated all ten verses by rote, and then helped them to memorize them as well. He also taught them other silly songs like "Rufus Rastus Johnson Brown."

After enjoying another sumptuous meal prepared by Mrs. Timm, the children had asked Mr. Larkin if he knew any other fun songs. So he performed a resounding version of "Hallelujah, I'm A Bum," which he sang to the tune of the old Presbyterian Hymn, "Revive us Again." The children's eyes sparkled and their cheeks dimpled. In high spirits this evening, Larkin made his youthful apprentices laugh, bringing him great delight. Will and Lena were not the type to be silly, yet even they smiled to see their hired hand interacting with their children and having fun.

Once again, Larkin surprised himself with what he could remember. He knew all the words to the poem and the song but had no idea where or when he had learned them. But although the recitation of the poem did not conjure up recollections of people or places, tonight, nothing dampened his enthusiasm.

Later, Dorothea and Sylvia sat at the kitchen table, folding paper. "Do you know origami?" Dorothea did not look up from her project.

Larkin scratched his head. "Can't say that I do. Who is she?"

"Not who!" Dorothea giggled. "Origami is Japanese paper folding, silly." Larkin could sense the delight in the voice of the twelve-year-old as she taught him something new. She showed him how to make simple flowers, a frog, and a crane.

"Am I doing this right?" Larkin made some primitive attempts, but was clearly out of his league.

But the girls were gracious. "Very good."

"Johnny," Larkin called. "Aren't you going to do some orgimommy with us?"

The girls tittered.

"Origami is for girls," the fourteen-year-old said. "And little kids."

"No wonder I'm so bad at this." Larkin held up one of his creations. "This is supposed to be a swan."

Johnny laughed.

"Don't laugh." Dorothea put a hand on Larkin's forearm. "It just takes practice."

"Come to think of it, I do remember one folding paper trick." Larkin took a fresh sheet of paper, folded it over about half an inch at one edge, and creased it. Turning the paper over, he folded the sheet over again in the same way. He repeated this process clear across the length of the paper, making an accordion shape out of it.

Dorothea's frown showed disapproval. "That's not origami."

"Why not?" Larkin made sure his folds were straight and parallel. "I'm folding paper, aren't I?"

"But it's supposed to be something, like an animal."

"Just wait. It will be something." When he had folded the sheet all the way across, he pinched it in the middle and fanned out the ends. He placed the fan-shaped paper at the part in his hair, like a big ridiculous bow. In a falsetto voice, he said, "I can't pay the rent. I can't pay the rent."

The girls giggled again.

He then moved the folded bow underneath his nose, becoming a giant mustache. In a snarling gravelly voice, he declared, "You *must* pay the rent. You *must* pay the rent."

Back to his hair and falsetto, "But I can't pay the rent. I can't pay the rent."

"You *must* pay the rent! You *must* pay the rent!"

He moved the folded fan to his neck, where it became an absurdly huge bow tie. In a deep heroic voice, he stated boldly, "*I'll* pay the rent!"

Back to the hair and falsetto. "My hero!" he said with a lilt in his voice, batting his eyelashes.

With the mustache and gravelly voice, "Curses! Foiled again."

The girls nearly fell off the kitchen chairs with laughter, enraptured by Mr. Larkin's performance. They asked him to do it again, which he did with great delight.

Lena finally interrupted the hilarity. "That's enough pandemonium for one night. It's past your bedtimes." All three children thanked Mr. Larkin for the fun evening, and the two girls even gave him a hug before heading off to bed. The hugs were uncharacteristic in this stoic German family, but the night seemed special. He was enthralled that he had made his way into their hearts.

When the children were gone, Larkin got up from the table, ready to head to his quarters. But Lena delayed him. "I want to thank you, too, Mr. Larkin."

"I should thank you," he said, smiling. "I don't imagine you normally invite your hired hands to spend the evening in your house. I feel like part of the family."

Will got up from his chair and approached the two. "You're right. We don't usually have our hired hands spend evenings with us. But with you, well, I can say we all had an enjoyable evening. You are welcome here anytime. And yes, you are part of the family."

"Indeed," Lena added. "The children adore you. I can see that you have a father's heart."

Although Larkin knew that she meant this as a compliment, the statement made his ears hot. Filled with embarrassment and guilt, he felt a lump in his throat and couldn't speak. When he did respond, it may have seemed a bit rude.

Pointing to the back door, he choked out, "I need to go."

Turning on his heels, he fled to his room in the outbuilding down the slope from the house. Once there, he slammed the door behind him, flopped facedown on the bed, and shed bitter tears.

How can I live with myself? I know I have a family out there somewhere, wondering where I am. No doubt, suffering without me. And I am here enjoying the company of someone else's family.

What kind of man am I?

DAY 22

FRIDAY, MAY 2, 1924

A knock came at Edward Olson's front door.

Annie sat up in bed and squinted at the clock. Close to eleven o'clock. "Who would be calling at this hour?"

"I haven't the faintest idea." Edward got out of bed and put a robe over his pajamas. When he came to the door he was surprised to see two uniformed men from the Spokane County Sheriff's office.

"We apologize for calling at this late hour," began a tall and dark officer. "I'm Deputy Sheriff Brower, this is Deputy Hadley. May we come in?"

Edward invited them in and asked them to have a seat, which they declined. Annie then appeared in her night clothes and both gentlemen removed their hats.

"So what brings you gentlemen here tonight?" Edward asked.

"Well," Brower began, "we had a report tonight of a man seen in this area. Someone said he might be your missing son."

Annie gasped. Edward raised his brows.

"He's been seen periodically a couple of miles from here in the Valleyford

104

area in the last week or so, and tonight someone spotted him in the hills near here."

"And they think it might be John?" Annie put her hand on Edward's arm.

"Hard to say." Brower pursed his lips. "Height and build seem to match, and he has dark-brown hair. Thing is,"—here, his voice lowered into a rather conspiratorial form—"he's hardly wearin' nothin'. He's bare-headed and barefoot and bare-chested. Just wearin' a pair of shorts."

Hadley, who had remained silent until now, spoke up. "Do you know the Pearsons over on Stoughton road?"

Edward glanced at Annie. "Yes, but not well."

"Well, they saw him—from a distance—and said it might be your son. They didn't get a good look at him, but they thought maybe we ought to check into it."

Edward nodded. "Who else has seen him?"

"Well, it's mostly been kids." Brower rested his hands on the front of his belt. "He approached a boy riding a pony in Valleyford a couple of weeks ago. It scared the boy and he ran away. Then some other kids saw him a few days later in the same general area, but they ran from him."

"Do you think I could talk to any of these kids?" Edward asked. "Just to ask them a few questions?"

Brower glanced at Hadley and shrugged. "I don't see why not. Maybe tomorrow. Anyway, we were thinking of gettin' up a posse. We were wonderin' if you wanted to ride with us."

"Absolutely." Edward couldn't wait to get going. "And I'll get some other neighbors to go along, too."

After the deputies left, Edward and Annie weren't feeling tired anymore. They sat out on the front porch for a while, wrapped in blankets on the chilly spring night. For a long while, neither one said anything. Finally, Annie broke the silence. "Do you think… he's gone mad?"

"Well, something is wrong in his head, I think."

Annie turned to Edward with a frightened look. "What makes you think so?"

"For one thing, I believe Mrs. Richardson's story. I am certain she saw John."

Frowning, Annie said, "But wasn't that on a Thursday night? He didn't disappear until Friday."

"That's what the police say. According to them, someone at the hotel saw him on Friday, but I don't know who, and we don't know for sure that he was in his right mind at the time. Things don't add up."

"What was the other thing?"

"Hmm?"

"You said, 'for one thing.' What else is there?"

Edward bit his lip. "The pawned watch. Why would John use an alias at the pawn shop?"

"I try not to think about that."

"There are only two possible reasons." Edward stood and looked in the distance. "Either the police are right and John is running away." He turned toward Annie. "Or he has forgotten who he is."

Standing, Annie took Edward's hand. "You mean the police chief may be right about amnesia?"

"Possibly."

She looked deep into Edward's eyes. "If he's near here, maybe he is trying to find his way home."

"I hope so," Edward said. "I sure hope so."

DAY 23

SATURDAY, MAY 3, 1924

It was late afternoon before Sheriff Brower came to the house to talk with Edward.

"Sorry we weren't able to get the posse going today." Brower held his hat in his hand. "Organizational issues. I promise we'll have it all worked out by tomorrow morning."

"Well, I guess it couldn't be helped." Edward slapped his thigh and stepped aside. "Who do you have with you today?"

A chubby boy, about eleven or twelve years old, Edward guessed, peeked out from behind the sheriff's leg.

"This here's Albert Hanson. Say hello, son."

"Hello." The shy boy still used the sheriff as a shield but poked his head out a bit more to respond. He wore a white button-up shirt and dirty brown pants held up by suspenders.

"Well, come on in, Albert. I understand you have something to tell me." Edward led the two to the kitchen table. Annie appeared and served milk and cookies to Albert and coffee for Sheriff Brower.

Albert tore at his oatmeal cookies as if it were his last meal. The sheriff took a sip of coffee and turned to the boy. "Tell Mr. Olson what you told me, Albert."

"I was jes' ridin' up Madison Road on Melba—that's my pony—after visitin' my Gramma." Albert swallowed. "And this nekked man came walkin' up to me and he wanted to talk but my mama said not to talk to strangers and he was mighty strange lookin'."

"How so?" Edward asked.

"Well, he wasn't wearin' nothin' but baggy ol' short pants. And his body was all hairy and kinda dirty and his eyes were kinda, well, kinda *wild.*" Albert's eyes flared while cookie crumbs flailed from his mouth.

"Wild, eh?" Edward frowned and squinted at the youngster. "Do you remember the *color* of those eyes?"

"I don't reckon so, no sir." Albert's curly hair rustled as he shook his head.

Edward nodded. "What did he say?"

"He asked me my name. But when I didn't answer, he jes said he liked my pony." Albert took a swallow of milk. "Then I rode off fas' as I could."

Edward glanced at Sherriff Brower and back to the boy. "How did he act? Was he nice?"

"He acted real friendly and had a big dopey grin on his face."

"Is that all?"

"I reckon so." Only crumbs remained from Albert's treat. Annie fetched another cookie.

"Let me show you a picture." Edward reached over and laid the reward poster in front of Albert. "Do you see any resemblance between the man in this picture and the one you saw on the road that day?"

Albert squinted at the pictures of John and frowned. "Not really. He was a lot hairier and *wilder* lookin'."

Edward rubbed his chin. "Do you like to draw?"

Albert tilted his head. "Sure."

"Well, here." Edward handed Albert a stubby pencil. "I'll let you draw on that picture." He pointed to the picture of John without the hat. "Can you draw his hair?"

"I'll try." Scrunching his mouth up in a likely attempt to stimulate his creative juices, he scribbled longer, disheveled hair on the picture. Then he added an unkempt beard and—with aplomb—made the eyes bigger. As a final touch, he turned up the edges of the mouth. Tilting his head in apparent appraisal of his handiwork, he passed the poster back to Edward.

Edward studied the artwork briefly. "So this is what he looked like?"

"Purdy much," replied Albert, talking through another bite of oatmeal cookie.

"Okay." Sheriff Brower stood. "Albert, why don't you go sit in the police car and wait while I talk to Mr. Olson?"

"Can I sit in the driver's seat?" he asked, wide-eyed.

"Sure. But don't touch any buttons."

Albert scurried out to the Model T paddy wagon, and the sheriff picked up the conversation from there. "So what do you think?" he asked Edward.

"I wish we could be out searching for him right now," answered Edward, a little irritated neither one of them could pull together a posse until tomorrow.

"Well, if you want my opinion,"—he pointed to Albert's artwork—"I don't think this guy is your son."

"Why not?"

"Sounds like a crazy man to me."

"But if John got hit over the head, or if he's just snapped, he may not be himself right now. He may be wandering off who-knows-where in a daze. Who else could it be?"

"I have a hunch." Brower shoved his thumbs in his belt. "There's this crazy guy that wanders around the county named Willie Willey." He pronounced the last name with a long 'I'. "He usually wears next to nothin'. It could be him."

"Willie Willey," Edward repeated the name. "I've never heard of him."

"Most people haven't." Brower got up from the table. "But the police know him. We've arrested him a few times."

"Hmm." Edward peered out the window at the police car. "Albert saw this man almost two weeks ago, just a week after John's disappearance. His hair couldn't have grown considerably in that time. Nor do I believe his beard could have grown out much, either. Yet I'm inclined to assume it could still be John, even if it's based on the testimonial drawing of an eleven-year-old. Anyway, whether it be John or whomever, maybe we can help you catch him.

Sounds like this Willie Willey is a bit of a trouble-maker."

"Oh, he's a bit eccentric, is all. He's actually pretty friendly to most people. He just doesn't like cops."

"Well, you can hardly blame him for *that*."

DAY 24

SUNDAY, MAY 4, 1924

ill cut the deck and drew the lowest card.

Sunday afternoon cribbage had become a tradition in the Timms' living room since the arrival of Mr. J.A. Larkin to the ranch three weeks ago. Larkin enjoyed the distraction from his troubles. His only apprehension was that the subject of his past would come up again. He believed he had won their trust, so he considered telling them the truth about his memory problems. But the fear that they might think of him as some sort of madman kept him from revealing the truth.

So far.

Will dealt six cards each to Larkin and himself. "More and more trains coming through Harrington all the time. Talk about a booming business." He studied his cards. "The railroads have all these lobbyists in Washington. Not only are they making money hand over fist, but they have the federal government helping them get rich. There never seems to be any funds to help the poor farmers."

"No amount of government money can bring rain." Larkin laid away two cards for the crib. "According to the papers, we got less than a tenth of an inch in April. It sure has been dusty."

"True enough." Will nodded as he laid a pair to complete the crib. "But they could at least help us out during the lean times. Lord knows those railroad moguls don't need more handouts."

"Four," Larkin said as he laid a four faceup on the table.

"Thirteen." Will added a nine. "Have you ever worked for the railroad?"

"Yes, I have, as a matter of fact." The answer came from his lips before he even had a chance to think about it. It almost startled Larkin to hear himself say these words without being prepared to give this answer. He realized it must be true. "Some years ago I was a fireman and a brakeman." He had somehow managed to reveal something about his past to the Timms—and to himself—without actually having to invent a story.

As the game continued, the subject returned to farming, but Larkin dwelt on this revelation throughout the day. *The railroad! Of course. Why hadn't I thought of that?*

That evening, lying in bed, he became more convinced than ever to change his strategy. Working on the farm gave him some money, but it didn't help him get back to the main business at hand, discovering his true identity. He had learned from reading the newspapers that Spokane was the railroad center of the region. If he had any chance of recognizing someone—or being recognized—it might be there.

******

Edward Olson was also frustrated with his current strategy. After a full day of over fifty riders searching every possible hiding place in the hills near Freeman, they were no closer to solving the mystery of the disappearance of John L. Olson.

He kicked off his boots and hung his hat on the hook by the back door. Releasing a heavy sigh, he plopped onto the bed. Since they had not found the man who had been seen in the area, there was still the possibility that it could be John. Not knowing was enough to drive a man crazy.

His face riddled with worry lines, he could not hide his frustration from Annie. She stroked his hair as he lay beside her, but it did not erase the furrow in his brow.

Edward Olson would not rest until he had answers.

DAY 25

Monday, May 5, 1924

"So, tell me about how you ended up in Harrington." Larkin asked the question to keep the subject off of his own past.

The children cleared the table while the adults conversed after another fine meal prepared by Lena.

Will set down his napkin. "Well, I was born in Germany, not far from Berlin. My Uncle Fred came to this area first and talked my father into coming too. I was eight years old at the time."

"How did you and Lena meet?"

Using a toothpick to dislodge the remaining bits of Lena's delicious pork roast, Will said, "My father went to work for Lena's uncle, not far from here. He had also recently emigrated from Germany. About fifteen years later, the rest of Lena's family came here from the old country."

Raising his eyebrows and smiling, Larkin said, "Ah, fate."

"Yes, it was all in God's plan." Lena smiled broadly. "A year later, I married Willie."

Larkin enjoyed hearing stories of the past. It made him wish he had one.

"What made your families leave Germany?"

Will turned to Lena to let her explain. "There was a great deal of turmoil in Germany in those days, before the war. So much political infighting." Lena shook her head. "Socialists, Marxists, Communists… all trying to get the upper hand. In our part of the country, Lutherans were persecuted harshly. We had to meet discreetly. And then we lost our farms to industrialists and aristocrats." Lena's eyes turned red and her voice faltered as she recalled the social injustices her family suffered. "It was illegal, but no one stopped them. But you see, everything happens for a reason."

"You really think so?" Larkin frowned.

"Sure." Lena pressed her hands flat to straighten the tablecloth. "If there's no plan, there's no meaning or purpose in life. God is in control. So I believe that all the hardships we went through brought us together." She pointed to Will.

Larkin wondered if God had a purpose in his life.

"All that we went through brought us here to the United States. It is truly the land of opportunity." Her face brightened. "Farmland was cheap and fertile. Here, we have religious freedom. And, with hard work, we can eke out a living."

Leaning back in his chair, Larkin said, "Sounds like a dream come true."

"I wouldn't go that far, Mr. Larkin." Lena shook her finger. "As you know, Germans have their share of trouble *here*, too. With the war and everything, some people in America are none too fond of Teutonic folk. I don't even go by my given name—Magdalene—because it sounds too German. So I go by Lena. I don't suppose you can go anywhere without experiencing persecution."

Larkin nodded. "True, but it's a darn sight better than what you experienced across the pond."

Lena put her hand on his arm. "Mr. Larkin, you don't know the half of it. I wish I could forget everything that happened over there."

"Oh, you mustn't say that." Larkin's eyes were wide and serious.

"Why not?" Lena crinkled her eyebrows.

"Because the past is who you are." Larkin spread his hands as if to say this simple declaration was self-evident.

"What *ever* do you mean?" Lena frowned.

Larkin knew exactly what he meant. But he had to gather his thoughts for a moment and weigh his words. "What I mean to say is, well, the events in your past have made you into the person you've become, the good things as well as the bad. The places you've been, the people you've met… all have had an impact and continue to be a part of you even now."

This time Lena paused, apparently considering her response. "Well, I'm not sure I can entirely agree, Mr. Larkin. The past affects everyone in different ways and to varying degree. But it is not who we *are*. Who I am is determined not by anything or anyone but myself. My decisions are what make me who I am. I am not a prisoner of my past. My path is not determined save by God in his sovereignty. The awful things done to me in my past in Germany could have caused me to become an evil person, choosing to do harm to others. But I chose to do what is right, despite the past iniquities I've suffered."

"Hmm." Larkin held a finger to his mouth, digesting what she said. "I understand what you mean. But you said you wanted to *forget* your past." He licked his lips, deliberating. Was the time finally ripe to tell the Timms about his problem? *Maybe they will understand. They might even be able to help.* "Try to imagine not *having* a past. What if everything that ever happened to you, everywhere you had ever been, everyone you had ever known… was nothing but a blank. If you *could* imagine such a thing, it would be like a nightmare, don't you think?" He leaned forward to emphasize his point. "You wouldn't even know *who* you are."

Lena stared back in a confused daze. "I'm sure I have no idea what you are talking about, Mr. Larkin. I suppose they would check me into Eastern State Hospital for the insane if I was in such a pickle. But what does that have to do with our conversation? I only meant I wanted to put my past behind me and get on with my life. All this talk of not knowing anything about my past is just… just mumbo jumbo."

Larkin did not know what to say. At the mention of the asylum, he stopped cold. He knew now that the Timms couldn't understand what he was going through. *Maybe I do belong in an institution.*

"I'm sorry." Larkin stumbled verbally. "I, I guess I just reacted to your statement about forgetting the past. I, I…"

"Mr. Larkin." She pointed at his face. "If anyone's past is a total mystery to me, it's yours. We know so little about you, and you seem to dodge the issue when we bring it up. We don't even know your first name."

Mr. Timm, who had been across the table listening to the interaction, shifted in his chair and drew a deep breath. He seemed uncomfortable.

Lena stood and put her hands on her hips. "Now, I don't know what has happened in your past, and it is surely none of my business. But I can see it troubles you. Whatever it is, I know God can forgive you. But you must confess it." She went to the sink and picked up a dishrag. Upon returning, she wiped the table with more exertion than needed.

Will and Larkin exchanged glances. It was clear Larkin needed to respond somehow. "Well..."

"Not to me." She pointed up. "To Him!"

The blood drained from Larkin's face. He held his bottom lip with his teeth to keep it from quivering. Hunching over, he stared at the floor with his hands folded in his lap.

"I just mean that," she continued, "well, what you were saying earlier. It really is true. You can't simply forget about your past." Her voice softened as she calmed and sat down again. "You need to *face* your past, whatever it is. But I don't see how you can do that from a farm in the middle of Lincoln County."

Larkin turned to her but could not speak. Her face had softened, expressing empathy, not condemnation.

Will, who had seemed almost frozen during their awkward discussion, finally spoke. "Mr. Larkin. You are the best ranch hand I have ever had. It is not our intention to upset you, and we don't want to see you go. But, if you have some unfinished business somewhere you need to take care of, I would be willing to give you a leave of absence."

This acknowledgment gave Larkin some strength, and he stood. "Thank you," he said, ready to retire for the evening.

Will stopped him with one last statement. "You rest on that tonight. We'll talk about it more tomorrow."

Larkin responded with one word. "James."

The Timms stared back with bewilderment.

"My first name. It's James."

DAY 26

TUESDAY, MAY 6, 1924

The next day, "James" went to work without a word about the previous evening.

Larkin knew the "J" in J.A. Larkin could have stood for anything. It was only a name that came to him from… who knows where? Even so, he had written it in the inside front cover of the little red book last night.

Jas. A. Larkin?

Driving a McCormick-Deering "Big Six" hay mower with a vertical lift sickle, he worked the south field. Two horses pulled the mower that cut the hay the work animals needed to keep the farm going. Early May was a bit early for the hay harvest, but the recent dry spell gave Will enough reason to put Larkin on the chore before the imminent rains.

The smell of freshly mown hay was invigorating and reminded him of… what? It reminded him of something just out of reach.

"What am I going to do, Penny?" The large draft horse glanced over her shoulder but continued with her work. "I think I have a family out there somewhere. How are they making ends meet?" Larkin clicked his tongue and pulled the reins, coaxing Penny and Missy to turn around for another pass.

"What if I do have a family, but I've been divorced or separated somehow? Maybe they don't want me to find them. What then?"

Penny was a good listener, but not much of a conversationalist.

"Worse yet, what if I'm some kind of outlaw? There could be wanted posters out there. If I show up in public, maybe I'll be arrested. On the other hand, if I don't do something, I'll never know." Larkin clicked again and the horses made another U-turn. Penny gave a little whinny.

"You're right, Penny. I've got to make up my mind soon. I'll go crazy if I don't. And worrying about it doesn't do any good."

He concluded there was nothing like a silly song to distract you from troubles.

"Alfalfa hay, alfalfa hay, alfalfa hay, alfalfa hay,

Alfalfa hay, alfalfa hay, alfalfa hay, alfalfa hay,"

He didn't know where he'd heard the inane ditty before, but the tune was catchy. It didn't lighten his heart, but it numbed it a bit. After one rendition of the song, he thought it needed a little more panache. He decided to shout the second word each time.

"Alfalfa HAY, alfalfa HAY, alfalfa HAY, alfalfa HAY,"

A quarter of a mile away, Will leaned against the well pump. Wearing a bewildered and rather pained expression on his face, he listened to his hired hand crooning to the livestock in the distance.

Straining to make sense of what he heard coming from the south field, he failed to hear Lena come up behind him.

"That man sure does love to sing."

Startled, he turned just in time for Lena to hook her hand inside his elbow. "Is that what you call that caterwauling? I worried maybe he got a limb stuck in the mechanism."

Lena smiled at Will. He didn't joke much. She changed the subject. "I'm preparing supper."

"Already?"

"Mm-hmm. Making his favorites. Ham, potatoes with gravy, and buttermilk biscuits."

Will raised one eyebrow. "What's the occasion?"

Lena responded with only a knowing expression.

"Wait a minute." Will cocked his hat. "What's going on?"

At about two o'clock in the afternoon, Larkin returned the Big 6 to the barn. He unhitched the horses and contemplated how he would word his explanation to the Timms.

He knew it was time.

His abrupt decision might leave them in the lurch, but he felt he had no recourse.

Will strode into the barn. "Everything okay?"

Hanging the bridles and reins in their proper places, Larkin replied, "Everything's fine." He removed his gloves. "With the horses, I mean."

"What is it?"

Larkin averted his gaze and stuffed his hands in his pockets. He kicked at the dirt like a schoolboy having to explain himself to the principal. "I just… well, I just have to get out of here."

"Oh?" Will put one foot up on a railing and rested an elbow on his knee. He waited while Larkin gathered his thoughts.

"I mean," Larkin stammered, "I mean, I don't want to let you down, but… Well, I've *got* to go find my family. I won't be able to make sense of anything until I do." He slapped his trousers. "You understand, don't you?"

Will nodded. "I understand there is nothing more important than family. Don't worry about us here. You need to do what's best for you and your kin."

"Thank you." He was relieved that Will wasn't angry with what appeared to be a snap decision.

"Where are you going to go?" Will asked.

"East." Larkin pulled a kerchief out of his pocket and wiped his brow. "Spokane, to start with, then maybe on from there."

"You aiming to leave tonight?"

"If that's okay."

The farmer rewarded Larkin with a warm smile. "Well, the Cascadian comes through Harrington about five o'clock. You'll want to be on that. Lena is making a special meal for you as a going-away present."

Larkin began to object when Will raised his hand up. "Don't say no. Somehow, she saw this coming. She would have my hide if I didn't let her see you off right. Now, go get your things together, and I'll tell Lena."

Everyone enjoyed all the fixings, including a scrumptious cherry pie for dessert. Larkin had his things together for his lift into town. But he wasn't emotionally prepared for his goodbyes to the kids. They had all grown to love each other.

"I enjoyed getting to know you, Johnny. Especially rabbit hunting and fishing." Larkin shook Johnny's hand, squeezing it hard.

The boy seldom smiled, but now he produced a toothy grin. "And horseshoes."

"Keep practicing, and maybe you'll beat me someday." They both laughed.

Dorothea presented a gift to Larkin. She had made an origami swan from a page in the Montgomery Ward catalog.

"It's beautiful!" declared Larkin. "I never could get the hang of orgimommy. Except for that hair bow ⊠ mustache ⊠ bow tie thingy."

"Anybody can do that!" Dorothea laughed. "But we had fun."

Finally, Sylvia had her turn. The youngest girl announced, "Mr. Larkin. I know where wind comes from."

"Oh, you do, eh?" replied Larkin with his arms akimbo and his hands on his hips.

"Yes, I do," she replied defiantly. "It's *not* from windmills!"

"It's not?" Larkin feigned surprise at this revelation. "Well, where on earth *does* wind come from, then?"

"Wind comes from God."

"I see." Larkin stroked his chin. "I suppose you are right about that after all. How did you get to be so smart, anyway?"

"My mom."

"Yeah, you can always trust moms to give you the right answers to hard questions." Larkin winked at Lena.

Sylvia took Larkin by the hand and escorted him to the Model T pickup. "I'm going to miss you." Her face expressed an adorable pout. "You know how to make me laugh."

She gave him a tight bear hug.

"I'm going to miss you, too, little darlin'." He wiped a tear.

Will cranked the starter on the truck and Larkin turned to Lena. "Thanks for putting up with me," he said. "I haven't told you everything, and, well, I know I haven't been an ideal guest."

"Oh, hush." Lena dusted an imaginary fleck off his shoulder. "Frankly, I don't know how we're going to get along here without you. I don't mean the work. We'll do fine. But we're going to miss your company."

She poked a playful finger to his chest. "The Good Book says *the wind bloweth where it listeth, and thou hearest the sound thereof, but canst tell whence it cometh, and whither it goeth: and so it is with everyone that is born of the Spirit.*"

Taking his hand, she squeezed it to her heart. "Let the Spirit guide you, Mr. Larkin. Only God knows what lies ahead for you. You must learn to trust him."

Larkin had no idea how to let the Spirit guide him. He responded with words that he thought she would like to hear.

"I will."

Part 2
Spokane

DAY 26

TUESDAY, MAY 6, 1924 (CONTINUED)

The setting sun glinted off the buff-colored masonry of the Great Northern Depot.

Larkin arrived in Spokane at seven-thirty in the evening. He had made eye contact with as many passengers as possible on the train ride in. He had hoped someone might recognize him.

No such luck.

Following a couple dozen passengers from the train, they herded like Holsteins to the milk barn. The depot was an impressive sight, a three-story brick edifice with a clock tower soaring twice as high as the main roof.

At the bottom of a ramp, the passengers turned left to cross the south channel of the Spokane River by way of the Stevens Street Bridge. A network of rails sprawled through the area like a brood of vipers. Cigarette smoke mixed with the acrid odor of spent diesel fuel.

To the south he took in Spokane's skyline. The multi-story brick buildings peeked at Larkin over a dingy railroad viaduct on the other side of the bridge.

The skyline did not seem familiar. *Darn.*

No one took note of a nearby bill affixed on a telephone pole with a single thumbtack at the top. It hung in a prominent location, but a breeze had flipped the poster up to obscure its report to the passersby. Larkin, following the crowd, passed by it last. He, too, missed its communique. Only after everyone had gone by the poster did the wind die down enough to reveal its message.

REWARD: DEAD OR ALIVE – JOHN L. OLSON

The notice included a description of the missing person and two photographs resembling Mr. J.A. Larkin.

He paused at the south end of the bridge and watched the rest of the crowd continue on ahead. He observed his surroundings again, hoping something would strike a chord. The Depot's splendid clock tower loomed in the twilight, gloomily reflected in the dark waters of the mill pond. Unfortunately, neither the tower nor its reflected image stirred the murky contents of his memory. He was unaware that almost a month earlier, many of the belongings of John L. Olson had been found strewn along the south bank a little over one hundred yards to the west of where he now stood.

He turned again southward, passing under the viaduct for the O.W.R.N. and Union Pacific Railroads. Emerging on the other side, he came to Front Avenue, marking the north edge of Spokane's "congested district." The former train passengers had now melded into the bustling crowds of a busy nightlife.

Larkin scanned the landscape to find the nearest place to rest his head. Across the street, he saw numerous hotels and restaurants. The most prominent accommodations were the American Hotel and the Hotel Dempsey. Reaching into his pocket, he counted his money again. Fourteen dollars and seventy-five cents. He knew it wouldn't last long if a job didn't materialize soon. Having to conserve funds, he sought something a little more… seedy.

He crossed the busy street and found a faded sign reading "ROOMS." At the unlikely address of W419 ½ Front Street stood the narrow façade of The Lea Hotel, opposite Union Station—the other prominent railroad depot in town.

He ascended a steep, narrow wood staircase that took him to the flophouse located above a jewelry store. At the top of the stairs, dingy tan walls were lit by a single bare bulb. The "lobby" consisted of a simple pine desk in a short hall with bare wooden floors. He expected to find Spartan accommodations. In reality, it was musty, cramped, and rundown.

Just what he was looking for.

At the desk sat a man who he assumed was the clerk. A heavyset man who hadn't shaved in a day or two, he wore a thin white skivvy shirt. Chest hair erupted from the top, and an equally hairy belly protruded from the bottom. Hunching over the desk, engrossed in a newspaper article, he did not acknowledge Larkin's presence.

A paragon of hospitality.

Larkin stood across the desk from him, wondering if he was invisible to the man. He searched for a bell to ring. Finding none, he cleared his throat.

"Lookin' for a room, pal?" The man did not turn his attention from the paper spread on the desk. The cigar he chewed appeared to be glued to his bottom lip and flopped up and down violently when he spoke.

"Yes, one night, please."

The clerk finally flashed Larkin a fake smile. "We got two-bit, four-bit, or six-bit rooms depending on whatcha need."

"I need a bed."

"They all have beds." He returned to his article.

"As I suspected." Larkin slapped a quarter on the desk.

Without getting up, the clerk reached behind him and tossed a key to Larkin. "Seventeen. Top of the stairs on the left." He coughed on his own cigar smoke. "Oh, and uh," he added with a tone laden with sarcasm, "I hope you enjoy your stay at the Lea."

He was already back to his paper.

DAY 27

WEDNESDAY, MAY 7, 1924

What's that sound?

He awoke to a rattle, quiet at first but then louder. Startled from his sleep, he sat up in bed. It took a moment for him to arouse from his sleep stupor to remember he had checked into a hotel room.

The rattling sound came from the door. *Someone is trying to break into my room.* Moving shadows broke the straight line of light emanating from beneath the door.

Without thinking, he jumped up and yanked it open.

A disheveled man stumbled into the room, key in hand. He barely caught his balance before noticing Larkin. With frightened eyes, he asked, "Who're you?"

"I was about to ask the same."

Sixtyish, the thin man wore a dirty overcoat that was way too big for him. What little hair he had stuck straight up. "I'm Kansas." He spoke with a southern accent, but it included a slur. It came out more like "Ahm Kanzush." Larkin winced when he got a whiff of him. He smelled like he had fallen into a vat of whiskey.

"What are you doing here?" Larkin held his hand flat on the front of the man's shoulder, preventing him from coming any farther into the room.

"I live here."

"I'm afraid not." Larkin pressed the man a little harder.

Kansas investigated his surroundings. " But…" He wiped his nose with his filthy coat sleeve. "But that'sh mah bed."

"No, that's *my* bed." Larkin pulled the chain on the floor lamp that stood by the door. The room filled with the glare of the bare bulb.

Kansas squinted and shielded his eyes with one arm and leaned against a wall. "Are you shurr?" He belched. "Can I just lay down on the bed?"

"What's going on here?" The skivvy-shirted desk clerk from downstairs appeared at the door. "Kansas, this is not your room."

"Yesh it izh."

"You're in nineteen." The clerk grabbed Kansas by the collar and dragged him out of the room. "This is seventeen."

"But it *looksh* lack mah room."

"Yes, it does." He pushed Kansas down the hall. "Two more doors down." Pulling the cigar from his mouth, he pointed it at Larkin. "Listen, pal, keep your door locked and don't be opening it to no strangers. Kansas is harmless, but the next guy could be a thug."

Not knowing what else to say, Larkin replied with a weak, "Thanks."

"Don't mention it." He put the cigar back in his mouth and stepped out into the hall, then turned back to Larkin. With a cynical expression, he added. "Consider it a service from the friendly staff at the Lea Hotel. Be sure to recommend us to your friends." As he headed down the hall, he shouted with exasperation, "Kansas, you went past it! Give me the key. I'll open it."

When the two had disappeared down the hall, Larkin shut the door and locked it. Grabbing his jacket from the floor, he dug in the pocket for his watch.

Four thirty-five.

Shaken, he didn't even consider going back to sleep. Instead, he sat down on the edge of his bed, taking in the windowless ten-by-ten-foot room. It smelled of urine, and paint peeled from the walls. The furniture consisted of a squeaky wood frame bed with a thin mattress and a table. The tall lamp stood by the door on a bare wooden floor. A cast iron radiator stood stout against one wall. The coolness of the room suggested the boiler had not fired up yet.

Larkin stood and stretched and thought about what he would do today. Scratching his head before putting his pants on, he ventured down the hall to a common bathroom containing a toilet and washbasin. Patrons on another level had the luxury of a shower for an extra fee.

These inconveniences did not go unnoticed by Larkin, but they didn't bother him much either. On a budget, he anticipated an austere existence; for now, at least. His immediate task demanded that he discover his true identity.

After splashing some water on his face, he returned to his room and dressed. Before leaving the hotel, he stopped at the front desk.

The same affable attendant greeted him. "Checking out, pal?"

"No," he replied, sliding a quarter across the desk. "Let's make it another night." Keeping his room for one more day allowed him to remain unencumbered while exploring the city today.

"Did you find everything to your satisfaction?" The unmistakable rancor in the clerk's voice did not escape his attention.

"My room is missing a chair."

"Dear me," the clerk said in mock concern. "I'll notify the concierge immediately to alleviate the problem."

Larkin waved him off. "That won't be necessary. Can you tell me how to get to the Great Northern freight yards?"

"Take the streetcars wherever you want to go. Howard and Riverside." He pointed his ever-present cigar in the general direction. "They'll show you which one to take."

Two blocks from the front door of the Lea, he found the hub of all streetcar activity. An agent waited in a small booth at the corner.

"Which one do I take to the G.N. yards?" Larkin asked.

"Take Hillyard to the end of the line." The agent gestured toward the car waiting across the street.

Larkin crossed Howard and climbed onto the back platform of the streetcar, easily finding a seat at this early hour. A sign across from him read, "It Is Absolutely Forbidden to Expectorate!" Five minutes after he sat down, the car jerked forward and proceeded north. As the conductor collected fares, Larkin could see each patron pay a nickel, so he did the same.

He continued his policy of making eye contact with as many people as possible, with no favorable outcome. By the time the car headed up Crestline, he had given up on that strategy and began to concentrate more on his surroundings. He thought some of the houses along the way were vaguely familiar, but it might be wishful thinking.

The streetcar turned right at Diamond Avenue and they were in the suburb of Hillyard, named after railroad magnate Jim Hill. He remembered how Hill had chosen this place on the outskirts of Spokane to build his roundhouse, machine shops, and freight yard. It serviced all rail activity eastward to Minneapolis, Chicago, and beyond, as well as westward across the Cascade Mountain range and on to Seattle.

The car came to a stop at Diamond and Market, at the curb right in front of "Schultz's Corner," a restaurant. The streetcar emptied while the conductor turned the roller on the destination sign from "Hillyard" to "Shops," meaning the return to downtown Spokane. Many of the riders became patrons of Schultz's, hoping to grab something for breakfast before going to work.

Larkin decided to wait until later to eat. Anxious to see the yards, he continued on foot for one more block. From the corner of Diamond and Greene Street, he could see the G.N. ice house to the north and the roundhouse and repair shops to the south. At six o'clock in the morning, the yards were already a flurry of activity, with switchmen pairing up locomotives with freight cars heading to various destinations.

He spent two hours watching the workers with pointed interest, noting that he could do any of the work he observed there—most notably, the task of switching cars to various tracks and lining them up for destinations. This particular yard wasn't familiar, but the activity seemed second nature to him. *Surely, I have done this before.*

Finding the main offices, he discovered a sign hanging on the door that read "Not hiring at this time."

Larkin snapped his fingers in frustration. "Nerts!"

After checking out the yard, he strolled up and down Market, browsing through the various shops. He finally returned to Schultz's to pick up a late breakfast. Most of the clientele were railroaders—dirty, trash-talking, hardworking train crews and shopmen. In conversation with the waitress, Larkin learned the restaurant had been a tavern in earlier years, but when prohibition was enacted in 1916, it converted to a diner with a candy counter and soft drinks.

Sitting at the breakfast counter, Larkin could observe everyone coming and going. He hoped someone might know him, but was disappointed. He ordered coffee and oatmeal while he read the *Spokesman-Review*. Nothing caught his interest in the news, but he saw Babe Ruth had batted in two runs and scored the winning run for the Yankees' win over the Philadelphia Athletics.

Taking the streetcar back downtown, he transferred to the Broadway car, taking him to the O.W.R.N. yards. After passing the impressive castle-like county courthouse, he hopped off at Maple Street and walked two blocks south to the yards. The Oregon-Washington Rail and Navigation Company had very much the same facilities in west Spokane as the Great Northern did in Hillyard. While there, he conducted himself the same way he had at the G.N. yards, with about the same results. No work and no acquaintances.

He gave a low groan and walked back downtown instead of riding the trolley. At this rate, he would have to save his nickels and reconsider his strategy. Not sure what to do next, he decided to take in a show. *Maybe that will cheer me up.*

A Girl of the Limberlost, based on the classic novel, played at the Casino Theatre about three blocks from the hotel.

With nothing else to do, he took in another show at The Majestic, also nearby. *The Exiles*—starring John Gilbert—headlined, but he chose the Majestic because of a short starring Harold Lloyd. *You can never get enough of Harold Lloyd*, he thought. His madcap adventures were even funnier than Buster Keaton and Charlie Chaplin.

Larkin laughed out loud watching his movie hero, but found the joy it brought him short-lived. Back on the street, his hopeless situation hit him again. He shoved his hands in his pockets and made his way to the hotel with his head bowed low.

When he came to the top of the stairs at The Lea, a surprise awaited him in the hall next to his door.

A simple oak chair.

DAY 28

THURSDAY, MAY 8, 1924

He was not alone.

Waking early again—this time it was five o'clock—he sat on the oak chair, watching his new friend explore every corner of the room. Instead of complaining to the hotel clerk about the infestation of vermin in his room, he saw this cute little gray mouse as a lonely drifter—like himself— needing companionship. Larkin could tell him anything, and the little rodent returned no judgment.

Last night he had made another entry in his journal, and before he turned out the lamp, he read it out loud to Leonard.

Leonard.

That was the name he gave the little fella. Leonard seemed to approve.

"So, where should I go today, my little friend?" Never mind that asking the counsel of a rodent could be confirmation that he indeed belonged in a sanitarium. He just needed someone to talk to. Leonard offered no advice, so Larkin left his friend behind and went outside before deciding where he would go.

The sky was clear and the sun sat low. He had to shade his eyes to see eastward. But it was shaping up to be a beautiful day. He took the East Sprague streetcar to the end of the line at Freya and then walked the last mile and a half to Yardley, the Northern Pacific yards in East Spokane.

Today's results were no better than yesterday's. Once again, he confirmed his rail yard experience in his mind, but this yard didn't seem like the one either. Couldn't someone just pipe up with, "Hey, Joe Yokel, where have you been?" or something like that?

He sat on a bench and threw his head back in dismay. Squinting into the sun, he began to wonder if he was ever going to find himself. He closed his eyes and determined that he would not give up.

Visiting the Milwaukee Yard, the only other major rail yard in Spokane, his expectations were low—and they were met. The initial enthusiasm that had accompanied him when he came into Spokane two days ago had disappeared, only to be replaced by despair. None of the railroads were hiring, and most other businesses he went by didn't seem to be seeking workers either.

He had developed a headache, and he rubbed his temples vigorously.

No wonder. It was nearly two o'clock in the afternoon, and he hadn't eaten anything all day. On First Avenue, he found Bob's Chili Parlor. Judging by the throng at the door, it was a popular choice. He bought a paper outside and waited in line. Before long, he was inside a plain, undecorated eating area.

Clearly, "Chili Bob" was a well-known celebrity in the area. Everyone seemed to know him personally, and he knew many of his patrons by their first names.

When Larkin finally got a seat at the bar, he opened the paper to the want ads. The smell of chili and spices made him even hungrier.

"What'll it be, friend?" Bob seemed to be enthusiastic about... well, everything.

"Chili."

"Excellent choice," Bob said. "Hot, medium, or mild?"

"Uhhh..."

Bob cupped his hand by his mouth and spoke in a conspiratorial tone. "I recommend the hot, but you'll want a glass of milk with that."

"Hot, please," Larkin raised one finger. "And a tall glass of milk to go with it."

"Bowl o' red!" Bob announced boisterously to no one as he ladled a big helping of his hot chili into a bowl. "By the way, our tamales are world-renowned," he said, waving one hand in an encompassing arc.

"Just chili, please."

"Suit yourself." Bob moved down the counter to other customers.

The want ads were *not* promising. The listings for "Help wanted—male" were only a half-column long. They needed boys to sell newspapers and experienced men in various occupations he did not qualify for.

"You look like you could use some more chili." Bob scooped more of his specialty into the bowl without waiting for Larkin's reply. "You trying to find a job?" Bob pointed to Larkin's want ads.

"Yeah," Larkin said. "Not much in the paper."

"I could've told you that." Bob went back to wiping the counter. "Spokane is growing faster than employment opportunities. Lots of people coming here looking for work, but work's not looking for them. What have you done in the past?"

"Railroading."

"Oh." Bob's face turned sour. "The unions are making it tough for the railroads these days. They want more pay for fewer hours and better conditions and all that. So what do the railroads do? They start laying people off." Bob shook his head. "I tell ya', unions aren't working for the workers. Is that what happened to you? I mean, did you get laid off?"

"You might say that," Larkin said.

"Where are you from?" Bob flipped his towel up onto his shoulder.

"Helena." It was Larkin's pat answer to that question.

Bob pointed an enthusiastic forefinger at him. "Last Chance Gulch."

"Huh? Oh, uh yeah," mumbled Larkin, not recognizing the reference to the history of the town.

"I have friends in Helena," Bob said cheerfully. "You're no doubt familiar with the Broadwater area."

"Well, I…"

"Bob, can I get some more chili over here?" A neglected customer was waving a hand at Bob. After serving him and helping a few other customers, Bob was back. Larkin quickly changed the subject back to jobs.

"So, if the railroads aren't hiring, who is?"

Bob stared off for a moment before replying. "Well, the match factories are sometimes hiring. They are Spokane's biggest employers."

"The match factories?"

"Oh, yeah," Bob said. "Almost all the matches made in the world come through Spokane. They have all that white pine around here, and they bring trainloads into the mills from the Idaho panhandle mostly. They don't actually make them into matches here, though. They cut the trees into blocks about like so." Bob used his hands to indicate blocks approximately six inches by six inches by three inches.

"Then they load up box cars full of those blocks and ship them back east where they cut them up into matchsticks. They have several hundred people working out there. They must have some turnover."

Bob turned to address one of his customers. "Hey, Gus! How many people have they got working out there at the match factories altogether?"

"A few hundred," came the reply.

"You see?" Bob patted his chest. "Like I said."

Another chap sitting at the bar chimed in. "Yeah, but paper matches are gonna put wood matches outa' business in a few years."

A groan came from the collective audience. Now everyone was in on the conversation.

"Git outta' here!" Bob waved a hand dismissively at the patron. "Wood matches are here to stay. Nobody likes those floppy paper matches. I never use them."

Turning back to Larkin, Bob said, "If you really want work, your best bet is to go west."

"What's west?"

"Lumber mills. They're so desperate for help they'll hire anybody with a body temperature."

"But you still think I have a chance at the match factories?" Larkin thought that if he got on with the factories, at least he would be close to the railroads, where someone might know him.

"It's worth a try," Gus said.

Bob scooped up Larkin's empty bowl and glass. "Good luck."

It was late afternoon, so Larkin gave up his job searching for the day. He would get a fresh start in the morning. At a loss about what he would do for the remainder of the day, he wandered the downtown streets and found himself back at the corner of Howard and Riverside, where the streetcar routes began.

Not wanting to spend more money on the movies—five cents even if you didn't buy any popcorn—he tried to think of something he could do that would be free. He overheard some people talking about going up to Manito Park, so he followed them onto the Manito streetcar that started heading up South Washington. It still cost a nickel, but he stood a better chance of being recognized than in a dark theater. Moving up to the front, he sat near the motorman.

The car chugged up the steep hill and turned onto Grand Boulevard for a short two-block flat stretch before it came to a stop right across from Sacred Heart Hospital to pick up riders. Larkin watched the motorman glance at his watch before he pushed the controller to maximum power.

He watched as the motorman carefully wound up the controller to ten points, cutting all resistors and putting the motors in parallel for full line current. Larkin knew if he made the motion too fast, it could cause a flashover that would result in a loss of power before the steep climb. *We're about to go up a steep hill.*

With this thought, it dawned on Larkin how much he knew about streetcars. *How would I know that unless I have experience operating a streetcar?*

The trolley made a right turn and began its ascent up Grand Boulevard. Larkin turned around and stared at the seven-story hospital situated at the base of the hill. It felt strangely familiar. But the sight of it made him feel a bit queasy. Sort of like déjà vu, but in a nauseous way.

Soon after the car started moving up the hill, it shifted over to the double track. Larkin saw the "inbound" trolley coming down the hill. He knew that it was on this incline that the two cars on the Manito line passed each other. Therefore, it was important that the timing be correct so that both cars would meet during this short stretch of double track.

The odd feeling he had soon felt more like sickness when he glanced at the brake bar next to the controller. His stomach quivered. Was Bob's chili having an adverse effect?

He watched the northbound car pass them on his left, then glanced over his shoulder again to Sacred Heart. The sight of it made his stomach do flips. Dizziness and motion sickness overwhelmed him. A sense of imminent doom crashed over him like a tsunami.

Everything went black.

******

Thursday, May 11, 1917 (Seven Years Earlier)

"So, how's married life?"

Motorman John Olson and Conductor Jesse Bolen chatted for a few minutes on the turnaround at the end of the Manito Line. They had finished taking a full load of passengers to their south hill homes and waited at Grand and Thirty-Eighth until time to head back down the hill toward downtown.

"I'm livin' the life." Bolen grinned from ear to ear in answer to John's question.

"You can't fool me." John leaned against the controller. "I know the real reason you got married."

Jesse's smile disappeared. "Really, now. You mean it can't be because I wake up every morning next to this gorgeous doll who fixes me breakfast and packs my lunch?" He shook his lunch pail in Olson's face.

"Nah. That isn't it. You haven't been married for even a month. You'll be packing your own lunch before long."

"Hah! That's what you think." Bolen pointed his right thumb at his chest. "Hazel knows who wears the pants."

Olson couldn't stifle a chuckle.

"Okay, wise guy. Why do *you* say I got married?" Bolen stood with his fists on his hips.

"To avoid the draft, of course."

Jesse waved his hand at Olson. "Shows what you know. We all have to fill out draft cards next month. Including you. Being married is no exemption."

"True enough." John glanced at his pocket watch. Two minutes before six in the evening. "But the single guys will get picked first. You know that."

"So you think I'm afraid to fight?"

"Not at all. You got married, didn't you?" John pushed the controls, and the streetcar began its return trip to the city center.

"Very funny, coming from you, John." Jesse held on to an upright as the trolley picked up speed. "Anyone can see you and Helen are happy together. You can't fake that."

Olson nodded. "True enough. But you can't be happily married unless you do whatever you can to make your wife happy." John maneuvered the streetcar northward. "That's the key, Jesse. We have our fights, but I only put up a fight if it's important to me. I let her win all the small battles, so I can save up for the big win. So sometimes I pack my own lunch."

No passengers boarded as they motored down the gentle slope past Manito Park. At this time in the evening, it wasn't unusual to head back empty. Soon they came to the crest of a steep downhill. John applied the brake bar to control their descent when it inexplicably snapped in his right hand.

He let go of the wooden handle, and it fell uselessly to the floor of the cab.

"No brakes!"

They had passed Thirteenth Avenue and their speed increased exponentially. John threw the controller into reverse, but the motor did not respond. The outbound streetcar must have wound up the controller to ten points, robbing the entire line of the power he now needed. Without brakes or power, all he could do was ring the bell and blast the horn to warn everyone ahead of a streetcar out of control.

Pedestrians and vehicles scattered when they saw thirty tons of steel and wood hurtling toward them down the fifteen percent grade. A man driving a carriage glanced over his shoulder and urged his frightened horse to the far right as the runaway car flew past them.

Once the street cleared of obstacles, John could see they were heading straight toward Sacred Heart Hospital at the bottom of the hill. There was no way the car could negotiate the sharp turn at high speed. It would either tip on its side going around the curve, or it would jump the tracks and crash into the south face of the hospital. Either outcome terrified him.

Then John saw an even more horrifying sight. The outbound Manito car appeared around the bend, coming straight toward them.

Full of passengers.

His only hope was that the outbound car would reach the double track before he got to the bottom of the hill.

He continued clanging the bell and blasting the horn, but if the outbound trolley didn't make it to the double track in time, there would be a head-on collision. He could now make out the terrified expressions of the commuters in the other car while his trolley careened down the hill at blinding speed. As the outbound car shifted to the other track, the passengers' screams came to a crescendo and then diminished as his cable car blazed past the other one, missing the back corner of the opposite trolley by inches.

As he neared the bottom, he could only hope he and Bolen would be only seriously injured.

"Hold on!" he yelled. Bolen hardly needed to be told; his white knuckles had been clenched around a vertical handrail at his post in the back of the car since they started their wild descent.

When the car reached the turn, John surmised he was about to meet his maker. A young nurse stood on the south fire escape of the hospital, holding her hand over her gaping mouth. An expression of utter horror contorted her face. The car lurched at the sharp bend and leapt the tracks—but not before it initiated the turn, just a bit to the left. It tipped about thirty degrees to the right before the weight of the car brought it back to an upright position. Still moving forward at high speed, it headed across the pavement straight for the six-inch curb.

A deafening crash shattered the air as the steel wheels exploded into the sidewalk, causing the car's front end to soar high. Completely disoriented, John expected the next impact would be the last one he would ever experience. But the angled encounter with the sidewalk caused the car to turn ever-so-slightly *farther* to the left, narrowly missing the southwest corner of the building.

Instead, the car came crashing down onto the hospital lawn to a sudden halt, jolting him and Bolen helplessly forward and downward. John lay motionless on the floor of the motorman's compartment. Stunned, he kept his eyes closed, afraid to move.

He heard voices.

******

"Sir. Are you alright?" He opened his eyes to see the motorman kneeling beside him.

Where am I? What happened?

The conductor came forward to investigate. "Sir? Do you need to see a doctor?"

Larkin blinked, trying to get his bearings. Sweat drenched his skin. The passengers stared at him, some wagging their heads and speaking to each other in hushed tones. When he saw they were stopped at the entrance of Manito Park, he finally spoke. "Uh, no. I mean, I need to get off here."

Standing, he wobbled his way to the back of the trolley and stepped off shakily. Tugging down the front of his shirt, he forced himself to stand erect in an attempt to appear normal to the onlookers.

That's the last time I eat Bob's chili.

He felt ill, but also fearful. Something happened on the streetcar he couldn't explain. He couldn't even *remember* what had just happened.

Except for one thing. He knew he not only had experience with railroads but with streetcars as well. Something about it terrified him.

Larkin wandered around the park for about an hour, trying to shake off the latest incident. He read a plaque stating that the word "Manito" meant "a supernatural force that pervades nature" in the native Algonquin language.

I could use a bit of the supernatural about now.

Passing ball fields, playgrounds, and a bowling green, a part of him admired the beauty. But a bigger part of him felt nothing but apathy. Everything seemed so pointless.

Picking up his pace, he walked briskly past rose and lilac gardens and a formal sunken English garden. The most popular attraction seemed to be the zoo. Bears, monkeys, buffalo, beaver, an ostrich, and many other animals populated it. Even the expansive park, with all its magnificent beauty, failed to move him. Shaking his head and grunting, he realized the superficiality of it all. Sure, it was lovely, but what did that matter? It made him feel even emptier.

He remembered now why he came. Hoping something might connect or strike a chord. Or someone might recognize him. So far, nothing.

After his mysterious experience on the streetcar, coupled with his lack of success at the rail yards, he felt despondent. The enthusiasm after first arriving in Spokane had completely disappeared, and he felt like he was wasting his time. Once again, his predicament seemed like a wide, yawning chasm.

He slumped down on a park bench by a mirror pond filled with swans and ducks and gazed into the reflective waters pensively. He tried to think of options. What could he do differently? *I can't go on like this.*

Nothing came to mind. His shoulders sagged as he glared off aimlessly. He felt like he'd swallowed a handful of worms now wreaking havoc in his belly. People-watching again, the carefree attitude of the park visitors stood in stark contrast to his own demeanor. *Why can't I be happy, too?*

A number of families picnicked near the pond as others strolled by. He found himself watching a woman with two children rather intently. She was an attractive brunette, thirtyish, and wore a flowered sundress. The boy with her seemed to be about twelve years old. His mother told him to quit throwing stones into the pond. The other child was a lovely, demure little girl with dark curly locks flowing past her shoulders. He guessed her to be nine or ten years old, and she held a leash with a small black schnauzer tethered to the other end.

Larkin imagined his beautiful wife and their two lovely children, spending the afternoon here at the park. Later, they would walk to their spacious Victorian south hill home and have a scrumptious dinner together.

But the fantasizing did nothing to bring him out of his depression. If anything, it brought him to a new low, because he knew it wasn't substantive. His life still felt meaningless and desolate, no closer to discovering his real self than ever. He held his head in his hands. *What's the use? I'm never going to find my family or my identity. I might as well turn myself in to the asylum and let them do experiments on me.*

Suddenly, something warm and wet touched his left hand. Deep in his funk, he hadn't noticed the girl with the schnauzer sit at the opposite end of the bench. The schnauzer had taken an interest in his hand, licking it with abandon. This went on for a minute or two as the girl's attention seemed focused on the ducks in the pond. When the dog had tired of his left hand, it moved to his right and repeated the process.

"Seems your dog can't hold his licker," Larkin quipped.

Ignoring his comment, she turned to him for the first time and asked, "Where's *your* dog?"

"I don't have a dog," he answered.

She tipped her head and gave him a puzzled expression as if his answer seemed illogical. "Well, where's your family?"

Good question. "I don't have a family, either."

This seemed to evoke a response bordering on shock mixed with disbelief. But her expression melted into one of deep sympathy. "You're here all by yourself?"

Her question almost made him cry. He blinked and shrugged. "Seems that way."

Her large, dark-brown eyes stared into his, penetrating his soul.

What's happening? Something... odd.

As Larkin stared back, he felt warmth. But it didn't come from the bright sun. It welled up from inside. Or, to be more precise, it seemed to be flowing from *her*, into his bones and his very essence.

The worms disappeared. The feeling of hopelessness waned.

The little girl and Larkin sat transfixed upon one another. All the anxiety, anger, and guilt drained away, replaced by peace, calm, and compassion, along with a sense of mercy and grace.

His perspective completely changed. His pessimism disintegrated, and a sense of hope broke over him like a rogue wave.

"Ursula."

He heard someone.

"Ursula!"

"Yes, Mommy." The little girl turned her head to her mother, and the spell was broken. Larkin jerked.

"We're going to the zoo now," her mother said.

The girl turned back to Larkin. "I have to go." Hopping off the bench, she tugged at her little schnauzer. "Come on, Schultzie."

"I want to see the monkeys." The boy drug a stick behind him, increasing his pace.

"You always want to see the monkeys." The girl gave Schultzie another tug.

"Well, you always want to see the polar bear."

"So? I like the polar bear."

The voices faded as they walked up the path toward the zoo.

Larkin watched in a daze as they receded from view. He had no idea how long the trance had lasted. It could have been moments, minutes, or even hours. He only knew he didn't want it to end. He opened his mouth to call out to her, but he seemed unable.

Before they went completely out of sight, the girl turned and looked back at Larkin with a solemn but peaceful expression. Without exactly smiling, her face beamed like the sun. She seemed to be saying, "Everything is going to be alright."

And he knew the truth of it. For the first time, he believed the end of this nightmare would come, and his life would be restored again. He sat on the park bench for several minutes longer, feeling almost paralyzed, trying to take it all in.

When he finally stood, a smile blossomed on his face. He walked back toward the park entrance with a spring in his step. Another trolley waited there for passengers at Grand Boulevard, but he didn't take it. Not because of fear.

He just felt like walking.

DAY 29

FRIDAY, MAY 9, 1924

NOT HIRING AT THIS TIME.

Perhaps Chili Bob was wrong about the success of paper matches after all. Turns out the production of wood matches had gone down recently. In fact, layoffs were imminent.

Squinting into the bright afternoon sun, he still felt energized by his experience at Manito Park. The strange encounter with Ursula felt like a sign. What else could it be? Instead of feeling defeated at every turn, he felt like God finally stood on his side. Maybe he would even go to church this Sunday.

Instead of taking the streetcar back downtown, Larkin decided to walk East Trent. It was an industrial area, and he wanted to see if any businesses might be hiring. He spotted a manufacturer of agricultural implements on his left. Having experience with farm equipment, he could offer his services. A large painted sign read "Northwest Harvester."

The front office was empty when he entered, but a man behind a large window at a desk talked on the phone. Gold lettering on the door indicated "Wm. H. Puttock. Manager." The man gave a little wave Larkin interpreted as meaning "I'll be right with you."

A young woman emerged from a hall smiling. "How can we help you today?"

"My name is J. A. Larkin and I am inquiring to see if you are hiring."

"I'm sorry, not right now." She gave her head a tilt. "Have you tried Carsten's?"

He returned a quizzical expression. "Carsten's?"

"Yes. They're a meat packing plant two blocks from here." She pointed westward. "They seem to need help all the time."

Larkin nodded. "Thanks."

He saw the sign for Carsten's down the street and headed there to inquire about employment.

******

Meanwhile, Mr. Puttock finished his phone call and came into the front office. "Who were you talking to just now, Etta?"

"Someone looking for a job." Etta had returned to her front desk and shuffled papers.

Puttock frowned. "Did you get his name?"

"Uh, Larkin, I believe."

"Hmm." Puttock appeared thoughtful. "He looked quite a bit like a former employee here. But his name was Olson. You may have seen the article in the paper about him last month, something about him running off with a woman." Puttock shook his head. "He seemed like a decent family man to me."

"Well, I'm sure his name wasn't Olson. I think he said Larkin."

DAY 30

SATURDAY, MAY 10, 1924

Helen Olson filled the watering can with the hand pump.

She loved her flower garden, especially her lilies. Now, tears filled her eyes in a medley of joy and deep sorrow. It had been exactly one month to the day since Helen had seen John. The last thing he did for her was water her lilies. So now they bloomed as a reminder of him and his love for her.

For the first couple of weeks after John disappeared, she had been highly motivated and knew what she had to do, leading a spirited search in Spokane and the surrounding area. But when Detective Bucholz expressed his belief that John disappeared of his own accord, it sent her reeling. Not that she believed John would run off, but she hated to lose the assistance of law enforcement in her quest to find her husband.

Setting the spent watering can down, Helen slumped onto a garden bench. *Why am I so weary? It's not like I've done anything today.* The stress was clearly wearing her down.

Since the Spokane Police Department put the case on the back burner, Helen had fallen into a deep funk. She kept thinking her tears had run out, but every day new ones found their way down her cheeks. Like now, as she watered the lilies.

But she determined things would be different. Instead of letting the depression make her lethargic and discouraged, she decided today she would do something. *I'm not going to sit around the house waiting for something to happen.* Helen resolved she would take the train this afternoon into Spokane to tell Detective Bucholz she had not given up, and he shouldn't either.

She still held out hope—didn't she?

Hope.

Sometimes it seemed like nothing but an irrational desire. Like hoping a long-lost relative would leave you with a large inheritance. Oh, she knew the scandalous stories were not true. The wagging tongues in Kootenai were working overtime, but she knew better.

It wasn't the rumors she worried about so much, but the desire to find out what happened to John overwhelmed her. She feared the worst. Still, she tried to hold out hope for another explanation. It was better than despair.

Done with her chore, she dragged her feet up the back porch and opened the door. She hesitated, leaning her forehead against the door jamb. She felt so worn out.

But then an idea came to her. Raising her chin, she went to the bureau, letting the back door slam shut. Grabbing some tablet paper and a fountain pen, she sat at the kitchen table. It sounded silly, but she had to talk to him. So she decided to write him a letter.

No, a poem.

Once the pen contacted the paper, it seemed to have a life of its own. Words came like a flood. It felt almost like she wasn't composing, but taking dictation. And yet, it came from her heart. She hoped somehow, someway, her words would reach him.

Lilies white and slender in my garden

Palely gleaming as the shadows fall

Seem to speak to me of you

And those wondrous days we knew

Joy and rapture gone beyond recall
For you my heart is breaking
I want you night and day
When dawn is slowly waking

When daylight dies away
My thoughts are all about you
In dreams your face I see
I cannot live without you

Come back again to me

******

"Why do I own this suit?" Larkin held his suit aloft for Leonard to consider. The mouse yielded no plausible theories.

"I mean, I wouldn't wear a suit to work if I worked on the railroad. Or for a trolley company. Did I become a lawyer or an insurance salesman? Not likely. A minister? Definitely not. I may have been attending a wedding or a funeral."

Larkin enjoyed talking things out with Leonard. It helped him to think. His failure to get a job yesterday did not extinguish his enthusiasm after meeting Ursula in the park. It had dampened a bit, though. He had to do something soon. Funds were getting low.

"Where should I go today, Leonard?" The cute little rodent seemed to turn his nose in a northerly direction. Larkin took it as a sign, and decided to go job hunting on the north side.

******

"We have nothing new."

Helen Olson sat across the desk from Paul Bucholz at the police station on Howard Street. "It's like I told you on the phone. If we come up with something, we'll keep you informed."

Helen knew this would be the line she would get. But she also believed if she kept showing up at Bucholz's door, he wouldn't completely forget about her.

Helen shifted in her chair across from the detective's desk. "But you haven't given up on the case, right? I mean, you are still looking for him?"

Bucholz started to say something, hesitated, then pointed over Helen's shoulder. "See over there by our front door, Mrs. Olson?"

She peered over her shoulder through the open door. A thick cloud of smoke created by various tobacco products filled the room. "What am I supposed to see?"

"Right there by the door is a bulletin board. Prominently displayed is the reward poster you had printed."

"What good does that do?" Helen's tone betrayed her irritation with the detective. He seemed patronizing.

"When you walk out of here today, you will see that poster with the two pictures of your husband on it." Bucholz drilled his forefinger into his desk to emphasize the point. "Our officers walk past that poster every day and are reminded of your missing husband. It is their duty to keep an eye out for him. If he is in this city, chances are, they will find him." He smiled, but it seemed forced. "The fact that a reward is attached to his discovery doesn't hurt their motivation."

Helen stared back at him, unmoved. "But you doubt he is in Spokane, don't you?"

"I have to be honest with you, Mrs. Olson." He leaned back in his chair. "My police instincts tell me he is nowhere near here."

******

Larkin paced the sidewalk outside of the front door to the police station on Howard Street. Wandering Spokane's north side all day brought discouragement once again. *Aren't there any jobs in this town?* He kicked the brick façade of the police station.

He also felt oddly homesick. Homesick for where? *How can you miss your family if you can't even remember them?* Yet he did miss them, whoever they were.

Doubts crept in about his encounter with Ursula. Did he imagine it? Was it nothing but wishful thinking? Whatever happened at Manito Park had brought him a ray of hope. But the hope that seemed so glorious two days ago had faded. Was God toying with him?

Shoving his hands deeper in his pockets, he began pacing again.

Before today, he had avoided the police for two reasons. First, if he told the authorities his story, they might take him for a mental case and throw him in an institution. At times, he suspected that might be a pretty fair assessment of his situation.

Second, he couldn't be sure he wasn't a wanted fugitive. For some reason he couldn't explain, he had a dreaded feeling his picture could be found on wanted posters. In either case, the result would be that he would be locked up and be worse off than now.

He continued traipsing up and down Howard Street. *On the other hand, could I be any worse off?* Wandering the countryside without a clue to your own identity posed another type of imprisonment. Maybe the worst kind.

There was yet another possibility. The police might know who he is and return him to his family. Since this best possible scenario remained, he had to take the chance. He cleared his throat and checked his reflection in a window to make sure his hair wasn't wild. He would go into the police station and tell them his whole story.

But he stopped before going in. How to do that? He walked in the other direction again, practicing in his mind what he would say. *Hello. My name is… well, that's the problem. I don't actually know my name.* No. That sounds like something someone would say if they really were loony.

Excuse me. I was wondering if you have a list of missing persons I could look at? Right. Like they are going to hand over a list of missing persons, no questions asked. *I just wanted to see if I made the list.* Somehow he didn't think that would work too well.

He walked up to Main, turned around, and strode back to Front Street. Over and over he paraded past the front door of the police station, deliberating with himself.

As he passed the station again, the door cracked open. The action spooked him enough to turn tail and start heading back to the hotel room, less than two blocks away. *Maybe tomorrow.*

******

"My instincts are seldom wrong, Mrs. Olson." Bucholz swung the door open for her, inviting her out to Howard Street. "But just the same, rest assured we have not put this case to rest. I know it seems like thirty days is a long time, but missing persons cases have been solved even after several years have gone by."

"If that is supposed to be reassuring," Helen replied, "I can tell you that you are sorely mistaken."

Bucholz looked chagrined. "What I meant is, as a missing persons detective, I am not likely to give up on a case after such a short period of time. I'm sorry if I sounded insensitive. It's just that I do have a professional opinion. I believe I owe it to you to express it frankly."

Helen broke eye contact. "I guess I don't feel like you are doing everything you can when your instincts tell you he is not even in Spokane." Her gaze came back to Bucholz. "The fact that you say the case is not closed seems like nothing but lip service."

"My instincts are one thing. My duty is another. As a sworn police officer, I am bound to stay on the case until it is closed. Now, if you can think of anything new that I could investigate in relation to this case, I would be happy to pursue it."

"Like what?" Helen asked.

Bucholz spread his hands. "Exactly."

DAY 31

SUNDAY, MAY 11, 1924

Larkin counted his money. $12.60 left.

Decision time.

Spokane wasn't working out. There were no jobs and nothing to show he had ever lived here. His only friend was Leonard. A mouse.

Pathetic.

He sighed and glanced around his room one last time. He'd already gathered his few belongings and hoped to say goodbye to Leonard. But the mouse must have been finding crumbs in someone else's room.

Leaving the Lea Hotel, he went down to the Great Northern tracks. Once there, he gazed eastward and sighed. The place names in that direction—Idaho and Montana—seemed somewhat familiar. But according to local sources, the jobs were west. He would need money more than anything.

Well, almost anything. If there was a guarantee he would discover his identity heading east, he would do it—job or not. But if he ran out of money before solving the mystery, then what? So he squinted toward the setting sun in the west, hovering his palm above his eyes like the bill of a cap.

The last time he'd copped a ride on a freight car, it had an unhappy ending. Nevertheless, he needed to save money, and clearly he had experience "beating the trains."

Finding a scrap piece of lumber, he scanned the yard for an empty car heading west. When the coast was clear, he climbed in a vacant reefer. Then he slid the door almost shut and stuck the piece of wood in the door so he wouldn't get locked in. Sadistic trainmen were sometimes known to lock a hobo in an empty car. This time he stayed alert. He didn't want an angry brakeman to surprise him again.

The train rolled westward during the night, stopping periodically on sidings to let other trains pass. It passed through Edwall and Harrington and finally came to a stop where it appeared to be unloading. He slid the door open a little wider and peeked out. It was almost daylight, but he couldn't see any "bulls"—railroad security agents.

He hopped out of the car and found himself strolling through an industrial area. A warehouse sported a sign reading "Wenatchee: Home of the Big Red Apple." Wispy clouds and a saffron sky to the east promised a beautiful day. Across the Columbia River, the sun had not yet peeked over the hills, but the already warm air felt good.

He found an apple orchard near the confluence of the Wenatchee and Columbia Rivers and sat in the shade, leaning his back against a tree trunk. He whiled away a couple hours, reading more in *John Halifax, Gentleman* while waiting for businesses to open for the day. There were no apples to eat, as the picking season was still four months off. His stomach growled. He hadn't eaten anything in the last twenty-four hours, but stores weren't open yet.

Taking a nap under a tree, he awoke to sweat dripping from his brow. He decided to look around town and remembered it was a Sunday, so most businesses were closed. Happily, he found a Piggly Wiggly store downtown that was open. He bought a *Wenatchee World* newspaper, a small block of cheddar cheese, and saltines. After inquiring with the clerk, he learned the lumber mills were still farther west, up the Wenatchee Valley.

He sat on the sidewalk and leaned against a cool stone building to devour the want ads and some of his rations. But nothing there showed much promise. Wenatchee was mostly comprised of fruit growers, buyers, and sellers. All the other businesses seemed to thrive on the back of the fruit industry. Since the picking season was still far off, job opportunities were slim.

Saving the rest of his food in his satchel for later, he decided to wander around Wenatchee to see what it was like. It seemed like a nice town, but hot. Ninety degrees.

After a couple of hours, he made his way to the bank of the wild Columbia River. He took off his shoes and socks, sat on a rock, and dipped his feet in the cool water.

He decided to stay one more night to see what Monday would bring; someone might be in need of a simple laborer. Under the shade of another apple tree, he opened his diary to add a new entry.

The paper says it is Mother's Day – Mother Dear – dead or alive, I am thinking of you. My heart nearly breaks, thinking that you are alive and wondering where your lost son is. Oh, it is an awful sensation to not know who you are. It wouldn't be so bad if I knew that there wasn't anyone to worry about me or dependent on me. But the torture I've been under the last month makes me sure that I have a Mother someplace as well as a wife and babies.

When the sun set, he curled into the fetal position and slept uneasily.

Part 3
Sky

DAY 32

Monday, May 12, 1924

Larkin spat on the ground.

Before the sun had reached its apex, Larkin knew Wenatchee had been a waste of time. So he hopped a local electric interurban railway that took passengers up the Wenatchee Valley and arrived in the logging town of Leavenworth less than an hour later. He found a padlocked gate at the entrance to the Lamb-Davis lumber mill.

"Looking for work?" An elderly white-haired man wearing a straw boater and holding a cane sat on a bench near the entrance to the mill.

"Yes. I'm surprised the mill isn't open on a Monday."

"River Rats!" The old man took an angry puff on his pipe. An earthy scent emanated from it.

"Pardon?" Larkin sat next to the gentleman on the shaded bench.

Despite the warm weather, the man sported a light-gray wool-worsted suit with a tie and cuff-bottom trousers. His weathered face wore a frown, and he seemed to be chewing on something. "Blasted River Rats shut down the mill. Don't know when we'll be open again."

"River rats?" Larkin pictured an infestation of large rodents besieging the area.

The gentleman pointed to the river. Larkin could see a log dam creating a mill pond on the Wenatchee River. But the pond remained as quiet and lonely as the moon.

"No raw timber, no mill." The old man apparently believed this explained everything.

Larkin stood up, improving his view of the river. "What happened to the logs?"

"The River Rats went on strike." Pulling the pipe from his lips, he gestured toward the river with it. His long mustache did little to conceal his sour expression. "They're the ones who guide the logs down the river."

"I see." Larkin seemed to recall seeing men standing on logs as they floated down a river using peaveys to guide them downstream to a mill. "That's a pretty dangerous job, isn't it?"

The gentleman eyed Larkin sharply and pointed his pipe at him. "They are well compensated."

After a pause in the conversation, the old man struck up again. "I'd hire you today if I could."

"Are you the boss?"

"You could say that." He took another puff from his pipe. "I'm the owner."

Larkin sat once again. "I'm sorry about the strike." Larkin felt his response insufficient but was not sure what else to say.

"Not half as sorry as I am. I just don't understand people these days. They want more money, but they want to work less. Well, where's the sense in that? Huh?"

Before Larkin could respond, the old man continued.

"In my day, if you wanted to have more money"—he tapped his cane on the ground—"you worked harder. And longer." He chewed on his cud with more enthusiasm. "Next thing you know, they'll want money to stay home. Now is that a good idea? Huh?"

Larkin didn't even try to interrupt his harangue.

"You know where money comes from, don't you? Huh? From labor, that's where. You work to provide a product or a service that people want. And they *pay* you for it. That's where money comes from." Each time he made a point, he tapped his cane again or puffed out a billow of smoke. Whatever he chewed on was a mystery.

"And I tell you what else. We worked hard in my day, and we were satisfied with what we got. You know why? Because we knew we *earned* it. And it was just a pittance of what this lacksa-daze-ical rabble gets today." He turned and gazed with droopy eyes toward his idle mill. "I fear for the future of this country if we keep down this path." Turning back to Larkin, he said, "Stand up, let me get a look at you."

Larking stood, and the old man tipped his head, sizing him up. "Let me see your hands."

Larkin held out his hands.

The mill owner set down his cane and held Larkin's hands in his, turning them over, examining them. "Hmmm. Yes, these are working man's hands. You've worked hard your whole life, haven't you?"

Having little recollection of his work history, Larkin nodded anyway.

The man let go and took his cane again. "Well, there's nothing here for a man like you, not today. But if you want a job at a mill, take the next train over the pass there." He pointed his cane to the Cascade Range. "There's another mill on the other side of those mountains that's hiring, last I knew. And if not, keep heading west; there are more mills. Somebody must be producing lumber. Lord knows I'm not."

"Thank you, I'll do that, Mr. uh…"

"Lamb. William Lamb." He put out his hand, and Larkin shook it vigorously.

"Larkin. J.A. Larkin."

Lamb shooed him with his cane. "Be off with you now, Mr. Larkin. It doesn't do to have fine workers like you wasting your time listening to bitter old fools."

******

An empty boxcar took Larkin westward toward the Stevens Pass. Once underway, he cracked the door to let cool air in and to take in the view. The dry, steppe-like terrain of the Wenatchee river valley with its shrubs and ponderosa pines gave way to more dense and diverse growth as the freight train made its way toward the crest. Spruce, tamarack, cedar, and other conifers populated the landscape, while stands of quaking aspen became more frequent.

By and by, the rush of the river disappeared, but smaller tributaries clogged by beaver dams became common. Larkin took in the flora and welcomed the cooler air as the train climbed the eastern slope of the Cascade Range. Making several switchbacks and traversing through tunnels and snow sheds, the tracks ultimately entered a two-and-a-half-mile tunnel. When it came out the other side, the train began its descent. Finally, it came to the town of Skykomish.

As the train entered the mill town, the fusion of dense smoke and steam gave Larkin the impression they had descended into the crater of an active volcano. The town could have been described with one word—gray. He almost choked on the dense diesel fumes mingled with the smell of burning wood. Did the slate sky indicate clouds, or was the blight billowing from the mill stacks and the train chimneys causing a permanent dense fog overhead? Even the buildings lacked color.

In addition, the town felt grimy and generally unkempt. It bustled with activity, however. It seemed to him about two to three hundred people had crammed into a densely wooded narrow valley. Several sets of tracks went down the middle of the main arterial known appropriately as "Railroad Avenue."

A bustle of people stood in front of a hotel called—no surprise—the Skykomish. He saw a few men waiting in line to talk to a young gentleman with green suspenders and a bow tie sitting at a table. A handwritten sign above his head declared, "Bloedel-Donovan Mills: Now Hiring."

Oh boy! He took his place in line.

He hadn't been there for more than a minute when he heard a voice call out from behind him. "Fisher!" A second time, "Fisher!" Larkin turned to see a man with a handlebar mustache approaching him.

Larkin's heart skipped a beat. *Could this be it? Has someone found me?* "Sir!" He replied.

"Beg pardon," the man said sheepishly. "I mistook you for an old acquaintance."

"From where?" Larkin asked.

"Durant, Nevada," he replied.

"And you are quite sure I am *not* him?" Larkin asked.

The mustachioed man laughed. "Oh, yes. Now that I see your face better, you don't look like him at all. But from *behind…*" He paused. "Well, let's just say I was quite surprised when you turned around."

Trying not to show disappointment, Larkin said, "Well, I hope you find your friend."

"I wasn't actually looking for him," replied the man. "I would have been somewhat surprised to see him here, to tell you the truth." Changing the subject, the man said, "Are you here for a job?"

"I sure hope so."

"Well, you shouldn't have any trouble with that. Nobody seems to stay here long, though. They come, make some quick money, and head back to their families. But you knew that, right?"

"Right." He didn't know, but thought he should.

After a few other pleasantries, they bade their farewells, and Larkin noticed he had advanced to second in line. He started thinking the name "Fisher" suited him well. He had made the name Larkin up while registering at the Harrington Hotel, not knowing its origin. Now, at least, the new name had been given to him in a way.

The friendly twenty-something young man in suspenders greeted him when it became his turn. "Welcome to Sky, sir. Let's start by getting your name."

Larkin hesitated as the man held his pencil poised above the paper.

"Fisher," he said. "F-I-S-H-E-R."

"First name?" responded the man.

"F-Frank."

"Is that with one 'F' or two?" The young man laughed good-naturedly.

Fisher laughed too. *Very funny.*

The gentleman took other vital information, but the assumption all along was that he had the job. It wasn't an interview per se, just the essential data needed to begin work.

Having been in Skykomish for only a few minutes, Larkin—a.k.a. Fisher—had a job.

"Your pay is four dollars a day and payday is Saturday. Now, you'll need a place to stay and eat." It wasn't a question, but the young man waited for a response.

"Okay."

"The Skykomish"—he pointed behind him with his thumb—"is where you'll stay. You need this to get a room." The bow-tied man handed Fisher a voucher. "This is good for two weeks' rent. After that, the mill will take it from your paycheck. You need this one, too." Now he received another voucher for meals. "The boarding house is up the street on the left, and they'll feed you lunch and dinner seven days a week. Start tomorrow morning at seven-fifty sharp at the main headquarters right down that road." He pointed to his right in the direction from where all the smoke originated. "Good luck, Mr. Fisher. Next!"

DAY 33

TUESDAY, MAY 13, 1924

Fisher peered out his hotel window onto Railroad Avenue.

His spirits were high. He had a job and a cooler climate than Wenatchee. The sun had managed to pierce the drab sky, making it almost cheery.

Men headed west down the mill road, and he followed suit. The main headquarters was only a couple blocks away. Four other men in work clothes waited in a small office.

A wall clock with Roman numerals indicated 7:50. A tall skinny gentleman with wire-rimmed glasses and gray overalls came in and introduced himself as Mr. McKenzie, the operations manager. All five men were asked if they had ever worked in a mill before. Fisher was the only one with no experience.

"No, sir, but I'm a quick study," he said.

"How about custodial work? You can push a broom, can't you?" the manager asked.

"I'm willing to do about anything." Fisher hoped his enthusiasm to work would impress McKenzie, but it was hard to tell. He wasn't very expressive.

The manager had all five men follow him outside. Fisher's nostrils filled with the pleasing scent of fresh-cut lumber. The sounds of band saws, circular saws, and other machinery made it impossible for the manager to communicate with the new hires without shouting.

He gave instructions to each man, assigning them to their tasks, as well as to the foremen in charge of each area. Each time he also explained to Fisher what the men were doing. From debarking logs to the main or "head" saw, to the edger and then the planer, and other processes—McKenzie made sure Fisher could see the basic steps that took place at the mill.

While doing this, he also showed Fisher what cleanup duties were necessary at each station. "While you are cleaning up," he said, "be sure and watch what each of the workers is doing. Soon you'll be expected to fill in at their jobs from time to time. Before long, you'll be doing one of those jobs on a regular basis. Right now, you're the low man on the totem pole, but if you're diligent and learn quickly, you won't stay there long."

Fisher found the work environment to be pleasant enough. McKenzie and the other supervisors seemed to be friendly and fair. His fellow employees were swearing, belching, bragging ne'er-do-wells for the most part, but he didn't mind. Mostly they ignored him, only occasionally having to give him additional instructions. He worked hard his first day, hustling from location to location, trying to keep up.

When the day ended at 4:00, he felt tired and hungry. After eating vegetable stew at the Mill Boarding House, he returned to The Skykomish Hotel, not knowing what to do. Many of his coworkers sat at tables playing poker in the common area. Some asked him to join in. He declined, explaining he wasn't good at cards.

"We'd be happy to show ya'!" The young man who signed him on yesterday smiled and gestured for him to come to his table. "Fisher, right? Fellas, meet F-frank Fisher." He introduced himself as Chet Lowry and then the other men at the table. They were drinking beer and hard liquor. Fisher wondered to himself if the constable might come in at any minute and arrest everyone.

Lowry held his cards close to his chest. "Aw, come on. We'll even let you win a few hands." Two other men at his table smiled and nodded.

"Sorry, I've got other things to do," he lied.

Up in his room, he admitted to himself that he felt a bit out of place here. He longed for the cribbage games with Will Timm. After writing in his little red book, he had run out of things to do. He thought about going to sleep, but darkness had not even fallen yet.

Pacing, he considered his situation. He missed Leonard, the mouse. Talking things out with him had always helped. Now he would have to analyze the situation without his rodent cohort.

"What am I doing here anyway? It's nice to have a decent job, and heaven knows I need the money. But I'm quite sure I've never been here before. How am I going to find out who I am if I'm in this remote place?" He examined himself in a dingy mirror on the wall. By now, the face was familiar, but there continued to be so much about himself he didn't know.

He'd heard railmen refer to towns like Skykomish as "bean eateries." Itinerant railroad workers came and went like circus performers through town. Section crews, mechanics, engineers, and conductors all stayed briefly, then moved on to where they were needed next.

Fisher continued his personal debate. "At least I have a chance of being recognized by a Great Northern employee. They come here from all over and they overnight at the hotel." He turned again toward the mirror. "Perhaps I *should* spend more time socializing downstairs. Nobody is going to see this face while I'm up here in my room. The more people I encounter, the greater chance of success."

But fear still nagged him, though he couldn't place it precisely.

"Maybe tomorrow night."

DAY 34

WEDNESDAY, MAY 14, 1924

It is still cloudy and cool. I like my work fine, same job as yesterday. I am still having trouble getting to sleep nights. I keep figuring out the possibilities of whether I have a family or not. I am trying hard to compose myself so I won't worry so much. But I have long evenings to myself. I have sent in a month's sub. to Spokesman-Review. And think I will send for some other local County papers in Northern Ida and East Wash. as those places in the paper seem more familiar to me than some others. I have maps of Ida, Wash and Mont, which I study.

Fisher shut his little red book and put it away for the night.

"Oh, almost forgot." He pulled it back out and opened to the inside front cover. Below the inscription of "Jas. A. Larkin," he added:

alias

Frank Fisher?

******

Helen fidgeted in her overstuffed chair opposite Pastor Munton and his wife.

"We've been missing you for the last couple of Sundays," Pastor Munton said.

Mrs. Munton added, "We stopped by to make sure everything is okay with you."

Her response was terse. "I'm fine." *Just fine and dandy! Chip, chip, cheerio and all that!*

The Muntons had dropped by unannounced, and Helen felt obliged to invite them in. They sat on the sofa while Helen limped to the kitchen and returned with coffee in her best china cups.

In their mid-fifties, the Muntons—rather new to the community—were still getting to know the members of their congregation. The pastor wore a black wool suit with a tie. His British accent added to his austere image. Mrs. Munton's slim figure was enhanced by her mild and soft expression. She wore a conservative ankle-length white dress and a large-brimmed garden hat with a black bow.

She was in no mood for guests, but Helen tried not to appear rude. She hoped her recalcitrance didn't show, but she didn't want to make them feel *too* at home.

The pastor forged ahead. "You know the community is behind you one hundred percent."

"Is it?" Helen asked. She knew the town of Kootenai was actually split about the disappearance of John Olson. To her, it seemed to be about fifty-fifty as to whether he had met with foul play or left on his own recognizance. Some days, she wasn't even sure which side of the fence *she* was on.

"What my husband means," Mrs. Munton said, "is that the entire church is praying for you." She paused, and when no one else spoke, she added, "And the whole Christian community here is praying, as well. Other churches, too. We are all praying for the safe and soon return of your husband."

"That's nice." Her reply left frost in the air.

"Helen," continued Pastor Munton, "please tell us if there is *anything* we can do. The congregation feels like they aren't doing enough. You have turned down numerous offers to help you."

"I'm not a charity case." Helen nearly stood. "I don't want your money."

The Muntons stared at the floor as Helen regained her composure.

"The Sampsons and the Gilbertsons and some others have brought by food, and—believe me—we appreciated it. I have family members in Hope and Spokane who drop by to help as well. The Bonner store has also been gracious enough to extend some credit."

The Muntons kept silent while Helen caught her breath and steadied herself.

"I am the center of attention when I go to church… or any other public place for that matter. At least here in Kootenai. I can't help but think people are judging me… *and* John. Perhaps it's my foolish imagination going wild, but… well, it's how I feel." Tears began to well up in her eyes.

Just what she wanted to avoid. Helen tried to appear adequate to face life's burdens, but her tears betrayed her weakness. *Why did they have to come here?*

"We want you to know we are here, Helen." The pastor sat forward, his palms pressed together as if in prayer. "Please don't shut us out. We want to be there for you, no matter what kind of need you have. It seems to me that, more than anything, you need encouragement. And you can't get that if you don't let anybody in."

Helen sat up straight in her chair with her arms folded across her chest. *If I let them get to me, I'll disintegrate.* No, she had to be hard.

"It seems to me, Pastor," she said, "that what I need more than anything is to have my husband back, and I scarcely see how you can help with that. I don't need sympathy. I know you are trying, but please, let me be. At least for now."

At that moment, a baseball rolled into the living room from the kitchen. They all turned to see Helen's oldest son standing in the doorway, looking embarrassed. "Sorry."

"Hello there, young lad." The pastor picked up the ball and handed it to him. "Do you like to play ball?"

"Sure," he replied. "My name is Charles."

"Of course." The pastor put his hand on Charles's shoulder. "Do you want to go out and play catch?"

Hesitating, Charles shrugged and said, "Sure."

"You'll excuse us, ladies?" Turning to Charles, he asked, "Where's your glove?"

"Don't have one."

"Well, we don't need a glove to play catch," Pastor Munton said as they exited through the back door.

Helen and Mrs. Munton floundered for a few moments, studying the wallpaper. Finally, Helen began, "Frances…"

"Frankie," interrupted Mrs. Munton. "My friends call me Frankie."

"Frankie, I really need to get back to my housework…"

Mrs. Munton interrupted again, "Tell me about him."

"Wh - who? John?"

The pastor's wife nodded and smiled.

"What do you want to know?"

Raising her shoulders, she replied, "Where did you meet?"

"High school." Helen wasn't sure she wanted to go down this road. She had built her wall and darned if she'd let the pastor's wife peck at it.

Finally, Frankie said, "Do you remember the first time you saw him?"

Helen stared at nowhere in particular, and her eyes began to mist again. Her throat tightened, and she took another sip of coffee. The hardness began to slough off as a medley of joy and sorrow stirred in her soul. She nodded in response to Frankie's question before she bowed her head and let out a sob. Frankie drew near to Helen to offer a shoulder, but Helen waved her off, not ready yet to be consoled.

At last, Helen choked out a single word. "Vividly!"

Frankie set down her china cup and crossed her hands in her lap.

"It was the first day of my eleventh-grade year." She cleared her throat. "School had not started for the day, and I stood out in front of the schoolhouse chatting with my friends. It was a cool September morning, but the sun raised the dew, creating a mist round about us. The schoolmaster was about to ring the bell, so we started inside, but we stopped and turned when we heard the sound of approaching hoof beats.

"And there he was. Breaking through the mist riding tall in the saddle, like some movie star or something." Both women laughed.

"Like Tom Mix, he dismounted even before the horse came to a complete stop. He hitched him to the post and tipped his hat as he brushed by us girls and entered the schoolhouse before we did. I knew he was showing off, but he sure did get my attention."

The atmosphere in the room had changed completely. Now the two ladies were giggling like giddy schoolgirls.

"Did you talk to him?"

"Are you kidding?" Helen gave a dismissive wave. "I couldn't talk to him. He was handsome and immediately popular. All the girls adored him."

"So what happened?" Frankie wiggled with anticipation.

"Well, a couple of weeks later, as I walked down the hall with some of my friends, this one boy named Arthur started making fun of me by using an exaggerated limp. You know how mean boys can be. It wasn't the first time." Helen waved her hand like she didn't care.

"Anyway, he and John were friends, and they were together at the time. When Arthur started mimicking me, John got furious and pushed Arthur into the wall—hard! Arthur got all indignant and said something like, 'Hey, what's a matter with you?' And John said, 'Nothing's a matter with me, and there's nothing the matter with *her*, either. But something's the matter with you.'"

Helen laughed at the memory. "They had more words, but that ended the fight. After that, John started carrying my books for me and doting over me. I couldn't believe it."

"Did other boys make fun of you after that?" Frankie picked up her coffee cup and took a sip.

"Not if John was around. That's the most violent I ever saw John get in his life. He's not one for fighting."

"So, if you don't mind me asking," Frankie ventured, "what happened to your feet?"

Helen glanced down at her deformed feet. Her ankles almost touched, while her soles splayed outward. "That's another story. It happened in a farming accident when I was twelve years old. It was late August, harvest time. My dad shared a combined harvester with some other farmers. The pricey machine took a half dozen people to operate it, not to mention thirty-two horses to pull it. None of the farmers in our area could afford to have something like that on their own, so several neighbors co-owned and operated it.

"Anyway, the men and my brothers got to work out in the fields to bring in the harvest, but I had to stay at the house with my mom to cook and clean." Helen shook her head in disgust. "It was a rotten deal, if you ask me. I was old enough and strong enough to help with the sack jig or the horses. But

I was just a girl, so I volunteered to bring lunch out to the crew.

"One day my dad went to town to get supplies. I brought lunch out to the men, and when they were finished eating, I asked if I could have a ride on the combine. At first they said no, but somehow I charmed them into letting me ride up in the crow's nest—the highest spot on the combine, right behind the driver of the horses."

Frankie held her china cup with both hands, eyes focused on Helen.

"Our farm was south of Spokane, down in the hilly Palouse country, and I have to tell you, to ride in the crow's nest is more exhilarating than any amusement ride I've ever been on." Helen smiled as she reminisced. "Sometimes, as you went over the crest of a hill, you could completely lose sight of the horses as they headed down the other side. Only sky could be seen. I held on tight to the bar in front of me as the combine swayed back and forth. I had the time of my life!" At this point, Helen stared off with a wide grin. She felt as if she was right back on that combine.

"But after about twenty minutes, my hands were starting to get tired of gripping. Of course, I didn't tell anyone. I just kept holding on. We started going on this side hill, and the combine tipped to the left like this." Helen used her hand to demonstrate about a thirty-degree angle. "I did fine until the left front wheel fell into a badger hole with a violent jerk. I screamed and went flying."

At this, Frankie gasped, almost spilling her coffee.

"Normally, I would have been fine, because the plowing of the fields would make for a pretty soft landing. But wouldn't you know it." Helen slapped her knee. "I landed feet first in an uneven rocky area they couldn't plow."

Frankie's eyes went wide. "Were you taken to the hospital?"

Helen shook her head. "My parents couldn't afford a doctor bill, and they didn't realize how hurt I was. They figured I would heal up."

"So what *did* happen? I mean, how bad was it?"

"Well, there were several broken bones in my feet, especially my left one. My doctor says over time they fused together in their own way."

"Can't something still be done?"

Helen shook her head again. "It's too late to do anything now. Anyway, for some reason, John was the only boy who didn't see anything wrong with me. Everyone else saw me as defective."

******

Storm clouds formed to the southwest across the surface of Lake Pend Oreille. Pastor Munton and Charles hardly noticed.

"Hey. Not so hard!" Pastor Munton laughed. "Remember, I'm not wearing a glove either."

"Sorry. Guess I don't know my own strength," Charles bragged.

"You have a pretty good arm," the pastor said. "You play baseball?"

"Yeah." Charles shrugged. "With my friends sometimes at school. I guess it's my favorite sport." He tilted his head to one side. "Hey, do they have baseball in England?"

"Well, we have cricket. It's a bit different than baseball. More exciting, if you ask me. But I've been in the states for fifteen years now, so I've learned to love baseball."

They chatted about sports in general for a few minutes, and then Pastor Munton changed the subject.

"So, I suppose you are the man of the house right now?"

Charles shrugged, responding with little enthusiasm. "Yeah."

"How is that going?"

"Fine, I guess. Mom has me doing most of the chores Dad did. You know, splitting the wood, getting the stove going, yard work, fixing things… all that kind of stuff. Plus I'm working now at the store for Mr. Bonner. He pays me twenty-five cents after school and fifty cents on Saturdays."

They tossed the ball back and forth as they conversed.

"What does he have you do?"

"All sorts of things. I help unload trucks when they arrive, help stock shelves."

"Sounds like a lot of heavy lifting."

Charles stood straight and threw back his shoulders. "Yeah. But he's also teaching me how to run the till. I might have to run the store by myself some days."

"Sounds like good training. How old are you now?"

"Twelve-and-a-half."

Pastor Munton raised his eyebrows. "That's quite a bit of responsibility for

171

a twelve-year-old."

"Twelve-and-a-*half*," the boy corrected.

"Still." The pastor stifled a smile. "Quite a bit of responsibility even for someone who's almost thirteen."

This time the pastor held on to the ball for a moment. "So, how are *you* doing? I mean, with your dad missing. It must be hard." He threw the ball back to the boy.

"I guess I'm getting used to it." Charles caught the ball with his left hand and tossed it over to his right. "But people say things."

"What kind of things?"

"You know." Charles kicked at the dirt and averted his gaze. "They say bad things about my dad."

"Things that aren't true," the pastor added.

Charles gazed at the dark clouds. "Right."

"And that bothers you."

"Sure it does." Charles still held the ball, seemingly addressing it. "Wouldn't it bother you if people were lying about your dad?"

"Yes, it would," the pastor confessed, catching the ball again. "What do you do about it?"

"Nothin'."

"Why?"

"'Cause my dad doesn't like me to fight."

The pastor let the response sink in. A distant roll of thunder punctuated the moment. He noticed the dark clouds were getting closer.

"Where do you suppose your dad is?"

Charles stared at the ground for a bit. "Who knows?"

"God knows," the pastor said softly.

"Lotta good that does." Charles's voice rose in anger. "He ain't tellin' us!"

The pastor drew near to the boy. "Charles, God knows what's going on. He knows what's going on in your life and your brother's and sister's. He knows how much your mom is suffering right now. And He knows where your dad is."

Charles blinked as it started to sprinkle. He stared out toward the ominous black cumulonimbus clouds. Was it the rain or tears rolling down his cheeks?

Pastor Munton stooped down and made sure they were eye to eye. His voice was just above a whisper. "God is working right now. He knows the truth about your dad, and that is more important than what anyone else thinks or says about him. But make no mistake. He's working powerfully, even if we can't see it."

"Doin' what?" Charles asked with a frown.

"Well, for one thing, He's making you into a man."

Charles wiped his cheeks and locked eyes with Pastor Munton.

"Mind if I tell you a story?" The pastor tossed the ball up and down with one hand. "It's a baseball story."

The boy offered a slight nod.

"It's a true story about a baseball player named George. He was the best player on his team—the most important one, too. But a couple of years ago, he missed the first couple months of the season."

"Was he injured?"

"No, he was suspended for breaking some rules in the off-season. But that's not important. The point is, he was *missing*. So you know what his team did? They played harder than ever. And even though he missed all that time, when he came back, they were in first place. They went on to win the American League Pennant."

"George?" asked Charles. "I've never heard of him."

"Sure you have. George Herman Ruth."

Charles's eyes grew wide. "Babe?"

The pastor stood erect. "The Sultan of Swat himself. But do you know why the Yankees did so well that year?"

"Because they tried harder." Charles squinted up at the pastor.

"Partly." Plucking the ball from Charles's hand, he examined it a moment. "But the real reason is they knew he would come back. They made sure to play hard while he was missing because they knew even the Babe couldn't dig them out of a hole. They had to play well during his absence because they wanted to be in a good position when he came back."

Pastor Munton stooped again and got close to the boy's face. "And you know what? *You* believe your dad is coming back."

Charles frowned. "Huh?"

"A little while ago, you said your dad doesn't like you to fight."

"So?"

"You didn't say 'didn't.' You said 'doesn't.'" The pastor paused. "You know your dad's alive out there somewhere, don't you?"

Charles dropped the ball and ran into the house.

It started to pour.

DAY 35

THURSDAY, MAY 15, 1924

A knock came at the front door.

"Now what?" In no mood for callers, Helen peeked through the curtains. Mrs. Hoover, the nosy, gossipy next-door neighbor, stood on her front porch. Tempted to not open the door at all, she resigned to comply when Mrs. Hoover saw her peek through the curtains. Her neighbor waved like an old friend.

Helen rolled her eyes and opened the door.

With a goofy grin and without a word, Mildred Hoover held out something in both hands for Helen to accept.

"What do you want, Mildred?" Helen spoke with a flat tone.

The grin disappeared, replaced with unconcealed woundedness. "Well," she gushed, "I brought this blackberry pie, fresh out of the oven, and I thought it would be the neighborly thing to do…"

Crossing her arms, Helen waited to see if Mildred had anything to add. The rich scent of the fresh-baked pie was not lost on her. She could see steam rise from under a white hand towel. It would taste good, she knew, but…

"You know, with the, uh, situation, and all." Another pause. "The one you're in."

Helen let her wallow in her awkwardness for several more seconds before replying. "Feeling kind of sorry for me, are you?"

"Well, I…"

"Maybe feeling a little bit guilty?"

"Guilty?" Mrs. Hoover presented an innocent, childlike face.

"Guilty about spreading rumors about John leaving me?"

"Well," she gushed again. Mrs. Hoover had a habit of starting sentences with the word "well" accompanied by an excessive breath of air. Helen found it to be another thing about Mrs. Hoover to detest.

"Well," she repeated, "it isn't a rumor if it's true."

At that moment, it took all of Helen's starch to not take the blackberry pie and plaster it directly into her self-righteous expression. She somehow managed to calmly utter, "You wouldn't know the truth if it smacked you flat in your lying face."

It appeared that the serenity with which she delivered her insult stung more than if she had applied the blackberry facial. Mrs. Hoover froze, open-mouthed.

"Your pie hardly makes up for the damage you and your tongue-wagging knitting circle have caused my family." Helen took a step closer. "So I'll thank you to move your foul carcass off my porch."

"Well!" Flabbergasted, the red-faced Mrs. Hoover hurried down the steps and rushed to the front gate. In her haste, she dropped the pie on the walk. She hesitated, but decided not to pick up the mess and made for home expeditiously.

Helen felt better than she had for some time.

******

After eating supper at the Mill Boarding House, Frank Fisher decided to explore the town instead of holing up again in his room. He had been in Skykomish for three days, and he determined to stop feeling sorry for himself. He would explore the town. Maybe someone would recognize him.

He started at the east end of Railroad Avenue, where the Mill Boarding House occupied a space in the Cascadia Hotel. Returning westward, he came to where the Maple Leaf Confectionary beckoned.

Mmmm. He could smell fresh brownies baking, mixed with the aroma of hot buttered popcorn. Through the window, peanut brittle and chocolate truffles beckoned him inside.

Railroaders and millworkers alike enjoyed patronizing the Maple Leaf. For the sweets, of course, but mostly because of the card tables and the illegal booze. A perky young blonde wearing a red-and-white striped apron greeted him when he came in. Her presence added to the patronage as well, Fisher was sure.

"You look like you could use a peppermint." She held a tray of hard candy wrapped in foil close to his nose. "Just a penny for two."

In Skykomish, a town populated mostly by men, the sight of a beautiful woman could take one's breath away. Fisher swallowed and glanced around the room. He didn't want to gawk. "Uh, how much for a pack of Beeman's?"

She tilted her head and smiled. "Today, it's free."

Surprised, he asked, "It is?"

"Yesiree," she replied with a merry lilt. "Only problem is, we're out." Her smile became an exaggerated pout.

"Oh." He furrowed his brow in confusion.

"Which is why we can sell it so cheap." Her smile returned.

Sassy. I like it. "Are you getting more in?"

Her effervescence never disappeared. "Next week." Some of the men at the tables turned their heads, apparently finding the conversation amusing.

"I don't suppose when it comes in it will still be free?"

"Oh, no," she replied. "It will go back to its regular price. A penny a pack."

He plopped down a penny for a pack of Wrigley's spearmint gum and decided he would make the Maple Leaf a regular stop. If for no other reason than to get another eyeful of the candy girl.

Continuing west, he passed the Skykomish and crossed Fifth Street. Maloney's

General Store stood on the corner. John Maloney, the founder and first mayor of Skykomish, was the first owner of the mill. Still the most prominent businessman in town, he owned the store as well as the post office inside.

Fisher strolled around in the store with its eclectic hodgepodge of almost everything anyone in Skykomish could want. From groceries and dry goods to hardware and electrical items, it stood as the center of retail business in town.

He had been in the store the night before to subscribe to the *Spokesman-Review* newspaper when he met John Maloney Jr., the acting clerk. This time he didn't buy anything but simply meandered the aisles for a bit and moved on.

Next door, an old warehouse had been converted into a theater. A Buster Keaton movie was scheduled for Saturday night. He decided he would go. Payday was Saturday.

Music came from the direction of Maloney's store. He headed back where he had come from to see John Jr. hovering over an Edison Blue Amberol Cylinder record player. It played a vaudeville comedy featuring dialogue by a couple named Susan and Elmer. Fisher marveled at the turning cylinder and the sounds coming from it. They both laughed as Susan and Elmer flirted with each other and even kissed. Frank's smile disappeared as he thought about how wonderful it would be to have someone to kiss tonight.

Orchestra music followed, and then a duet by the two.

"Just got it in today." John Jr stroked the side of it. "Do you like it?"

"It's a beaut." The tag said thirty dollars.

Another song began, and Frank said, "Hey, I remember this song. It's called 'Si Perkins' Barn Dance.'"

"That's right." Junior read the tube the cylinder came in. "Featuring Ada Jones and Len Spencer." When the four-minute recording finished, they played it again so Frank could hear it from the beginning.

When Fisher returned to his room, he slammed the door behind him. Pacing the room and talking to himself, he seethed about the perplexities of his memory. "Why do I remember the name Si Perkins, but not my own name—or the name of any friend or relative? If I ever did hear my *own* name uttered, would I recognize it?" He returned to the dingy mirror perched on his dresser, studying his features again.

"I don't even know my own nationality. I would have to guess I am of northern European descent, but who knows?" He gritted his teeth in frustration. "Do I have a family somewhere looking for me and praying for me right now? Do I own property somewhere? Do I have money saved up in a bank?"

The more he mulled these questions over, the more his rage grew. He turned to the mirror again, searching for answers, and was startled when the mirror shattered into a thousand pieces. Trembling, he stared down at his hands, clutching the dresser in front of him.

His knuckles were bleeding.

DAY 36

Friday, May 16, 1924

The broken mirror sat in a garbage can.

So Fisher examined his physique in the reflection in his window. Not skinny, by any means, but trim enough. He flexed a bicep, impressed.

His physical condition was one thing; his mental state was quite another. Most nights, he lay in bed for hours, tossing and turning, before finally getting two or three hours of honest sleep. How long could he keep it up?

What will become of me? He had grown tired of the charade of pretending to be someone he wasn't. But what choice was there? While in Skykomish, he felt farther from the truth than anywhere else he'd been.

Flicking the light off, he crawled into bed, staring at the dark ceiling. *Maybe after a couple more weeks of saving money, I can head to Idaho or Montana and search there.*

Tonight, melancholy replaced the anger of last night. Longing for home, he wondered again how you can desire something you know nothing about. Yet it was there.

After less than an hour, he crawled out of bed, giving up on sleep. Gazing out his window to the railroad tracks below, he watched the activity at the station across the street. Even past midnight, passenger trains and freight trains came and went, making the small village of Skykomish seem like a major destination.

He blew out a deep breath and sat on the floor with his back against the wall, hugging his knees. The light of a nearly full moon cast its beam across the windowsill. The back of an oak mission chair split the single beam into seven, creating an odd image against the wall.

Fisher examined the image with hypnotic indifference, the shadows changing as time passed. He barely moved for what seemed like hours. The chair no longer felt the moon's touch, and instead, the moonlight favored the foot of his bed. As night marched on, he studied the moon's influence on his room.

My loved ones—if there are any—are they feeling the same?

Lost.

Were they, like him, hoping for illumination in a dark world? Or were they moving on with their lives without him, sleeping soundly, unmoved by the passing of the moon?

He thought again about Leonard, the mouse. At least the little rodent was someone he could talk to.

******

Helen could have pulled the floral patterned curtains shut. But she knew the moonlight wasn't what kept her awake. With all the emotions she had felt over the past few weeks, tonight simply felt empty. She moved with difficulty, her weariness sapping her. Her shoulders sagged as she got up and slid open her window, letting cool night air in. Hearing a train whistle as it passed through Kootenai, she stared up at the moon.

What secrets could it tell?

DAY 38

SUNDAY, MAY 18, 1924

He hated Sundays.

It was his first one since starting at the mill, but he knew they were going to be the end of him. *At least Monday through Saturday I can concentrate on my job. I have no idea what I'm going to do today.* A distraction was in order.

He tried to sleep in late, but his mind couldn't rest. Out his window, he saw townsfolk dressed in their Sunday finest headed to church.

Not him.

At church, friendly people introduce themselves and want to know all about you. *Then what do I say? My name is Frank Fisher, but that's only been my name for the last six days. Before that, I went by J.A. Larkin for a few weeks, but before that, who knows?*

Or he could be ready to answer with a bunch of lies, but that wouldn't be right. Not in church. Better to avoid any social gatherings.

With nothing else to do, he hung around in his room, as usual. The hours dragged on. He had yesterday's *Everett Herald*, which he had already read. Twice.

What is my family doing today? Where are they? Are they looking for me? The same questions haunted him daily. Hourly. Every minute.

The mill paid for two meals a day, lunch and dinner. They did the same on Sundays but called them dinner and supper. Dinner was the main meal, with supper being lighter, maybe cold meat sandwiches. But Sunday dinner was always special. Like roast chicken, mashed potatoes, and gravy with corn. It also included fresh fruit and a dessert of some kind. Even so, when noon came, it wasn't so much hunger that drove him there as something to do.

The boarding house served dinners family style, so he ate all his meals with fellow workers at the same table. Chet Lowry was a regular.

"I see the Yankees beat Saint Louis yesterday." Chet wasn't speaking to anyone in particular, just the table in general as he read from the *Everett Herald*.

"Yeah," another said. "Still in first place."

"Uh-huh." Lowry continued to read. "Says here they knocked out Danforth in the fifth. That's his first loss."

Heads nodded. More baseball talk continued, but Frank didn't hear it. He busied himself by staring at his food and wallowing in self-pity.

"What do you think, Fisher?"

He noticed Lowry and the others eyeing him, apparently expecting a response.

Frank glanced down again at his untouched plate. "Uh, yeah, I suppose so."

"You suppose what?"

Hiding his inward torment, Frank couldn't make eye contact. "Oh, I don't know."

Chet set down his coffee cup. "You're a regular chatterbox, you know that, Fisher?"

Some of the men laughed, but Fisher couldn't think about baseball right now. *Do I have a wife worrying about me? Children missing me? Is there an empty chair haunting my household?*

The food in front of him blurred, and he wiped his eyes. With no appetite, he sat there, afraid he might start blubbering. Getting up from the table, he tried not to make a scene.

"Hey, you gonna eat that chicken?" someone said. But he took his full plate to the return window and walked out.

Instead of returning to his room, which was beginning to feel like a cell, he strode out of town. He didn't know where to go, but had to get away from everyone and everything.

The double-decker Mill Bridge had railroad tracks on top and a walking bridge below. The lower level also accommodated horse and buggy traffic.

A stiff wind blew northward—at his back. As he crossed the bridge, he stopped to gaze at the roiling water of the Skykomish River, contemplating what would happen if he jumped in. *Should I go through with it? Would it end my sorrow or just be the beginning of it? If I do have a family, would they ever know my fate?*

Only questions—no answers. And that only magnified his angst.

Bunching his hands into fists, he threw back his head to gaze up through the ties on the upper deck of the bridge. "Why are you doing this to me? How long must I go on like this?"

He bowed his head again and stared into the raging water for a while as it forged westward to the sea. A leaf drawn downstream was gone again in a flash to some unknown destination, helpless to do anything about it. The thought of it made him pound his fists against the handrail.

Fleeing across the bridge, he went up a logging road for about two miles. The landscape in every direction consisted of nothing but stumps and weeds left over from clear-cutting. The road came to a sudden end, so he continued up the mountain, following a deer trail into virgin woods.

Brushing undergrowth to the side, he continued onward and upward. When a branch appeared beside the trail, he picked it up, thinking he might use it as a walking stick. But it was too flimsy, so instead, he swung it brutally against a nearby tree with a loud crack. He turned when he heard another sound, but then realized it was probably just the echo of his frustration.

The wind blew more violently now, weeds flopping to their sides and trees nodding in obedience to the gusts. Ripping dandelions from their roots, he tossed them to the side, persisting in his quest to—do what? He had no idea.

Retreating ever farther from Skykomish, he came to realize he didn't know his way back.

He didn't care.

******

The Olson family sat at their table in Kootenai, about to partake in Sunday dinner. Friends from the church had stopped by that morning to leave a chuck roast. They said it was no trouble; they had extra and couldn't use it.

Charles, the oldest, would ask the blessing. He was used to it now. Since his father disappeared, his mother had become more distant—detached from the family, church, and spiritual matters. She stared blankly ahead.

He had already lost his father. He worried now that he might be losing his mother.

"Dear God. Thank you for this food. And please bring Daddy home soon. We really need him. Amen."

******

The winding trail up the mountain brought Fisher to an overlook giving him a panorama of the verdant Skykomish valley. He stopped briefly to observe the mountains that prevailed above the meandering river far below. From this vantage point, there was no civilization evident, only endless forest. He saw nothing but a vast and empty chasm.

He was alone.

No one in Skykomish knew him. Some knew his name and his face. But if they ever knew of his troubles, they would not care. Or, if they did, they would only retreat from the presence of a madman.

Another mile or so later, the trail came to a cool spring bubbling to the surface of the ground. He hadn't realized how thirsty he was until he came upon it. Now he cupped his hands in the small pool of clear water and drank from it greedily.

After getting his fill, he sat by the pool. His thoughts turned to his mother. Any mother would be beside herself with fear if her son were missing. The idea of his mother suffering because of him brought a whole new level of culpability and shame. *What have I done to deserve this purgatory?*

He heard another sound on the trail behind him. He waited for a bit, his attention drawn in the direction of the sound.

Nothing.

Probably a bear or mountain lion, knowing his luck.

When nothing appeared, he was alone again with his torment. He lay on the rough ground and shed bitter tears before finally falling asleep.

******

Edward and Annie Olson sat at their dinner table in Freeman. Annie had prepared Edward's favorite: liver and onions with green beans. Only the ticking of the kitchen clock broke the silence.

With thirty-seven years of marriage behind them, each knew the other's thoughts. After a few bites, the tears began to well up in Annie and she turned to Edward, her face melting to one of utter despair.

Edward dropped his fork onto his plate and grabbed Annie, giving her the hug he knew she so desperately needed. It was not a selfless act.

******

When Fisher woke, it took a moment to get his bearings. He pulled out his pocket watch. Past four o'clock already. He must have been sleeping for almost three hours.

First he noticed the wind had died down some. But then he was startled to see a man sitting on a rock not three feet from him.

Tall and thin, the man wore blue denim overalls with a plain white work shirt and a red ball cap. He was about fifty years old, with a large Adam's apple and a long sprig of grass that had gone to seed dangling from his mouth. At his feet, a small pile of wood shavings had accumulated from a stick that he was whittling into… something.

Fisher cleared his throat. "Who are you?"

The man smiled, revealing a sizable gap between his two front teeth. "Name's Joe Clyde Mailer, from Kye-en-tucky," he said, stretching his home state's name into four syllables. He extended his hand for Frank to shake.

Frank returned the gesture. "What are you doing out here?"

"I follered ya."

"Why?"

Removing the sprig of grass from his mouth, Joe Clyde adjusted himself on the rock. "Whell, I noticed you were lookin' kinda fretful back at dinner and saw the way ya left the table. I was just a mite concerned. The name's Frank, right?"

Then Fisher thought he recognized him from the mill. "Yeah, it's Frank. You work in the planer room, right?" Before the man had a chance to answer, he asked, "How do you know my name?"

The man glanced around. "I pay attention."

"And you say your name is Joe?"

"Joe Clyde. That's what they call me." Joe Clyde continued his whittling.

Frank sat up straighter. "Okay, Joe Clyde. So you say you were worried about me?"

"Yes, indeed. You look like a soul with a lot of troublin' goin' on. I wondered if there was anything I could do." His tone of voice was very calming and friendly.

"I hardly know where to start," Fisher said. "But you see, I... I..." Words seemed inadequate. Joe Clyde waited and whittled. Fisher didn't know what it was, but even though Joe Clyde was a total stranger, there was something about him that made him trust him.

With great moral effort, Fisher finally reached into his hip pocket and pulled out the little red book. With trembling hands, he handed it to the hillbilly.

Joe Clyde set down his knife and stick. He beheld the book in his hands, looking back at Fisher before opening it and beginning to read. Expressionless, he read without uttering a word for ten minutes. Fisher watched him, wondering what the man was thinking.

Finally, Joe Clyde said, "Whell, I don't blame ya for bein' weepy. Looks like y'all have been goin' through the Valley."

More like a canyon. A deep, dark canyon. Fisher could only nod in response. A knot formed in his throat, making him feel like the devil himself had his hands wrapped around his larynx.

Rubbing his chin thoughtfully, Joe Clyde arose from the rock and began to pace with his grass sprig firmly planted between his teeth. "I've heard about perdicamints like this."

"You have?" Fisher stood to pay close attention.

"Oh, it'taint common, to be sure," he replied. "But tisn't permanent, either."

"It isn't? How long does it last?"

"Varies," he said with a shrug. "Days, weeks, months. With some only a few hours or minutes. It could even go on fer years."

"Years?" Fisher shoved his hands through his hair.

"Now, now." Joe Clyde gestured with his palms down. "I said it's not common, and it's even less common for it to go on and on like that."

"Well, what causes it?" Fisher asked. "I can't even remember what happened to me."

"Could have been in an auto accident," he offered. "Or maybe you were struck by a car 'n' they thought you were dead and to keep away from police had you put in a box car."

Fisher shook his head. "How does a person get his memory back?"

"I've heard tell that sometimes it's necessary to be knocked senseless a second time to place your memory back where it was."

At this statement, Fisher started searching the ground. He walked over to a rock about the size of a cantaloupe and picked it up. Marching back to Joe Clyde, he said in a desperate, raspy voice, "In that case, my prayer is that I get knocked out as soon as possible, just to satisfy myself as to whether I have a mother, father, or family of my own. Now, you said you came here to help. Are you going to help me or not?"

Wide-eyed, Joe Clyde stretched his arms in front of him and shook his palms at Fisher. "Now see here, I'm not going to… Hey, stop that!"

Fisher—when he saw Joe Clyde wasn't about to partake in head clobbering—took matters into his own hands and began to bang the rock straight into his forehead.

The hillbilly lurched forward and, with a struggle, seized the rock from Fisher's hands and dispatched it directly to the nearby woods. Fisher fell in a heap to the ground and dissolved into tears.

As Fisher lay on the ground, Joe Clyde glanced heavenward and spread his arms apart. With pity in his voice, he said, "I'm sorry, Frank. I don't know why I said such a foolish thing. I really don't know if anybody has ever been helped by getting hit agin'. It's just somethin' I've heard, and it probly tisn't even true. I didn't know you'd act all crazy like that."

Joe Clyde sat on the ground beside Fisher, who had assumed the fetal position. He set his hand on Fisher's shoulder, trying to calm him down. They stayed that way for a few minutes while Fisher got control of his emotions again. Only the sounds of the bubbling spring and the breeze rustling through the aspens could be heard.

Finally, with a stern yet kind expression, Joe Clyde turned to Fisher. "Yup. It's called the Valley of the Shadow of Death. And you're in it."

Fisher quaked at the sound of those words. He knew them from the Bible. The Twenty-third Psalm. He sat up. "Well, what did I ever do to get here?"

Joe Clyde shook his head. "Nothin'. The Good Shepherd guided you here."

"But why?" he asked as he stood. "What did I do to deserve this… this punishment?"

"I told ya'. Tisn't a punishment. I reckon maybe ya' had it too good. Forgot how much ya' needed Him every day. He's taking you down a path of learnin' to trust 'im."

Frank walked over and kicked the bashing rock. "Feels more like I'm wanderin' through this canyon all alone."

"Doesn't have to be that way." Joe Clyde picked up a paper bag sitting next to him. "Are ya' hungry?"

He hadn't thought about that. He hadn't eaten anything all day. He had only picked at his meal at the boarding house—too upset to think about food.

Joe Clyde produced an orange from the bag. He extended it to Fisher.

Fisher sat on the ground facing Joe Clyde. He blinked and, with a sheepish grin, accepted his offer without a word. As he peeled the orange, the scent of citrus filled his nose and lifted his spirits. "This orange," he said through a mouthful, "is the best orange I have ever tasted."

Mailer produced a slice of rhubarb pie from the same bag. Frank eagerly accepted that as well.

While Frank stuffed the food in his mouth, Joe Clyde said, "You know what you need more than anything?"

Through a mouth full of pie, he answered, "Yeah, my memory."

"Nah." Joe Clyde slapped one knee. "You need a friend."

Frank swallowed. "Maybe. But I sure could use a big dose of recollection."

Shaking his head, the hillbilly said, "I've seen the way you are. You don't say much. Yer not unfriendly, but yer not zactly sociable either. After work, ya' hole up in your room and…"

Frank frowned. "How do you know about that? Have you been watching me?"

Joe Clyde spread his hands. "Like I told ya. I pay attention."

"Why does it matter? I mean, is it so important to have a friend?"

"Yer memory will come back when it comes back. But right now, you've got to do something to keep yer sanity." Joe Clyde pointed his long index finger at Fisher. "If all you ever do is feel sorry fer yerself, you may not make it back to the real world."

Fisher thought about his pause at the bridge. The fact that he would even consider suicide sent a cold shiver down his spine.

"Why are you so afraid of making a friend?" asked Joe Clyde.

"Because of what people will think of me if I tell them the truth. I could become the laughingstock of town."

"You told *me*." Joe Clyde sat back down on the rock and returned to whittling.

"Yeah. But you're… different."

Joe Clyde smiled. "I've been called worse."

They both laughed for the first time.

"*You* could be my friend," Fisher said. "You are the only person I've ever told the truth to."

"How did that make ya feel?" Joe Clyde peeled another strip from his stick.

Nodding, Fisher said, "Better. I feel a sense of relief like I just unloaded a sack of potatoes."

"That's how it is to have a friend." Joe Clyde shifted on his rock. "A true friend helps you carry your burden. It's someone who can help ya through a tough time."

Wiping pie crumbs from his mouth, Fisher asked, "So, how about it?"

Joe Clyde stopped whittling. "How about what?"

"Being my friend."

"Whell, my time here is about up. I need to go back to my family. That's where I belong."

Fisher hung his head. "I wish I could get back to my family."

"You will." Joe Clyde patted his back. "But if we don't head back down soon, we'll be too late for supper."

The two of them rose to their feet. Fisher felt… light. As they walked, they talked about friendships and even sang a couple of hymns. Finally, they paused at the same vantage point Fisher had stopped at on the way up. Now the sun was lower, and the valley had filled with shadows, but it still shone brightly on the two men.

Fisher said, "It's beautiful."

Mailer removed his ball cap and scratched his head. "From up here you get a whole different perspective."

They both stood there admiring the idyllic setting they were living in. The Skykomish River could still be seen in the dusky light, splitting the deep valley in two.

When they proceeded again, Fisher said, "Hey, the wind stopped."

Joe Clyde started another hymn, and Fisher joined in.

Amazing grace, how sweet the sound, that saved a wretch like me.

But Fisher couldn't choke out the next line. Joe Clyde sang it solo.

I once was lost, but now I'm found. Was blind, but now I see.

DAY 39

MONDAY, MAY 19, 1924

"So, what happened to your forehead?"

A bemused Chet Lowry took a bite of corn on the cob while he and Fisher ate supper at the Mill Boarding House.

"Oh, that. I, uh, ran into a pole."

Chet laughed. "Looks like you were running pretty fast. That's quite a goose egg."

"I can be a bit clumsy." Fisher changed the subject. "I started in the edger room today."

"So I noticed," Lowry said after swallowing. "How do you like it?"

"A whole lot better than the custodial work."

"Really? Seems like the custodial work is pretty easy." Chet put down his finished cob and sprinkled pepper on his mashed potatoes.

"It is more demanding. Heavier work, too. But I think I like it." Frank spoke through a bite of corn. "I'm lining up for the edger man. So after the band saw does the initial cuts, the half-round logs come to me…"

"The cants," Lowry said.

"Right. The cants. So, I lay the lumber flat side down on the belt, and the edger man makes them into dimensional lumber. Pretty interesting."

Lowry yawned. "Yeah, fascinating."

Frank decided to change the subject again. "Do you know anybody named Joe Clyde?"

"No. Should I?"

"I think he worked in the planer room. But I asked some of the men from there, and they didn't seem to know who I was talking about."

Scratching his head, Lowry looked toward the ceiling. "Seems like there used to be a guy named Joe in there."

"He goes by Joe Clyde." Frank started to take a bite of potatoes but finished his thought first. "Last name Mailer."

"Hmm. I would have remembered somebody with a name like Joe Clyde." Lowry turned to the next table. "Hey Hank, you ever hear of a guy named Joe Clyde working around here?"

Nobody seemed to know the name.

Chet returned to his corn on the cob. "Where'd you find this fella?"

"I took a hike yesterday and ran into him."

"I thought you said it was a pole. Was he Polish?" Chet laughed at his own joke.

"No," Fisher stopped eating and glared at Lowry. "I mean we had a conversation."

"And he said he worked here in the planer room?"

"Well, no. But it seemed like I saw him there once." Fisher took another bite.

"What did you say his last name was? Mailer?"

"Yeah."

"Mailer… Mailer…" Chet wiped his mouth. "Mailer like uh, a messenger? That kind of mailer?"

"Yeah, like a…" Frank dropped his fork. "Like a messenger."

DAY 40

TUESDAY, MAY 20, 1924

Helen hesitated as she reached toward the shelf at Bonner's store.

I think I can do without baking powder just yet.

Mary Bonner came to her side. "Helen, let me hold the baby so you can shop."

"I'm just getting a few things." *I can't afford much.* She handed baby Mary over to her namesake. "Anna May! Don't touch."

Toddling by the apple barrel, the two-year-old's big hazel eyes grew wider and wetter as her mouth contorted into a pout.

"Oh, she can't hurt anything," said Mrs. Bonner with a wave. Holding the baby with her left arm, she used her right hand to write Helen's items in a ledger.

Frank Bonner appeared from the back room. "Mary, let me do that. You can't hold a baby and write at the same time."

"You want the baby or the ledger?" Mary tried to hand him baby Mary.

Frank frowned. "I'll take the ledger, if you don't mind. Besides, I can hardly read your writing." A smile developed on his face as he turned to Helen. "Mrs. Hoover came in earlier. She told me that you're an 'ungrateful ol' bitty.'"

Helen laughed. "She sure does like to talk. And I seem to be her favorite subject nowadays."

Just then, a familiar boy emerged through the batwing doors leading to the storeroom, carrying a push broom. When he caught sight of Helen, he dashed into the back room with great haste.

Helen froze. "Charles?"

Frank and Mary exchanged confused glances with Helen as Charles slowly returned from the back room with a sheepish grin on his face.

"Yes'm?"

"What are you doing here?" asked Helen. "You're supposed to be at school."

"I'm working here at the store now." Charles thumped the broom on the floor.

"Is that a fact?" Helen glared at him and then turned her gaze to Frank.

His mouth gaped open but no speech poured forth.

Charles spoke again, a pleading tone in his voice. "Mom, we need the income, and Principal Nogle says I already have enough credit to go on to eighth grade next year."

Helen scanned all three. "Seems everyone knows about Charles's newfound vocation but me."

Both Mary and Helen turned their gaze to Frank.

"Helen, I, I thought you knew…"

"Frank, you know how I feel about charity."

"It isn't charity if you're working for it." He put his hands on his hips.

"Just how much are you paying him, Frank?"

"Ten cents an hour."

"That's almost as much as John made working for the railroad." Helen slapped her hand on the counter.

Bonner folded his arms. "It's the same I'd pay anyone doing the work he's doing."

"He's only twelve years old."

"He's doing man's work, and he has a man's responsibility." This time Frank slapped the counter.

Taking a deep breath, Helen said, "Put these on my tab, Mary." She collected her things.

"You don't have a tab here anymore," Frank declared.

"What?" Slack-jawed, Helen couldn't believe her ears.

"Everything you buy here is taken directly from Charles's pay." Mary nodded in agreement.

Helen was steamed about Charles not telling her about school, but she was proud of his industriousness. She didn't want him to see her ambivalence, so she continued to glare at him for a moment. "In that case, I need a pound of roast beef, too. We're having stew tonight." She didn't take her eyes off of Charles, suggesting he may be one of the main ingredients.

Frank, looking embarrassed, said, "Helen, we'll get it all bagged up for you and I'll send Charles home with it. You've got enough to handle with two little girls in tow." Then he turned to Charles. "Put the broom down and help your mother. Once that's done, I need you back here Jack Sprat to set up that soup can display."

DAY 41

WEDNESDAY, MAY 21, 1924

Fisher maneuvered a wheelbarrow full of wood scraps down the path. Encountering three men smoking and chatting outside the band saw before the start of the workday, he announced, "Wide load coming through."

One of the men, Chet Lowry, stepped aside. "Yeah, plus you're pushing a wheelbarrow." The men guffawed.

Stopping in his tracks, Fisher feigned indignation and dropped the wheelbarrow handles. "Very funny, Lowry. You should take that act to Vaudeville."

"I think I will," Chet replied. "The wages are probably better, especially after the pay cut."

Fisher had raised the handles on the wheelbarrow but dropped them again. "What pay cut? Is this another one of your jokes?"

"I wish I *was* joking." Lowry crushed out a cigarette with the toe of his boot. "You must not have heard. The rate goes down to three-sixty a day starting next week. Half the mill is talking about quitting." The other men grumbled in agreement.

Wiping his brow, Fisher said, "That's forty cents less a day."

Lowry turned to the men. "Well, boys, Euclid here did the math for us." More laughter. "So what's with the wheelbarrow?"

"They started me on the boiler room today. They got me out of bed at two o'clock." Everyone knew steam powered everything at the mill. The fuel for the boiler was the most plentiful resource in the valley—wood.

"Hot work," Lowry said.

"Sure is. I just got done taking a break down by the river to cool off, but I've had it. I think I'm going to have to tell the foreman to find someone else."

"I'm not surprised." Lowry opened the door to the band saw shed. "They have a hard time keeping anybody there for very long. But you may set the record for the shortest stint."

******

Spokane Police Chief Wesley Turner took a seat across the desk from Detective Paul Bucholz. The detective removed the pipe from his mouth. "What's up?"

Turner put his hands on his knees and took a deep breath. "Where are we on the Olson case?"

"You got a call from Helen Olson, didn't you?"

Nodding, Turner said, "She thinks you're not doing anything."

Bucholz smiled. "So she called *you*. What did you tell her?"

"I told her we are doing everything we can. She asked me what I meant. I kind of fumbled around because I really didn't have a good answer." He let out a sigh. "I told her I would talk to you and get back to her. What do I tell her?"

Shrugging, Bucholz said, "She is quite a handful, isn't she?"

"Paul, I have to admit she has a point. You've given up, haven't you?"

Bucholz held his palms up. "What do you propose, Wesley? He's been missing for over a month. We drug the river, and we have questioned every witness. Our officers are on the lookout for him every day. We have sent notices to every police department in the Pacific Northwest." He took a long drag from his pipe and sighed. "Given up? No. But I don't have a crystal ball. Is there room in the budget for one?"

"Tell me the truth, Paul. What do you think happened to him?"

"Frankly, I think he bugged out. We had several witnesses say he and his wife had an argument that morning…"

"Wait a minute. I thought there was only one witness saying that."

"Only one woman reported the altercation itself, but several witnesses say they saw him at the train station in Sandpoint a few minutes later, and he was clearly agitated. They say he tried to pick a fight with someone." The detective frowned and shook his head. "Besides, you've talked with Helen Olson. Doesn't she seem like someone you might bail out on?"

Turner scowled back. "Could it be Helen Olson seems cantankerous to you because she thinks you've been uncooperative?"

"Are you saying I haven't been doing my job?"

"I'm *saying*, Paul, that you could try a little harder to be a bit more winsome."

Bucholz blew out a large puff of smoke. "Winsome?"

"Winsome, yes. You know, engaging, friendly…"

"I know what winsome means, Wesley." The detective got up from his chair and came and sat on the corner of the desk. "I thought my job was to solve crimes, not to be a public relations agent. That's what you're good at."

The chief stood and began to pace. "I'm just saying my job would be easier if you could work a little bit on your relationship skills. Like right now. I just wanted to have a serious conversation with you, but you're being antagonistic and defensive. You don't have to be confrontational about everything."

An awkward silence punctuated the moment. Bucholz wiped his hand across his mouth, searching for the right words to appease his young police chief. Glancing down at the paperwork on his desk, he said, "What about the Peterson case? You want me to back off on that and devote more of my time to the Olson case?"

Turner had been pacing away but turned and faced Bucholz, pointing a finger at him. "You know what your problem is, Paul? You are a pessimist. You always think the worst in people. If you had a more positive outlook, you might not be so sure about John Olson, and maybe you'd see Mrs. Olson in a different light as well. Why do you have to be so negative?"

Bucholz scoffed. "Because I'm a cop. People have a public face, and they have a private life. The two are very different. When *you've* been a cop for twenty-four years, you'll see the dark side everyone hides. It's my job to ferret that out." He went back to his chair and faced the chief. "I'm a detective, Wesley. It's my job to *detect*. I don't deal with the obvious and the superficial. It's my job to dig and find out the truth. Believe me, John Olson is not the church-going, goody-goody choir boy Helen Olson says he is. He is an angry, tormented man who needed to get out of a miserable existence. Nobody will find him. He's gone for good."

DAY 47

TUESDAY, MAY 26, 1924

Philip Matthews propped his brogue wingtips on his desk at the Home Telephone and Telegraph Company on South Howard Street in Spokane.

A broad smile lit his face as he leaned back in his leather office chair reading last evening's *Spokane Daily Chronicle*. He had already read the article—twice—but he was re-reading it a third time to absorb every detail.

His electric table lamp flickered periodically and sometimes went out entirely. He bumped the base a time or two and it would work again—for a while. But this inconvenience did not dampen his spirits. He was in a jubilant mood because, as director of H.T. &T, he could now declare the spending freeze over.

The problems all started when H.T. &T.—the telephone company for the Spokane region —filed for a rate increase with the Washington State Department of Public Works. First it was denied. Then a smaller increase was approved, and then the district court denied *that*. Finally, they appealed to the Supreme Court of the United States of America.

Yesterday, Chief Justice (and former President of the United States) William Howard Taft wrote in a majority opinion that the telephone company was within their rights to ask for increases. H.T. &T. had won. After losing money for three straight months, the company was well on its way to solvency again.

"Sir." It was Matthews's secretary, Miss McClary. "There is someone here to see you."

"Who is it?" he asked.

"It's a fire extinguisher salesman, sir."

"Miss McClary, you know that I don't see solicitors without an appointment." He tapped a pencil on his desk. "What company?"

She smiled sheepishly. "I'm sorry, sir. It's the Fyr-Fyter Company. I thought you might make an exception."

He thought for a moment. "Olson?" he asked.

Nodding enthusiastically, she said, "Yes, sir."

"Well, send him in." Matthews put his feet down and sat up straight, anxious to see John Olson and find out what had happened to him. He had been ready to say yes to him weeks ago, and then he disappeared. The papers had a story about him running off with a woman, but Matthews knew that the papers were likely to print any juicy rumor that came along. The family had probably been right in assuming he had fallen to foul play. But what kind of explanation could there be for his sudden reappearance? Besides, with the Supreme Court decision, now was the perfect time to pull the trigger on fire extinguishers.

When his office door reopened, it was not John Olson who came through it. It was a woman carrying sample bags and brochures from the Fyr-Fyter company. She had a pretty face, her dark hair pulled back. She also had a distinctive limp, though it did not diminish her all-business expression.

Sticking her right hand forward, she said, "Good morning, Mr. Matthews. My name is Helen Olson. Thank you for seeing me this morning. I am here to present to you the Fyr-Fyter brand of fire extinguishers, which are the most superior firefighting equipment that you can buy. They are all U.L. approved and suitable for industrial and automotive applications."

Because of his buoyant mood, he allowed her to go on with her sales presentation uninterrupted. He sat in his office chair with his hands cupped together in front of him, his fingertips touching, maintaining an attentive expression. Periodically the lamp would go out, and he would bump it again.

She stood across from him reciting her rehearsed lines, using meaningful gestures and keeping eye contact throughout. She was not a polished salesperson, but she held his attention.

"So," she concluded, "you can see how Fyr-Fyter would be beneficial to your safety needs here at Home Telephone and Telegraph."

There was a pause as Helen waited for Matthews to absorb the information. Finally, he responded.

"Mrs. Olson," he began. "I'm sorry, what did you say your first name is?"

"Helen."

"May I call you Helen?"

Hesitating, she said, "Yes."

"And can I assume that you are John's wife?"

"Yes, I am."

Matthews didn't quite know how to approach this next question. But he had to know. "I am assuming that you are taking his place until he…"

She filled in his blank. "Returns. Yes."

He asked his next question slowly and with trepidation. "And… where are we on that? I mean, do we know anything?"

"No," Helen replied simply and without emotion.

"Hmm." He tapped his fingers on the desk. "Helen, I was ready to buy Fyr-Fyter extinguishers six weeks ago when John first came to me. I was impressed with the product and, frankly, with *him*. But… there were problems."

"Problems?" Her eyebrows arched.

"Yes. The first problem was that before I could finish my interview with him, our time ran out. I had another appointment, and I asked him to return the next day so that we could discuss installation. He agreed to do some demonstrations of the product for me and for our operators, lineman, and other employees. But, as you know, he was not able to do that. I was ready to sign a contract, but…." He left the sentence hanging, with his palms up.

Helen started to respond, but Matthews continued.

"The second problem was that, even though we have an obligation to employee safety here at H.T. &T, we were having revenue issues. I was willing to buy some product at the time, say eight or ten extinguishers to start. Three for this building and five for our fleet, with a view to adding on later. But soon after that, our money problems got worse, and buying extinguishers became simply out of the question."

"But now it seems you can afford them," Helen said, pointing to the front page article that he left sitting on the desk.

"I see," said Matthews. "So, may I assume that your appearance here on this particular morning is not coincidental?"

"Not entirely," admitted Helen. He detected the hint of a smile.

"But we still have one problem," said Matthews.

"What kind of problem?"

"Well, John had promised me that not only was he the salesman for the company, but the serviceman as well."

"Yes," she said. "I know."

"So he was going to personally install the extinguishers when they arrived, and regularly come in and test them. And as I said before, he was going to demonstrate to the employees how they are operated."

"He will still be your serviceman," she responded. "As soon as he's back."

Matthews waited for her to elaborate on what she meant by that. *When is he coming back? Will he ever come back?* But she did not say any more, and he did not care to ask the embarrassing questions.

"Well, then," he continued, "until he comes back, who would fill that role?"

"I will, of course," she said, standing straight.

Matthews hesitated, not sure if a woman had the mechanical skills to do the job. Just then, the lamp went out again. He reached over to bump it, but she stopped him.

"Let me see that," she said. She picked up the lamp and studied the underside, then pulled some wires out of the bottom.

"I've already changed the bulb," he said. "It didn't make any difference."

"No, it's not the bulb. Could be the switch." She examined it closely. "No. Look at this." She pointed to a small break in the wire at the base and wiggled it, causing the lamp to flicker on and off. "There's your problem. Have you got any friction tape?"

"Uh, probably downstairs."

She unplugged the lamp and produced a knife from her purse, cutting the offending wire. "I can fix it for you," she said. "It will only take a few minutes. If I just had some friction tape."

Matthews grinned broadly. "I would like that. And let's schedule a time for you to come in and show everybody how these fire extinguishers work."

Now Helen was also smiling.

"I'll go down and get that tape." Matthews rose from his chair. "Why don't you get the contract ready, and we will discuss numbers when I get back."

DAY 54

TUESDAY, JUNE 3, 1924

"This is our 'Super Model' half-quart extinguisher."

Twelve Home Telephone and Telegraph employees watched as Helen wadded up a piece of paper and threw it in a metal wastepaper basket.

"As you will soon see, it shoots a continuous stream of foam to smother a fire." Choosing a young man standing close by, she handed him a stick match and striker. "Will you do the honors?"

After he lit the corner of the paper, she let the fire grow to its fullest. "You simply turn the top handle and..." Pumping the plunger of the fire extinguisher, she ejected an impressive stream of foam which quenched the flames instantly. Several people gasped. Helen let the stream flow for a few more seconds than she needed to for maximum effect.

"Once the fire is out, make sure to turn the handle in again so the plunger is secure." Walking over to a wall bracket she had previously installed, she added, "The Fyr-Fyter extinguisher is now ready to place back in its holder like this." She deftly snapped it into its bracket.

Philip Matthews, witnessing the demonstration, asked, "What do we do with the mess?"

"I'm glad you asked," Helen responded. "In this case, there isn't a mess because I confined the fire to this can. But in real life, you could end up with this foam all over the place in case of a larger fire. Most of this foam will evaporate in a matter of minutes. As you can see in this can, the foam is already beginning to disappear." She showed the inside of the can to the employees. "However, there is some residue left by the foam afterwards. Simply use a solution of vinegar and water to clean up almost any surface."

After her exhibition, employees went back to their various duties and Matthews took Helen aside. "I'm giving you a list of some other businesses here in Spokane who would be delighted to see you and your fire extinguishers. I suggest you make appointments with each one within the next few days."

Helen perused the list of potential customers with wide eyes. The list had the names of six prominent businesses along with phone numbers and contacts for each one.

"I've already told them about Fyr-Fyter," Matthews said. "They are expecting you."

"Old National Bank? Washington Water Power?" She spoke the names with almost a holy awe in her voice.

He nodded. "These are friends of mine. We share information like this all the time. As you know, safety in the workplace has become a big push these days. Your timing couldn't be better."

Helen somehow controlled her enthusiasm until she had left the building. Phillip Matthews did not witness her leap awkwardly for joy on South Howard.

DAY 55

WEDNESDAY, JUNE 4, 1924

The whistle blew at five o'clock, bringing the end to another day of work at the Bloedel- Donovan Mill.

"Hey, Frank! You want to do something tonight?"

Chet Lowry and Frank Fisher walked together down Railroad Avenue to the boarding house. It was the third evening this week they had enjoyed each other's company. Telling Fisher he had recently come out west from Saint Paul, Lowry added that he was "dee-vorced." He promised he would never make the mistake of getting married again.

"C'mon, let's play cards tonight," Lowry said.

"Doesn't anybody play cribbage around here?"

Chet just about fell over laughing. "Are you kidding? Maybe at some ladies' guild meeting at the town hall. Or you could learn to knit! C'mon, it's nineteen-hundred and twenty-four, for Pete's sake. Men don't play cribbage."

Fisher had already gotten used to Lowry's ribbing. He knew he didn't mean anything by it. It was just his way.

"Actually," Lowry continued, "I'm more of a pinochle guy, myself."

"I thought your game was poker."

"Not really." Lowry kicked a small rock down the road. "I've just learned to play poker since I've been here. It's what everybody does."

"So I've noticed." Fisher shoved his hands in his pockets as they walked together. "But I'm not anxious to lose what little money I've got. I need to save up."

"The trick is to get at the right table. I know better than to play with the card sharks. Once you know who's good and who's not so good, you'll do fine. Besides, unless you're playing with the real pros, the stakes are low."

"But I don't even know how to play." Of all the things that had been wiped from Fisher's memory, playing crib was not one of them. But poker he apparently had never played.

"Tell you what." Lowry slapped him on the back. "I'll teach you how to play poker. A couple hours of lessons from me and you'll be one of the guys."

"Maybe. But aren't you afraid of getting caught with the booze?" Fisher asked.

"Is that what you're afraid of?" Lowry kicked the rock a little further. "Look, prohibition has not made drinking illegal. *Selling* it is illegal. *Making* it for the purpose of selling it is illegal. But drinking it—no problem. Besides, prohibition is not really enforced around here. Heck, the town marshal drinks with us sometimes."

"Really? Things sure are different here."

"Are they?" Lowry laughed. He stopped walking, forcing Fisher to wait. When the other men on the road were far enough away, Lowry spoke in a low voice. "So tell me, what's with you?"

"What do you mean?"

"I mean, you act kind of strange. Standoffish, you know? Are you just shy or what?"

Frank blinked. "Not really."

"Then what is it? I got to tell you, some of the guys are talking."

"People are talking?" Fisher frowned. "What are they saying?"

"Well,"—Lowry glanced around—"some people have guessed that you might be a fugitive or something."

"A fugitive?" Fisher was aghast. He had no idea. "Why on earth would they think that?"

"You know. A stranger comes to a remote town, keeps to himself." Chet cocked his head to one side. "Makes people wonder, is all. I'm not saying that's the consensus opinion, and I never believed it. It's been mentioned, is all." Chet shrugged. "I wouldn't make too much of it."

After dinner, they went up to Fisher's room and Lowry broke out a deck of cards that he kept in his shirt pocket. "You ready to learn?" Frank sat cross-legged at the head of his bed while Chet straddled an oak chair backwards at the foot of it. Lowry dealt five cards each on the blanket.

"So." Lowry held his cards to his chest. "You never did answer my question."

"What question?"

"What's with you? You said you're not shy. So what's your story?"

Fisher hesitated. "So a full house is better than a straight?"

"Don't try to change the subject." Lowry pointed a finger at Fisher's chest. "Sooner or later I know you're going to tell me, so let's hear it."

Taking a deep breath, Frank peeked at his cards and back at Lowry. "Can you keep a secret?"

Lowry hunched forward and made a motion that he was buttoning his lip.

For the second time in just over two weeks, Frank was about to share his deepest secret. The first time, with Joe Clyde, he felt so much better after sharing his diary. But would Chet react positively? He knew that Joe Clyde was right about finding a friend that could help carry his burden. But he wasn't sure if Chet was the right one to bring into his confidence.

After wiping his brow, he decided that it was time to gamble. He knew he had to let go of his fear. Pulling the little red book from his hip pocket, he handed it to Chet without a word.

Lowry opened it and read a couple pages. He glanced up with a serious face and asked, "This is you?"

Fisher nodded.

He continued reading and made no other comments until finished. "Hmm. Now that's some story." He pondered a bit before handing the book back. "But why didn't you go to the police?"

"Well, you know how I came to the train station in Edwall?" he asked. "At the beginning?"

"Yeah."

"The stationmaster gave me an odd look when I told him that I didn't know where I was from. He looked… I don't know… frightened… and suspicious. Like I was some kind of threat or a crazy person. I'm afraid if I tell the police or just about anybody, they'll think I belong in an asylum or something." After a pause, he asked, "Do *you* think I'm crazy?"

"Sure I do. But I like crazy people."

"No, seriously."

Lowry tilted his head. "I don't think you're insane or anything like that. You don't belong in one of those hospitals for crazies, that's for sure. But…"

Fisher leaned forward. "But what?"

"You *do* need help." Fisher could tell that Lowry wasn't making another joke. He was serious.

"What kind of help?"

"I only know one person who can help someone like you."

"What's his name?" asked Fisher.

"Chet Lowry."

DAY 58

SATURDAY, JUNE 7, 1924

Helen caught herself smiling.

Then she felt guilty. *How can I be happy when God-knows-what has happened to John?*

But she had to admit that her success at H.T. &T and the leads given to her by Phillip Matthews had her feeling pretty lofty.

It was good to feel good again. She would not be miserable forever, after all. It had been almost two months since her husband's disappearance, and the pain she felt was as real as ever. But as she peered out of the train and pine trees whooshed by on her way back home to Kootenai, she remembered a Bible verse she had learned as a little girl. It had always just been just another memory verse. But now, she felt God speaking to her in her time of need. He had come to her rescue.

> *Have not I commanded thee? Be strong and of a good courage;*
> *be not afraid, neither be thou dismayed; for the Lord thy*
> *God is with thee withersoever thou goest.*

Courage. That was what she needed now as she returned to her children. It is not something you can just decide to do. It could only come from God. She realized that the success in Spokane hadn't brought this indescribable joy. It was merely a manifestation of it. And the courage she now felt did not come from her own ingenuity. It was divine.

After getting off the train in Sandpoint, she took the streetcar to Kootenai, two and one-half miles. When she stepped off the trolley in front of Bonner's Store, she had less than two blocks to walk home. Despite the Humbird Lumber Mill just a few blocks away, the air here smelled fresh and sweet.

She was home.

Four days gone from her family was too long. When she opened the front door, her children came running to greet her, multiplying her cheer. Her mother, May Belle, had agreed to stay with the children, and she greeted Helen with a hug.

But she noticed that one was missing. "Where's Leonard, Mom?"

"He went to bed early," May Belle said. "He complained of a sore throat. I suspect he will feel better in the morning after some rest."

"Well, I'm exhausted." Helen plopped into an overstuffed chair. "I think that I'll be going to bed early myself."

At nine o'clock, she sent everyone to bed. "I know it's a little early, but everybody needs to get a good night's sleep. I don't want anybody else to catch Leonard's cold, and we are all going to church in the morning."

DAY 59

SUNDAY, JUNE 8, 1924

"Just stay hidden from the door opening," Fisher said.

Trying to catch his breath, Chet Lowry asked, "What happens if we get caught?"

A sudden lurch caused the two men to hold on to the sides of the empty boxcar as the steel wheels strained against the rails. The train rolled westward out of Skykomish and disappeared innocently from the town's sight. The two men sat and faced each other on the floor with their backs against the walls of the boxcar, their arms wrapped around their knees.

Lowry let out a nervous laugh. "I can't believe I let you talk me into doing this." His fingers twitching, he glanced toward the door. "We could get arrested."

"Oh, come on." Fisher grinned. "Where's your sense of adventure? Besides, they never arrest hoboes."

"They don't?"

"Well, hardly ever," Fisher said. "Sometimes they beat them up, though."

"Oh, that's a relief." Lowry rolled his eyes and fanned himself with his hat.

"I'm kidding. All they do is kick you off."

"But we're not hoboes," Lowry said. "If they realize we're working men stealing a ride, they might get real sore and report us."

"Relax! Like I told you before, I know how they work." Fisher shook his head. "First of all, we won't get caught. But if we do, let me do the talking. I know how to talk to the railroad bulls."

"Oh, you do, do ya?" Lowry slipped his hat back on. "Since when have you been such a talker? All this time you've been keeping to yourself, avoiding conversations and everything. Now you can talk your way out of trouble?"

Fisher stared at the far wall as he thought about that. "I guess I just feel more confident around railroad people."

Scooting his butt around on the floor, Lowry said, "The seats on a Pullman car are a bit more comfortable than this one."

Frank raised his finger to emphasize a point. "But we saved eight bits."

The train passed through Index without stopping. Lowry stood and watched the scenery through the partially opened door. "I know this area. I used to come up here and go fishing at Twin Lakes with my Uncle Bert. Sometimes I'd spend the whole summer up there with him."

Fisher nodded. He wished he could have memories like that.

Soon, the train stopped in Gold Bar, about twenty miles from Skykomish. "It's unlikely they'll drop off empties here," Fisher whispered. "Most likely they'll take them in to Everett or Seattle. But it's possible they will inspect them here, looking for hoboes."

"What do we do?" Lowry stood, apparently expecting trouble.

Frank motioned for him to sit. "Stay low and keep quiet."

After about ten minutes, the train started moving again.

"Next stop," Fischer said, raising his eyebrows.

Lowry blew a sigh of relief and smiled. "I have to admit, it is a bit exhilarating."

"And don't forget about the fare we saved," Fisher said.

Ten minutes later, the train slowed, coming to another stop. Lowry started to get up, but Fisher put a hand on his shoulder. "Wait 'til the train comes to a full stop, and then follow me."

The train finally halted with a jerk, and the two got up. Fisher poked his head out the opening. "All clear," he said and jumped off, scurrying into a stand of trees.

Lowry followed close behind, noticing two other trespassers jumping off a couple of cars down.

They waited for the train to move on, then strolled into downtown Sultan. Frank immediately noticed the familiar sawn lumber smell, reminding him of Skykomish.

Asking around, they found out where to find the ball field. The two showed up there in time to see the visiting Skykomish team come in and play against Sultan. The clean white uniforms had large blue letters across the front reading "SKY." Chet knew several of the players, and he and Frank cheered them on to victory.

After the game, the two asked around again and found out the nearest movie house was in Monroe. After some discussion, Chet talked Frank into walking instead of hopping on another freight train. They had been told Monroe was another five miles west.

They lied. The walk was actually over seven miles. But they made it in time to the Monroe Theatre to see Tom Mix in an action-adventure titled *North of Hudson Bay*. The fifth installment of the Jack Dempsey serial *Fight and Win* was also featured.

When they left the theater, they were surprised to see that darkness had already fallen. In high spirits and feeling adventurous, they caught the "Number Two" freight train back to Skykomish.

As the train rumbled through the dark valley, Lowry came back to a subject they had talked about a few days ago. "You know why you should come with me to the poker tables?"

"Not really."

"Because people notice your absence."

Fisher cocked his head. "What do you mean?"

"You can't be a mole, Frank. You need to be a chameleon."

"Huh?"

"Hiding just makes you more suspicious." Lowry shifted again. "If you want the talk to stop, you gotta blend in."

"By playing poker?"

"Exactly." Lowry added an exclamation point by slapping Fisher on the knee.

The car rocked at a joint in the tracks but continued its hypnotic clickety-clack as it rolled down the rails. Fisher asked, "What do you guys talk about when you're playing cards?"

Chet shrugged. "The usual. Baseball, women, life…"

"You see?" Fisher interrupted. "Life! But what if you know nothing about your life? I avoid people because they ask me questions about my past and then I have to lie."

Getting out a cigarette, Chet said, "And you don't like to lie."

"Well, let's just say I'm not very good at it."

Lowry grinned.

"What?"

"That tells us both something about you."

"What's that?"

The two locked eyes. "You're a good person Frank."

Fisher realized it was the first time Chet had paid him a genuine compliment.

"But," Lowry added, "we can still be friends anyway."

DAY 60

MONDAY, JUNE 9, 1924

It was embarrassing.

Appointments with Washington Water Power and Old National Bank had to be rescheduled. Helen had a sick child to attend to. *This is why women don't get the same treatment men do in the business world. A man would never reschedule for a sick child.*

In reality, Helen worried about Leonard even more than her missed appointments. His cold hadn't gotten better, and now he had a low-grade fever. Most concerning, her son had not eaten for three days, complaining his throat hurt too much.

Calling Doctor Wendle, Helen made an appointment for the following morning.

A knot tightened in her stomach.

DAY 61

TUESDAY, JUNE 10, 1924

The sun glinted off Annie's teacup as she sipped from it on the front porch.

Other ladies enjoyed knitting or crochet. But Annie enjoyed watching the eastern sky darken, bright colors in the clouds turning to pastels and then grays before turning black.

She could now go an entire day without shedding a tear about her missing son. But it still hurt terribly—not knowing. It would be better to know they had found his body. Or whatever may have happened to him. Anything was better than no news at all.

Setting her cup down on a tiny wooden stool next to her rocking chair, she realized the tears had been replaced by a bitterness that wouldn't quite go away.

Edward joined her on the porch. He dusted soot off of the matching rocker next to her before plopping in it. The brick plant down the road left a bitter organic smell and a thin film of clay dust when the winds blew to the south, as they did today.

Without him uttering a word or even a sigh, Annie could sense his melancholy.

"Who was on the phone?" she asked.

He stared ahead as a motorcar passed by on the dirt road below. "Helen."

"She is so excited about the fire extinguisher sales." Annie brightened. "I'm so happy for her. Is she coming to Spokane tomorrow?"

"No."

The dull tone of his voice told her Edward had some news—and it wasn't good. Annie feared the worst. *Did they find John's body?* She wasn't sure now if she really wanted to know.

"It's Leonard," he said.

"Leonard?" She turned to Edward with a start.

Edward took her hand and looked into her wet eyes. "He has diphtheria."

DAY 62

WEDNESDAY, JUNE 11, 1924

Fisher sat cross-legged at the head of his bed, stroking the slick surface of the new cards he was dealt.

Since there was no table in his Skykomish Hotel room, they used the bed as a makeshift poker table. Lowry crouched at the foot of the bed. "I dealt like there are four players. You focus on your hand, I'll play the other three. Let's split our pennies and nickels four ways."

"I don't know how I'm going to remember all this." Fisher counted out his change. "When to hold, fold, check, call… It's complicated."

"You have to play… *a lot.*" Lowry looked at Fisher through his eyebrows. "Besides, I'm only showing you how to play Five Card Draw. Sometimes they play Five Card Stud or even Seven Card Draw."

"How do you play those?"

"All in good time." Lowry gestured to 'slow down' with his right palm toward Fisher. "You need to learn Five Card Draw first. Right now, I'm only teaching you how to play poker. You still need to learn the *real* game."

"Whad'ya mean?" Fisher eyed Lowry over the top of his poker hand.

"I mean," Lowry said, "that poker is not about playing cards."

"It isn't?"

"No. It's about playing people."

Frank frowned. "I don't know what you're getting at."

"Well, let's get the basics of the game first. It's time for you to bet."

Checking his cards again, Frank said, "Okay, I'll raise you ten." He threw in two nickels.

Chet said, "We all fold."

"What? Why?" asked Fisher.

"You have the best hand."

"How do you know?"

"Because of your tell."

"My what?" Frank still held the cards close to his chest. "Did you peek?"

"Nope. When you looked at your cards,"—Chet gestured with his hand—"you covered your mouth with your hand, like this. It's called a tell."

"I don't get it," Frank said.

"You were hiding a smile." Lowry turned the cards of his three imaginary players faceup. "Now, let's see your hand. I'll bet you have at least two pair, if not three of a kind."

Fisher showed his three Jacks and said, "How did you know that?"

"Because you took three cards on the draw, which probably means you kept a pair, and when you raised the pot, I figured you got at least another pair or your third card."

Fisher threw his cards down. "I'll never be as good as you are."

"Most likely," Chet said. "But remember, I just learned how to play a few months ago. Don't worry, you'll get there. But in any case, you need to work on your poker face."

"I don't know." Fisher's shoulders slumped. "I may not ever play poker."

"But you still need a poker face."

"What for?" asked Fisher.

"For everything."

Fisher stared at Lowry, knowing that elaboration was forthcoming.

"You see," Chet said as he stacked and reshuffled, "your problem is that people can tell you're hiding something. So people are always trying to guess your hand. Thus, they talk about you being a fugitive or something."

Frank thought about that and gave a little nod, still not sure where Chet was going with this.

"But I saw a side of you on Sunday nobody else around here sees. I saw confidence."

"You mean on the train?"

"Right." Chet stood and peered out the window at the activity on Railroad Avenue. "When you showed me how to beat the freight trains, I saw a guy who knows how to bluff. You were ready to do the talking if we got caught."

"I guess so." Frank shrugged.

"But," Lowry said, "you still need more practice. So don't give up on poker yet. It may be the way you start fitting in. You've got to learn how and when to put on a good bluff."

Chet returned to the bed and dealt four hands again.

"Hmm," Frank said. Putting two of his cards face down on the bed, he said, "I'll take two."

Lowry continued. "Someone once said that it's not about getting a good hand, it's what you do with a bad one." He dealt two more cards to Frank.

"So that's the key to winning at poker?" Frank reached for the two cards.

Chet slapped his hand on the cards before Frank could get them. "I'm not talking about poker."

DAY 63

THURSDAY, JUNE 12, 1924

It was half past ten when Helen heard a knock at her door.

Mary Bonner greeted her with a hug. No words were needed as Helen stepped aside and let her in. Mary sat on a small sofa while Helen took up an armchair across from her. They were situated close to each other, practically knee-to-knee.

"I came as soon as I heard." Mary held a handkerchief which she used frequently.

Helen held back the tears but kept a hanky nearby. "They call it 'The Strangler,' and I can see why. He has such trouble breathing."

"After everything you've been through…" Mary choked the words out.

"I was just learning to cope without John." It had been two months. "Now another setback."

Mary reached over and squeezed Helen's hands. "I honestly don't know how you do it."

After letting out a heavy sigh, Helen said. "I'm not sure I *can* do it. How are we going to make ends meet? Until Leonard gets better, I won't be able to make sales calls in Spokane. I don't know how much more I can take." Her voice ended in a whimper.

Helen appreciated that Mary didn't try to quote some platitudes about faith or hanging in there or "everything will turn out fine, you'll see."

"I was just starting to feel good about things again. Right when I had something positive going on—with the fire extinguisher sales—this happens."

After blowing her nose, Helen said, "I'm angry, Mary. I'm angry at God because He keeps pulling the rug out on me. I hate living here in Kootenai, you know that. The church people try, but they don't understand." She wrung her hands. "And I feel guilty."

"Guilty? Whatever for?"

Clearing her throat, Helen said, "I snap at the kids. They don't deserve that. It's not their fault. They need me to be strong! I'm a terrible mother."

Mary cocked her head. "You're being too hard on yourself."

"I can't help it. It's how I feel." Hot tears streamed down her cheeks. Mary took her handkerchief and gently dried them. If it had been anyone else it would have seemed maudlin. But it was different with Mary.

"Mostly," Helen added, "I am so angry with John." She pushed her fists into the sofa. "How could he leave me alone now? In the time of our greatest need?" She knew there was no answer.

Helen composed herself and spoke again. "But I can remember the good times. They were not long ago." She stared out the window absent-mindedly. "It seems like a lifetime. I wish things could be that way again. I guess I didn't realize then how happy we were." She turned to Mary. "I'm so sorry, I didn't even offer you coffee…"

"No, no," Mary said. "I didn't come here to be waited on."

"But I've been a terrible hostess. Here I am whining, and you… well, you've been such a good friend."

"Don't make me blush. Let me perk a pot of coffee and let's spend some more time talking."

"Oh, Mary. I'm such a wreck. I don't know why you put up with me."

"Nonsense." Mary slapped the sofa cushion. "I know you would do the same for me."

"Yes, I would."

They went into the kitchen, where the fire still burned in the stove. Helen added wood while Mary prepared a pot on the stovetop.

While the pot percolated, Mary asked, "How is Leonard doing?"

"Well, he has to remain isolated. So, he's sleeping in my bed for now. I'm taking the sofa. The other children had to visit Dr. Wendle to get a Schick Test."

"A what?"

"It's an injection that determines their susceptibility to diphtheria. Meanwhile, they have to stay clear of Leonard." The aroma of the coffee alerted them that it was done, and they returned to the living room.

Mary brought the cup to her lips to take a sip but stopped. "Poor Leonard. Won't he get lonely?"

"I try to keep him company, but mostly he sleeps. When he's not coughing." Helen cleared her throat and her voice became husky again. "Dr. Wendle said nearly fifteen percent of children who get diphtheria—" Her voice caught.

Mary put her hand on Helen's forearm.

"Of course, he couldn't have said over eighty-five percent recover." Helen set down her cup harder than she meant to.

"Sounds just like Dr. Wendle's bedside manner." Mary fondled the handle on her cup. "Can your family come and help?"

"There's nowhere for them." Helen gestured with an open hand around the room. "But John's parents have offered to take us all in down at Freeman until Leonard gets well."

Mary raised her eyebrows. "They have plenty of room?"

"It would be tight. But my parents live in Kiesling, less than eight miles away from John's folks. Some of us could stay with them instead."

"You should take them up on their offer."

"Don't get me wrong," Helen said. "It is tempting. A chance to get away from Kootenai—present company excepted."

Mary nodded in agreement.

"And the children love Annie's baking. John's brother, Eddie, lives next door and drives a Nash Roadster the kids like to ride in. And John's mother could keep an eye on Leonard while I take the commuter train into Spokane to continue my extinguisher sales."

"Sounds like you've made up your mind to go to Freeman."

"I turned them down cold."

"Why?" Mary's face twisted with confusion.

Helen stood up. "Do you want a refill?"

"Sit back down!" Mary playfully slapped Helen's hand. "Tell me what your problem is."

She did as she was told. Fiddling with a loose thread, she said, "I don't want the dependence. I'm trying to be strong, and I don't like the feeling that I need someone's help."

Mary folded her arms. "You are the strongest woman I know. But even the strongest women need help sometimes. If you don't accept help from John's parents, I'll hogtie you and take you down there myself."

DAY 64

FRIDAY, JUNE 13, 1924

"But I thought you said I wasn't ready."

"And you're not. But you never will be if all you do is play pretend poker games." Lowry opened the door to Frank's room and stepped out. "Nothing can prepare you for the real thing except for the real thing."

Fisher followed him out the door. "But I'm going to lose my shirt."

"Don't worry. There are several tables to choose from, and I will get you one that will have some chumps. And by chumps, I mean guys that are still better than you." Lowry proceeded down the hall as Fisher followed.

"But…"

Lowry stopped at the top of the stairs. "How much can you stand to lose?"

"Nothing."

"Now c'mon. Would you really miss three bucks?"

"Three bucks! That's almost a day's pay."

Motioning with his hand to lower his voice, Chet said, "Two dollars?"

Frank leaned against the wall at the top of the stairs. "Why don't you go ahead and play while I watch. I can learn that way."

Lowry shook his head. "Nobody wants anyone peering over their shoulder, least of all me. It's a huge disadvantage."

Leading Fisher down the stairs to the smoke-filled lobby, they noticed only three tables going, not many for a Friday night. But it was still early. A large railroader with striped overalls lumbered in, followed by a thin man wearing suspenders. They scanned the room.

"Here's your chance," Chet said. "These guys are new. We can start a table." Turning to the newcomers, Lowry said, "You guys in for a game?"

After some discussion, they decided to play Five Card Draw. "We're a couple of greenhorns, so I'm hoping to keep the stakes low," Lowry said.

The two railroaders exchanged glances, and one said, "Sounds fine to me." The other nodded. They emptied their pockets of loose change at a round mahogany table. Four padded chairs surrounded it.

Everyone anted up a penny. The big man chewed on an unlit cigar, grunting periodically but saying little.

Each of them ordered a drink. Frank drank root beer while concentrating on everything Chet had taught him. On the third deal, he won a hand. Seven cents. *I'm actually ahead. Maybe I'm not so bad at this after all.*

But two hours later, he glanced at his little coin pile and realized he'd lost nearly two dollars. Running his hand through his hair, he checked his cards for the third time and anted in. When the betting came around, he raised it a dime, the most he had bet so far. Everyone else did too. On the draw, Chet took two, and both railroaders took three. Fisher asked for one card.

On the second round of betting, the big man raised the stakes by twenty-five cents. Suspenders folded. When it came to Fisher's turn, he hesitated, then saw the bet and raised it another two bits. Chet folded and sent him a stunned expression.

The large man in overalls chomped hard on his cigar and glanced back and forth between his cards and Fisher. He threw in the twenty-five cents while his eyes burned a hole through Fisher. Finally, he raised another fifty cents. "You're bluffing." The tough railroader glared at Frank, daring him to go higher.

Covering his mouth with his hand, Fisher swallowed hard and put fifty cents into the kitty. "I'll raise you another fifty." With shaking fingers, he dug in his pocket, pulling out two more quarters. He felt sweat form on his upper lip.

The railroader squinted at his cards and then at Fisher and Lowry. "Low stakes, eh? Greenhorns, my eye!" He threw his cigar to the floor. "Fold." Scooting his chair back, he stomped away from the table. Suspenders picked up his few coins and followed his friend without a word.

Lowry blew out a deep breath. "You came in pretty big there. But do you realize you had that tell? You covered your mouth again. You probably could have won even more. What did you have?"

"Well, I started out with these four spades." Frank showed him a Jack, a ten, an eight, and a seven. "I threw out a two of hearts and got this."

Frank showed Chet his card, and Lowry burst out laughing. "I can't believe it. You did a fake tell? You learn fast."

Fisher grinned. "You didn't teach me that."

They both walked up to Fisher's room with the fifth card lying faceup on the table.

A seven of diamonds.

DAY 65

SATURDAY, JUNE 14, 1924

Like every Saturday, the mill shut down at 4:00.

Frank stood in a line of workers waiting to get paid.

"Hey, chum!" Chet slapped him on the back. "Weekend's finally here. Thought it would never come."

"Same here." Frank bounced on his toes as he moved closer to the front of the line. "Nice to get paid for a full day." Though the mill shut down an hour earlier on Saturdays, the workers got the same pay.

"Yeah. Everybody's in a great mood, and not just 'cause it's payday."

"You mean the wedding?"

"I mean the reception." Chet punched the air like he was warming up for a boxing match. "Free food and booze. Nobody's gonna miss that."

"Here comes another train full of people." Frank nodded toward the Great Northern depot.

"Hmm. Murray and his fiancée must know a whole lotta people. That's the second train-full today." Chet wiggled his eyebrows. "Maybe some eligible females coming to see their friend get married?"

"I thought you weren't interested in getting married again."

"Who said anything about marriage?"

The ceremony at the Catholic Church preceded the anticipated reception at Maloney's warehouse, where they were going to show a movie afterward.

It was a simple wedding, highlighted by a stunning bride. A shapely brunette with Mediterranean features and a gorgeous smile, she wore a silk wedding dress featuring French lace and a plunging neckline.

Later, at the reception, Frank sat at a table with Chet and some of the other mill workers he was familiar with. Frank noticed that after a while, some of his coworkers were beginning to feel the bathtub gin. The conversation turned bawdy, and men told off-color jokes about spending the night with the beauty in the evocative dress.

At about 11:00, Frank leaned over to Chet and said, "I'm going to head back to the room. You ought to turn in soon, too, if we're going into Everett tomorrow. We want to get an early start."

"Wait," Chet said, "here comes the happy couple. You don't want to go before you wish them your best, do you?"

The bride and groom made their way over to their table to greet the guests. Albert, the groom, proudly introduced his new wife, Sophia, to each of his friends from the mill. Frank rose and shook her hand politely. When he stood, dizziness almost overcame him, and his peripheral vision went dim.

He winced as her appearance changed. Before his eyes, her hair shortened, and the shape of her face altered. Her skin became pale, her dress a creamier color and much more conservative. She was still beautiful, but she had transformed. He inhaled, and a familiar perfume took his breath away.

As he continued to hold her hand, she seemed to be beckoning him to come with her. Her lips moved, but he could not hear her. She squeezed his hand harder and tugged at him to follow her down a hall toward a bedroom, her hazel eyes pleading.

His attention never strayed from her, but he became aware that the place they were in was not Maloney's but a very small house. It somehow seemed familiar. The simple furniture, the wood floors, the drab walls, the floral patterned curtains—he had been here.

He ached to come to her as she called him, but his legs felt burdened with heavy weights. Seemingly paralyzed, he tried to speak, but could not utter a single thing.

To his great dismay, she let go of his hand and limped down the hall to the bedroom—alone. He gasped, not understanding what was happening.

"Hey, Fisher! It's not polite to stare," a voice from Maloney's warehouse called out.

The dark-skinned bride reappeared in front of him, struggling to extricate her hand. He realized that everyone was laughing, except the bride. She examined him with concern on her face. "Are you alright?" she asked.

His heart pounded in his chest like he had run a race, and the dizziness returned. "I'm sorry." Breathless, he could only say it again. "Sorry."

The bride and groom excused themselves stiffly and moved on to another table. Conversation resumed, everyone seeming to want to move past the awkward moment. Haltingly, Fisher sat back in his chair, relieved the attention had turned from him.

Later that night, Frank lay in bed, too excited to sleep. He could not stop thinking about the beautiful woman in the vision. It filled him with equal amounts of excitement and great sorrow.

But he had noticed her unusual gait. Something about it was oddly attractive.

I have to find her. The beautiful woman—is she my wife?

DAY 66

SUNDAY, JUNE 15, 1924

"So, what was last night about?"

Frank and Chet had sneaked onto another freight train and were hiding out in a boxcar.

"What do you mean?" Fisher asked.

"You know what I mean. Last night, at the reception. You appeared to be in a drunken coma there for a minute. But I don't think you had a drop of gin."

"I don't know." Fisher shrugged, hoping Chet would drop the subject.

Chet smiled. "Man, you are stuck on her, aren't you?"

Fisher glanced away.

"I got to admit. She was a choice bit of calico." Chet removed his hat and fanned his face.

"I wasn't even looking at her. I mean, you know how sometimes you are daydreaming and, you know, you just stare?"

"Uh-huh. I *know* what you were daydreaming about," Lowry said, wiggling his eyebrows.

"No. It wasn't that." Frank closed his eyes. "Not really. I mean… oh, you wouldn't understand."

"Oh, I understand, all right." Lowry returned his hat to his head. "You need a woman."

Fisher didn't reply, but he had to agree. *Yeah. But first I have to find her.*

"It's too bad we got up so late." Fisher altered the course of the discussion. "But this will be fun today."

They had scrapped their plans of going to Everett because they knew they wouldn't have time to enjoy it. After staying out late the previous evening, they were not anxious to get up and go out this morning. Especially Lowry. After the reception, he had played a few hands of poker at the Skykomish Hotel.

As a result, they decided to head the opposite way—east—toward Stevens Pass. Chet had told Frank about a scenic trail near the tunnel. So they decided to go to the top for a while and return later to take in a ball game and a picture show in town.

"It's beautiful up there," Lowry said, "but I liked the scenery last night, too." He wiggled his eyebrows again.

About a half-mile before the tunnel at the top of the pass, the train took a siding and stopped, allowing a westbound train by. The two got off there and spent a while exploring a path leading to an idyllic alpine lake. Glaciers gleamed from the highest peaks.

Even though they were only about ten miles from Skykomish, they had ascended more than 1700 feet into the Cascade Range. "It's definitely cooler," Frank said.

Lowry took a deep breath of the pine-scented air. "I like it up here."

Frank nodded and took in the lush greenery. "Wish I had my coonskin cap."

"You own a coonskin cap?"

Frank thought about that. "I think I used to."

"Why doesn't that surprise me?" Chet led Frank up the trail.

"Do you think there are any bears out here?" Frank asked.

"Sure. I've seen bears up in these mountains." Lowry stopped along the path. "See here." He pointed to the ground. "Bear sign."

Fisher came over to examine the scat. "Are you sure?"

"I've seen it often enough."

Surveying his surroundings, Fisher said, "Do you think we're safe?"

"Yeah." Lowry spoke with confidence. "In all my years in the woods, I've never been attacked by a bear."

This brought little comfort to Fisher.

"Now *people*, on the other hand… sometimes *they* scare me." Lowry stopped on the path and gazed intently at Frank. "You never know their motives. People hide behind masks and can sometimes not be who they want you to think they are. They are much more unpredictable than bears."

"Yeah," Fisher said. "With bears you always know they want to eat you."

They both laughed, although Frank's laugh was a bit more nervous.

After about an hour and a half, a westbound freight train came along and they jumped on. As had become their custom, they sat across from each other with their backs to the wall. The train jerked and began its descent. Chet rubbed his chin and scrutinized the ceiling.

"What's on your mind?" Frank asked.

"I've been thinking," Lowry said. "You need a story."

"What do you mean?"

"Background. You know, for when you're at the poker tables."

Frank shifted his feet. "Like I said, I'm not good at lying."

"Mm-hmm." Chet squinted. "Answer this: what is a lie?"

It seemed to Frank to be a rhetorical question, but when Chet didn't elaborate, he held his palms up. "It's when you don't tell the truth."

Chet pointed to Frank. "Exactly. But what if you don't know the truth? If you tell a plausible story, is it still a lie?"

"Yeah, I think it is."

"No." Lowry pointed again. "Not if it *could* be true. It's only a lie if you intend to deceive. Think about it. Didn't you say in your journal you might be from Helena?"

Frank tipped his head. "Possibly."

"Let's just say you are. Since it *might* be true, it's not a lie. But here's the key. You have to *believe* it. You can do that, can't you?"

Rubbing his temples, he shook his head. "I don't know."

"And you're not married."

"What? Why?"

"You've got to keep your story simple." The train jostled over a hump in the tracks. "Imagine the questions you'll get if you're married. 'Where is she? Why aren't you with her? Any kids?' Oh, don't get me started on kids! Believe me, you are better off without a family, or your story gets bigger and more complicated."

Frank didn't like the sound of this. "I don't know…"

"And you're a farmer. A wheat farmer near Helena."

"Why not a railroader? I know about that, too."

"In case you haven't noticed, this town is crawling with railroad men. The railroad is a network stretching clear across the west. There are guys here in Sky right now from Helena. You want them to ask you about Helena or the railroaders there?" Lowry shook his head in an exaggerated motion. "Huh-uh. You're a wheat farmer."

Frank took a deep breath and let it out again.

"Keep it simple, and believe it. You do that, and you'll be ready for anything. Besides, if people keep asking questions at the table, I'll be there to change the subject."

Frank didn't feel confident. What Chet said made sense, but he *wanted* to be married. The perception would be hard to ignore.

He could not get the limping woman out of his head.

DAY 69

WEDNESDAY, JUNE 18, 1924

Helen Olson had experienced many emotions over the last ten weeks.

Shock, depression, anger—even apathy. But in the last few days, one emotion stalked her. Fear.

She feared the future, not knowing what might become of her family. Would John ever return? Would they ever know his demise?

But her greatest fear concerned Leonard. He could be dying.

Her phone rang, and she jumped. It was her mother calling to check on her. "Fine, just fine," she lied. But she knew now that her fears had started to become irrational. Trusting almost no one, she could not shake the feeling that someone would come into their house and violate her or her children. So she kept a constant vigil.

Dark circles had formed under her eyes because of sleeplessness. She didn't know if the lack of sleep drove her crazy or if the delusions were what kept her awake. It seemed to be a vicious circle.

No longer using the sofa in the living area, she lay down fully dressed on a cot next to her bed where Leonard slept. She stared into the darkness, wondering what tomorrow would bring. Tossing back and forth, she finally got up and opened the top half of the double-hung window to let some cool air in. Lying back down on the cot, she hoped for some rest.

All kinds of ideas raced through her head, many of which were senseless. Her heart beat fast and hard. When she opened the window, she had been hot; now she shivered.

She reached for a light blanket and then thought she heard something. A scratch at the window? She thought she saw movement in the darkness. *Is it my imagination? Am I going mad?*

She groped for the baseball bat kept by the bed and heard something fall to the floor. It sounded like her vanity mirror had fallen off the dresser. Someone *had* broken in!

Feeling the smooth wooden bat handle in the grip of her left hand, she sprang to her feet. "Who's there?"

More things fell when—whoever broke in—attempted to make an escape. As fearful as Helen was, she determined not to let anybody intimidate her. Holding the club with both hands, she crouched between Leonard and the window, ready to defend her family.

She wanted to turn on the Tiffany lamp at her bedside but did not dare take her eyes off the movement happening near the chest of drawers. Straining to see in the blackness, she began to realize the intruder appeared very small, certainly not an adult. Helen gritted her teeth, finally working up the courage to take one hand off the bat. Reaching over, she pulled the chain on the lamp.

When light filled the room, it revealed her jewelry box on the floor, but no intruder.

Then she saw him.

Mrs. Grave's black cat scurried up the curtains and dashed out the window. He had apparently gotten curious enough to scramble up the outside wall so he could see what he could see in the Olson house.

Her chest still pounded, but Helen let out a heavy breath of air and leaned against the wall. Checking over her shoulder, she saw the commotion had not disturbed Leonard at all. He still slept soundly, for once. His chest rose and fell in a slow pattern.

That does it! Tomorrow I'm going to call John's parents and tell them to prepare for company.

DAY 73

SUNDAY, JUNE 22, 1924

"Well," Lowry said, "this is Everett. What do you think?"

"It's beautiful!" replied Fisher.

"Beautiful?"

But Fisher wasn't facing the city. His eyes were on the water. "I've never seen the ocean before."

Chet came and stood by Frank. "It's not really the ocean, you know. It's actually Puget Sound, which is a tiny part of the ocean. In fact, it's only a small part of Puget Sound called Port Gardner."

"I know it's not the open ocean." Fisher's attention turned to various shorebirds pecking at the sand along the water's edge. "I just mean I've never seen salt water before. It smells so… different."

"Yeah, it's kind of a fishy sm… Hey! Wait a minute. How do you know?"

"Know what?"

"How do you know you've never seen salt water before? For all you know, you were born in a German U-boat."

"No." Fisher shook his head and spoke with confidence. "I don't know how I know. I just do."

Chet removed his hat to scratch the top of his head. "You *are* an oddball."

The two had jumped out of an empty boxcar after the fifty-mile trip into town from Skykomish. The tracks took them right to the shoreline before turning south to Seattle. When the train came to a stop at a siding, they found themselves at the very busy Port of Everett.

A ship bristling with booms, cranes, and rigging bobbed at a nearby pier. Chet had a passion for ships and led Frank closer to the action. Dozens of men were busy loading a steam freighter, the words *Horace Luckenbach* painted on the bow. Chet learned in a conversation with one of the men that the ship would contain more than two million board feet of lumber by tonight. Tomorrow it would head for the east coast via the Panama Canal.

Burly longshoremen unloaded flatbed railcars loaded with lumber while more dock workers wrapped cables around bundles of lumber. Steam-powered cranes hoisted the bundles onto the deck of the ship. There, stevedores manipulated the bundles into place for stowage while a foreman barked out commands like the choreographer of a stage play.

After watching for a while, Frank and Chet spent most of the day exploring the rest of the shoreline. Frank took off his shoes, rolled up his pants, and tested the water. He laughed when the sand beneath his feet tried to suck him down as the waves went back out.

When the shadows lengthened, they went into the town of Everett. Chet kept an eye out for a speakeasy, while Frank hoped to find a movie house. In the end, they settled on a soft drink establishment with pool tables, where Frank found out Chet played Eight-ball even worse than him. But Chet didn't complain. The server had some whiskey behind the counter.

"Okay," Chet said. "So I agreed to take the freight train in, but now you have to keep your part of the deal. We're going back to Sky the way civilized people travel."

They found their way to nearby Bond Street and the mission-style Great Northern Railroad Depot. Many had gathered at the station for the G.N.'s latest luxury passenger train, the *Oriental Limited*. There were actually eight Orientals running between Chicago and Seattle at any given moment. The railroad had placed them in service on the first of the month.

The two men stood on the platform admiring the sparkling new train as it came to a stop. The Pullman sleepers, diner, and observation car were painted with a fresh green and black color scheme. The lettering for "Great Northern Railroad" and *Oriental Limited* gleamed in gold leaf on the side of each car. Frank paid special attention to the oil-fired engines. Not steam!

"When will it all end, Chet?"

Lowry shot Frank a perplexed stare. "When will what end?"

"Progress."

"I beg your pardon?"

"Think of how much progress there has been over the last few years." Frank waved his arms around him. "Thirty years ago, this was nothing but frontier. People came by wagon train or ship. It took *months* to get here from the Midwest. Now you can get on this train in Chicago and come to Seattle and be back to Chicago in less than a week."

"It boggles the mind," Lowry admitted.

"And with the trains came the telegraph." Fisher pointed to the lines overhead. "Communication could be made clear across the continent thanks to the telegraph. But now, you can actually call someone and talk to them on a phone." Frank pointed to a pay phone on the wall next to the platform.

"Right. And think of how many people have automobiles now." Chet got into the spirit of the conversation. "You can even drive a car over Snoqualmie Pass from Seattle to get to the east side of the mountains, and someday you'll be able to do the same up at Stevens Pass."

"You would never catch me doing that," Frank said.

"Why not?"

"Are you kidding? Can you imagine breaking down up there in the middle of nowhere?"

"Is this about bears again?" Lowry nudged Fisher with his elbow.

"I'm just saying the train is still faster *and* safer *and* more reliable. Give me the train anytime."

The conductor checked his watch. "All aboard!"

When Frank and Chet boarded the train, they were overwhelmed by the extravagance and appointments of the interior. The rugs and art hangings on the walls were of Asian themes.

Frank rubbed the palm of his hand on the plush upholstery of a chair as he sat in it. Bamboo board games with polished marble game pieces sat on mahogany tables between overstuffed armchairs. Two elderly men played the ancient Asian game of Go! at one table.

"If you want," Chet said, "you can go get a haircut or a massage."

"How much does *that* cost?" Frank asked.

"No extra fare."

Frank's eyes widened. "You've got to be kidding."

"Nope. Although they are probably already booked up. The passengers in the sleeping cars have valet service and maids, and there's even showers and bathtubs back there." Chet motioned with his head to the Pullman sleepers two cars back. "Do you want to check the stock market?"

"I don't own any stock," Frank said. "Well, not that I know of."

"You can even get that right here on the train."

The two of them sat in upholstered chairs facing each other. They felt like royalty.

Frank smiled. "It's certainly more comfortable than a covered wagon."

"It's even comfier than an empty boxcar." Chet laughed. The train left the station with a small jerk. "Now this is the way to travel."

After a bit, Frank decided to broach a new subject. "You've never mentioned why you're divorced."

Chet scowled at Frank. "That's funny." A sarcastic tone lurked in his voice. "Why wouldn't I want to chat about *that*?"

Frank blinked at the rebuke, not knowing what to say. He immediately wished he hadn't brought it up.

Lowry let out a sigh, and his visage softened. "You see, that's the difference between us. You're trying to remember your past." His eyes glistened and he turned away. "I'm trying to forget mine."

DAY 78

FRIDAY, JUNE 27, 1924

Helen held on tight to Baby Mary as they jolted over a bump. "Sorry," Edward said as he swerved around another rut. Anna May, sitting in the middle of the front seat, giggled each time the Model T clattered over another obstacle.

"These roads are terrible." Helen pulled Mary even closer, partly to protect the baby but also to have something to hold on to. "I still think it might have been better to take the train than two cars."

"Now, Helen, we've talked about this." It was apparent that Edward's attention was divided as he talked while keeping a sharp eye on the treacherous road. "I can't picture you herding your whole family to the train station and then changing trains in Spokane. Especially with five kids, including a baby, a two-year-old, *and* a sick child."

Glancing over her left shoulder, Helen could see Leonard still slept soundly in the back seat. His head rested on a valise. Except for an occasional cough, he seemed to be taking the trip well.

"Besides," Edward said, "I thought you were anxious to get out of Kootenai."

"I was… I mean, I am." Helen shifted in her seat, pursing her lips. "It seems like such an imposition."

"Oh, pish." Edward took one hand from the wheel to wave her off. "We have a big empty house, and you know how Annie likes to fuss. John and Eddie's old bedroom will be the quarantine room where you will stay with Leonard. The girls can stay in Millie and Beulah's old bedroom, and Eddie has a bed for Raymond next door."

"I know all that." She didn't mean to dismiss it so rudely. "I'm sorry, I'm just not myself."

Edward slowed down as Eddie, who drove his Nash ahead of them, decelerated while passing through Rathdrum. A train whistle indicated that they would have to wait at a crossing. When they stopped, Margaret and Raymond turned and waved to their mother. She knew they enjoyed riding in Uncle Eddie's fancy Nash Roadster.

"That's why we want to help, Helen," said Edward, bringing her attention back to the subject at hand. "You can't take all the pressures yourself. Let us help share the load for a while."

"For how long?" She knew no one held the answer to that question.

"Let's just take it a day at a time."

Helen thought Edward might be getting tired of her negativity, so she kept silent for a spell. The train passed, and they moved on. "I don't mean to sound ungrateful. It's just that I worry."

"You have much to worry about." Edward cast a warm, deferential smile.

"And I'm not sure leaving Charles at home was such a good idea." Her voice cracked and she fought back tears.

"Charles is practically a man."

"He's twelve!" Again, she regretted sounding so vociferous. But she was fighting with herself more than anything.

"Twelve-and-a-half, as he likes to say." Edward managed to get Helen to let out a little laugh with that. He chuckled himself and sighed. "I still remember being that age, back on the farm in Wisconsin."

Edward remained silent for a few moments, and Helen let him dwell on his thoughts before expressing them.

"Sometimes, my dad would take odd jobs for weeks at a time in Saint Paul or Madison and leave me to run the farm. God knows we needed the extra money."

Helen saw another smile come across his face, which seemed odd, considering the circumstances.

"I had charge of all the crops, feeding and caring for the animals, everything."

"But your mother was home," Helen said.

"Yes, she still took care of things in the house, but my point is..." He didn't finish his thought.

"What?"

His smile never disappeared. "It was good."

Helen frowned. "You enjoyed it?"

"I wouldn't say that. I just mean that I became a man at age thirteen." He shook his head and let out a breath. "It felt good to be responsible. It made me who I am."

"But Charles is alone. I can't stop worrying about him."

Edward nodded. "Nothing will ever keep a mother from worrying about her child. But he is not *all* alone. You told me the church people and the Bonners are checking up on him. He's got a job at the store now. And"—he raised his forefinger to make a point—"you have a phone now. You can call him every night."

"I can't afford the charges—"

"*We* can afford the phone charges. Talk as long as you like."

DAY 83

WEDNESDAY, JULY 2, 1924

Frank and Chet were about to embark on a new adventure.

Before they left Skykomish, he made a new entry in his diary.

The Mill shut down today until after the 4th. My I wish I could be with Mother on that day and wife and Babies if I have any. I have quit grieving as much as I used to, but I think of who my dear ones are every day. Lowrie and I are going to Seattle tonight and I am praying that some one I know will recognize me and be able to tell me weather I have any dear ones or not and if I have O Boy won't I be a happy one and if I belong in the Northwest, I'll have a good chance of some one knowing me in a big city. I will try to locate a better job there. I only have about $50.00 clear and here since May 12th. But if I find none I can come back and go on repair work.

Part 4
Seattle

DAY 84

THURSDAY, JULY 3, 1924

They planned to get up late, but Frank couldn't sleep.

The anticipation of the new day caused him to rise at his customary time, and he went out to explore the vicinity. It was a regular workday in Seattle. Motorcars filled the streets, and the sidewalks bustled with pedestrians. The aromas from a nearby cigar shop mingled with exhaust fumes. A half dozen Makah Indians sat in a semi-circle on the sidewalk selling handmade baskets.

A ride on the *Jim Hill Special*—named for the founder and owner of the Great Northern Railroad—had taken them the night before into King Street Station. The two were lucky to get a room at the New Arlington Hotel at First Avenue and Spring Street, considering the holiday. It cost more than Frank would have liked, but Chet liked being "close to all the action." Although they traveled light, Frank carried all his earthly belongings—as far as he knew—including his enigmatic suit.

Even considering the everyday turmoil of the city, Frank knew in twenty-four hours, Second Avenue would be total mayhem as the big Fourth of July Parade passed right by the front doors of the hotel. The *Post-Intelligencer* promised it would be the biggest celebration ever. The parade featured over

5,000 people marching, not to mention spectators.

After strolling past the piers on Elliot bay, Frank headed back to the room.

"You're wearing your suit?" Chet assessed Frank with drowsy eyes and a cocked eyebrow.

"Why not? It's either this or my work clothes. Besides,"—Frank straightened his cuffs—"it's my first chance to wear it. Thought I'd try to look a little ritzy for the big city."

Chet raised his eyebrows. "You look like a drugstore cowboy."

Frank felt slightly hurt by the comment, but he tried not to show it.

Chet stood at the mirror, shaving. "Just make sure at the ball game there's a few inches of space between us on the bleachers."

Soon, the two were out exploring the town. First, Lowry showed Frank around Pioneer Square and the downtown area. Then they took a streetcar south on Rainier Avenue to Dugdale Field. Here they would see some "real" baseball, according to Chet.

"Follow me," Lowry said. Instead of going to the front gate, Chet led Frank to an area behind the left-field bleachers. He stood there for a moment, glancing around.

"Where are you going—"

"Now!" blurted Chet, pulling open a break in the chain-link fence. He ducked into a dark corner under the bleachers.

Frank hesitated, his eyes darting to each side. Cautiously, he followed. "What are we doing?" he whispered, knowing they were now within earshot of dozens of baseball fans seated right above them.

Without a word, Chet moved to his left, motioning Frank to follow him. They came to an opening that allowed them to enter the general seating area near the outfield.

"I've been doing this since fifth grade." Lowry winked. "You've been jumping on freight trains, I've been getting into baseball games for free. Worst that can happen is they'll kick us out. It's not like they put trespassers in the slammer."

The Seattle Indians hosted the next-to-last place Los Angeles Angels. Chet explained that the Indians were in second place, trying to catch the San Francisco Seals in Pacific Coast League Triple-A action.

The two settled into seats near center field. "I played minor league baseball for a couple of years down in Tacoma," Chet said.

"You never told me that," Frank said.

"There's a lot you don't know about me." Chet winked again.

Unfortunately, the lowly Angels whupped the Indians 9-1. After the game, the two headed back downtown to catch a movie at the Liberty Theatre, across from Pike Place Market. "Wait 'til you get a load of the pipe organ in here," Chet said as they entered. "They actually built this theater around the organ."

The organ was indeed the centerpiece of the 1700-seat auditorium. *The Perfect Flapper* played that night, a comedy starring Colleen Moore. She was adorable. But the organist stole the show, managing to make the black-and-white images come to life as he not only played traditional organ music but, when necessary, contributed dozens of different effects. At one point, he added the sounds of cooing doves and, later, of surf crashing on shore. In addition, the organist gave the impression that a string orchestra accompanied him. It thundered loud enough to shake the entire building. Fisher found the experience enthralling.

When they emerged from the theater, they discovered it was almost dark. They made it a double-header by walking down to the Strand Theatre to watch another movie.

"Where ya' goin'?" asked Lowry when they left the Strand.

"The hotel is this way." Fisher pointed to the Arlington one block away down Spring Street.

"You calling it a night? It's only ten o'clock."

Fisher shrugged. "Do you have something in mind?"

Chet touched the side of his nose. "I've got a surprise for you."

Frank followed Chet to a streetcar heading east on Yesler Way. They rode it to a park at the end of the line, next to Lake Washington. A sign read "Leschi Park."

"We're going to a park?" Frank asked. "At night?"

"You'll see." Chet led Frank from the trolley to a winding gravel path past manicured flower beds and trimmed shrubs. In the distance, they heard jazz music playing.

Chet stopped in a grassy clearing and pointed toward the source of the music. A large brick building with several spires and a grand entry loomed a few yards distant. "They have a great dance hall here. Live music, single ladies." The word "ladies" he pronounced with a provocative lilt in his voice, and he wiggled his eyebrows in his trademark gesture. He stretched his left arm outward like a circus ringmaster introducing his next act.

"Oh, I don't know, Chet." Frank put his hands in his pockets and his toe scraped the ground. "I'm not much into dancing."

"You're not listening to me, pal. I'm talking about *girls* here. We came to have a good time, right? Let's have a little fun."

"Baseball was fun. The movies were fun."

Chet leaned in close. "I'm talking about *real* fun, Frank. C'mon! The night is still young. There's no harm in it."

In reply, Frank stood there, scrunching his face.

"Listen, it won't hurt anything to go inside, listen to some music, have a couple of drinks. You don't have to do anything you don't want to."

Frank turned his face back uphill toward the path they had come down. "When's the last streetcar? We don't want to miss that."

"At least another hour." Chet squeezed his hat on his head. "Besides, we can always take a jitney."

"I'm kind of tired," Frank moaned. "You go ahead. I'll meet you back at the hotel."

Chet pulled off his hat and threw it on the ground. "I don't understand what your problem is. Let me see if I have this straight." Pacing the lawn, he gesticulated with his arms and talked a bit too loud, Frank thought. "You don't drink, you don't smoke, you don't chew or run with women who do. Have I got that right?" With each point he counted on his fingers almost maniacally.

Before Frank could answer, Chet cut him off. "No, wait! You don't run with women, *period*. Am I right?

"Well…"

"You *do* like girls, right?"

"Chet!" Frank looked indignant. "You know better than that."

"I know, I know. I'm just trying to figure out what we're doing here, Frank." Chet put his hands on his hips. "What is tomorrow?"

"It's the Fourth of July…"

"Right. Also known as…"

"Uh, Independence Day."

"That's what I'm talking about, here. *Independence.*" Chet still paced and fumed but calmed down some, reminding Frank of a preacher, albeit a backslidden one.

"Take me, for example." Chet gestured with both hands pointing to his chest. "I am an independent man. I've got no wife telling me *when* I can come and go, *where* I can go, or *who* my friends are. I've got no church telling me what I can and can't do. In-de-pen-dent."

He continued, "Now, let's consider your situation. You have no wife… that you know of," he added before Frank could object. "Remember, we decided you are a single man. No commitments. No church affiliation. You are about as independent as anyone I have ever known." He put his hand on Frank's shoulder as if giving a pep talk to a prize fighter in the neutral corner at the end of the ninth round.

"*But* you act more like an inmate at Walla Walla. You might as well be shackled. Why not live a little. Loosen up. Be a man. Make your own decisions."

Frank found it ironic that Chet tried to persuade him to make his own decisions, so long as they agreed with Chet's. *On the other hand…*

"I guess it wouldn't hurt to go in." Pensively, Frank glanced toward the dance hall.

"Now you're talking."

"I suppose it's possible I might see someone who knows me…"

Chet slapped him on the back. "That's why we're here."

Frank held up one finger. "But only for a while."

"Sure, sure," Chet assured him. "We won't be out too late."

"Because we still have a big day tomorrow, and we're going to need our sleep."

With excitement, Chet took Frank by the arm and led him toward the alluring brick structure, continuing the conversation. "Right, big day tomorrow. But no sense in wasting the evening, either. You should take advantage of every opportunity to meet people who might know who you are."

Chet opened the large wooden door for Frank to enter. In stark contrast to the peaceful park setting outside, the large hall was chaotic. Smoke filled the noisy hall and raucous music blared in a room crushed with people. Chet led Frank through crowds to a punch bowl which he partook of without hesitation. After taking a gulp, he turned to Frank. "Have some." Ladling out the punch, he poured it into a crystal cup for him.

Frank picked it up tentatively and sniffed it. "Is it spiked?" he asked.

His friend laughed. "Is there another kind?"

Frank took another sniff and sipped it. Raising his eyebrows, he said, "It's good," and took another sip.

Chet scanned the room. Swallowing the last of the punch from his cup, he said, "I think I see a few prospects." He set the cup down and made his way into a bevy of ostensibly eligible females, leaving Frank by the punch bowl. Chet seemed to be chatting amiably with some young ladies and, in less than thirty seconds, made his way to the dance floor with one.

How does he do that? Frank realized he had finished his cup of punch and filled another. He watched Chet and the woman dance for a second number, standing alone near the punch table. Then, partaking of some hors d'oeuvres at the table, he browsed the room, hoping to find a familiar face.

His gaze kept returning to a pretty woman amongst the bevy where Chet had found his dance partner. She had shoulder-length brunette hair, loosely curled, framing a face with high cheekbones and an engaging smile. Wearing a royal blue chiffon tubular dress with beads at the hem, she looked charming. She had a kind and innocent face that Frank found magnetic. As she chatted with one of the other girls in the group, Frank couldn't help but notice she kept glancing in his direction. He swiveled to see if someone else might be near him, but there didn't seem to be another prospect.

Brushing his hair back, he summoned the courage to approach her. When he neared her, she averted her gaze.

"Ahem. Excuse me," he began.

"Yes?" She turned toward him with a disarming smile.

With one word, she took his breath away, and his heart skipped a beat. He realized he had not given a thought as to what to say once he got her attention.

She took a sip from her crystal cup while he found his voice.

"Well, um, you see, I was just wondering…"

"Yes?"

"Uh, do you know me?"

"Should I?" She tilted her head.

Her response caught him off guard. *Maybe I should've stayed at the punch bowl.* "Um, well, I thought that as I was standing over there that I knew you from somewhere."

"Possibly." She took a sip of punch. "Where are you from?"

Good question. "All over, really. Maybe from Montana."

"Maybe I've never been to Montana." She flashed a bemused smile. "You should probably start by introducing yourself."

"Oh, sorry. How silly of me. I'm Frank. Frank Fisher." He held out his hand to shake.

Examining the chandelier above his head, she ignored his outstretched hand. She repeated the name slowly. "Hmm. Frank Fi-sher. No. The name isn't familiar."

"Oh…" Frank glanced away, trying to imagine what to say next.

"I thought"—she brought his attention back to her—"that you might be coming over to ask me to dance."

"Oh, yes. By all means. That is, if you would like to."

The band played "The Blue-Bird Waltz."

Grabbing his hand, she guided him to the center of the dance floor. He followed like a dog on a leash. When she turned to face him, he stared back, unable to move.

She took his right hand and placed it on her back, and then grasped his left hand with her right and held it extended out to their sides. She pulled him closer.

Frank gasped at the warmth of her body next to his. He didn't know the last time he had been so close to a woman. His knees felt wobbly.

"Do you know the waltz?"

He blinked and gave a sheepish grin. "It seems not."

She giggled. "You're funny. First of all, you need to stand up straight."

He squared his shoulders, but then she pulled him closer again. "Upright does not mean apart."

Beads of sweat formed at his temples.

"Now you move your feet in a box step, like this."

Stumbling a bit, Frank followed her example

Bringing her face close to his ear, she whispered, "*One*, two, three; *one*, two, three…" He struggled to keep up.

After another waltz, the band went into a lively rendition of "The Charleston."

Smiling up at him, she asked, "Do you want to sit this one out?"

"But I was just getting the hang of it."

"Well, you can hardly waltz to 'The Charleston.'"

"You never know until you try." He proceeded to waltz alone as onlookers stared inquisitively. She doubled over, holding her laugh in with her hand.

"You're so silly." They both laughed. She took his hand and led him to the punch table. He poured her a cup and partook of another one himself. They made small talk about the weather and holiday events.

Chet arrived with his date. "Well," Chet said, "I see the two of you have become acquainted. Tell me who this lovely lady is, Frank."

"Chet, I'd like you to meet…" He stopped short. "Uh…"

"Wanda," she said.

"You forgot her name?" Chet asked in surprise.

Frank's face went flush. "I, uh, actually forgot to *ask* her name."

"You'll have to forgive my friend here," Chet said. "Forgetfulness seems to be his specialty." Chet introduced Lu.

"Nice to meet you, Lu." Frank nodded. *Attractive, but not as petite and spritely as Wanda.*

Lu chimed in. "Wanda and I already know each other. Actually, we came here together after work. We both work at the Oyster House on First."

"How about that?" Chet said. "The pair of us paired up with a pair." Nobody laughed, and Chet cleared his throat. "So, Lu and I were talking about stepping outside for a few minutes. Get a little fresh air." Chet winked at Frank. "Care to join us?"

"Sure." Wanda answered for Frank and took him by the hand again, something he rather enjoyed. He pulled at his collar, happy to go outside where it was cooler. They left through the large, wooden double doors and descended wide concrete steps to the spacious lawn of Leschi Park. Chet and

Lu headed for a park bench and sat on it, almost immediately engaging in passionate necking.

Wanda raised her eyebrows and led Frank a few yards away. She stopped and turned toward him. Rubbing the lapel of his jacket between her thumb and forefinger, she peered up into his eyes. "I like your suit. Where did you get it?"

"Uh…" *How do I explain that I found myself wearing it one day?* "I just… have it."

A wry smile crept across her face. "You're kind of a puzzle, aren't you?"

He chose not to answer the question. "Um. *You* look fabulous. I love your dress."

"Thanks." Wanda bounced up on her toes once. "Do you want to look at the stars?"

"Sure." Frank was happy to do anything as long as it was with Wanda.

They found a clearing just a few yards away, giving them the most panoramic view of the night sky. She lay down on the manicured lawn in her long dress, somehow managing to do it with grace. She patted the grass beside her and smiled up at Frank. He took the cue and lay on his back beside her as they gazed skyward.

To Frank, it felt like a dream. "It sure is a beautiful night."

Wanda pointed skyward. "Do you see those stars over there, which makes a kind of 'W'? That's called Cassiopeia."

"I didn't know that. The only one I know is the Big Dipper."

"Ursa Major. The Great Bear."

Frank pointed. "No, I mean the one that looks like a dipper."

Wanda giggled again. "Yes, it does look like a dipper. I don't know why the ancients thought it looked like a bear."

"You sure do know a lot about astrology."

"Astronomy," she corrected.

"Huh?

"Astrology is superstition," she replied. "Astrologists believe the stars determine our destiny. Astronomy is science. It is the study of the stars and constellations and so forth."

"I always get the two mixed up."

"Looking at the stars is a way to see into the past." She stared upward dreamily.

"What do you mean?"

"Since the stars are light years away, the light we see burned thousands of years ago. So it's like looking back in time."

Frank scratched his chin, contemplating. Sitting up on one elbow, he eyed Wanda. "I like that." He wished the stars could help him see into his past. "Have you ever…?"

"What?"

"It's silly." He shook his head.

"No, tell me." Her eyes pleaded with him.

"Have you ever wished upon a star?"

"That's just more superstition."

"I know. But when you really need a wish to come true, well, you have to try something." Frank lay back down, staring up at the inky sky.

"Do you want to know what I do when I need something?" Wanda asked.

Frank sat up again and nodded.

"I pray." Wanda beheld his gaze.

"Does it work?"

"Yes." She nodded. "I mean, it's not like God is a genie who grants all my wishes. But I always have whatever I need. He's never let me down."

The only sounds for several moments were a mild breeze through the willows and the muted sounds of the band inside.

Frank wanted to believe in prayer. He had tried it, but God's seeming indifference to his problem made him feel like a fool to believe that God cared.

"Have you ever seen a star in the daytime?" she asked.

It seemed like an odd question. "No. Have you?"

"Never. You know why?"

"Because it's daytime, I guess."

"Right." She reached out and stroked his hair once. "The stars are still there. You just can't see them because it's all bright outside. But when things get dark, that's when you see the stars."

Frank frowned and waited for her to explain.

"That's how hope is. When everything is right with the world, people don't reach out for hope. They think since everything is fine, they don't need anything. But when darkness comes, fear comes, too. And then,"—her eyes turned to the skies again—"people look to the heavens. And there's hope."

He remembered what Joe Clyde had said. About having it too good, and the Good Shepherd guiding him into the Valley of the Shadow of Death.

"So, what's your wish?" Wanda asked finally.

A waxing crescent moon filtered through the trees, softening her already delicate features. She had put a spell on him, making him forget about his greatest desire, thinking now of a more immediate one. His focus darted from her hazel eyes to her rosy cheeks and her soft lips. Her angelic visage and the hypnotic scent of her perfume made him feel weak. His heart felt like electric shocks were pulsing through him. He couldn't remember ever feeling this way before.

Shifting, she asked, "Is something wrong?"

"No. Not at all," he said quietly. "I'm just…"

"What?"

"You're just so… beautiful." Frank could tell, even in the dark, that she blushed. This made her even more endearing. He reached over, touching the hair behind her ear delicately.

After he gazed at her for a few more moments, she finally spoke.

"Aren't you going to kiss me?"

He needed no further motivation. Leaning over, he kissed her gently on the lips. Then gazing at her one more time, he closed his eyes, engaging in a very long and passionate kiss, holding her bare shoulders. Her skin felt warm compared to his cold fingers. He realized the blood had rushed from his extremities to… well, elsewhere.

But something else intruded without warning. Frank pulled back with astonishment.

Alarmed, Wanda asked, "What's wrong now?"

Frank jumped to his feet and paced in all earnestness, brushing his hair back with both hands. "Oh my gosh! Oh my gosh!"

"What happened, Frank?" Wanda stared at him wide-eyed.

The commotion got Chet and Lu's attention as well.

"What's going on?" Chet rushed over to his friend. "Tell me what's wrong."

Frank let out a breath of air and declared, "I'm married."

Wanda sat up straight, slack-jawed.

With a pained expression, Lu asked, "What?"

Stretching both arms out as if making a public announcement, Frank said, "I'm married."

Wanda continued to sit on the lawn in what appeared to be a state of shock. Lu stood and put her fists on her hips. "Waaait a minute, what are you two up to?"

"No, no, no!" Chet waved his arms. "Frank, you don't know that. Not for sure." Turning to the ladies, Chet repeated, "He doesn't know that for sure."

"What are you babbling about?" Lu eyed Chet with suspicion.

"Well, my friend here, he's…" Chet seemed to be grasping for the right word. "He's touched."

Wanda and Lu exchanged perplexed glances.

Regaining his composure, Frank said, "What he's trying to say, or rather, trying *not* to say, is I have no memory of anything that happened in my life before April."

"Oh, no." Chet buried his face in his hands.

Lu stared, frowning, apparently trying to comprehend the new developments.

"That must be horrible." Wanda's eyes were wide.

Throwing up his hands, Frank said, "You can't imagine."

"You're buying this?" Lu asked Wanda incredulously.

"Wait a minute, Frank." Chet grabbed Frank's lapels. "How can you suddenly know you're married?"

Frank gazed back at Chet with a crooked grin. "I just do."

"Really?" Chet pointed his finger at Frank's chest. "Then who are you married *to*?"

"I haven't the foggiest." Frank shook his head.

"You see?" Chet poked Frank in the shoulder. "You can't be sure you're married if you don't even know your wife's name, can you?"

"I *know* I'm married." He spoke with confidence.

"Stop saying that. How can you know you're married, just like that?" Chet snapped his fingers. "A few minutes ago, you had no idea, and now—right in the middle of uh…"

"A kiss," Wanda said.

"Yeah, right in the *throes* of passion, you remember, 'Oh, yeah, I'm married'?"

Frank stared at the manicured lawn, contemplating.

"That does it." Lu slapped her knee. Marching over to Wanda, she took her by the hand and helped her from the ground. "We're leaving. Sorry, *Chet.*" Lu spoke in a sharp accusing tone. "*If* that's your real name. Bank's closed."

"No, no, wait a minute." Chet pressed his hands together as if in prayer. "Just because *he* has…"

Lu drug Wanda up the path to the streetcars. Wanda turned her head. "I believe you, Frank. I'll pray for you."

Chet yelled in desperation as they disappeared from view. "But there's nothing wrong with *me*. I'm not married. I remember everything!" It appeared that Chet would start to bawl at any moment. They were already out of earshot when he whined, "My name really is Chet."

The two men stood silently for a while. The breeze continued to blow through the trees. The band struck up "Somebody Stole My Gal" from beyond the walls of the dance pavilion.

"I'm sorry, Chet."

"Yes, you are!" Chet plopped down on the bench he and Lu had been using. "This is the thanks I get for all I've done for you."

Frank had nothing to say in response. He could only wait for Chet to calm down.

"I had a wonderful evening," Chet continued, "until you were assaulted by your conscience."

Another period of awkward silence followed. Finally, Frank said, "It wasn't my conscience."

"What?" Chet's exasperation was still evident.

"It wasn't a feeling of guilt or anything like that." Frank stared down at his feet. "It was more like… Well, when my lips touched hers, I just somehow *knew*. It was like a revelation."

"I see. Like Joseph Smith, you're a latter-day prophet."

"It's not like that," Frank said.

"What else did God tell you, Frank? Did he tell you who's going to win the World Series this year? Because that kind of revelation I could use."

Frank thought for a minute. "The New York Yankees."

Chet started. "He told you that?"

"No. I just know it's going to be the Yankees."

"Oh, right. You just happen to *know* this information. The guy who *knows* he's married, but doesn't know who he's married to or where his bride is."

A young couple descended the stairs to leave the dance hall.

"Hey!" Chet called in their direction. "Come meet my friend here. He knows nothing of the past but can tell the future. Go ahead, ask him anything."

The couple whispered to each other and hastily left in the opposite direction.

"It's not like he *spoke* to me, Chet. It's more… I can't explain it."

"Neither can I." Chet threw his hands in surrender. "I can't figure out *what* happened tonight. I just know it didn't end well."

They were lucky to catch the last Yesler Way streetcar of the night. Frank was in a better mood than he'd been in a long time.

"What are you smiling about?" Chet asked.

"I'm married." Frank grinned even wider.

Chet slugged him in the shoulder. "Shut uuuup!"

DAY 85

FRIDAY, JULY 4, 1924

Helen poured the pancake batter and watched it sizzle and pop on the griddle.

After staying a week with her in-laws, *she* was feeling the heat, too. Since coming to Freeman, Leonard had gotten worse. His coughing spasms were more prolonged, and he hadn't spoken a coherent word in two days. In addition, there seemed to be an underlying current in the house she couldn't quite put her finger on. She didn't feel exactly unwelcome, but… what was it?

Trying to sleep on a cot squeezed between a wall and Leonard's bed began to seem like purgatory. It made her cranky. She couldn't blame her in-laws if they were growing tired of her.

Lost in thought, she was running her finger up and down the wooden handle of the ladle when she was startled by a voice.

"You're up early." Annie entered the kitchen.

"Thought I'd get breakfast started." Helen wiped her hands. "Try to get ahead before everyone starts getting up."

Reaching into an upper cupboard, Annie pulled out a larger griddle. "I like to use this one when I have company. I can do four pancakes at once instead of only one."

Helen grunted. It was just like Annie to politely point out her mistakes. Annie took over the cooking duties with her large pan, giving Helen the impression she wasn't considered skilled enough to prepare breakfast for her family. Helen plopped down in a kitchen chair and stared at a shelf containing her mother-in-law's collection of china. A heavy sigh escaped her lungs.

Glancing over her shoulder, Annie flipped the pancakes and then came and sat across from Helen. She reached over and put her hand on Helen's. "Honey, I know how you feel."

Do you? Helen didn't look at her.

"I know it's not the same, but Leonard *is* my grandson, and I'm suffering along with him. And John is my son. His absence is tearing me up inside."

In a mechanical response, Helen said, "I know."

Annie got up, put the pancakes on a plate, and laid a kitchen towel over them to keep them warm. Then she started four more. "Edward!" she shouted toward the back hall. "Get the children up. The flapjacks are getting cold." She fussed some more at the oven before turning her attention back to Helen. "Can I tell you about a dream I had? It was months ago, but I have been thinking about it lately."

Helen finally turned to her. "What was it?"

Sitting back down, Annie smiled at Helen. "I dreamt that after nearly three months, John came back to us."

"Why have you never told me about this?" Helen furrowed her brow.

"Well. It was just a dream." Annie shook her head as if shaking off a silly notion. "I didn't put much stock in it. Besides, if I would have told you two-and-a-half months ago John would come back in three months, that wouldn't have been very encouraging, would it?"

"I guess not." Helen let out an uneasy breath. "It's been close to three months now."

"Eighty-five days," Annie said.

Helen widened her eyes. "You've been counting the days?"

Getting up, Annie walked over to a roll-top desk and opened it. She produced a calendar with black X's covering blocks of days. "See? Today's the

Fourth of July. Day eighty-five." She pointed to the calendar. "It will be three months on the eleventh."

"Still, it seems far-fetched to think your dream might be fulfilled." When Leonard's illness became her paramount concern, Helen had stopped counting the days John had been missing. She had resigned herself to the idea of facing life's challenges without a husband. She doubted she would ever know what became of John. But now, she had to admit, Annie's enthusiasm buoyed her spirits a little.

Annie rushed to the skillet, realizing she had left the pancakes there a bit too long. "It's okay. Edward likes them a little bit crunchy." Brushing a curl from her face, she continued working at the stove. "I know it's kind of crazy. But now that the time is coming close, I've been praying more. Getting closer to God, I think. And I've been encouraged by it. I believe something is going to happen." She sat back down across from Helen. Her face shone. "Soon."

******

People jammed the sidewalks in anticipation of the beginning of the Independence Day parade in Seattle. Frank and Chet were having a difficult time finding a place where they could get an unobstructed view. When five DH-4 biplanes from the Great War flew low overhead, every eye turned skyward, and cheers erupted as if celebrating Armistice Day all over again.

Frank and Chet stood on their tiptoes as the parade began, trying to see as sailors, marines, and soldiers marched and saluted, followed by their accompanying bands. Various floats representing a multitude of clubs and organizations passed by, as well as the float carrying Miss Liberty and her court. Cops on motorcycles and horses also populated the parade contingent, not to mention the endless number of policemen patrolling on foot, keeping an eye on the crowds.

"Hey," Chet said, "let's get away from all these people and head down to the water." Frank was happy to oblige. His habit of making eye contact with every person seemed fruitless. Everyone was a stranger, and he was a stranger to everyone.

"In these crowds, it'd be easy to get separated." Lowry snapped his fingers. "Tell you what. If we do, let's make this spot, Second Avenue and Spring Street, our meeting place. If I get here first, I'll make a mark in the sidewalk like this." He rubbed his heel against the curb, making a distinctive black signature. "If you get here first, rub it out."

"Okay," Fisher replied.

A wry smile formed on Chet's face.

Then Fisher laughed. "I get it."

Chet's pace quickened as they moved north along the wharf. When they came to the foot of Pike Street, they went out to the end of the pier to get an eyeful of the *U.S.S. Pennsylvania*, the flagship of the Navy's Pacific fleet.

"Those are fourteen-inch turrets." Lowry's voice filled with awe.

"Gosh." Fisher assumed that must be big.

Lowry impressed his friend with other technical details of the *Pennsylvania*, while Fisher continued to be inspired by his enthusiasm. Frank found Chet's extraordinary command of naval trivia interesting, if not terribly meaningful.

After some time at the wharf, Frank said, "What beach did you say we were going to go to today?"

It took two streetcars to reach Alki Beach in West Seattle. With temperatures in the high seventies, there wasn't a cloud in the sky—unexpectedly pleasant weather for Seattle, even for July. Sunbathers filled the beach, and the large natatorium housed heated freshwater and saltwater pools. It wasn't as crowded as First Avenue and the parade, but a popular destination, nevertheless.

Since they had no swimwear, they spent the afternoon beachcombing. They carried their socks and shoes, rolling up their pant cuffs before splashing in the salt water. Later they headed for the main event of the day, held at the University of Washington stadium.

While waiting for the next streetcar, Frank noticed an ache in his gut. He put his hand on his belly but had a feeling he wasn't actually sick.

Chet, climbing onto the trolley, asked, "Are you okay?"

"Yeah. Fine"

Getting to the stadium from West Seattle required two transfers and took almost an hour, but they arrived before five o'clock.

Husky Stadium, only four years old, was a sight to behold. With 30,000 seats in a U-shape—the open end of the "U" facing Union Bay—it afforded every spectator a beautiful view of Lake Washington.

The program commenced at seven o'clock sharp with the landing party from the *U.S.S. Pennsylvania* accompanied by their "Crack Band." Sundry military exercises were next, followed by presentations of awards for the best floats in the morning parade, equestrian stunt riding, bike racing, more bands, dancers, drum brigades, and comics.

Frank fidgeted, the ache becoming worse, but he tried not to show it.

"Mink de Ronda's next." Chet looked to the sky wide-eyed with expectation. "There he is." The one-armed daredevil made a grand entrance by parachuting into the stadium. Everyone stood and pointed, roaring with appreciation and applause.

"Now that was something!" Chet rocked on his heels.

Frank still sat.

"Hey, what's the matter?"

"I don't know." Frank spoke soft and low. "I'll be back." He stood and left his seat.

"But you're going to miss the fireworks."

Finding a shadowy spot of ground next to a booth where vendors sold American flags and patriotic noisemakers, he got down on his hands and knees. He was light-headed and wracked by dry heaves. An immense weight pressed down on him, making him feel weak and oppressed. Sweat poured from his brow. He became convinced of the source of the pain. It wasn't from food or the grippe.

It was guilt.

He'd experienced it before whenever he had fun. It didn't feel right to celebrate when his family must be suffering without him. They had come to Seattle to celebrate the holiday, yes. But his primary goal had been to see and be seen. Someone here had to know his identity and help him find his past. But so far, nothing.

Fireworks exploded, and cheers followed by oohs and ahhs erupted from the far side of the stands. Colored light flashed in his peripheral vision, and the smells of popcorn and sulfur magnified his nausea.

On the farm in Harrington, Lena Timm had told him that everything happens for a reason. Doubting it at the time, he thought about it now, wondering. *What reason would God have to afflict me so? If it's not a punishment, is it a lesson of some sort?* Pondering if he would ever know the truth, Frank conjectured that God might want him to be content with never knowing about his past.

Then Wanda's advice came to mind. She had told him that when she was in need, she prayed. She had made it sound so easy.

Still on his hands and knees, he tried to concentrate, but words would not come. *I don't even know what I truly need.* Salty drops from his temples pooled in his eyes, causing them to sting. His lungs filled with huge breaths, and he wiped sweat from his face with violent strokes.

If I pray that I want to know about my past, but God doesn't want me to know, will He get angry? In desperation, he uttered the only words that came to mind.

"God, help! Please help me."

The prayer was lame, he knew, but he couldn't think of anything else. He looked up to see if God had answered his prayer, but nothing became evident. Disappointed, he changed positions, lying on his back. Staring up at the stars, he wondered. *Why can't I look into the past like Wanda can? Why won't God answer my prayers?*

The burden still remained, and he did not feel better. The cheering stopped, and the hum of murmuring multitudes followed as spectators poured out of the stadium.

"There you are." Chet stood over him. "I've been searching all over for you. You missed the best part of the show."

Chet sat down next to him. "You sick or something? You're white as a baby's butt."

"I'm fine." He stood the moment Chet sat next to him. "Let's go."

Getting back to downtown afterwards took some time. The city's arteries were clogged with all modes of transportation attempting to depart the University District. Frank and Chet hung to the sides of an over-full streetcar taking them to Pioneer Square, where they continued on foot.

As they walked, Chet gestured wildly as he described the pyrotechnic display Frank had missed. "You should've seen it. They even reenacted war battles."

Frank stayed mum.

Halting him with the back of his hand, Chet stepped in front to face him. "Hey, is it something I said?"

The two stood there in silence for a few moments. Pops, crackles, and sparks interrupted the quiet as revelers shot their own fireworks.

A cool breeze came up from Puget Sound, and Chet grabbed his hat just before a gust blew it down the street. They were still about a block from the hotel, and Frank stared down Spring Street toward the dark water of the Sound.

"No." Frank tried to wave it off.

"Then what is it? You might as well tell me. I can see you're ill or sad or mad or... something. We had a good time today, didn't we?"

Shrugging, Frank stuffed his hands in his pockets. "Sure." He stared at a space of sidewalk between his feet.

"Well, try to dampen your enthusiasm, will you? You're making a scene." More of Chet's sarcasm.

Frank sighed. "It's just that, well, it's been a waste of time."

Puckering his lips, Chet formed his mouth into a shape that suggested a reply, but he only shrugged.

"We had fun, but I'm no closer to knowing who I am than when I came." Frank sniffed. "I doubt I'll ever figure it out."

Chet put his hands on Frank's shoulders. "This is my fault."

"Your fault?"

"I'm the one who talked you into coming here." Chet shook his head. "Seattle was a bad idea. We should have gone east. Like to Helena or Idaho or someplace like that. We still can. Somebody is bound to know you there."

With disbelief, Frank said, "But... but you have to get back to the mill."

"Who says? I got nothing tying me to that place of torment. Let's beat another freight train and head east. Whaddya say?"

Frank gaped. "You'd do that for me?"

Chet spat on the sidewalk. "No, are you crazy? Not for you. I'd just do it for the adventure."

"Olson!"

Fisher and Lowry ignored the sound of someone calling out. They continued chatting in earnest about their new plans.

"Hey, John Olson!" The voice came closer.

They turned to see the source. A beat cop twirling his baton walked straight toward them. Blinking, Frank replied, "Sir?"

"Excuse you!" laughed the policeman. He took off his cap. "Don't say you don't recognize me. I'm Bolen. Jesse Bolen."

"I guess you have me wrong." Frank took a step backward.

"No, I don't." The cop narrowed his eyes and cocked his head. "I knew you well back in Spokane on the streetcars. Last time I saw you was 1917. You were a motorman and I was your conductor." He bumped Frank's elbow. "I know it's you, Olson. You've always been a kidder."

Frank and Chet regarded each other with big grins.

"I think the time has come," Frank said. They slapped each other on the shoulders.

Officer Bolen squinted toward Frank, then Chet, and back again. He scratched his scalp before putting his cap back on. "What's going on here?"

As if on cue, bombs burst in air, celebrating the occasion.

DAY 85

PLUS ONE: SATURDAY, JULY 5, 1924

"I'm a wanted man?"

At half past midnight, Officer Bolen showed John the flyer. The policeman had escorted John and Chet six blocks south to City Hall, a five-story building at Fifth Avenue and Yesler Way. The triangular building looked like a four-layer slice of wedding cake. It held city offices, the police department, and a small jail. An infirmary known as City Hospital occupied the third floor. Once they were inside the police station, Jesse found the poster behind other notices on the bulletin board.

"You're wanted, that's for sure. Just not by the cops." Bolen pointed to the bold, large print at the top. **REWARD.** "Looks like Helen wants you back."

"Hmm." Chet peered over Olson's shoulder and pointed to a picture on the flyer. "That's your ugly mug."

"I still can't believe you don't remember anything." Bolen had mentioned the names of several people they both knew, but Olson didn't find any of the names familiar. "What about Hazel? You remember Hazel. You were at our wedding."

John shrugged and kept studying the reward poster. "It's me alright." He looked down at his left wrist, noting the birthmark described on the poster. It seemed so strange and dreamlike. Or a motion picture about someone else, except for color and sound. But slowly, it all began to feel real.

"We've got to call the number on this poster." Urgency rang from John's voice. "I need to talk to my family."

"The front desk has already tried the number, but the exchange seems to be down." Bolen motioned for John to follow him. "We'll keep trying. In the meantime, you need to see a doctor."

"What for?" Olson and Lowry followed Bolen down a hall. "There's nothing wrong with me."

The police officer talked over his shoulder as he came to an elevator and pressed the up button. "Yeah, except for the little detail of you not knowing anything about your past. That's not normal, is it? A doctor is going to have to examine you."

Bolen swung a hinged door and then slid open the cage. All three men hopped aboard. After the doors closed, Jesse pushed the lever forward and took them up two floors to the infirmary.

The infirmary at City Hall had the familiar hospital smell of antiseptic and urine. In the wee hours of Saturday morning, City Hospital bustled with activity. Several people had been injured in various holiday accidents the night before, including some people seriously hurt when hit by automobiles or when fireworks went awry. Bolen went off shift after he got Olson settled in.

"I feel kind of stupid wearing a hospital gown and being in a hospital bed." Olson flattened the sheets.

"Yeah, you look kind of stupid, too." Chet chuckled.

"You don't have to stay here all night, you know."

"I already have." Chet opened a curtain on a nearby window. "See? It's already getting light."

Olson stared at a corner of the room, lost in thought.

"You okay?" Chet asked. "You look like you dropped your ice cream cone on the beach."

After glancing at Chet, Olson smiled. "Sorry, just thinking."

"I thought you would be excited. This is what you've been waiting for. All you've talked about since I met you is how you need to find out who you are. Now your dream has come true, and you're all glum. What gives?"

Olson closed his eyes and rubbed his face with both hands. "I'm scared."

"Scared?"

"I'm afraid of what everyone will say when I get back home. It's such a cockamamie story. Will my family accept me back? Will they be angry? Will I even know them? I have no idea what to expect."

"Mr. Olson?" A nurse popped her head in the door. "You need to follow me."

******

Annie jumped when the phone rang. She shook Edward to awaken him, but he was already moving. Padding into the kitchen, he picked up the receiver from the candlestick hook. "Hello."

Four-thirty. Who can be calling at this hour? Annie had followed Edward out to the kitchen, expecting bad news. Some sort of emergency. Standing in the doorway, wringing her hands, she knew it *could* be good news. Maybe even the best news. But she was afraid to be too optimistic. She couldn't bear to have her heart shattered again.

"Hello? What?" Edward shoved the phone close to his ear. "I can hardly hear you. Who is this? You want to talk to who? Helen, you say?"

Turning to fetch Helen, Annie found her standing right behind her.

Edward handed the phone over. "Someone in Seattle wants to talk to you."

"This is Helen. Yes, Helen Olson. Who is this? Jesse Bolen? Yes, of course I remember you. What? Did you say you're a policeman now? I'm sorry. Why are you calling?" Helen turned to her in-laws, puzzled. "He's giving the phone to someone else. Hello?"

She shuddered and plopped down in a nearby chair.

Annie and Edward held on to one another for support.

She took in a sharp breath. Then, in a shaky, halting voice, she said, "Oh, John! John! It's you!"

******

John set the phone down on the hook and looked at his two friends.

"Well?" Chet asked.

A smile crept across his face. "You were right. She wants me back."

DAY 85 PLUS TWO

SUNDAY, JULY 6, 1924

"I'm beginning to think there is no doctor."

John spoke to the same nurse he had yesterday morning. Her hair seemed to be pulled back even tighter, if possible. "You are just holding me here hostage. Tell me the truth, am I one of those experimental guinea pigs they talk about?"

She glared at him. "It's still the weekend, so we are shorthanded. This hospital is full of people needing more urgent attention than you. I'm afraid you are not very high on the priority list."

"But just think." Olson pointed his index finger straight up. "If you let me go, that frees up a bed for a more urgent patient."

At that moment, Chet Lowry walked into the room. To the nurse, he said, "Mornin', Sunshine!"

She grunted and left the room without a word.

Turning to John, he said, "And to you, too, Mr. Olson. Still have a hard time calling you that."

"I'm starting to get used to it. I think it fits me."

Chet sat down. "I've got to be heading back to Sky. I still have a job there, for now."

"For now?"

"Yeah, I'm going to be moving on from there soon. I decided I want to be closer to the water, and my family."

"Your family?"

After taking a deep breath, Chet walked to the window and looked out. Without turning, he said, "Called my ex last night." He spun toward Olson. "She's in Saint Paul. Haven't talked to her for over a year." He lit a cigarette.

"Saint Paul is not closer to the water."

"I'm not going to Minnesota. She's coming out here. With our son."

Olson stared back with wide eyes and an open mouth. "You have a son?"

"Yep. His name is Charles. He's nine."

Olson tilted his head. "You haven't talked to your son for over a year?"

Chet turned toward the window again. "I know. You must think I'm a real piker. But I had to get away from Millie. She drove me crazy. *And* she was seeing another man." He took another drag from his cigarette. "But I *do* miss Charles."

After a moment of silence, John said, "It sounds like you're going to get to see him again soon."

"Yeah. In about three weeks. She's going to move to the Portland area. I'll probably move down there to be close by. There are lots of jobs there working on the ships." Chet paced near the window. "To be honest, I'm rather scared, too. Do you think Charles will forgive me?"

"You and I seem to be in the same boat." John got up and looked out the window with Chet. Yesler Way bustled with traffic on a Sunday morning. "I guess we just have to go see."

"You want to hear something crazy?" Chet slowly blew a lungful of cigarette smoke and turned to Olson. "All this time I've known you, I've been jealous of you."

"Jealous? Of *me*?"

Chet nodded. "Well, you had no knowledge of your past. I was *running* from mine. I *wanted* to forget how bad I was at being a husband and father. And then I saw your face the other night on Second and Spring, when Officer

Bolen told you who you were… Well, I realized maybe I needed to reconnect with my past, too."

Olson patted Chet on his shoulder. "We have much in common, Chet. You want to hear another one?"

"Sure."

"Jesse told me my oldest son's name is Charles."

"How 'bout that?" Chet turned and sat on the windowsill. "We're like long-lost brothers or something. Strange how the two of us ended up being friends."

"I thought the same thing." Olson rubbed his chin. "You don't suppose it was Divine intervention, do you?"

"Normally I'd be ready with a sarcastic retort for that." Chet smiled. "But I'm inclined to agree with you. Somebody is looking out for both of us."

The two spent some time talking about the good times they had and the laughs they'd shared together. Then Chet picked up his bag. "Well, I guess I'd better be going, Fisher."

"Name's Olson!"

"I know, I know. Just had to call you that one last time. But you'll always be Frank Fisher to me."

"Thank you for being my friend." Olson reached out to take Chet's hand. "I never would have gotten here without you."

Lowry took the hand and pulled John in close. They patted each other's backs. "Turns out," he said, "we needed each other."

******

"I'm telling you, he is one of the most belligerent patients I have ever had to deal with, doctor." The stern nurse walked into the room with a doctor in tow.

"Della, you say that about every patient." The gray-haired doctor plopped his bag on Olson's bed. "I hear you're anxious to leave."

"I've been in here a day and a half!"

"That's why we call you patients." The doctor didn't smile. "I'm Doctor White. Happy to meet your acquaintance." Wearing a white coat and a stethoscope hung around his neck, he appeared to be in his mid-sixties. He smelled of hair tonic and seemed a kindly gentleman, so John decided not to let him have it with the tirade he'd been reserving for him.

In all, the examination took about twenty-five minutes. Fifteen minutes of questions and answers and ten minutes of poking and prodding.

"Well," the doctor concluded, "I see no evidence of a recent blow to the head. I see an old scar on the back of your head, but it is evidently from many years ago. I don't suppose you remember how you got that."

John shook his head. "Remembering things is not something I'm very good at, I'm afraid."

"Amnesia is a very mysterious condition." Doctor White snapped his bag shut. "Nobody knows what causes it most of the time. It's so rare that, well, you are my first amnesia patient, and I've been around for a long time."

"How soon will I remember again?"

"Hard to say, hard to say." The doctor closed his bag. "Maybe when you see your family, it will all come back to you."

"Does that mean I can leave today?"

"Nosiree."

"Why not?"

"Your condition is very unstable, Mr. Olson. Your amnesia has not gone away, and even if it had, there is no telling when it will reoccur. What if you forget where you are going on your way back home?"

"So, what am I supposed to do?"

"If there is not someone here you can ride back with, you will need someone to come get you. Until then, I'm not releasing you. I can't be held responsible for what happens."

Suddenly, a man came in and pointed a camera at him. A bright flash blinded him momentarily. "Are you John Olson?"

"Who are you?" Olson asked.

"I'm with the Seattle P-I. Are you amnesia man?" He produced a notebook and pencil.

"Excuse me," the doctor interrupted. "I'm this man's physician. I don't want him disturbed unless..." He turned to Olson.

"It's okay," Olson said, "I'll talk to him."

DAY 85 PLUS THREE

MONDAY, JULY 7, 1924

"I'm going stir-crazy." John Olson pounded his fist into the bed.

"How long have you been in here?" Jesse Bolen had come for a morning visit. "Forty-eight, plus…"

"Sixty-one and, uh, a half hours." Frowning, he leaned toward Bolen and said, "C'mon, I know you can get me out of here."

Bolen laughed. "No thanks! I'd like to keep my badge, thank you." After a pause, he asked, "Has anybody else been to see you besides your friend from Skykomish?"

"Just nurse Carry Hatchet Nation."

"I heard that!" the nurse shouted from somewhere down the hall.

They exchanged wide-eyed glances. Olson finally said, "Oh, and a reporter from the P.I."

"Yeah." Bolen produced a newspaper from under his arm. "I brought the article with me. You made the front page."

Olson read the article with astonishment. Bolen let him read it in silence. "Well, I'll be. President Coolidge's son is on his deathbed."

"Are you reading the right article?" Bolen batted the paper with the back of his hand. "You are the main headline right there on the front page."

"Yes, right next to this article about Calvin Coolidge Jr," he said. "He got an infection from playing tennis? Strange."

"Yeah, it's strange," Bolen said flatly. "And the article about you? Did you read that?"

"Think of it, Jesse. The most powerful man in the country, maybe even the world, but he's powerless to save his own son." He glanced down at the article again. "What would you say to your son who's dying? I can't imagine."

"That's all very interesting." The cop snatched the paper. "But I bought this paper for you to keep as a souvenir. Not because of Calvin Coolidge Jr., or because of the weather or sports either. I got it for you because John Olson is the main story on the front page of the Seattle paper. I thought you might take notice."

"Oh, I noticed it." Olson grabbed the paper back. "He got it about right, at least. You know how reporters are. They like to juice up stories sometimes. But he did alright. A reporter from the *Times* said he's coming over, too. I'm expecting him any minute."

"You have company." Nurse Hatchet walked in, unsmiling.

"That's probably him," Olson said.

"It's not a 'him,'" she said.

"It's a her?" asked Olson.

"It's *two* hers. I'm quite sure you would like to see them."

John raised his eyebrows at Bolen. "Okay. Send them in."

Soon, Wanda and Lu appeared. They had a copy of the paper, too.

"Well, this *is* a surprise." John grinned from ear to ear.

"After the way we left the other night," Wanda said, "we thought we owed you an apology. We saw the article."

"No apology needed." John smiled. "Since we last talked, I've had a glimpse of my past. Not light years, just a brief conversation with my wife. Officer Bolen here has helped fill in some blanks, and I'll be learning more soon—if they ever let me out of here. And I have you to thank."

"Me? Why?"

"I thought about what you told me that night. And while we were lying on the grass in the park, I prayed."

"What did you pray?"

"I prayed I would see into my past. I needed to find out who I was."

"You hadn't already tried praying?"

"I did at first. But I felt like something blocked me. Like I was being punished for something. I thought God was mad at me."

A thoughtful expression crossed Wanda's face. "Sometimes God allows things to happen to us so we can learn. It's not always punishment, even though it may seem like it. He was probably trying to get your attention."

"Well, it worked, I guess." John scratched his head. "Maybe soon I'll be able to figure out what I needed to learn."

"I am so excited for you, Mr. Olson. I'm sorry we didn't listen to your story then."

Lu chimed in. "Actually, I'm the one who owes you an apology." She wore a sheepish smile. "Wanda believed you all along. But the whole story sounded so far-fetched to me."

"I know." John shook his head. "The whole experience feels like a bad dream."

"Anyway." Wanda stepped closer. "We wanted you to know how sorry we were about the other night."

"You *and* Chet," Lu said. "Where is Chet? I feel bad for him."

"He went back up to Skykomish."

"Well, if you ever hear from him, tell him to look me up at the Lion Oyster House on First," Lu said. "I'll fix him a nice seafood plate."

Another man appeared at the door and cleared his throat. A distinguished-looking gentleman, he wore a dark suit and a bowler.

"Oh, you must be from the *Times*," Olson said.

"No," replied the man. He stepped forward and removed his hat, revealing a shock of black hair. Holding the bowler against his chest, he said, "My name is Edward Olson. I'm your father."

******

Spokane police Chief Wesley Turner opened the door to his office and asked Bucholz to come in. The detective knew why the chief wanted to see him. He noticed the front page of the *Spokesman-Review* sitting on the desk.

"You saw it?" Turner asked.

"I saw it." Bucholz picked up the paper. He knew Turner would rub it in his face. "You don't actually buy it, do you? Amnesia?"

"Why not?" Turner held his palms up. "It can happen."

"No it can't. I don't believe something you can't prove. And remember, the whole theory of amnesia got written up in the paper weeks ago. What's to say Olson didn't read it himself and decide it might be a convenient story if anyone ever found him."

Turner sat on the edge of his desk, but Bucholz remained standing.

The detective continued. "What was he doing in Seattle anyway? Sounds like he was celebrating the Fourth of July holiday with a friend. Having fun, it seems. Don't think for a minute the escapades of John L. Olson are over."

"Spoken like a true skeptic," Turner said.

Bucholz began to walk out, but turned to his chief. "No. Spoken like a true cop."

From there he went to his desk for a few minutes, brooding. He lit his pipe and tried to concentrate on another case but couldn't. Something troubled him. Tapping his fingers on his desk, a thought occurred to him. He pulled some keys from his desk and went down a back hall to a door marked *Evidence Room*. Once accessing the room, Bucholz went to a large wooden cabinet and opened a drawer about halfway down. Pulling out a cloth bag, he closed the drawer again and set the bag on a nearby table.

He pulled off a large tag reading *JL Olson*. When he opened the bag, his nose curled at the foul, musty smell emanating from it. He didn't pull out the matted coonskin cap he'd discovered by the river. Instead, he glanced at it and closed the bag again, tying the top into a knot. He considered returning the cap to the Olson family, but what would they do with a stinky old hat? He had never told them about his discovery, and producing it now might cause them to accuse him of withholding evidence. Which, in a way, he was. Taking the cloth bag to an outdoor garbage can, the detective disposed of it there.

Case closed.

******

The train jostled over the tracks.

John held out an object for his father to take.

Looking curiously at John across the aisle, he took the little red book and opened it.

The younger Olson studied his father's features as he read, hoping to discern any kind of emotion. The train had left the King Street Station in Seattle at seven P.M. sharp and headed north toward Everett. From there it would turn eastward to cross the Cascade Range.

Edward read with a frown and a wrinkled brow. When he finished, he closed the little red book and pursed his lips.

"So, you know who the president is, and you know who the governor is." Edward pulled on his chin.

John nodded, saying, "Coolidge and Hart."

"And you know the names of all the Yankees and numerous movie stars."

John continued nodding.

"But you don't know who I am. You don't know your mother or wife or children?"

John shook his head.

"I have never heard of such a thing. How is it possible?"

"I don't know." John shrugged. "*You* talked with the doctor. *He* doesn't know either."

His father glanced out the window. "And we don't know when or *if* your memory will come back."

"Apparently not." John couldn't prevent his voice from shaking.

Edward appeared to be agitated. "Well, we will just have to make the best of it. I can't imagine what this family reunion will look like."

"I've been wondering about that."

"Everyone is going to be in Freeman to meet you. Mother, Helen, kids— even your brother and sister and in-laws." He turned to face John. "You didn't recognize me. You're not likely to recognize them. Doesn't sound like the makings of a joyous celebration, does it?"

The club car they were riding in suddenly felt smaller to John. The conversation had become uncomfortable, but he had to know more. "Can you tell me about them?"

"What?" Edward, apparently lost in his own thoughts, didn't seem to comprehend the question.

"Please," John said. "Tell me about every one of them. I want to know everything."

For the next few hours, Edward went into detail about each of the kids. He told anecdotes and gave descriptions of how they looked, their personalities, and their dreams. He said Charles had stayed in Kootenai, being the man of the house. When he mentioned Leonard, John smiled.

"What?" Edward asked.

"Oh, nothing." He thought about his mouse friend. "I just like the name Leonard."

"So does your mother. It's your middle name."

Edward told him about his mother, how much she had worried about him all this time, and how she greatly anticipated his arrival. She and Helen were preparing a grand meal. He told John about how brave Helen had been while he was missing, how she had even sold fire extinguishers in his stead. His father talked about how smart and beautiful she was and what an ideal wife she had been for him.

John's heart swelled.

His attention turned suddenly. "Wait. Look out the window. This is Skykomish coming up."

When they stopped in the smoky, dirty town, Edward turned up his nose. "Not much of a place to live, is it?"

"I'm not going to miss it." But John knew he really would. He had grown up there, in a way. He gazed up and down Railroad Avenue. The Skykomish Hotel, the candy store, and the Mill Boarding House to his right. To the left, Maloney's store, where he could see Junior nailing a new sign out front. What kind of memories would he have of Sky? He looked for Chet, but he was nowhere to be seen.

Edward opened the diary again. "You have a mistake here," he said.

"Where?"

He pointed to the inside front cover where John had written,

Jas. A. Larkin?

 alias

Frank Fisher?

"You can fix that now," Edward said.

John's eyes brightened. "You're right." He got out his pencil. It hovered over the page for a few seconds, then he pulled it away.

"What's wrong?" Edward asked.

John bit his lip. "Do you have a pen?"

Edward nodded, reached into his inside coat pocket, and pulled out a fountain pen.

Excitedly, John wrote his signature below the two other inscriptions in indelible ink.

John L. Olson!

With an exclamation point.

Part 5
Home

DAY 85 PLUS 4

Thursday, July 8, 1924

“Tell me more about my mother.”

It was past midnight now as the passenger train descended into the Wenatchee Valley above Leavenworth. It seemed they had exhausted things to talk about. Or maybe they just needed time to digest everything. In either case, both men had fallen silent for a while, staring out the window into the darkness, neither falling asleep.

John wanted to know everything he could about everyone before they got to Freeman, still nine hours away. “I don't even know my mother's first name.”

“She goes by Annie.” Edward pulled out his Velvet tobacco tin and filled the bowl of his pipe. “It's not her real name. She was born in Germany. You know how Germans are disparaged around here since the war. So she changed her birth name…”

“Let me guess…” John interrupted. “Ursula.”

Edward pulled the unlit pipe from his mouth and smiled. “I read in your little red book the name ‘Ursula’ seemed to ring a bell for you. Yes, that is your mother's real name, but I cannot for the life of me understand why it would be the one thing you would remember. Nobody has called her that for years. Can you give me a light?"

John reached into his pocket and pulled out a matchbox. Retrieving a stick match, he struck the side of the box and lit his father's pipe for him.

"Let me see that matchbox." John set it on the table between them. "Where did you come up with the name Larkin?"

"It just popped into my head."

Edward pulled out his own matchbox and set it beside the other one.

"Hey, it's the same brand," John said. "Where'd you get it?"

"A pawn shop. Look carefully at the box. What does it say?"

John read it aloud. "The martyrs. Made in Ireland."

"These matches commemorate the martyrs of the Irish labor unions. Whose portrait is on there?"

John squinted at the smaller print. Looking up at Edward, he gasped, "James Larkin!"

The two of them fell into another long silence. John noticed that most people on the train were snoozing away the hours, stirring only when the train made stops in Leavenworth and then Wenatchee. But he could not sleep. Too many thoughts were rushing around in his brain. With the destination growing nearer, he bit his nails.

As the train left Wenatchee station, John asked, "Why do you think I chose Helena as my hometown? Did I ever live there?"

"Yes, for a few months." Edward looked out the window, apparently in thought. "When you were eighteen, you worked for the Northern Pacific Railroad there before you decided to come back home." He turned back toward John. "It's funny, isn't it?"

"What?"

"You do remember *some* things. Even some personal details. But they seem to be a few pieces of a large puzzle. They don't connect."

John nodded. "Yes. It is like that."

"Of course, your wife's name is Helen. Maybe Helena sounded somewhat familiar because of her name."

"I thought about that. It's a possible explanation."

"There is one other thing," Edward added. "In a way, you kind of are from Helena."

"What do you mean?"

"In Kootenai, your address is 318 North Helena."

John raised his eyebrows and nodded. But he liked to think it was a latent memory of Helen that caused him to think of it.

The eastern skies began to lighten as they neared Harrington. John's emotions ran high, thinking about his time there and all the Timms had done for him as he worked on their farm. As they pulled into town, John pointed out the Harrington Hotel, where he'd spent his first night as an amnesiac.

He remembered how fearful he had been at the time. He had even considered the possibility he had gone to hell and would never know anything about his family ever again. The fear he experienced now could not compare to the terror he felt that first night.

The next stop was Edwall, where he'd first been booted off the train. In full sunlight, the town looked very different. Before, it had been terrible and strange. Now it actually appeared to be a normal little town, with a mercantile and a post office. A church and a hotel were close by the depot where his nightmare began. It had happened just three months before, but it was already a distant memory.

When they arrived at the Great Northern Station in Spokane, Edward pointed to a man outside. "That's him."

"Eddie?"

Edward nodded.

Leaning against the front fender of his Nash Touring Car with his arms folded across his chest, Eddie sported a satisfied smile. "John! I never thought I'd be so glad to see your sorry face."

"I could say the same." John said this despite the fact that he didn't recognize his brother. It just seemed like the proper response. He held out his hand to shake, but Eddie grabbed it and pulled him in for a quick embrace.

Eddie drove them the last thirty-some miles to Freeman. John sat in back while Edward sat in the front passenger seat. They rode mostly in silence, apparently not knowing what to talk about. A few pleasantries were exchanged about the weather, a few comments about the dusty, potholed road, but mostly they remained quiet.

When they neared Freeman, Edward turned his head around. "When we get there, I want you to wait in the car for a moment. Give me a chance to prepare everyone. Then I'll give you a nod and you can get out. Okay?"

John agreed, but wasn't sure what his father meant by "prepare everyone."

******

"Here they come!" Helen had been watching out the bedroom window to the north, knowing Eddie's car would be coming from that direction. She came bursting out to tell Annie and the others. She flattened her tan stylish summer wash dress she usually saved for Sundays. "How do I look?"

Annie put her hands on her hips and stepped back a bit to give her appraisal. "Honey, you make Mary Pickford look like a washer woman."

"Oh, please." She fluffed her hair with the palm of her right hand. "How about my hair?"

"Like it did ten minutes ago when you asked me."

Helen sighed and took a step toward the back door, but stopped and turned around. "Should I wear a hat?"

Giving an exasperated sigh, Annie said, "Helen, there's no time for that. Now get out there and meet your husband. We'll be right behind you."

As Annie gathered the children, Helen stepped out onto the covered back porch. The gravel driveway went up beside the house to where cars parked in back. Eddie's black Nash came to a stop just as Annie, carrying baby Mary, and the others stepped out onto the porch. Besides the kids, Helen's parents and John's sister, Millie, were all gathered there. Even the large porch made for tight quarters with so many people.

Once Eddie cut the motor, all that could be heard was the sound of a murder of crows quarreling in the distance. Everyone seemed to be holding their breath.

Eddie and Edward got out of the car and approached. Helen could see a figure in the back seat, but she couldn't see his face. She couldn't understand why he wasn't getting out. "Is everything alright?" Her voice shook with anticipation.

Edward put his palms facedown. "Everything's fine. I just wanted to speak to you beforehand." He instructed Helen's parents and Millie to wait inside. "We don't want to overwhelm him." Only Annie, Helen, and the children remained.

"You need to know John has experienced some sort of trauma. His amnesia appears to affect every area of his personal life. He may not recognize any of you. He didn't know who I was. Or Eddie."

Gasping, Helen steadied herself. Annie held her hand over her gaping mouth.

"Try not to be too disappointed or shocked by it. Otherwise, he appears normal—himself." He glanced over his shoulder. "Are we ready?"

Helen nodded and leaned against the porch post to brace herself.

Turning toward the car, Edward gave a slight nod.

The car door opened. First a foot appeared, then he stood and looked at Helen. Like a stone rolled away, Helen witnessed the resurrection of John Olson.

Her eyes gushed. As fast as her crippled feet would let her, Helen hobbled down the three steps and threw her arms around him as they met halfway up the walk. "Oh, John." She buried her head in his chest, making his shirt wet with her tears.

No one spoke for a long time, and Edward kept everyone else at bay for a few minutes, leaving this moment for Helen and John. Then the children came and each embraced their father in turn. First Margaret, then Raymond, and even little four-year-old Anna May.

"I missed you, Daddy." John picked her up and kissed her on top of her head.

"I missed you, too." He trembled and his eyes were wet.

He then came to the porch to greet his mother. She handed him baby Mary, and he squeezed her close to his chest, his tears moistening her bonnet.

Helen took her, and he turned to his mother. No words were exchanged at first, only a long embrace. Then she placed her hand on his chest. "I am so glad to see you are here in one piece. We worried so."

"I'm sorry." His voice cracked. "I never meant to put you all through such trouble."

"Oh, shush." Annie waved him off. "There are others inside waiting to see you."

More embraces commenced upon greeting Helen's parents and his sister Millie. Through it all, Helen never let go of his hand. She thought she would never let go of it again. She noticed he kept swiveling his head like he had lost something.

"Is everything alright?"

"Well…" John glanced around again. "Someone's missing. Where's Leonard?"

"He's sick!" Raymond blurted.

Helen shot a glance to Edward, who shook his head almost imperceptibly. And she realized John didn't know.

Tugging at his hand, Helen jerked her head toward the back door. "John, let's step outside for a minute."

"What's wrong?"

Guiding him out the back door, she wasn't sure how to tell him, and a little miffed Edward hadn't done so. She took a deep breath and held him by the lapels of his suit as she examined his face. "Leonard is very sick."

He returned a worried expression but waited for her to complete the thought.

"He has diphtheria."

******

Like a forging hammer had slammed him upside his temple, he felt dizzy, closing his eyes. He had started the day fearful of how he would be received and then rode an emotional high, seeing how accepting everyone was. But Helen's revelation took his breath away, worse than the swift kick to his side he'd received from the train conductor in Edwall. He knew diphtheria was a serious illness that oftentimes resulted in death.

"How bad is it?"

Helen's lip trembled. She rested her head against his chest. "It's bad. We've been praying he would make it until you came home. He's been delirious at times, and even calls out to you."

"Where is he?" John asked.

She led him back inside to the bedroom acting as a quarantined area. John entered the room alone as Helen waited at the door. It smelled of menthol and medicine. He approached the bed where a still, almost lifeless seven-year-old boy lay. Looking closer, he could see the rise and fall of shallow breathing as Leonard lay on his back. Each breath gurgled like he was underwater. He approached the bed and gently laid his hand on Leonard's shoulder.

"Leonard." He spoke in a low voice.

Leonard's eyes popped open immediately, and he coughed and sputtered. "Daddy? Is that really you, Daddy?"

"It's really me."

The boy sat up in bed, put his arms around his father's neck, and held on. The embrace was so tight it would have been uncomfortable if it hadn't been so endearing.

When Leonard finally let go, he leaned back and stared into his father's eyes. "It took you so long, Daddy. But I knew you would be back."

"And I'm here to stay, Leonard." John found it surprising how alert he was, considering what Helen had told him. "How are you feeling today?"

"I'm feeling better." His eyes were bright. "And I have not been a coward. I have been very sick, but I was never afraid."

Indeed, Leonard's appearance improved, even by the moment. His face had been white, but now it had color. His voice was rough, but the coughing had subsided. John mussed Leonard's hair. "You make me very proud, son."

Leonard's expression turned serious. "But I will be meeting God soon."

John, taken by surprise, paused for a bit before he made a reply. "You know, you don't have to go to heaven to meet God."

"You don't?"

"No."

Leonard coughed again but managed to ask, "Have you ever met God?"

John smiled. "A couple times."

"Really?" Leonard cocked his head. "What did he look like?"

"Well, one time he looked like a hillbilly."

"A *hillbilly?*" Leonard's eyes widened.

"Yep. But a wise hillbilly. And he came to me at a time when I needed help. I was at my rope's end." John wasn't sure if Leonard knew what the expression meant, but he was met with understanding eyes.

Leonard nodded. "God's like that."

John marveled at the wisdom in this seven-year-old. "You're right, God is just like that."

"And there was another time?" Leonard asked. "Did he look like a hillbilly then?"

"No." John sat on the side of the bed, his hand resting on Leonard's shoulder. "The other time, he looked like a little girl."

This time, oddly, Leonard didn't act as surprised.

"And I needed help then, too. I was feeling very… sad. And lonely. I didn't know where to turn." He didn't know how to make a seven-year-old understand his consternation.

Leonard furrowed his brow. "Did she have a dog?"

Unable to suppress his shock, John said, "Why, yes! Why do you ask?"

"A little black dog, with a waggy tail?"

John replied slowly, "Yeah. How…"

"Was she wearing a yellow dress and have black curly hair?"

Breathless, John asked, "How do you know all this?"

With confidence, Leonard replied, "She came to see me too. While I was sick. Really sick. I don't think she's really God. But God sent her. She told me everything would be okay." After a pause, he added, "She didn't say it with her mouth. She just kind of said it with her face. Ya' know what I mean?"

Stunned, John replied, "I know exactly what you mean, Leonard."

"Anyway, I told Mom, but I don't think she believed me."

John turned his shoulders to the door and saw Helen, who stood there, her mouth agape, tears streaming down her face.

"She does now, Leonard. She does now."

DAY 85 PLUS 5

WEDNESDAY, JULY 9, 1924

Despite being exhausted, John didn't get to sleep until about five A.M. The gray Chesterfield sofa in the parlor had been his overnight accommodations. It was comfortable enough, but he couldn't stop thinking about his re-found family. It wasn't until he heard people stirring in the kitchen that he fell into a deep sleep.

And he dreamt.

******

Flashback: Thursday, April 10, 1924

"Mr. Olson," the deskman at the Arlington Hotel called out.

John was returning for the evening. "Yes?"

"You have a message."

John retrieved an envelope from the clerk and opened it as he went to his room via the elevator. He found a typed message enclosed.

Mr. Olson,

I heard that you were in town selling fire extinguishers. I wish to inform you that the Great Northern Depot is in need of extinguishers, and very soon. I hope you are not busy this evening because I am here at the depot until midnight, after which I will be gone for several days. I can assure you that if you can come at once, I will make it worth your while.

It was signed "Henry Benson, Great Northern Depot Maintenance Chief."

"Hmm." *Nine o'clock at night and I've got a sales meeting? These fire extinguishers practically sell themselves.*

Ten minutes later, Olson found himself fumbling with all his Fyr-Fyter paraphernalia as he walked the six blocks to the station. *Couldn't have been the N.P. depot across the street. No, it had to be the G.N.!* Because the night was chilly, he wore his coonskin cap. He would take it off before going into his meeting.

There was tightness in his chest that had been there all day. The fight he'd had with Helen this morning, then the altercation with Preston at the train depot in Sandpoint. The meeting with the telephone company hadn't gone quite as planned either. Now this. *What an odd invitation.* He didn't know what to expect.

Just as he passed under the Union Pacific viaduct and was about to cross the Howard Street bridge, he heard someone call out to him.

"Psst. Olson!" A dark figure stood below him and to his left.

"Who is it?"

"I'm supposed to meet you here."

This seemed unusual, to say the least. "Not at the depot?"

"No. Down here. Please."

Olson stood there wondering what to do. The surreptitious meeting made him feel like a black marketeer. "Benson?"

"Yes, please. Hurry."

Olson walked down the gentle gravel slope with his bags to the shadowy area where the mysterious man stood. When he got close, he saw who it was. "Preston! What are you doing here?" He set down his heavy bags.

"I'm here on business just like you, Olson. Except I found another opportunity while I was here." Preston was wearing his fancy suit and smoking a cigarette.

"I haven't got time for your puzzles, Preston. I have an appointment—"

"He won't be there."

Then it became clear to Olson. "You sent me the note?"

Preston laughed. "You catch on quick, Marshal! I'm surprised you didn't get promoted to chief investigator on the Kootenai police force!" He took one step back and chuckled. "Look at you in your ill-fitting suit and your raccoon hat. A consummate professional if I ever did see one."

John made a motion like he was going to pick up his bags to leave.

"Wait a minute! I wanted to show you something." He crushed out his cigarette with the toe of his oxford and pulled something from his pocket. Between two fingers, he displayed a folding knife with a six-inch blade. It was open, and John's eyes grew wide.

"Hah! I knew you'd recognize it. It's identical to the one Sam Clark used to kill Bert." He feigned a somber face. "Funny how the outcome of Sam's trial was never in doubt. The law and the courts were in cahoots."

Preston waved the knife around as he spoke. "Bet you didn't know that Bert Partridge and I were business partners. Well, almost. See, he had money and I have brains. We were going to start a housing development right along the lake. Nice houses with views, worth lots of money. But when Bert breathed his last, the money was gone, and I'm still getting ten percent of the profits from each ten-cent magazine I sell. I think even you can calculate how much that is."

"Look, Preston, I'm sorry about Bert—"

"Shut up, Olson!"

A train going by on the viaduct made so much racket that the two had to shout just to hear each other. Olson knew that no one could hear them if he tried to call out.

"Liar!" Preston sneered. "You never cared about Bert." Spit flew from between his clenched teeth. "You stood and watched Sam murder him in cold blood and you never even tried to stop him. You call that justice?" He held the knife now firmly in his grip, standing two feet away. "Sometimes justice can only be served by the people."

Olson had been looking for an opportunity to get away, and now that he saw the desperate rage in Partridge, he tried moving toward the path back up to the bridge.

Preston stepped in front of him. "Not so fast, my friend." Gesturing with his hand, Preston said, "Now, hand over your wallet."

"Seriously? You're robbing me?"

"We-lll. Let's just make it look that way."

Olson swallowed hard. He handed him his dilapidated wallet. It was nearly falling apart. "There's not much in it." Earlier, he had moved his money to his satchel, thinking it would be safer there than in his fragmented wallet.

Preston searched it with his free hand. "Whadya mean? There's no money in here. C'mon. Hand it over."

"No."

"Tough guy, eh?" With a sneer, Preston put the wallet between his teeth and yanked, rendering it in two. Spitting out one half, he threw the other to the ground in rage. Then he seemed to suddenly calm down.

"Heh. Doesn't matter. I can get the money off your body later. Remember? I'm the one with a weapon. You're unarmed. And this knife knows what to do." Preston made a thrusting motion. Olson backed up another step, but he was against the concrete bridge abutment. He was cornered.

"Just under the rib cage and then up to the heart… and *twist!*" The veins popped from Preston's temples. "Just like Clark did it."

Olson focused on the blade, his heart pounding. Even in this dark area, the blade glinted light from a distant streetlamp.

Then, Preston made his move. He made the same thrusting motion as before, but Olson darted to the side just enough. Preston came at him again and again, but he kept dodging. When the attacker came again, Olson was able to grab his wrist and pull Preston away from the bridge, closer to the river. Now, both men had the knife, four hands on the white pearl handle at once.

"You know you can't win, Olson! You don't have it in you to kill a man. But I do!" Preston yanked to one side, and both men lost their balance and fell to the ground, scattering the grip and cases that held the fire extinguisher samples. Now the two salesmen in suits sprawled side-by-side next to the river, grasping onto the same switchblade. Preston used one hand to try to punch Olson in the face, but it glanced off the top of his head, knocking the coonskin cap into the waters.

Olson used both hands to wrest the knife away completely, but when he tried to get up, Preston shoved him into the concrete of the bridge. Using his free hand to catch his balance, Olson couldn't keep his enemy from ripping the knife out of his other hand.

Preston came at him again, flailing the point wildly as he pressed his victim closer to the bridge abutment. Once more he drove the blade directly for the chest, and Olson, stumbling, was caught off guard. He tried to grab the handle, but the blade hit him square, right below the sternum. Exhaling, he felt the pressure of the blade and knew that Partridge had won. He had taken his life from him.

At that moment, something in his head snapped. All the pressures of the day culminated in this climactic moment. He no longer even knew who he was. He couldn't think of anything but how to make it all stop.

Grabbing at the knife handle, an adrenaline rush gave him the strength to push the blade and Preston away. He struggled to bend his wrist enough that he would release the weapon.

It was quieter now since the train had passed. Muscles shaking, the two continued to struggle for control when they heard voices of women approaching the bridge.

The sound distracted Preston enough that Olson was able to nick his forearm, drawing blood. The knife fell to the ground about five feet away. Glancing down, he was surprised to see that blood was not gushing from his chest. *The knife must've hit a button in my vest.*

Preston dove for the knife, and Olson used it as an opportunity to scramble up the bank to the bridge deck. Breathing hard, he cut in front of the two women, who gasped, thinking he was an assailant. He ran as fast as his weary body would let him, north across the bridge, not looking back. He turned left at the end of the bridge and frantically ran toward the dam through the Phoenix Lumber Company's lot at the river's edge. That's when he looked back.

Strangely, the women were following him, calling out.

"Don't jump!"

The adrenaline rush had caused him to be so out of breath that he couldn't even reply. When he saw Preston walking behind them, he searched for the best getaway. The dam was a dead end. His only chance was to head back toward the women and turn north. He hoped Preston wouldn't spot him and start coming after him again. His peripheral vision had turned black, like he was looking through a tunnel.

In a fog, he didn't know what else to do. He was in a nightmare, and his only chance was to run.

******

"John, wake up."

Helen Olson hovered above him. Delirious, it took him a few moments to get his bearings.

"Are you okay? You were tossing about. And you're covered in sweat."

John sat up and rubbed his temples. "I'm fine now. More than fine, actually. I had a bad dream, I guess."

"What about?"

"I - I can't remember."

"That's probably a good thing. Now wash up. Breakfast will be soon."

His heart was racing, but whatever his nightmare was about, it was over now. He took a few deep breaths, and soon John was thinking about the events of the last two days.

It all seemed so dreamlike. When he arrived in Freeman, the house he'd grown up in since thirteen years of age was completely unfamiliar. Thanks to his father's detailed descriptions of everyone, he had successfully faked his way with family members. But he still didn't recognize anyone.

Except Helen.

When she first appeared on the back porch yesterday, he knew it was the girl he had seen in his vision at the wedding in Skykomish. Dark hair, hazel eyes, high cheekbones, a wry smile. And a limp. It was her, alright. The girl of his dreams, literally. Could he be this lucky?

His world was dreamlike again. But not a nightmare like when he had been kicked off the train in Edwall. Instead, it was a dream he hoped would never end. *Please don't pinch me; I don't want to wake up.*

"Feeling better, sleepyhead?"

There she was again. Standing over him with an adorable smile and a cup of hot coffee in her hand.

"Very much." He accepted the cup and took a sip. He grinned so wide some dribbled from the corner of his mouth. She wiped his chin with a cloth napkin from her apron pocket. The warmth of the coffee didn't compare to the heat he felt from her touch. He thought his heart would explode with delight.

"You want to know something funny?" He set the cup down on an end table and beheld her eyes while she stood over him. "I slept horrible. You would think after being up all night on the train the night before, I would have slept well. But I didn't. You know why?"

She shook her head, tilting it to one side.

"Because I was too excited thinking about the day ahead. Being with my family and going back home to Kootenai." Not to mention spending the whole day with Helen.

Anna May wandered out of her bedroom still wearing her night clothes and rubbing her eyes. She climbed into his lap and leaned her head against his chest without a word. Having her on his knee seemed so natural.

While holding her, his attention turned back to Helen. "I couldn't stop thinking about everything. It wasn't until I heard activity in the house I actually fell asleep pretty hard. Isn't that strange?"

Leaning down, she held his face in both hands and kissed him gently on the lips. Electricity shot through him, and the smile on her face struck him as so inviting, he broke into a cold sweat. Without saying a word, she made him feel special. Could this be what he was supposed to learn from his terrible experience? Had he taken all these blessings for granted?

Her hand lingered on his left cheek while they gazed at each other for a few moments.

"What's that smell?" he asked, still smiling.

"The bacon? The coffee?" She started to pull her hand away, but he grabbed it.

"No." He took a whiff of her wrist. "Here."

She blushed. "Oh, that. It's Chanel Number Five. You gave it to me for an anniversary gift two years ago. It's very expensive. I only wear it on special occasions." She turned back to the kitchen with a most attractive limp.

Can a limp be attractive? Yes, indeed. Standing, he followed her to the kitchen, where his mother stood over her Wedgewood cook stove. Annie and Helen were busy frying bacon, ham, eggs, and fried potatoes.

"You'd better get people to the table, Helen." Annie slapped more bacon into the pan. "We don't want the food to get cold." She turned and smiled.

"Good morning, John. I trust you slept well."

He nodded without elaborating, took a strip of bacon, and put it in his mouth.

"Well, it seems like your memory problems have made you forget a great many things." She frowned and flipped some bacon. "You've forgotten your manners. We raised you better than that."

Casting his eyes downward, John stopped mid-chew, unsure of his offense. He spoke around the morsel resting on his tongue. "Please?"

She crossed her arms and shook her head.

"May I? Thank you?"

Pointing a metal spatula at him, she said, "You haven't said grace. Did you forget to thank God for the food you were about to eat?"

"No," he lied. He didn't know what to do with the strip of bacon in his mouth. Savoring it seemed inappropriate, and spitting it out would be rude. So he swallowed it whole. It stuck in his gullet. "I… just figured we would have prayer as soon as everyone gathered, and that would count."

"Count for what?" Annie swung the spatula around animatedly, gesturing as she spoke. "You don't thank God posthumously, like He's some sort of afterthought. 'Thank you, God, for the food we already ate?' We might have to train you all over again. Now get over to the table, everyone's gathering." She used the spatula to herd people like lost sheep.

The whole family gathered around the pine table, but no one sat yet. They stood in a circle near the table and held hands.

Edward cleared his throat, and everyone fell silent and bowed their heads. "Father, we thank thee for the abundant blessings thou hast given us. We are truly thankful for thy grace and mercy to us all."

It suddenly struck John as odd how people prayed in seventeenth-century English, as if God hadn't learned modern language yet.

"We especially thank thee for bringing John back to us. And we ask thy forgiveness for our lack of faith in thee. We confess that we believed that thou hads't abandoned us and would not answer our prayers. But thou hast delivered in thy way and in thy time. And thou hast brought manifold blessing and abundance to our humble home."

It seemed like a long prayer, and like a lofty one someone might hear in church by some hifalutin preacher. But it was his father. He dared to sneak a peek and saw the adults and older children were moved by his words, with tears and quivering lips.

"And we ask, dear Father, for thy healing and comfort on behalf of thy beloved child, Leonard. As thou hast restored one family member to our fellowship, we could not bear to have another torn away. But thou only knoweth what is best. Thou dost know our desires. We thank thee again for this bounty and bless the hands that have prepared it for us. In Jesus' precious name we pray, amen."

The first one out to the car after breakfast, John paced in front of Edward's Model T, anticipating the trip to Kootenai. Last night John had talked with his son Charlie on the phone. John had promised to take him fishing once everyone was back home.

At Annie's insistence, Leonard would stay on a little while longer in Freeman. Although his health had improved, room was tight in the cars, and Annie believed it too soon to keep him in close proximity to the other children. Helen acquiesced, promising to return shortly to bring him home and have the whole family back together again.

That night in Kootenai, after the children were all in bed, Helen told John about how they had met at Latah High School, about their wedding, and their early days of marriage. She described places they had lived, the births of their children, their struggles, and their triumphs.

They didn't discuss recent events. Nothing about Helen's trials during John's absence or Leonard's illness. They didn't talk about the places John had gone or the troubles he had, or his amnesia episode. Helen hoped to help John remember things from the past.

"I have something for you," Helen said. She reached into a nearby drawer and set a hunter-case railroad pocket watch on the table between them.

He pushed the button on the stem, opening the front cover. An engraving on the inside read "John L. Olson."

"Now *this* is a quality timepiece." John pulled his other pocket watch out. "Much better than this cheap one. When did you buy this?"

"I bought it five years ago. You, uh, left it behind." She winked. "But the engraving I had done a couple months ago."

They talked well past midnight. It felt right to get to know each other again. Still strangers, the idea of sleeping together still seemed a bit awkward. Besides, Helen could tell John enjoyed the conversation, finding out more and more about himself and his family.

After a lull in the conversation, John asked, "What else do you want to talk about?"

"I don't know." Helen shrugged. "What do *you* want to talk about?"

"Well," John said, "what were we talking about the last time we talked—before I disappeared?"

"Hmmm." Helen folded her hands in her lap. "We were talking about moving to Spokane."

"Really?"

"Yes." She displayed a crooked smile. "You almost had me talked into it."

FIFTEEN DAYS

AFTER DAY 85

SATURDAY, JULY 19, 1924

"Ashes to ashes, dust to dust…"

Reading from a little black book, the Baptist minister stood by a small wooden casket at the Evergreen Cemetery in Freeman. The sun struggled to break through the early morning mist.

Helen stood with her hand hooked in John's elbow, resting her head against his shoulder. Her grief was immeasurable, yet tears would not come. Not long ago, she'd believed if Leonard died, she would lose all hope. But she was surprised to find she didn't know how to feel.

On the one hand, God had taken her seven-year-old son from her. She felt robbed. It was unfair to her *and* her dead son. But that emotion mingled with the joy of John's return. Standing next to him, Helen felt she could stand up to any calamity.

As a result, two extreme emotions seemed to wash into a neutral numbness. She knew the tears would come, but not today. Glancing up at John, she saw his eyes were dry as well. *I wonder what he is thinking.*

The pastor led the little congregation in The Lord's Prayer. "Our Father, which art in heaven, hallowed be thy name…"

If anything, she felt a bit guilty. Several people in the small congregation were crying; why couldn't she? Maybe all the highs and lows experienced over the last three months had limited her ability to feel at all. John's disappearance, the lack of cooperation from the police, the scandalous gossip, Leonard's illness, and John's return—all had taken such a toll on her. Helen felt like she was going through the motions. An observer, unattached to the circumstances.

Oddly, hearing other people sob brought her some comfort. As if they were mourning in her stead. And John's presence gave her strength. His memory had not returned, but the family had regained a sense of normality because John was determined to learn everything about his past. Even more remarkable was his commitment to her and the children. Even though they were still strangers to him, he genuinely loved each of them and took every opportunity to spend time with them. She marveled at his ability to display his affection without an established intimate connection to them.

Helen had been so absorbed in her thoughts, she hadn't noticed the final phase of the funeral had started. The pallbearers lowered the casket into the grave with ropes, and the minister handed Helen a shovel. She and John each scooped a bit of dirt onto the casket, and the preacher gave a final prayer.

The pastor and others patted them on the shoulder or offered condolences on their way out of the cemetery. With Edward and Annie's home within easy walking distance, everyone would meet there afterwards. But John and Helen lingered, watching the grave digger finish filling in the hole.

For a long time, neither one of them said anything. Finally, John broke the silence. "He was a remarkable boy."

She nodded.

He turned from the grave to Helen. "He was so spiritual." John's brown eyes seemed to bore deep into her soul.

"He had a special connection with God." Her gaze turned from him to the fresh dirt. They were alone in the cemetery now. "I rather thought someday he would be a pastor, or maybe a missionary."

"Yes," John said. "I thought that, too. And he was so brave."

"Uh-huh." The fog had lifted, and it became sunny and bright. Helen shuddered despite the warm air. "He faced his illness like a soldier."

"He told me so," John said.

"What?" Helen shifted her gaze from the ground to John's face. "Told you what?"

"That he was a brave boy."

They turned face-to-face as she fingered the lapel on his suit jacket. Puzzled, she cocked her head. "When?"

"The morning before I left for Spokane to sell fire extinguishers. He told me he was not a coward."

With the sun behind John, Helen squinted up at him. "You remember that?"

"Of course I do. How could I forget?"

Helen pulled him closer. "But… what about your amnesia?"

"Amnesia?" John blinked and his forehead wrinkled. "What amnesia?"

THE END

POSTLUDE

On January 21, 1926, just a year-and-a-half after John's reunion with his family, he and Helen gave birth to a daughter. They named her Ruth Wanda Olson – my mom.

She had fond memories of her "daddy." How he struggled through the depression, but afterwards paid all his debts. He sang in the choir at Hillyard Baptist Church, which was right behind their house at that time. He read to her and taught her silly songs and poems which she remembered until her dying day. In turn she taught them to me.

On December 30th, 1939, tragedy struck. Just two blocks from their home on North Regal, John was crushed between a railroad car and a helper engine in the Great Northern yards in Hillyard where he worked as a switchman. The brakes on the engine "dynamited" (malfunctioned). The next day - New Years Eve - he passed away. My mom was just thirteen at the time.

When she was seventeen, she was "snooping around" in the parlor at their home and found a little red book in the drawer of a bureau. She opened it and began to read. She realized it was the diary of a man who had lost all memory of himself and traveled the Pacific Northwest in search of his identity. She cried because she felt sorry for him. No one had ever told her of her father's amnesia or disappearance. It wasn't until the end that she discovered she was reading about her dear daddy.

Ten years ago, she gave the diary to me, and that's when I started my writing adventure. Although he died seventeen years before I was born, I have come to know my grandpa through my research and writing as if our lifetimes had overlapped.

My hope is that I have made him alive to you as well.

CONTENTS OF JOHN L. OLSON DIARY

(Transcribed as written, including misspelled words and lack of punctuation. A few dates are off.)

[Special thanks to Raymond L. Olson, who did this originally]

On the inside front cover was found the following notation:

Jas. A. Larkin?

alias

Frank Fisher?

John L. Olson!

Harrington, Wash. Apr. 13 – 1924

Here I am on a ranch 6 miles from Harrington on a wheat ranch. I hired out as a farm hand at $45 a month. Will try to handle 9 horses on a plow tomorrow. But where did I come from? Where is my home? Have I father, mother, bros., sisters, wife or children? Is anybody looking for me? I can think of no place where I might have lived. Nor can I think on any one who might be a relative or friend.

The first thing I can remember was a kick in the side, and some one said get to hell out of here. If you can wear cloths like that you can pay your fare. I got up and was dizzy. My head was splitting with a headach something fierce. as soon as I got my bearings, I saw I was in an mty box car. I got out. The man who woke me up threw a small satchel out after me.

I walked toward some lights, about a quarter of a mile, and came to a depot marked Edwall. I sat down on a truck for 30 or 40 min. and examined my possesions. I could not find anything with a name on it. The satchel contained a shirt, collars, socks, and shaving kit. In my pockets, I had $7.20, a knife, match box, comb, 2 pencils and a fountain pen. Also a cheap watch.

As I was looking through the satchel, a man came up to me and asked me where I was going. I told him I didn't know. He asked me where I came from. I told him I diden't know. He opened up satchel and looked in and asked if it belonged to me. I told him yes. Just then, a passenger train pulled in. He told me to get on and stay out of town. This happened between 9 and 11 p.m. When the conductor came along, I gave him a dollar. He asked me where I was going. I told him next stop. He gave me back 40¢. I got off next stop. Harrington, Wash. I went to first hotel I saw and asked for a room. When he showed register to me to sign, I was stumped. I put first name that came to mind. Larkin, J. A. Helena, Mont. I went to bed but diden't sleep until after 5 oclock. I was puzzled. Was Larkin anyone I knew, I was satisfied it was not my name and I had no recent recollection of Helena tho it seamed to me I had been there. I finally slept about 2 hours. I got up and was hungry I had breakfast and wandered about town for a couple of hours. What should I do. I was afraid to go to police, for fear they would lock me up as an insanity suspect if I told them my story. I finally decided that if I was to eat very long or get any place, I had better get some work if I could. I stopped at a blacksmith shop and asked the boss if there was any work to be had in the neighbor hood. He said the only work was ranch work and that I had better go to the pool rooms, as the farmers went there when they wanted help. I did this and finally got a job about 4 P.M. I hired out to J. W. Timm.

I went out bought a jumper overalls, 2 shirts and 2 prs. socks. I had 50¢ left. I left it at drug store for 2 weeks sub. for a daily paper. It was a Spokane paper.

I went out to ranch in a Ford. There was a boy and 2 girls in family from 10 to 14 years old. I was real hungry as I haden't eat since morning. I eat a good supper. I still had a headache but not bad. after helping Mr. Timm I went to bed early.

This A.M. I got up at 6 oclock after a fitful sleep. No one else up yet as it was Sunday. I fed the horses about 12 altogether.

I picked up a Twice a Week Spokesman Review and read it. I saw names of dozens of towns and places, the names of which seamed familiar but could not remember being at any of them.

Some of the National topics of the day were familiar as well as some of the national known persons. But there was nothing to give me a clue as to my residence, or family if I have any. The day dragged along slowly. I played cribbage with Mr. Timm after noon and evening.

The Timm's are Germans. I went out a while with the boy Johnnie and hunted Jack Rabbits also played horse shoe with **him.**

Mon. Apr 14

I've got my first day in. I plowed today with 9 horses – am sure I worked on a farm before as I had no trouble. Did not have a headach for the first time.

Tues – 15th

Same as Monday – Very blue. I started to hum some familiar tunes and had to cry like a baby. There is something wrong some where. I've lost something dear to me.

Wed – 16th

The wind and dust blowing so bad today I did not go out after dinner, but helped Mr. Timm hang wallpaper and paint wood work. I could see that I had done such work before. But where? And under what circumstance.

Wed. Plowed all day. No change.

Thursday 18

High wind again helped Mr. Timm on harvester. He began to ask me questions as to what I had been doing. (I told him quite a lot about having been a drinking man, and had lost my family six or seven years ago.) But how long have I lost my memory. I can't recall, a place I've lived in or the name of a single aquaintance.

If I have a mother she must be worried to death. It nearly breaks my heart to think that some loved ones may be looking for me. I don't even know how old I am. Must be between 32 and 36 years old. Have I a wife and babies any where? And if I have, what will they do without me?

Sat 2oth

I plowed all day. After supper I went to Davenport with Mr. Timm I bought a Spokane Chronicle. It looked familiar, but could find nothing of interest.

Sunday 21

Quite and Lonesome. I cleaned up my room and washed my cloths. Mr. and Mrs. Timm send to a mail order house for some food – I sent for some underwear and gloves. Played cards a good part of evening.

Monday 22

New team today and bad hill to plow, kept me busy.

Wed 24

I just had first bath and change of clothes. I got a bunch of Spokesman Reviews today to see if I could find anything to draw my attention, but was disappointed the names of several towns were familiar. I can remember of being in 4 states, Ida, Mont., N.D. & Wash. And maybe Oregon.

Sunday 28th

Another week gone and if I don't get away from here or locate myself I will go mad. Have felt sick and blue for 3 or 4 days now. Will try to stay out the month and then go to Spokane. If I don'tk now any one, maybe some one will recognize me. I am satisfied that Larkin is not my name.

I have started to read a book called John Halifax Gentleman. The girls name is Ursula, a name that struck a responsive chord in my memory but I can not place it.

Sunday May 4

Have made no record for a week. Mr. Timm and I go to taking about railroading today. He asked me if I ever railroaded. I spoke right up and told I had been a fireman and a brakeman years ago and I feel sure that I have been now since I try to think of it. But can't remember where, or how long ago. I haden't even thot of having done anything like that until he asked me.

Wed – May 7, Spokane

Well here I am in Spokane. I coulden't stand it any longer on the ranch, I worked last 2 days for Mr. Timm on his harvester. I tryed to be as cheerful as possible, but would worry nearly all night, I got into Spokane last night, very tired and went to bed. Today I visited Hillyard and OWRN yards took in a couple shows. I saw no one I knew but am sure I have worked on railroads.

Thur May 8

Another fruitless day. I visited N.P. and Milwaukee R.R. yds, was at Manito park nearly all P.M. I am only eating twice a day so as to conserve my funds. Will try to find a job tomorrow.

Sat May 10

Have spent 2 days looking for a job I was all over east Spokane, to Match factorys and packing plants. All so Harvester works. I spent this P.M. wandering around on North Hill. I am getting awful discouraged and homesick. Homesick for where? Who? I started to go to Police station this evening but got so nervous I backed out. I have decided to go, West tonight. I have $12.60.

Sunday May 11 Wenatchee, Wash.

The Paper says its Mothers day – Mother Dear – Dead or alive, I am thinking of you. My heart nearly breaks, thinking that you are alive and wandering where your lost son is. Oh it is an awful sensation to not know who you are. It wouldn't be so bad if I knew that there wasn't anyone, to worry about me, or dependent on me. But the torture Ive been under the last Month makes me sure that, I have a Mother some place as well as Wife and Babies.

I beat my way here last night on a freight train in an Nite Reeffer. got here at 4 a.m. got a bed and slept until 10:30/a Best sleep Ive had for over a week. As near as I can find out there is no work here but have been advised that one may find work in Sawmills west of here. Will start traveling tomorrow again.

Monday May 12 Skykomish, Wash.

Here I am in a town I don't remember of ever having heard of before. And I have a job to go to work at in A.M. I left Wenatchee at noon today on a local and went to Leavenworth 30 miles. Mill shut down there acct. strike of rivermen. I took next train and got off here. 30 min. later I landed my job. I have $5.10 left. Hope I like the work, all tho I can't say I like the town. It has 2 or 300 population and is at foot of Cascade Mts. West side.

Tues. May 13.

My first day is in and I am tired, but I think I will like my work. The foreman asked what I could do I told him it was my first experience in a sawmill. and I guess I was right as none of the work seams familiar. He put me to cleaning up around saws and conveyers. and told me to watch different machines so that I could fill in when necessary. The pay is $4.00 per day – We go to work at 7:50/a and quit at 5P except Sat. when we quit at 4 P.M. It is nice and cool here compared to Wenatchee. It was sure hot there. It has been cloudy here.

Wed May 14

It is still cloudy and cool. I like my work fine, same job as yesterday. I am still having trouble getting to sleep nights. I keep figuring out possibilities of weather I have a family or not. I am trying hard to compose myself so I won't worry so much. But I have long evenings to myself. I have sent in a months sub. to Spokesman Review. And think I will send for some other Local County papers in Norhern Ida and East Wash. as those places in paper seam more familiar to me than some other I have maps of Ida, Wash and Mont, which I study.

I am rooming at the Skykomish Hotel. and board at Mill Boarding house, Meals are served family style Quite a few R.R. men stay at Hotel Locals and Helpers tie up here. Who knows some RR Man may recognize me

Thur May 15th

I will make a little note for record hear before I go any further. When I got off train here Monday a man spoke to me and called me Fisher, I said sir! He looked at me second time and said Beg pardon. I mistook you for an old acquaintance, I asked from where, He said Durant Nevada. We talked a few Minutes He said then that there was quite a difference. Then when I went to register I put Fisher down as my name It sounded better than Larkin. For first name, I am using Frank. When I had J. A. Larkin. I diden't know weather it was Joe, Jim, John, Jess or what it was. What's the difference in name for me tho? Might just as well be Si Perkins I don't even know my nationality. It looks awful queer to me that I remembered most of big things and national figures, and can't remember my own name - nationality weather I have a family —Mother Father Sisters or bros. or a single place where I might have lived. Something tells me tho that I have a family and Mother some place and that they are, looking and praying for me. I have often wondered if I have any money any place or any property. I have no recollection of any what soever.

Fri May 16

Well I have 4 days in on this job and like it as well as could be expected under the conditions, under which I am laboring. I was pretty tired first 2 or 3 days. But am in good shape physically. But mentally, I don't know how I'll come out if I don't find out who I am. I'll go to bed sleepy at 9 or 10 oclock. but will toss about and Fret for 2 and 3 sometimes 4 hours before I go to sleep.

Sun – May 18

This has been a hard day on me I got up at 8 a.m. and did not eat until noon. I had just started to eat dinner, and got to thinking, if I had a table of my own with wife and kiddies. I broke down and cried, and had to leave table. I started out walking on a Log road which went 2 miles out of town. at end of road I struck a trail and went up a Mountain about a mile, I stoped to rest by a spring and, thot of Mother Dear Old Mother and family, for I surly must have a family somewhere. on account of thinking so much of them. I cryed myself to sleep. I woke up at 4 P.M. and there was a man sitting beside me. He works in the planer here. He is about 50 years old. He said he noticed me leave table with tears in my eyes. and had followed me. He asked me what was the matter and if he could help. I started to tell him and broke down, then handed him my book. This book. He read it, turned to me, then said son I don't blame you for crying. He told of other such cases he had known, and thru different agencys had found themselves. He suggested I might have been in an auto accident. and lost my identity, He said some one may have, struck me with a car and thot me dead, and to keep away from Police had put me in the Box car. He said often times it was necessary to be, knocked sensless second time to place memory where it was. I told him that my prayer then would be to get knocked out soon as possible, just to satisfy myself as to weather I had a Mother, Father or family of my own.

He finally got me calmed down and gave me an Orange and piece of Pie he had brought along. We strolled back to town, had supper then he took me to a picture show. after while I went to Bed and had the best sleep Ive had since I struck Harrington. It was a relief to tell my troubles to some one.

Mon. A.M. [*no entry*]

Wed May - 21st^{t}

Well Little red book, we haven't much to Chronicle tonite. I was called on to Fire the boilers in the mill today, but had to quit after 2 hours work acct of sever heat. I went down to river to cool off. stayed an hour than, back to mill at old job. I had change of work Monday. working on edger. I sent to Sandpoint Ida for Official County paper for 6 mo, Thot Maybe I would see something that might jog my memory. If not will send for some other local from East. Wash Nor Ida or Mont. Because those places in general seam more familiar to me. I have been more composed this week than anytime I can remember. My only hope is, is that if I have a family and they are in a position so that they won't be subject to the necessity of excepting charity.

Sunday June 1st

Well little Red Book it has been some time since I talked to you. I have a regular job at Mill now. Lining up for edger man. The cut in wages takes effect in a.m. so will get only $3.60 per day. Think I will stick it out until 4th and then go on to coast. I am thinking every day of a Mother, Wife and Babies, waiting for me some place and have figured it won't pay to stay to long in one place. on the other hand from the amount of Men looking for work, one had better have a little ahead before he quits a job where he gets his bread and butter. I am sleeping fairly well again and am eating like a workman should. I only weighed 170 lbs. when I came here but weigh 178 now. Still my suit I had seams a little large for me.

Sunday June 8 -24

This has been my best week as far as feeling fit is concerned. In fact I can smile once in a while without forcing it. I got acquainted with a young fellow by the name of Chet Lowrie. He has been married but is devorced. We visit together every evening. Today we got a Freight train and went to Sultan Wn. about 30 miles west to see a ball game after the game we walked to Monroe 7 miles – took in a picture show and got back here on #2 10:40/p. Next Sunday we plan on going to Everett. I have told him my story. If I have wife and Babies I hope they have got over their greif and am praying that we will be reunited soon.

Sunday June 15

Well I did not get to Everett today as I had planed. But Mr. Lowrie and I got on a Freight and went up the mountain about 10 miles until we met a west train and came back. There is sure some pretty scenery in those hills. We took in a ball game here in the evening then went to a picture show.

I have finally got to a point where I am quite positive that I have a wife some place. or have had one some time in the past. The reallity of it came to me just thru a joke. One of the Mill hands, was married Saturday, one of the boys, while kidding him reminded me of the first night I was married But I can't place time place or girl. It will come to me someday tho. And in the Mean time Dear Wife, if you still belong to me, my prayers are that you are not suffering. And that we will meet soon.

Sun June 22 -

Another week has slipped by, and am still in same old place Lost and seams like lost for good. My friend and I got a Local Freight and went to Everett today. This was the first time I ever saw salt water. We visited along seashore and took in sights on a large Freight ship the Horace Luchenbach an 8000 ton ship. It was loading lumber. We got back to Sky on Oriental Limited at 10:50/P.M. Lost pen this week.

Wed July 2 -24

The Mill shut down today until after the 4th My I wish I could be with Mother on that day and wife and Babies if I have any. I have quit grieving as much as I used to, but I think of who my dear ones are every day. Lowrie and I are going to Seattle tonight and I am praying that some one I know will recognize me and be able to tell me weather I have any dear ones or not and if I have O Boy won't I be a happy one and if I belong in the Northwest, I'll have a good chance of some one knowing me in a big city. I will try to Locate a better job there. I only have about $50.00 Clear and here since May 12th. But if I find none I can come back and go on repair work.

Seattle, Wn. July 3rd 24

Seattle today – Came down on Jim Hills special last night.

Lowry and I still sticking together. I saw my first battleship in Seattle harbor. The Pennsylvania. Am going to pay it a visit tomorrow. Will also go out to U. of W. and probably some Beach. Today we saw Los Angeles beat Seattle playing ball. This evening we took in 2 picture shows and took a cable ride to Leschi Park and Lake Wash

July 5 -24

Hello Mr. Olson. I have a new name As Lowry and I were coming down 2nd Ave. this P.M. a Policeman stepped up and said Hello Olson. I told him I guessed he had me wrong. He said no, but that he knew me well. Lowry and I looked at each other and I told him I guess the time has come. The Policeman turned out to be a Mr. Bolin formerly of Spokane. He said I used to be a motorman on Street cars in Spokane from 1912-17 and that he was my conductor a good part of the time. He named over a dozen men that's working there now that knew me well. and said there was 5 or 6 here in Seattle that knew me. after he had heard my story and he told me what he knew of me. He advised me to go to Detective headquarters and tell my story -

Lowry and I went there, they than advised me go back to Bolin and have him write to some of these men in Spokane and see if they can have any dope on my disapearance and see if any one was looking for me. Bolin said that I had a wife and 2 children when he last saw me in 1914. So I'm on my Way now to see Bolen again.

[End of diary]

NEWSPAPER ARTICLES RELEVANT TO JOHN OLSON STORY

Streetcar accident

"Car Leaps Track to Hospital Lawn." *Spokesman-Review,* May 11, 1917, p.1.

Clark Trial

"Men Fight to Death." *Northern Idaho News,* Mar. 14, 1922, p.1.

"Men Fight to Death in Kootenai." *Pend Oreille Review,* Mar. 17, 1922, p.1, 4.

"Clark Preliminary to Be Held Monday." *Pend Oreille Review,* Mar. 24, 1922, p.1.

"Clark Must Stand Trial." *Northern Idaho News,* Mar. 28, 1922, p.1, 4.

"Clark Held to Face Second Degree Murder." *Pend Oreille Review,* Mar. 31, 1922, p.1-3.

"Clark is Freed on Murder Charge." *Pend Oreille Review,* Oct. 13, 1922, p.1, 4.

"Clark Not Guilty Verdict of Jury." *Northern Idaho News,* Oct. 17, 1922, p.1.

Olson Disappearance

"Man Gone; Fear Foul Play." *Spokane Daily Chronicle,* Apr. 15, 1924, p. 1 Night Extra.

"Fear Salesman Foul Play Victim." *Spokesman-Review,* Apr. 16, 1924, p.1.

"Seek Mystery Woman in Missing Man Case." *Spokane Daily Chronicle,* Apr. 16, 1924, p, 1. First Edition.

"'Mystery Woman' in Disappearance Case." *Spokane Daily Chronicle,* Apr. 16, 1924, p.1. Fireside Edition, Second Edition.

"Find New Angle in Olson Search." *Spokesman-Review,* Apr. 17, 1924, p.7.

"John L. Olson of Kootenai Missing Since Last Friday." *Pend Oreille Review,* Apr. 17, 1924, p.1.

"Get New Clew to J.L Olson." *Spokesman-Review,* Apr. 18, 1924, p.6.

"River Dragged for Missing Man." *Spokane Daily Chronicle,* Apr. 18, 1924, p. 3 Late Edition.

"Missing Man Pawned Watch, Police Find." *Spokane Daily Chronicle,* Apr. 19, 1924, p.1, Fireside Edition, p.3, Second Edition.

"Missing Man's Relatives Offer Cash Rewards." *Spokane Daily Chronicle,* Apr. 22, 1924, p.1, Second Edition,

"The community has been deeply stirred…" *Northern Idaho News,* Apr. 22, 1924, p.4.

"Posse to Search for John Olson." *Spokesman-Review,* May 3, 1924, p.5.

"Search Hills for J.L. Olson." *Spokesman-Review,* May 4, 1924, p.8.

Olson Found

"Olson Not Dead; Was in Seattle." *Spokesman-Review,* July 7, 1924, p.1.

"Finds Lost Son in Seattle." *The Seattle Star,* July 7, 1924, p.1,16.

"Seattle Cops Help Idahoan Identify Self." Seattle P-I, July 7, p.9.

"Mrs. J.L. Olson left for Spokane." *Northern Idaho News,* July 8, 1924, p.6.

"John Olson, Kootenai, Found Victim of Amnesia." *Pend Oreille Review,* July 10, 1924, p.1.

"Kootenai Man Victim of Amnesia." *Northern Idaho News,* July 15, 1924, p. 1.

Leonard's Death

"Young Leonard Olson Dies." *Pend Oreille Review,* July 24, 1924, p.1.

Olson Death

"1 Dead, 1 Hurt in G.N. Crash." *Spokesman-Review,* Jan. 1, 1940, p. 1.

"Olson Victim of Accident." *Spokane Daily Chronicle,* Dec. 31, 1940.

"Olson Funeral is Held Today." *Spokane Daily Chronicle,* Jan. 1, 1940, p.5.

THE CAUSE OF JOHN OLSON'S AMNESIA

The actual cause of John Olson's amnesia is unknown.

For almost one hundred years the primary theory proposed by family members was that he was struck over the head, robbed, and thrown onto a boxcar by thieves that tried to hide their deed.

It's a simple theory, but as I researched this out, I became convinced that this could not possibly be the explanation for several reasons.

According to his diary, he found seven dollars in his pocket. Thieves would not have left that.

He mentions a headache for the first two days, but never a word about a bump on his head or blood in his hair. The doctor in Seattle found no sign of recent head trauma.

Very little was known about amnesia in 1924. But the symptoms displayed by Olson seem to point to a condition known today as Dissociative Fugue. This psychological state is never caused by a blow to the head. Read a short description of the disorder here:

https://www.webmd.com/mental-health/dissociative-fugue

Others have dismissed the John Olson case as a fake; that he ditched his family until he got caught. After all, it is a rather handy excuse for a man that needs to take a break from the stresses of everyday life. No doubt, some have done that very thing.

There are a variety of reasons that I have dismissed this notion. First of all, a reading of the diary usually convinces most people that he could not have been the evil person he would have to be to do such a thing. Everyone I have known that knew him has given testimony that he was not capable of such a ruse.

Furthermore, I would have to ask why a man that is hiding from the authorities in Spokane would deliberately come back there for four days. While there, he made himself known in public places that he felt likely he would be be seen by someone that knew him.

Another interesting fact that I came upon, is that the famous writer, Agatha Christie had a similar experience two years after John Olson's episode. She disappeared for eleven days, leaving her belongings in a state of confusion. She took an alias and stayed at a health spa. She was already famous at the time, so some people recognized her, but she insisted that she was someone else. Naturally, most people thought she was faking it, but many psychologists today attribute it to Dissociative Fugue.

So, what caused John Olson's fugue? Doctors agree that it can be caused by a variety of traumatic experiences and pressures. But no one really knows what happened to John Olson the night he disappeared.

So I made up a story.

Yes, there were many factors that were stressors in his life at the time. Not the least of which was the fact that he had enemies at the time due to the results of the murder trial from two years earlier.

But who knows? Maybe the cause of his amnesia is even crazier than the one I conjured up.

ACKNOWLEDGEMENTS

It doesn't take most writers ten years to write their first book. But I'm not like most. I didn't even put pen to papers (finger to keyboard before two year of research. And I still kept researching even after I started writing.

The idea for the book began when my Mom, Ruth Haglund (1926-2014), reminded me of the diary her father had written. Then she became very excited when I told her I wanted to write a book about it. She was a huge source of information about family lore. I went to her often when I first started my research. My only regret is that she was not able to see it to its completion. I guess that's what happens when you take ten years to write a book.

I talked with aunts, uncles, and cousins that were familiar with the story and some of them even remembered my grandpa. They told me stories and helped me get to know people who have long since died.

I spent hours researching information at the Northwest Room of Spokane's Public Library, and traveled to the Seattle Public Library to pore through newspaper microfiche. I visited the Bonner County Museum in Sandpoint, Idaho and the Lincoln County Washington Museum in Davenport, just to name a few research centers. Thank you to all of the nameless people that helped me there.

I got a wealth of information on the Timm family of Harrington from their grandson, Jerry Jantz. Karen Allen, who is restoring the old Harrington (Electric) Hotel was very helpful with research about my grandfather's first night as an amnesia victim.

I had a delightful time interviewing Chet Lowry's son and daughter, Chet Lowry Jr. and Lonnie James. They welcomed me into their homes in Seattle, even though they had never met me before. They were very curious what I was up to, but shared everything they knew.

Many others helped me with research, but I should also mention my good friend, Davis Eyre. If something can be found out, Dave can do it. Thanks, Dave.

Besides researching history, there was something else important I needed to do. I needed to learn how to write. I read a couple books that were helpful, but things really turned when I lucked upon the Red Ink Fictioneers writers group and found out how much I didn't know. They were a wealth of criticism, mostly good. These good people included Pat Pfeiffer, Carol Crigger, Karen Parks, Kathryn Robinson, Jim Alexander, Steve Hughes, Fred Jesset, Bruce and Carrie McBride, Joyce Nowacki, Steve Stuart, and my good friends Carrie and Ricky Parks.

Many friends and family have cheered me on through this process, one that was much more involved than I realized. I can't name you all, but a big thanks go out to you.

I needed a good editor and found one in Calee Allen. She was the perfect mixture of cheerleader and hard case.

I especially need to thank my family. They put up with all my journeys and my endless hours at the laptop, scrutinizing details. Especially my wife, Lisa. She had to put up with an awful lot over the years. She encouraged me when I thought I would never finish, and went along with me on the same tracks from Spokane to Seattle that my grandfather took. She pretended that she was just as excited as me when I discovered new information. I never could have done this without you, honey.

Now that I'm done, maybe we'll do some traveling that has nothing to do with book writing. Although I have to do some research in Wisconsin for my next book. Hope it doesn't take ten years.

Randy Haglund